CW00431869

Like Sophie Rivers, Judith [...] the Black Country and taught for many years in a Birmingham further education college. She has lectured in Creative Writing at Birmingham University and in such different locations as a maximum security prison and the Greek island of Skyros. When not writing novels she returns to her first love, short stories, many of which have won prizes or been broadcast.

Judith has now adopted a more rural life, but there is no likelihood of Sophie Rivers doing the same.

'From PD James onwards, British detective writing is crammed with feisty young female sleuths. But in Cutler's Sophie Rivers we are undoubtedly dealing with the *crème de la crème*'   *The Times*

'The narrative is, always, witty and erudite, moving with assurance'   *Nottingham Evening Post*

'Thoroughly sharp, modern, witty and literate'
                                                  Margaret Yorke

'One of the most appealing newcomers on the crime fiction scene for years'   F.E. Pardoe, *Birmingham Post*

'Judith Cutler's Brum-based crime novels are a hit'
                                                          Crime Time

Also by Judith Cutler
and featuring Sophie Rivers

Dying to Fall
Dying to Write
Dying on Principle
Dying for Millions
Dying for Power
Dying to Score
Dying by Degrees
Dying by the Book

Dying in Discord

Judith Cutler

headline

First published in 2002
by HEADLINE BOOK PUBLISHING

First published in paperback in 2002
by HEADLINE BOOK PUBLISHING

A HEADLINE paperback

10 9 8 7 6 5 4 3 2

ISBN 0 7472 6785 5

Typeset by
Avon Dataset Ltd, Bidford-on-Avon, Warks

Printed and bound in Great Britain by
Clays Ltd, St Ives plc

HEADLINE BOOK PUBLISHING
A division of Hodder Headline
338 Euston Road
LONDON NW1 3BH

www.headline.co.uk
www.hodderheadline.com

For all my friends in the City of Birmingham Symphony Orchestra and Birmingham Chamber Music Society, with thanks for the lifetime of pleasure they have given me.

Acknowledgements

Two extraordinary buildings are featured in this novel, both real and both of historical importance. I am deeply indebted to the people who took enormous trouble to show me both.

The Birmingham and Midlands Institute is a precursor of Birmingham Conservatoire. It is housed in a wonderful Victorian Gothic building, with Arts and Crafts additions, in the centre of Birmingham. I had the assistance of two devoted employees, Philip Fisher and Andrew Peet, both of whom gave unstintingly and enthusiastically of their time. Thank you both: may your efforts to secure the future of the Institute be successful.

Even more important – a national, indeed an interntional site – is Matthew Boulton's Soho Foundry, Smethwick, currently in the care of Avery Berkel Ltd. Thanks to the vision of people like Tony Adcock, who has encouraged archaeological exploration of what are currently derelict buildings sitting alongside the modern Avery Berkel works, there is hope that members of the public will eventually be able to explore and appreciate the work of one of the fathers of the Industrial Revolution. I was shown round by a man with a passion for preserving the past and who knows more about the Soho Foundry than anyone else, George Demidowicz. He makes a brief appearance as himself in the text. Thank you very much: may your dreams for the future of the works come true.

I am also most grateful to Louis Ullman, formerly of

Birmingham University's Heywood Quartet, for his insights into the life of chamber musicians, which is, generally, unlike what I have depicted here – I hope.

Chapter One

'Give it your best shot, Sophie,' Mike had urged as he kissed me goodbye at Heathrow, as he and the rest of the England cricket team had waited for their flight to Pakistan to be called. 'I shall be back for Christmas, remember, and when you've got your dissertation sorted, you'll be coming out to Sri Lanka for the spring tour.'

I'd nodded. We'd had so many important things to say in our last two minutes together. Except we hadn't been able to say them. We'd been tongue-tied, like all the other cricketing couples about to be separated for several weeks. Our only claim to special sympathy was that we'd been married just ten days, stealing a moment in the pre-tour match-free slot demanded by the England and Wales Cricket Board for the tour players to relax. As yet, only three people knew: the registrar and two witnesses we'd borrowed from another wedding party. No, we hadn't had the meringue-dress wedding we'd talked about – but at least we could dress up for the big post-blessing reception we now planned.

Several weeks later, though neither of us was enjoying the long separation, we were both acquitting ourselves as best we could. Mike was toiling away in the hot Pakistan sun, with the sort of dedication, if not always total success, we'd come to expect of England cricketers recently. Meanwhile, I was at home, struggling with an M.Ed. dissertation. I'd started it the previous year at the University of the West Midlands before my studies had been rudely interrupted by the illegal activities of some of the staff. To do them justice, the university authorities had not only waived my fees for my repeat year, they'd also made an *ex gratia* payment to thank me for my part in exposing a nasty fraud. This helped support me in the absence of my income from William Murdock College. I'd have liked to report a series of impassioned letters from my College beseeching me to return to the classroom, but its finances were still so dodgy that every penny saved by my protracted sabbatical was welcomed with hand-rubbing glee. There was even some doubt as to whether there'd be a William Murdock College for me to return to when I'd completed my Master's – there were rumours of bankruptcy and merger, takeover and collapse.

So it really did behove me to get my head down and study. An M.Ed. would make me a much more marketable prospect should I have to find a new job. Enjoyable as my home catering sideline might be, I didn't want to spend the rest of my life dishing up canapés to serve at other people's parties: catering might have its charms, but it also had its attendant problems, one of which was that I had to engage in constant guerrilla warfare against the calories now viciously assailing me. If you're a cook, you need to keep tasting, and what was once an admittedly skinny size eight to ten Sophie was now a cuddlier size ten to twelve Sophie. And from cuddly, as I warned Mike when he claimed to prefer the new me, it was but a short step to tubby. People as short as me can't afford middle-aged spread – especially if they're not quite middle-aged. More to the point, without a regular salary, I couldn't afford an entire wardrobe of new clothes.

Whether it was a consequence of the previous year's dramas, or merely one of those quirky decisions for which educational managements are notorious, the University of the West Midlands had moved its education department, where I was based, from its unattractive home in West Bromwich to a much more attractive site in Smethwick, another Black Country town. This particular venue was a cluster of Victorian houses overlooking West Smethwick Park to the front, and their own extensive and well-maintained grounds to the rear. They'd been converted so beautifully that from the outside no one could have dreamt of the reorganisation within demanded by a music department – specialised practice and rehearsal rooms, not to mention the sound-proofing they all required. Don't ask why education should be combined with music: it was possibly a result of having a spare house and a half, but no one was sure. And no one in their right mind would argue. The West Bromwich building had been a miserable example of sixties Brutalism, and while here there were excesses in the way of curlicues and capitals, not to mention a particularly gormless crop of Burne-Jones lookalike stained-glass knights, Smethwick won hands down.

The student facilities were enviable. Both the music and the education faculties had post-graduate study rooms, with computers for each student and plenty of lock-up space. Our canteen – no, in this sort of august setting it was surely a refectory – was immaculately clean, and the food cheap and wholesome. The library was unexpectedly well stocked, after the discovery of a hidden cache of government resources for people returning to study. There was even adequate parking.

As for the teaching staff, so far I had no complaints there either. Practising teachers are notoriously – but perhaps rightly – critical of those who try to teach them. Our eyes gleam when an infinitive is split; we pounce on hanging participles. But my new tutor was professional and extremely hard-working. She'd already inspired in me a belief completely lacking last year – that while I'd never be a top-of-the-trees academic, I was on the way to producing a competent dissertation well ahead of schedule. Thanks to one of the wettest summers and certainly the wettest autumn on record, I'd completed all the reading I'd shied away from before, and started to make sense of all my notes.

To while away any spare time, and also to bring me somehow closer to Mike, with his passion for the recent past, I'd joined a university society that would have been dear to his heart – the Local History Group. I'd even found time to rediscover my singing voice – at one time I'd been in one of Birmingham's leading choral societies – and had been recruited into the university choir as a back-row soprano. Someone had also discovered that I played the piano, and had inveigled me into accompanying a couple of would-be recital singers: the ability to move between the rigours of dissertations about multiethnic language skills and the pleasures of playing Schubert was a huge bonus. Yes, even though I missed Mike with a pain that was physical, in many ways I was enjoying a full life.

As I reported to him in our daily phone call.

'We're actually working towards a series of concerts,' I told him. 'There's going to be a mini-music festival in a couple of weeks—'

'Haven't you had enough of festivals?' he demanded.

I took his point. My involvement with the Big Brum Bookfest had not been without incident. 'This is music,' I protested, 'well known for its power to sooth the savage breast. A number of small local choirs are going to band together with the Midshires Symphony Orchestra.'

'Wow! Sounds good. What are you doing?'

'Beethoven's Choral Fantasia—'

'That piano piece that sounds as if it's about to break at any moment into the Choral Symphony?'

'That's the one. It'll be wonderful: singing in Symphony Hall!'

There were other venues in use too, including the Birmingham and Midlands Institute, where I was coincidentally doing the post-concert catering the evening the UWM's own quartet, the Boulton, had been booked to play.

Mike and I concluded our conversation with the sort of exchanges no third party would care to hear. As usual, our desire not to upset each other had carried us through. Poor Mike had to go off and be manly, organising, for the sake of team morale, the stiffest of upper lips. I didn't have to. To be honest, my mascara was running something shocking. I blotted it firmly and straightened my shoulders. What a good job I had a rehearsal to go to.

It had to be admitted that Marcus French, the UWM Choral Society's conductor, was not universally popular. For a start, he was actually the music department's professor, so he held a great deal of academic as well as musical power. Secondly, he suffered from what Mike, a clear six-footer, described disparagingly as 'little man's disease': he was a slight, balding five foot four, and tried to make up in noise what he lacked in inches. Lastly, he prided himself on the sort of sarcastic witticisms long ago favoured by Sir Thomas Beecham. Had he had Beecham's panache with words and skill with the baton, he might have been positively applauded for them. As it was, he was loathed, his *bons mots* received with sulks. But not overt sulks, not if you wanted to escape a further withering.

'And if you think you've got away with it now,' Dawn Harper, the red-headed soprano next to me, said over a half-time coffee, 'you'll find he comes up with it at your next tutorial. He criticises everything till you feel so big.' She put her thumb and forefinger together, allowing a paper-thin gap.

'Can't you argue back?' I asked. I'd never tried the tactic of humiliation on any of my students, and could imagine the reaction if I had.

'Music's such a subjective thing,' she pointed out. 'If French says I'm playing badly, I can't point to scholarly references to show I'm right. All I can do is try to play how he wants me to play.'

'You're a full-time music student?'

'Of course. Oboe and piano. I have to sing in the choir because French says I have to. I thought you were too – a post-grad, of course. Aren't you?'

I explained my status.

'I'm surprised he let you in the choir, then. He's normally very picky about non-music students. My friend Doug – there he is, over there –' she pointed to a large young man – 'the prof said he didn't really want him, because his voice is like a foghorn. Not that he can really afford to be choosy – the numbers wanting to join a choir in a place this size are pretty limited.'

'He might have let me in, but he didn't exactly welcome me. He informed me that he supposed I could hold a line, but that I'd one of the tiniest voices he'd come across and it was a sign of our times that he'd have to condescend to admit me.'

'But you still joined?' She opened huge greenish eyes wide.

'Put together in the same phrase and join with a preposition the words "glutton" and "punishment", and apply them to me.' I grinned. 'No, I enjoy singing too much to be put off by an old misanthrope like him.'

'He's not all that old, though, Sophie – he can't be much more than forty-five,' she said doubtfully, pulling a face I couldn't interpret.

'You're right. He's not the generation where men were expected to be bullies. Maybe to become a conductor you need a big ego. What's the betting his name's not Marcus, but really Mark?'

She didn't respond.

'And you certainly need ambition and energy to become a prof.'

Dawn teased out a lock of hair and proceeded to chew it. 'I still wish I could opt out. But music students can't – we have to be in either an orchestra or a choir. Or, in my case, both.'

'Sounds reasonable – after all, you all want to become performers.' Oh dear, there I was, Sophie in bracing-mode again! *Slow down, woman, she may be a student but here you're not staff. You're a student too. And don't forget she's an oboe player – they're supposed to be the most neurotic of musicians: something to do with their reeds.* 'But not very good,' I temporised, 'if you have no option about working all the time with someone you really don't like.'

She nodded gloomily, and then pulled herself to her feet. 'Best be getting back. Nothing gets up his nose as quickly as people coming in late.'

Well, that was one thing I did, as a teacher, sympathise with. 'If we're all nice and prompt, I'm sure he'll turn out to be a real pussycat.'

I was less sure ten minutes later, though the sopranos escaped the worst of his tongue-lashing. He was after the tenors, and eventually made each man sing solo the problematic phrase.

'There is not one Welshman, not one in the whole benighted principality, who couldn't do better than that. Where's your sense of pitch?' To another, he said, 'Tell me, you are a Catholic, are you not? I hope for your wife's sake she has a better grasp of rhythm than you do!' There were too many references to underpants, tight and loose, to bother documenting.

By the end of the evening we'd all had enough of it. There wasn't even any wit to relish, at least in retrospect, just verbal bullying. We felt like a bombarded city: it might not have been our suburb that came under fire tonight, but our turn would inevitably come. It might be the basses next time, might be the contraltos – but sure as God had made little apples it would be the sopranos one day soon.

So when, as we streamed off to the student bar, we heard someone declaring, 'Another session like that and I'll bloody kill him,' we didn't take any notice – except, perhaps, to join the queue to hold down Marcus French in readiness.

Chapter Two

The one thing you never mention to viola players is the ream upon ream of Internet jokes about them. Humour isn't supposed to be racist or sexist these days, nor does anyone with any sensitivity mock people's physical characteristics. None of this consideration seems to apply to poor viola players (Internet-type joke: *Is there any other sort?*), who invite both real and cyberspace mockery.

Viola player or not, James Hallam didn't seem at first glance the sort of person to invite anything except respect. A man in his early forties, I'd say, with a full head of brown hair, he was the same sort of build as my Mike – tall, broad-shouldered and slender, with arms long enough to deal with a big fiddle. He was one of the university's Boulton Scholars, he explained, as we walked across the university car park together.

'Boulton? As in Matthew Boulton?' I asked. It was the obvious question given the great man's links with the area.

'That's right,' he agreed, making a grab for his viola case as the wind threatened to gust it into the side of a Fiesta. 'In fact the scholarships derive from a Black Country industrialist who wanted to remain anonymous and to celebrate another famous Black Country industrialist.'

'Not so much Black Country as world class – though perhaps when all's said and done the two terms are synonymous,' I said, not entirely joking. We Black Country people know we're the salt of the earth, after all.

He looked at me as if not at all sure how to take me, a state of affairs with which I was perfectly happy. After all, he'd only scraped my acquaintance when his car door was blown into mine. It might have been a lot less friendly had any damage been done, since the new Mazda was my pride and joy, and I begrudged the tiniest squashed gnat space on my otherwise pristine windscreen. But, smiling as if we were old friends, he'd immediately engaged me in conversation, falling into step with me as I headed for the rear entrance.

'So what does being a Boulton Scholar involve?' I shouted over Wuthering Heights-type gusts.

'Both playing and teaching,' he yelled back. 'I play in the Boulton Quartet and teach viola and violin the rest of the week. I've seen you with Dawn Harper, haven't I? You're a pianist on the accompanists' course, aren't you?'

'No, I'm accompanying one or two of the singers, that's all. It's just that my sight-reading's good.'

'How come? Sight-reading's an unusual accomplishment.'

I laughed. 'I never practised as much as I should have done when I was young and I had a martinet of a teacher, so if I wanted to survive, my sight-reading had to be spot-on. It's a skill you seem to keep.'

'Like cycling and swimming,' he said, opening the music department door for me. He touched my arm lightly. 'Fancy a coffee?' His voice was unnaturally loud in the calm of the corridor, his smile now distinctly that of someone determined to make a new friend. 'Please? Pretty please?'

Pretty please! What was in this man's head? Teachers weren't supposed to say such things to students, not in a manner more suited to a singles bar. Students were young, impressionable. As far as I was concerned, it wasn't a problem: when you're still single in your thirties you get the hang of evading would-be flirts. I certainly wasn't going to wear Mike's ring as either a trophy or a keep-off sign. But it was there, on my other ring finger, as it happened, the socking great emerald he'd bought right at the start of our relationship. There'd been talk of a proper engagement ring, but I truly wanted no other. What we both wanted now was to see a nice old-fashioned gold band on my left hand, but until we'd broken the news to all our nearest and dearest, probably at a party to end all parties, we maintained the pretence of singledom.

'No, thanks,' I said. 'I'm off to see my tutor – I've hit a snag in my Master's dissertation.'

He looked confused. 'You're not a music student at all, then?'

'Education. I play in my spare time. And sing. In the choir, at least. Now,' I said, looking at my watch, 'I really must push off.'

'Who's your tutor?'

What was it to him? But I was brought up to be polite, even when late, so I said briefly, 'Carrie Downs.'

'Oh. The temporary appointment.'

'I thought most people had short-term contracts in higher education these days,' I said. Security of tenure in universities was a thing of the past, with no huge marketplace salaries to compensate.

'But she's only here to cover for that guy who's supposed to have had his hands in the till, isn't she?'

I nodded. It was not my job as prosecution witness to say anything.

'What's she like? Apart from being young and disconcertingly pretty?'

Oh dear.

'Extremely alert, highly qualified, an excellent teacher. Oh, and she's a stickler for punctuality,' I added with a meaningful glance at my watch. 'See you,' I added dismissively, because that's how we say goodbye in the Midlands.

'Indeed you will,' he said.

Next time he'd get the most formal of farewells.

* * *

11

Dr Carrie Downs was indeed everything we'd both said. She was about thirty, pretty in a dizzy-blonde way that concealed a mind and memory I envied. She was also tidy to the point of anal retentiveness, and had a shrewd eye for modern art, if the gallery posters on her walls were anything to go by. They might be at odds with the prevailing Victorian ambience, but they certainly brought light and even a sense of movement to a room otherwise completely dominated by books and her state-of-the-art computer. She'd made herself very much at home in a way the university authorities might have found disconcertingly permanent for someone supposed to be on a temporary contract.

'I've found that Internet material I mentioned,' she greeted me. 'Here's the reference. Any problems?'

'None,' I replied equally briskly, copying the information on to my pad.

'Because now's the time to discuss them. You don't want to discover glitches when you're actually writing the thing. I notice you weren't at the lecture the other evening.' The rebuke was obvious.

'I covered that area last year,' I reminded her.

'Of course you did.' She clicked her mouse. 'Ah, and you got a distinction in the summer assessment. And in the research procedures module. No need for me to chase you, then. It's really just the dissertation you've got to cover. Excellent. I'm surprised you bother to come in.'

No need to tell her about the awful emptiness of my house. 'Discipline,' I said.

'Good. Now, how are you going to integrate the latest Inigo and Humphrys research into your material . . .'

Half an hour later, feeling as if my brain had been ploughed, I was relieved when someone knocked on the door.

Carrie rapped out, 'Come!'

Such an invitation always sounds friendlier with a preposition, to my mind, but the man obeying her injunction showed no signs of resenting her brusque efficiency.

'You know Marcus French, don't you, Sophie?'

I nodded hello. So did he. As if sure of his welcome, he sat down in the spare armchair and picked up Carrie's *Guardian*. Well, I could take a hint. And my session was officially over. I stowed my papers and fixed the next session. But I was surprised that such an assertive young woman as Carrie let him get away with such behaviour and turned, as I left, to talk to him with every appearance of delight.

If I was going to have to share a lunch table with James Hallam, and it looked as he slipped into the seat opposite mine very much as if I was, then we'd talk about music, not about his colleagues, past or present.

I waited while he took an identical lunch to mine – a salad, water, an orange – from his tray before asking, 'So how does playing in a professional quarter fit in with your teaching?'

'Actually,' he said, unwrapping the knife and fork from the paper napkin, 'the teaching fits round the playing. Our contracts stipulate minimum and maximum numbers of concerts, so much rehearsal time per week, with extra in the run-up to concerts, and then a bit of research – well, you know how highly research is rated these days, and UWM certainly needs to shin up the league tables a bit – and finally the teaching.' He smiled engagingly, letting his crow's-feet deepen round his eyes. I could imagine such a movement setting aflutter the heart of many a student. Unfortunately, I was sure he could too.

'A busy life,' I remarked, also unwrapping my cutlery. 'So how many concerts are you required to do? And do they have to be in any particular venues?'

'Well, you know we're doing one at the Birmingham and Midlands Institute – my God, in ten days' time?'

I nodded, but didn't mention my part in the evening.

'That's the biggie, of course, given that it's part of the

festival. Then we've got to fit in another couple before the New Year. But they can be here or in Staff House, over on the Oldbury site. We used to have to offer one a week, but we negotiated round that – after all, a public concert needs more rehearsal and brings in more prestige than a purely in-house one.'

'Of course. How long do you get to rehearse?' Many of my friends were orchestral musicians, but I'd never had much to do with people who played more intimate music, where every note was exposed. There's no hiding in the back row of what's called the tutti or rank-and-file desks if there are only four of you.

Hallam snorted. 'Two hours a week! Ridiculous, isn't it? And only four for a public performance. Whereas the real top chamber players get to play six, eight hours a day with each other. And they don't have to practise within earshot of the prof, either!'

I dropped my knife. 'You're joking! You don't have to do that!'

'Don't we just! It was in the original trust document setting up the Boulton Foundation,' he explained.

'But that's the sort of condition Mozart might have had imposed on him!'

'Quite. The last prof ignored it, but French has to have his finger in every pie. A real control freak. He checks on how many hours we practise on our own too – separately and together. Just as if the scholarships were in his personal gift!' He returned his attention to his salad, stabbing at an errant piece of celery so viciously it ricocheted across the table and on to the floor. I retrieved it, dropping it into the ashtray that graced the table despite the 'No Smoking' notices everywhere.

'So who is responsible for dishing them out?' I asked.

'Well, I suppose he is. We have to have a good track record of performing and of scholarship before we're considered.'

'Not teaching?' I asked, suspecting the answer before it came. One of my friends teaching on some self-improvement course in one of the warmer and more agreeable parts of Europe had been asked to suggest potential colleagues with good reputations and high moral standards – the words *teaching skills* hadn't even appeared in the job description.

'Not teaching. Though that's what the department's best at. Churning out more highly qualified kids for more highly qualified orchestras in the hands of highly qualified accountants pointing out that they're about to be swallowed in debt. Redundancy fodder.'

Despite my reservations, I found myself warming to him. But then, I'm prejudiced in favour of anyone who realises young people are our future. Especially someone who seems to like them too. We ate a few mouthfuls in silence.

'This quartet,' I said. 'Do I gather you're recruited separately, then? Not as a unit? So you end up with each other willy-nilly?'

'Not quite. The existing members do have some say in the final selection of any new candidate. You see, there is a certain flexibility about the scholarships. We're supposed to have five years' tenure, but obviously some people want out earlier, and some people get extensions. It's all a bit higgledy-piggledy, and I'm sure it ought to be rationalised somehow. They should sack us all and start again, or something!'

'But you don't actually choose the replacement cellist or whatever? So you could end up with someone you loathe. Or someone who just doesn't fit in with the quartet's style.'

'Absolutely. *Huis Clos*: you know, hell is other people.'

'So how do you get rid of someone you're incompatible with?'

'I'll let you know if the problem ever arises.' He smiled suddenly, dazzlingly, his crow's-feet highly active again.

This time he was smiling at someone over my shoulder. Two

someones: two women. 'Two of my colleagues,' he said. The shorter had an appearance and demeanour of an archetypal second fiddle: she blushed and wriggled when Hallam introduced her as June Tams. The taller – oh, yes: she had to be a cellist, probably in the Jacqueline du Pré school of playing posture, with her long blonde hair, permatanned complexion and huge blue eyes. Caz Byrd. She nodded at me as if accepting homage.

Hallam got to his feet. 'But now, I'm afraid, I have to go and rehearse with my colleagues. Within earshot of the prof.'

I finished the work I'd set myself to do, returned and renewed some library books, and told myself it was time to go home. As I let myself into the car, however, I recognised my usual reluctance to go back to the empty house. We were buying a new house in Edgbaston, but hadn't yet completed – someone way back in the chain was being awkward. So we'd been living one week at my house, one at Mike's. As a consequence, my whole domestic life was out of kilter. I couldn't settle to either garden, though given the incredibly wet weather it would have been impossible anyway, I suppose, to get them to my usual pre-winter standard of tidiness. And what was the point? Well into October the lavateras and fuchsias were still going strong – it would be a shame to cut them down, especially as the lawns were waterlogged and best not walked on. And although one day I would have to go to check out the BMI, the venue for the Boulton Quartet's concert for which I was doing the catering, there was no point in going into the city centre on just one errand.

So what, in the absence of any good ideas how to spend my time, should I do now? I was even denied a restorative cup of tea with my old mate Chris Groom at Smethwick's Piddock Road Police Station. He'd been seconded temporarily to the West Midlands Police's Murder Investigation Unit, and it looked horribly as if temporary was turning into permanent.

Another gust of wind, this one bringing great dollops of heavy rain, almost took the car door off. I grabbed it, and shut myself in. It had better be home, hadn't it?

Chapter Three

What amazed me was that James Hallam hadn't mentioned his part in an open rehearsal the following evening. I only found out about it because I happened to be talking in the loo to a double bass player. In my experience women bass players tended to be the most diminutive women around, even smaller than me, as if making a point. This one was the opposite, nearly six foot tall and broad with it – what we call in the Black Country a strapping wench – rejoicing, according to the name on her file, in the inapposite name of Rose. Her surname was more down to earth: Dungate. According to Rose, the idea was that various students would play solo with the departmental orchestra throughout the year, one eventually being chosen to perform at the end-of-year concert. Wherever possible they were paired with a member of staff, presumably for support and criticism.

'There can't be all that many concertos for two players,' I said absently, thinking more, to be honest, about Mike's current innings in Pakistan.

Not surprisingly, Rose sighed, splaying muscular fingers and beginning to enumerate: 'Mozart Flute and Harp Concerto, Mozart Sinfonia Concertante, Bach Double Violin Concerto . . . *Everyone* knows those.'

Everyone who was anyone, her sneer said. Which I clearly wasn't. Well, at her age I suppose I'd have felt the same, that the older you got the dimmer you got.

Trying to laugh, I joined in. 'Plus the Brahms Double – though surely no one would tackle that with a chamber orchestra – and all those baroque concertos. I get the picture.' I smiled. 'Didn't Dittersdorf write some stuff for double bass plus friends?'

Perhaps I might not be the ignorant twit I'd seemed at first, but her huge grin seemed an overreaction.

'And tonight it's . . .?' I prompted her.

'The Mozart Sinfonia Concertante – violin and viola,' she said.

One of my very favourite pieces: perhaps I should go along and hear how it was put together. 'So who's involved?'

'Neil Wiltshire – he's the leader of the departmental orchestra – and James Hallam.'

'Can anyone turn up and listen?'

She pulled a face. 'Anyone in the department who isn't actually playing *has* to. No option. It's a real pain – we all have to have jobs to keep going, and yet they insist on having events in the evening. Makes it really bad for people working shifts.'

'Shouldn't the student representative point this out in your staff-student forums, or whatever you call them here? Boards of Study? You know, where you discuss quality issues?'

She obviously didn't know. 'Hey, you haven't got time to tell me about these forums? Over a coffee, maybe?'

'Yes, a coffee would be fine,' I agreed, checking my watch. She could have five minutes of Sophie in education-mode. And then I really must concentrate on my own work. The way the music department ran itself was truly no concern of mine. But I might just turn up for the open rehearsal.

I didn't realise that such pretty boys existed these days. Oh, at William Murdock we had our share of handsome ones, and I suppose pretty ones to. But the vast majority of our students were Asian or African-Caribbean, with the appropriate sort of beauty. So the sight of Neil Wiltshire startled me. Although he was nearly six feet tall, he could have modelled as a stereotypical choirboy – angel, even. His hair palest gold, he had the most delicate pink and white complexion, the sort that would flush painfully if ever he were embarrassed, which was probably often. He had the sweetest Cupid's bow of a mouth. To complete the perfection nature had fringed his dark blue eyes with thick brown lashes. The sight of such glory in the mirror each morning hadn't, alas, inspired him with the confidence it would have given a girl. More likely it had reminded him of the day's bullying ahead. The poor kid looked gentle, vulnerable – and, to be perfectly honest, quite terrified. Every light in the auditorium was trained on him. The fact that it was really just a very large room, ideal for chamber works and an audience of about a hundred, was irrelevant. It might have been Symphony Hall in all its grandeur, full to capacity, as far as he was concerned.

'He's a wonderful fiddler,' Rose Dungate whispered in my ear as we took our seats. 'They were bound to make him leader,' she added naïvely, as if leading an orchestra weren't less about playing than about personality. All the orchestral leaders I've known have had a certain panache – they're chosen to lead because they can do just that: lead.

But not happy about taking a big solo. No doubt this mentoring and sharing scheme was designed to alleviate such anxiety. If you had to work together rehearsing and then actually performing, no doubt the professional would coax and support – and eventually, I trusted, stand back to let the youngster take the plaudits at the end.

So why the poor kid was having to hang round like a spare dinner was beyond me. While also waiting, the orchestra had at least music stands to hide behind, and could occupy themselves tuning up and gossiping, in whichever order. To my amazement – wouldn't he need it to refer to, bar by bar, with the conductor? – Neil had brought in no music, so didn't need to adjust the height of a music stand. It would have been much better for him to complete his tuning elsewhere – even in the corridor outside, for goodness' sake – and make an entrance, which would in itself be excellent preparation for his professional life. James Hallam was making one, anyway, bringing in a score as well as his fiddle and bow. And got a round of applause from the audience and a rattling of bows and stamping of feet from the orchestra. I rather expected him, given his previous pro-student attitude, to acknowledge Neil with a sweep of the hand. But he simply placed the score on a stand, and stepped forward to speak to the audience.

'Ladies and gentleman,' he announced, 'I'm afraid Marcus French is indisposed this evening, so I shall endeavour to direct the orchestra as well as take the solo viola part.' A smirky smile suggested he'd have no difficulty doing both, probably while riding a unicycle.

Hm. Self-effacing he was not. And why, when his news had clearly nonplussed the orchestra, which was, after all, just a bunch of students, not a body of hardened professionals used to dealing with last-minute changes, should he address himself to us? My opinion of James Hallam – I'd not disliked him, remember – was going down by the minute.

I had to admit that he was a very fine viola player. The trouble with the viola is that it's heavy and cumbersome, which places physical demands on the player. For some reason most violas don't project very well, so they produce a very small sound – I have known even professional performances where the soloist has been amplified. Hallam was big enough not to be disturbed by the length and bulk, and managed to get enough volume out of it to compete with the much stronger violin. Of course, Mozart had already thought of the problem, instructing the viola soloist to tune his strings up a semitone, the extra tension brightening the sound. Quite how the violist then fingers the piece I'm not at all sure – but then, I am a mere back-row soprano, not a string player.

What I did know very quickly was that Neil was not getting

the support he expected. The very nature of the piece, two solo instruments playing with each other and an orchestra, demands very close co-operation between the two principals. They have to watch each other as well as listen – first one plays a phrase, then the other expands or reflects on it. Mozart went against tradition and gave the initiative in most cases to the viola: well, he was a viola player himself, and no doubt thought it was time to have something other than the chum-chum-chum-chum, chum-chum-chum-chum of its usual accompanying role. But the violin gets to lead as well. The whole work celebrates partnership. For that reason – apart from my loving it anyway – it was one of the first pieces I'd given Mike: we had his and hers CDs, one at each house. I'd played it a great deal in his absence.

But I digress. It wasn't Mike I should be thinking about but poor Neil.

By now it was apparent that Hallam was concentrating on giving a performance. Despite orchestral rough edges, he was ploughing through the first movement without stopping. Neil was doing his best, but since Hallam either stared resolutely at his music stand or turned to bring in orchestral sections on time, it was a very unsupported best. How could a man who was supposed to be a chamber player systematically avoid eye contact with another player? Either he was a very bad chamber musician, or there was some history between him and Neil I wasn't privy to.

At last the first movement ended. Now Hallam would stop, surely, to discuss problem passages: phrasing, bowing, breathing – that sort of thing. There'd been a number of dominoes – wrong notes – that he'd want to eradicate too. At last he'd have to bring Neil in, as his fellow soloist with as much right to comment and criticise as he.

Wrong. He did all the conductorly stuff, as I'd expected, picking out meticulously passages that needed work. But Neil might as well not have existed. The poor kid tried once or

23

twice to make points, but Hallam took as much notice as if the music stand had started to speak – rather less, come to think of it. At long last he suggested a break, and the orchestra – and Neil – bolted as one.

'What the hell's all that about?' I asked Rose, as she got to her feet, stretching.

'All what?'

'The ritual humiliation of your colleague?'

Rose looked completely blank.

'Didn't you notice?'

'Notice what?'

'The fact that Hallam was completely upstaging someone he should have been supporting. Not just supporting: encouraging.'

'Well, Neil was playing all right.'

I gave up. Whatever Rose had been concentrating on for the last forty-five minutes, it certainly wasn't what was going on in front of her eyes. Perhaps she was simply tired: she'd mentioned shift and evening work on top of the studying and playing load imposed by the course. I remembered the happier and more generous days of student grants, wondering yet again how many of the politicians and civil servants who'd devised the current scheme had had to pay for their higher education and were now landed with appalling debts after a hand-to-mouth existence.

'Let's have a coffee,' she said.

'OK,' I said, without enthusiasm. It would have to be from a machine: UWM's excellent facilities didn't run to having the refectory fully operational in the evenings. 'Look, there's Dawn!' I lifted a hand to wave.

'Oh, do come on, Sophie.' Rose stepped between me and Dawn, then seized my arm, propelling me from the hall.

I was disconcerted, to say the least. Feeding coins into the machine and having them steadily rejected, I felt very tempted simply to abandon the rehearsal – I was under no compulsion

24

to stay, after all – and to push off home and see if I could catch any interesting cricket coverage. But I wanted to hear other people's interpretations of what I'd just witnessed, though couldn't with Rose standing guard. Eventually she went off to the loo. Rejecting her suggestion I might want to go too, I looked about me. Neil's own reaction might be interesting. He was standing alone, staring dismally at his coffee, so I had every chance to probe. But he had another hour or so to get through, so I merely smiled at him, saying, 'You're playing beautifully.'

He blushed to a rich peony.

'You've actually memorised it, I see.' Now was clearly not the time to ask him how he would clarify details.

'It— I find— You see—'

Lead? This poor kid could scarcely follow, yet he had to go on for the second half and give his all in two more movements. I said brightly encouraging things about his interpretation, his tone, his sensitivity and his general musicality. With each word he brightened, his smile increasingly in evidence. He looked more and more every mother's favourite son.

I thought with a pang of Steph, my own son by my cousin Andy. Steph had been adopted at birth. He'd sought me out, and at last met his father too. Thinking it was time to get him away from his indulgent adoptive parents – no, his real parents – and bond with him, Andy had whisked him off to Africa. Andy had thought that a stint working for his trust in Mwandara would enable them to get to know each other and teach Steph how privileged he was in every sense. I gathered from what little either let drop that father-son communication wasn't at all easy, but that at least Steph was showing talents he'd never dreamt he possessed. One was for teaching with infinite compassion and humour children orphaned when their parents had died of Aids. Now I felt the guilt Andy had expressed: it was easier for me to talk to this clean and tidy young man than it was to talk to my own son.

25

Neil talked animatedly about his choir school, his music scholarship to a specialist school, and his disappointment at not getting into a first-rate school of music – glandular fever before A levels, he said. All this in the space of about five minutes. I was touched but anxious that he should reveal so much to the most casual of acquaintances. Clearly I couldn't abandon him now.

Rose was hovering by my shoulder, her face heavy with resentment.

'It's time we were going back in,' she informed me.

'Hang on,' I said. I stepped towards Neil, taking his arm and turning him slightly. 'No, don't dash in first,' I urged. 'You're entitled to walk in alongside him. It's your show too, you know. Don't let Hallam up-stage you.'

If a rabbit in a car's headlights could have smiled, it would have looked like Neil. Maybe the poor kid had forgotten he had another hour to go.

'Come *on*, Sophie,' Rose said, tugging the shoulder strap of my bag. 'For goodness' sake!' Then, hand on my shoulder, she started to propel me back to the rehearsal room.

I didn't know whom to be more irritated with, her for behaving as if she owned me or me for letting it get to me. After all, she was just a kid with poor social skills. She was trying to be friendly.

The funny thing was that my William Murdock kids and I had always been on the easiest of terms, but I couldn't imagine any of them bossing me around. Then the penny dropped. I wasn't staff any more, was I? I was a student. But I was also a human being, not a wagon to be shunted. Should I make a professional lift of the eyebrow to tell Rose she'd overstepped a mark I could see quite clearly, even if she couldn't? Or should I simply not give her the opportunity in future? I couldn't stop myself trying to shrug her off. But she gripped all the more tightly.

'Rose, there's something I have to say to Neil.'

'But you've been talking to Neil all evening!' Reluctantly, she let me go.

In fact, all I did was wink and grin at him, but even that was enough to make Rose rigid with sulk throughout the second half of the rehearsal. I was too much interested in the continued interplay between Hallam and Neil to worry about her then. I could scarcely believe it was the effect of the pitifully few kind words I'd offered him, but Neil was a different player. Perhaps it was in the hope of uncovering this potential that some imaginative teacher had made him leader. Now, instead of stolidly following Hallam's lead, he started to push forward his own personality, and, since the band were taking his phrases as their model and ignoring Hallam's none-too-obvious beat, Hallam had to follow him or look a fool. Stamping my feet – I didn't want to give the game away by doing anything as obvious as clapping – I led the orchestra in what they thought was a spontaneous round of applause for the two players.

But maybe I'd done the wrong thing. It might have sent Neil home a much happier young man, but I suspected that Hallam had a long memory. The next few weeks might be distinctly unpleasant for the student violinist.

Chapter Four

As the wrinkles era approaches, rather more briskly than I care to admit, I spend more and more time on my skincare and, it has to be admitted, the same phrase without the word 'time'. The products that seem to suit me best – and I know the whole beauty business may be an expensive con – require a journey into Birmingham's steadily improving city centre. On the grounds of economy of stones in bird-killing, I thought I'd also check out the catering facilities of the Birmingham and Midlands Institute, a Victorian Gothic pile in Margaret Street.

The receptionist put me into the hands of an alert man in his forties, hair cut army short, called Peter Andrews. He described himself as an admin assistant, and ushered me through one of the many sets of doors with which the BMI seemed to be blessed.

'It's pretty unusual to have refreshments after a concert, isn't it?' he asked as we started down the long, elegant stairway to the subterranean bar, under the gaze of Victorian worthies in heavy gilt frames. On the landing was a little collection of plastic flowers in a sixties wrought-iron stand. Still, however much I'd have preferred to see something living, I suppose that with no natural light not many plants would have survived.

'It's not often this quartet goes public,' I replied. 'And I fancy it's a bit of a PR thing. After all, the UWM's not the best-known—'

'UWM?'

'There you are! I rest my case. The University of the West Midlands – the music department's based in Smethwick—'

'Smethwick!' His lip curled. 'But Smethwick's . . .' He seemed lost for words.

Feigning my most didactic manner, I said, loosely referring to Jane Austen's Mrs Elton, 'There may be people out there who believe that nothing good can come from Smethwick –'

Andrews narrowed his eyes as if trying to place the allusion.

'– But they would be the victims of age-old prejudice, which, though I come from Oldbury, the neighbour and long-standing rival of Smethwick, I strive to overcome.'

'You Black Country people.' He shook his head.

I could have embarked on a learned disquisition concerning the Black Country's general superiority to Birmingham, but thought it was time to get back to the point. 'I know UWM isn't the best known of our Midlands universities, and I think it wants to put itself more on the map. And however big it may be in the Black Country – and it's bigger than Wolverhampton Uni, I believe – it wants to muscle in on the territory of the Birmingham unis.'

'Hmm.' Peter Andrews pulled a face. '"Pride goeth before destruction"—'

' "And an haughty spirit before a fall",' I completed for him, delighted to find someone who knew his quotations.

I doubt if he considered my price far above rubies, but he let me into a spacious seating area, divided by upholstered benches into U shapes, echoed at the far end of each by U-shaped niches. Like the seating, they were much more recent than the building itself. They were the right size for statues, but were currently unoccupied.

He coughed apologetically. 'A bit naff, maybe, but better than the area windows they cover.'

I looked around. 'The UWM people told me there was a restaurant with a functioning kitchen.'

'There was. But it's not been used for some time. We took

away the counter and supposedly mothballed the kitchen. But I'm not sure it will be usable.'

Nor was it. Not unless someone moved out an assortment of easels and folding desks. And I didn't think I'd want to put them to that trouble. There was an air of sadness about the place – actually, on reflection, the smell of long-expired cooking oil – which confirmed my resolution to prepare all the nibbles at home.

'How many are you expecting?' Peter asked.

'Between fifty and a hundred.' I surveyed the available space. 'Plenty of room.'

He nodded. 'Better to have a crowd than to have too few rattling round. What about waiters and waitresses?'

'UWM students, glad of the chance to make an honest penny.'

'Even the amount waiters are paid?'

'I build their wages into my estimates,' I said. 'So I know exactly how much they get paid. They're happy, even if my customers might not be.'

He nodded thoughtfully, then smiled. 'The bar's still operational,' he said. 'Do you fancy a drink? I'm afraid I can't offer you draught anything, though we used to buy beer by the barrel. There's a chute in the boiler room they used to roll down, and then we'd trundle them into here.'

Just at that moment nothing seemed nicer than a drink, so I sank down on one of the benches and watched him retreat behind the bar. I have very firm ideas about wine that might have been open some time. So I plumped for a bottled lager. That seemed to suit him too. He brought the bottles and a couple of glasses over to the little table and sat beside me.

'I don't know when I last came in here,' I said. 'I've an idea I did some sort of oral exam here when I was at school. French or German, maybe.'

'We still use one of the big rooms upstairs for exams,' he

said. 'And we rent rooms to the College of Food. We have to make money where we can.'

'The membership needed to sustain a place like this must be enormous,' I suggested.

'That's right. We've got about four hundred. We need far more, of course. But people don't seem to join things any more.'

I nodded.

'It's such a waste,' Peter continued. 'We've got a most magnificent library here, hopelessly underused. I don't mean just the lending library, which is well stocked. But we've got a rare books section – volumes going back to 1779.'

'So can people use it for research?'

'That's what's primarily attracting new members: the research material. Want to look round?'

If I have a weakness, it's nosiness. I love poking round any building, and when it's one like this, the invitation was irresistible. 'Have you got time? In that case, yes please!'

'Are you up to the stairs?'

'Try me!'

My heart went out to the poor building. It cried out for money to restore it to its former glory, or at least to de-restore it from its nineteen-fifties' and sixties' 'improvements'. Even some appropriate carpeting would have been better.

I spread my hands sadly.

'Yes, it would be nice to do it justice,' Peter said. 'But it's a matter of funds.'

'Lottery?' I suggested brightly.

'We can't even afford the money for the feasibility test they want,' he said. 'Meanwhile, perhaps our future lies in the past. I'll show you the library in a minute. And it's this way to the theatre where your quartet will be playing.'

Despite a sign pointing to the theatre, he led me up the stairs again. And another flight.

'I thought—' I began.

'That's the John Lee Theatre down there. Your quartet's using the Lyttelton. Here you are.' He disappeared into another bar – the theatre bar – and thence through a door into a modern auditorium.

So there I was, cheek by jowl with a grand piano, staring up at the ranks of seats, some of which were in need of repair. But the rake was good, and the brick walls beautiful, despite some recentish paintings best not commented on. I projected in a manner which would have made an Actorrr Managerrr proud:

> 'I wonder by my troth, what thou, and I
> Did, till we lov'd? Were we not wean'd till then,
> But suck'd on country pleasures, childishly?'

The acoustics were fine for speech, but, I thought, might turn out to be a little dry for music. Certainly they wouldn't forgive any uncertainties of intonation or ensemble. The quartet had better make sure they used every moment of that pitiful amount of rehearsal time.

Peter looked reasonably impressed with my recitation, and I could see him fossicking in his memory for something to cap Donne with. His smile of triumph worried me. He stepped forward too:

> 'Your smiles are not, as other women's be,
> Only the drawing of the mouth awry;
> Parts wanting motion, all stand smiling by.'

As I feared, he had me there. I suspected from the way he'd stumbled between lines two and three that he'd missed a bit, though whether by accident or design I wasn't sure.

'OK, you've served an ace there,' I said. 'Are you going to tell me or do I have to guess?'

'Why not look it up,' he smiled, 'in our library?'

From the stage we progressed to the green room, a narrow

corridor-like place with no room to swing a piccolo, let alone a cello. It broadened out, however, the wall bending to follow the curving lines of the theatre wall. My eyes caught glimpses of greater days: the Evelyn Laye Room, the Wynford Vaughan-Thomas Room.

'Just storerooms now,' Peter said, not opening them.

There was a clutter of furniture at the far end of the green room, and a built-in cupboard. Except it wasn't built in, but built out, projecting two or three feet into the room. Big enough for Rose's bass, nearly.

Peter opened a door at the far end. 'There. Now, if we just go down *these* stairs, I can show you the library. Unless you'd prefer the lift?'

I thought of the calories I should be burning off. 'Stairs, please.'

This flight was much less distinguished than the first grand staircase – the equivalent, perhaps, of the back stairs in a country house. At the top, Peter pointed out, were some loos. But he led me – by now throughly confused – to the library, a room with a pleasant seating area and some formidable ranks of bookshelves off to the right. An iron barrier and a locked gate prevented access to the specialist library he was clearly so proud of. Feeling like Alice, I gathered my skirt and followed him down a circular staircase. For no apparent reason, the iron was painted bright orange. Be that as it may, I could see why he should be so proud of the place. My Mike, with his passion for local history, and indeed for literature, would have thought he'd died and gone to heaven. All round the circumference, for instance, were biographies and autobiographies in alphabetical order. I plucked a book at random – 1919 Commemorative essays on W. G. Grace.

'So where do I start?' I grinned. 'You'll have to give me a clue. It's years since I read the Metaphysicals properly.'

'Bonus marks for spotting it was a Metaphysical. And it was a first line.'

You could probably have heard the groanings and creakings of my brain. The volume I found offered authors and titles, but no first lines. I ran through all the names I could remember, almost at random – lovely names, designed for poets! Lovelace; Herrick; Suckling; plus all the more famous ones, like Carew or Waller or Marvell. At last he led me back upstairs and pressed into my hand a book I'd kept beside my bed when I was a teenager for ever in love: Helen Gardner's Penguin edition. And there it was – Aurelian Townshend.

'I don't recall ever having heard of him,' I admitted, 'though I must have done – I actually had this very book.'

'Not the greatest nor the most fashionable of the Metaphysicals,' he laughed. 'Now, apart from music – did I tell you we have fortnightly lunchtime chamber concerts? No? Well, apart from that and the regular Monday lecture, we run occasional study days on literature. It's really geared for sixth-formers but other people are welcome too. There's one on the Metaphysicals coming up – now, it's either late February or early March.'

'Sounds wonderful,' I said. But by then I'd probably be in the witness box at an unpleasant trial. I think I even shivered. Nothing like being a witness and having to recall things best forgotten for unsettling you.

'You look – troubled,' Peter said, eyeing me with concern.

I was going to quip about someone walking over my grave but found I didn't want to. 'I'm fine,' I said rather brusquely.

'Want to see the rest of the place? It's a rabbit warren because three buildings were knocked into one . . . Look – this was one of the dividing walls.'

So while I indulged my passion for sniffing round strong rooms and staircases, he indulged his for the building: yes, he obviously loved the place, seeing under the sixties' stuff its potential for real beauty. I was almost tempted to chuck in my course to come and help fund-raise. Now, that corridor there . . .

'Now, Peter,' I said, pulling myself together, 'what I need to know is when I can have access to the bar on the evening of the event.'

Brought back to reality, he pulled a face. 'Well, when the concert hall's open, I suppose. Though the building will be open during the afternoon so that the quartet can rehearse here. Would that be better?'

'Much,' I said. 'Do you have tablecloths or shall I bring . . .?'

I should have relished the calm and tranquillity of the BMI while I had the chance. I was due back to UWM to play for Leonore, a young black soprano soon to embark on a Grieg and Tchaikovsky recital, sharing the platform, with – wait for it – a male member of staff. If Bob Heywood was anything like James Hallam, she'd need all the support she could get – and your accompanist was the foundation, the buttress or whatever architectural image you preferred.

I arrived in plenty of time, to find Rose in tears. She could have wept all she wanted, had she not chosen my chair in the post-grad workroom to do it. My fellow post-grads were shuffling with embarrassment, feigning great interest in their computers or their notes.

The first thing to do was get her outside. As I did so, Myra called me back, tapping a book as she did so. I peered. Jane Austen's *Persuasion*. Myra leant towards me, mouthing, '"Taste cannot tolerate a large bulky figure in deep affliction".'

I was shocked: Myra herself was a earth mother figure, comfortably built, and normally very kind. It was unlike her to relish one of Austen's tarter observations. Saying nothing, I followed Rose into the corridor.

At William Murdock I seemed to spend most of my life counselling students in the loo, so that was where I urged Rose now, as she quivered with emotion. Oh dear. Why hadn't Myra kept her mouth shut? Poor Rose wasn't mourning a dead son whom alive nobody had cared for. She was an unhappy kid.

36

But her tears seemed more angry than sorrowful, when it came down to it. I calmed her as best I could. It seemed she had been given a bad grade in her most recent assessment while Dawn had been given a good one.

'We worked together on this, right the way through. It's just favouritism, isn't it?' she sobbed. 'Just because Marcus bloody French's got his hand in Dawn's knickers, she gets good marks and I get crap ones. She's nothing but a whore. And he – he's a—'

Oh God. The sort of allegation every teacher at whatever level dreads, the sort that has to be dealt with with utmost discretion and there's Rose yelling it at the top of her not inconsiderable voice. *Sophie, Rose is not Mrs Musgrove!* 'That's a terribly serious allegation to make, Rose,' I said. 'Now, calm down and tell me what sort of assignment it is.'

'What does it matter what sort of assignment it is? She's cheating, that's what. Nothing but a sex-mad cunt.'

Oh dear.

'Her and Neil. Just because they're pretty and can wheedle their way into anyone's bed. How do you think Neil got to be leader?'

'Because of what you said yourself: he's a good musician. Now, Rose—'

'No, he's a bum boy, a rent boy, whatever you call them—'

I took a deep breath. 'We shouldn't be talking about other people. We're hear to talk about your work. Just tell me what the assignment was about – and what sort of comments you got, both of you.'

The direct instruction seemed to calm her. 'It was an essay on changes in ornamentation between Bach and Mozart. And she gets an A and I only get a C. She's just a tart.'

'You mustn't go round saying things like that. Not without evidence. It's libellous. What did French write on the bottom of your assignment?' I was hoping for some comments on style or structure, anything to suggest that it was Rose's literary style rather than Dawn's sexual one that had made the difference.

'What does it matter?' The sobs were louder, more hysterical. 'Oh, Sophie!'

She cast herself upon me. I don't exaggerate when I say I staggered under her weight. She stood a good ten inches taller than me, after all, and probably weighed in three or four stone heavier. I patted her back ineffectually and tried to return her to the vertical. But it seemed to me as I did so that I was being clung to with more than the misery of a girl with a bad mark. If it had been a bloke, I'd have said he was trying for a quick squeeze and that his hands were in grope-mode.

'Come on, Rose,' I said firmly, 'pull yourself together.' I tried to disengage myself from her grip. 'Get some cold water on those eyes of yours and then you can come down to the refec and have a coffee while I look at that assignment. Right?'

I grabbed a fistful of paper towel and thrust it at her. She had to let go of me to grasp it. I was torn between a strong desire for the quickest of escapes, sympathy for someone perhaps unjustly treated and anger that what she was accusing the revolting French of might just be true. And deep down I was uneasy. I'd never had to cope with anyone quite like Rose without the back-up of my college, where I'd have bolted to a counsellor for help.

'Black or white?' I opened the inner door and stood in the little lobby waiting for her response.

'Don't leave me!'

'I'm not leaving you. You're coming with me,' I said. 'I'll get you black, shall I?'

I let the door shut on her, then let myself briskly out of the other and headed, as I'd said, for the refectory. What had happened to me? Where was my sympathy for a kid who needed calm encouragement? Why could I befriend young Neil when he needed it and not help her? Ashamed, I made it two black coffees. Large ones.

Chapter Five

I didn't know much about the changes in ornamentation between Bach's time and Mozart's, so I couldn't judge Rose's essay on content. Its structure wasn't too obvious, but it was the style that really let it down – it was dreadfully stodgy and lumpen. So I wasn't surprised she only scored a C – the equivalent, she told me, of a 2.2 degree. Not an ungenerous mark, then.

I couldn't spend long with her, however, given my prior arrangement with Leonore, who was already doing warm-up exercises when I found her in the practice room we'd booked. She was embarrassingly grateful to me for giving up my time, as she put it, to help her.

'Wait till you hear me,' I laughed. 'You may regret asking me. I'm very rusty. More to the point, I've always played solo or in a small ensemble before – and neither for absolutely ages, remember.'

It certainly took time to get going, both of us hesitant and awkward. But at last we managed to synchronise quite well, only to find that our session was over and that someone else was already rattling the door. We left together, checking our diaries so we could fit in another session as soon as possible, and laughing over the apparent impossibility.

I ran into Neil on my way back to the post-grad study room. He was leaning against a window overlooking the autumnal garden, looking as pensive as one fancies Donne must have looked – something he did extremely well. Had it not been for the different colouring, Neil would have been wonderfully like the romantic young man in that famous Hilliard miniature. He'd have looked so good in a white doublet and hose, clutching a wistful rose – always assuming his legs were good enough, of course. My Mike, now, he'd have been wonderful as a swashbuckling adventurer, complete with thigh-length leather boots.

Neil was embarrassingly not clear who I was, but it was obvious from his hesitant smile that he'd filed me somewhere under 'Friendly'. I produced the staff-to-good-student grin I'd perfected over so many years, remembering too late that I wasn't staff at all. Anyway, it reassured him enough for him to peel himself from the window.

'You did very well last night,' I said truthfully. 'Sophie Rivers – we spoke during the interval.'

'Oh, yes. Oh, thanks. Thank you very much. It's all down to my tutor, of course,' he said. 'Alex Fisher. He's a wonderful teacher.'

'Clearly.' But if he was so good, why hadn't he been at the open rehearsal to cheer Neil on? I would have been, and I'd have had the strongest of words with Hallam afterwards. I asked, 'What did he think of your efforts?'

'Oh – well, he couldn't be there. He did tell me beforehand, actually. Family party or something. He was terribly sweet – offered to try to get out of it. But of course he had to be there – his kid's birthday. That's the trouble with having these things in the evening – people have other things on.'

'I was telling Rose yesterday about the staff-student forums at my old place. Why not talk to her?' I suggested, not wishing to go over the same material again. 'They'd be just the place to raise issues like that. You'd have to sort out a departmental rep or two, and the staff would do the same. You could talk about issues raised in the quality question-naires too.'

'Quality questionnaires?' His eyes widened.

'Yes, you know the sort of thing: how the course is going as a whole; weak points; strong points; problems with the environment. That sort of thing.' I didn't mention essentials like the quality of the teaching and other tendentious issues. Not my business.

He shook his head. 'I've never seen anything like that.'

Hadn't the place had a quality assurance inspection recently?

'I'm sure you will. But as far as the forums are concerned, talk to Rose.' I looked at my watch. Time to do a bit more work.

'I will. Yes, of course.' He flushed. He looked over my shoulder and beamed, looking like a vulnerable eleven-year-old. 'Hi, Alex,' he said shyly.

I turned. Oh, yes, if I'd been his age I might have blushed too. Alex Fisher, perhaps a year or two my junior, was a god in human form – certainly the sort of person to stand out if he'd been to the open rehearsal the previous night. Heavens, he'd have stood out anywhere! Six feet tall, with dark curly hair, eyes nearly as blue as Mike's and a wonderfully sensitive mouth – oh, yes: he was noticeable.

He gave Neil a brief smile, and a more extended version to me. What worried me was the quality of the smile – there was a distinctly interrogatory angle to it. Appraising, even. And, despite the warmth around the mouth, those beautiful eyes seemed decidedly cold.

'Alex,' Neil said, 'this is – er, Sophie. Sophie, Alex is my tutor and the leader of the Boulton Quartet.'

So the quartet sported three good-looking players and one poor mouse.

Alex nodded easily and shook my hand.

'I gather you missed Neil's big moment,' I said.

'I'm hoping he'll be doing a repeat performance in the summer,' he said, his voice kinder than his face. 'He's a very talented fiddler, as I'm sure you heard.'

41

'Extremely.' Having agreed on that, I thought it was time to take myself off.

'Are you our mysterious pianist?' Alex asked, as I turned.

'I helped Leonore out, and I've got a couple of sessions with Dan Langley next week.'

'But I've seen you around a great deal. I feel I know you – even if no one's introduced us till now. Welcome to the faculty,' he said, holding out his hand, 'oh, mysterious pianist!'

'Thanks, but I'm an education student – which is where I'm off to now.' I smiled and set off down the corridor. Why couldn't young men – even attractive ones – realise how naff all this talk of being mysterious was! Any moment the silly sod might want to plumb my depths. Or, indeed, those of any other woman under seventy.

An awkward silence greeted me when I entered the post-grad room. Since I'd heard voices as I opened the door, the silence had to be something to do with me. I plonked my bag on my desk, slung my coat on a hook and burrowed in my cabinet. The silence persisted. Yes, it was something to do with me. I hadn't been in a position like this since my schooldays. At William Murdock we'd been mates enough to fire up straight away if there were a problem, have a good row, and retire to the pub to cement the friendship again. Not that we'd had much energy for rows, and, when management had tried to divide and rule, it had been in our interests to keep everything as low key as possible. Whatever the cause and the end result, however, the silent treatment was rarely if ever meted out. Neither were audible sniffs and noisy exits, which seemed to be the order of the day here.

Soon only one post-grad was left: Greg, a serious-faced man approaching fifty with whom I'd had very little to do hitherto – we both used what time we spent on university premises to work.

He coughed with more embarrassment than catarrh.

'What's going on, Greg? You seem to have picked the short straw,' I said.

He pulled a face, getting up and prowling round the room, hands in pockets.

'It's obviously me going on. What have I done?'

He stopped prowling and settled, if uncomfortably, on a chair next to mine. I swung to face him.

'We feel – we all feel – that you should keep your private life separate from your college life. What you do in your spare time is up to you, but we don't want any part of it. We've all given up a year's pay to be here, and we'd rather not have our work interrupted.'

'I can quite appreciate that. But could you be more specific?' I was genuinely puzzled, and also distressed. My heart was pounding as in the old school-bully days: I fought hard not to wipe my palms or straighten my hair.

'I'm sure you know what I mean,' he said awkwardly.

'I assure you I don't. I'd much rather you spelt it out.'

There was a knock at the door. I'd have ignored it, but Greg seemed relieved to be let off the hook.

Rose. More recent tears on her face. I got to my feet to back her out of the room, but she didn't seem inclined to back.

I pulled a semi-comic face at Greg. 'See you in a minute,' I said. 'And I meant what I said.'

No answering smile: all I saw in his face was anger and exasperation.

'Oh, Sophie—'

'This is a workroom, Rose,' I said. 'We can't talk here. It disturbs my colleagues. Come on—'

'But it's private!'

'All the more reason not to talk here. Come on.' I ushered her briskly out, but dodged back. 'Sorry, Greg. You see how it is. But I meant it – I really want to know what's bugging everyone.'

Greg snorted and turned an unfriendly shoulder. My God,

was that all? That Rose's visit earlier had got on his and the others' nerves? Maybe she'd returned. And returned . . .

My mind only a tenth on Rose, I propelled her once again to the ladies' loo. 'I'd like to help, but I really am very busy,' I said.

'You've got time to spend on Leonore,' she sobbed.

'I'm accompanying her,' I said. 'And Dan.'

'You never offered to accompany me!'

'You're not required to offer a recital programme, are you?' I could have pointed out that I wasn't a very good bet anyway. 'Anyway, what's the problem you wanted to talk about?'

'It's this essay. I really need to get a good mark for it and I wondered if you'd help.'

'My degree's in English, Rose – I can't possibly help with a music essay.'

'But you could if I explained it to you. And you could check my spelling and stuff.'

Oh dear. It wouldn't take me long, but it was technically cheating, and I'd been in education long enough to hate the very thought. I said patiently, 'If you have a problem with content, talk to someone in the music department. As far as spelling and grammar are concerned, all you need to do is use the spell-check on your computer. You are supposed to word-process essays, aren't you?'

'But you'd do it better.'

'But then it'd be my work, not yours. Come on,' I said bracingly, 'you're – what – a second- or third-year student?'

'Second.'

'Well, you must have written good essays before to have got through the first year. Don't let one bad grade get you down.'

'It's not just one bad grade. I'm *hopeless* at essays!'

I told her what I'd have told any of my tutees back at William Murdock. 'In that case go and talk to the Student Support staff and get some professional help.'

'Next thing you'll tell me to let that bastard Marcus French fuck me – that way I'll be sure of getting a good grade.' Her voice rose alarmingly.

'Nonsense. I want you to get a good grade because you've worked hard for it,' I said quietly and reasonably.

'If I let French fuck me I'd certainly be working hard.' Her voice was now full volume.

I said urgently, 'Be quiet. You're making allegations that could ruin a man's career. If you have evidence, it should be taken to the right people, not shouted out in a toilet!'

'You don't believe me – I knew you wouldn't.' Her face was awash with tears.

'I don't believe or disbelieve you,' I said, still trying to keep calm. 'All you've done is get angry and upset, and said things to make me get angry and upset. If there's a problem with French or any other teacher, of course I'll support you, provided you go through the correct channels. You'll need support,' I added darkly, 'because it's a very grim business for all concerned.' I grabbed some paper towel and thrust it at her. 'Now, come and have a coffee, and then we'll go and find what the university offers in the way of Student Support.' What she needed was more than academic support – but how could I possibly suggest she ask for professional counselling? No. I couldn't help her myself. For all I pitied her, I couldn't like her. And if I wasn't terribly careful to help her stand on her own feet, she'd come to depend more and more on me.

I had something else to worry about too: there was something missing in me that had always got me through in the past. It was as if I'd given and given and had nothing more to give.

By the time I'd sorted everything out, it was well after five. Predictably, the post-grad room was empty. Everyone had packed up and gone home. Sighing, I gathered my things. I might as well do the same, mightn't I? Except there was a meeting of the Local History Group in a couple of hours' time, at the Oldbury Campus. Mike would certainly have wanted to hear the local history lecture, about working conditions for nineteenth-century glassworkers in Stourbridge. I'd go and minute it for him. Should I stay here and work till it was time to set out, or go home and then have to double back?

The choice was between a warm but hostile room and a dodgy rush-hour journey. Think green, think petrol. I'd better hang on here. Yes. A decision made.

But I didn't want to stay in the workroom. What I might do was find an empty practice room. Despite myself as soon as I sat at the piano I started worrying about Rose: I was sure that she was at the bottom of my problems with my colleagues. She and her incursions into the workroom. Poor kid. At least she was so off the wall I didn't even have to consider taking her allegations about French to the authorities.

Right: now for some scale and arpeggio work, to warm up the fingers and switch off the brain. And, since the rooms were lockable and soundproofed, be completely inaccessible.

Of course, even a soundproofed room is only soundproof if you shut the door on yourself. If you leave it ajar it's as prone to eavesdropping as any. Having exercised my fingers and wrists till they'd started to ache, I called it a night – the last thing I wanted was tendonitis, after all. I was standing in the corridor, tossing up between a refectory snack and half an hour with the *Guardian* in the library when I heard voices. A man and a woman. I didn't recognise the latter. But I rather thought the man might be Marcus French.

There was little doubt about the other speakers I tried not to overhear, because they were actually emerging from a practice room in mid-bicker. Nice young Neil, the violinist, and his sexy teacher, Alex Fisher.

As soon as Fisher saw me, he said curtly, but with no more vehemence than I'd have used to shut up an importunate student, 'I think we should leave it there, Neil. You've got a tutorial tomorrow. That's really the time and place to raise problems. OK?' He'd perfected that teacher's 'OK?' It was the polite, professional 'Sod off'. I'd used it myself times beyond count.

Neil flushed to the ears and, eyes down and shoulders bowed, headed off down the corridor towards the refectory.

Fisher caught my eye. 'The joys of teaching.'

'Tell me about them. I'm trying to tell myself I miss the classroom, but I find the withdrawal symptoms have almost disappeared.'

'You did get withdrawal symptoms?'

'For all of ten minutes.' And then an enormous sense of relief that I was free, at least temporarily. 'But to be honest, I think my place was more testing than this. William Murdock College,' I explained.

His eyebrows shot up. 'But it's tough there. Wasn't there a drugs raid the other day?'

My eyebrows' turn. 'You're joking!'

'Not if you believe the *Evening Mail*.'

Fisher – and the *Mail* – might have been right. There'd been some violent incidents while I was there, and constant rumours about a subculture that was getting out of hand. If I needed encouragement to press on with the dissertation, what could be better than that?

'Looks as if I may have to find another job, then,' I said, as much to myself as to him.

'Stay in teaching? Or move out altogether?'

Somehow we had fallen into step and were heading in the direction Neil had fled in – the refectory.

'I don't know,' I said, still really ruminating. 'I suppose with my M. Ed. and my teaching experience I could always head for a place like this – teaching teachers.'

He shuddered. 'It's still people, Sophie. All their little angsts, all their tantrums, their—'

'Their genuine needs,' I concluded, didactic as ever.

'Of course. But their imagined needs too. God, sometimes I

47

get sick of it all! I'm a musician, for God's sake, not a bloody nanny!' He lowered his voice. 'It's a sort of compassion fatigue – as if no one wants to recognise that I have needs too.'

Before I could say anything – and what could I have said to such a baring of the soul? – he said, 'Sorry. I didn't mean to— Oh, God.' He stopped short, looking around the refectory. Neil, Rose, Leonore, and a whole bunch of other kids I didn't know. 'Protect me, Sophie: join me in a coffee.'

Self-protection for me too. I nodded.

As I unwrapped a baguette I cast around for something to say. At last I managed to ask casually, 'Any particular nannying problems?'

'Young Neil for a start. You won't let this get any further? It's just such a relief to talk about it to someone not in the department!'

'Lips sealed,' I said.

'He's got a chance of going professional now. Joining one of the London orchestras.'

'Wow!'

'But only as a rank-and-file second fiddle. And you know the state of the London music scene. He comes to me for advice. I tell him that with a completed course under his belt he could do better than that.' He paused to strip cellophane from his sandwich.

'But couldn't he work his way up? After all, a job in the hand is worth two in the Job Centre.'

'There's a huge pool of musicians waiting for better jobs. And can you imagine that poor kid cast adrift in London? Living away from home, working the most god-awful hours? And then losing his job because the orchestra goes bust?'

'Oh,' I temporised, 'surely the Arts Council wouldn't let—'

'It's been on the cards for years. Anyway, every day I get young Neil coming to me to be told I've changed my mind, that he's good enough. And I can't do it. Shit, looks as if he's coming over now.'

48

He was. With that big lad, Doug, Dawn Harper's friend, carrying a bassoon case. Neither seemed to be enjoying the other's company.

'Avoid,' I whispered, 'all eye contact. And drop your voice and tell me what you know about Rose.'

'Rose?' And a deep red flush stained his whole face.

'Rose the bass player,' I said, as if I hadn't noticed. Out of the tail of my eye I could see Neil approaching our table. But I returned my gaze to my baguette. He could surely tell he wasn't welcome.

His feet took him reluctantly away.

'She should have failed last year. But – you know how it is . . .' Fisher flashed a comradely smile. 'I pushed and shoved and somehow got her through. Her tutor this year's cursing me, though. Because if she's to get through this year – and the Uni doesn't like losing students at this stage—'

'Recruitment, retention, outcomes,' I murmured: it was the William Murdock mantra.

'Quite. So if she's to get her degree, in fact, her tutors this year and next are condemned to the same sort of struggle as I had. Only more so as the work gets more difficult. You end up wondering who's doing the degree, her or you.'

'Poor kid,' I said reflectively. 'No wonder she's scratching round for help.'

'Don't get sucked in, Sophie: she's a real pain. Believe me. Oh, believe me. I've got the T-shirt to prove it.'

'You're sure she's not – well, between you and me – a tad unbalanced?' After all, he'd known her a lot longer than I had. 'She seems to want to get very close to – to certain of her female colleagues.'

'And her male ones. The poor thing had a terribly unrequited crush on Neil Wiltshire last year. Well, she would, wouldn't she? And it would be unrequited. And she's been – well, one or two women on the staff had cause to complain last year.'

'And men?' I asked.

He said shortly, 'French knows all about it.'

All of which made it sound as if the University was aware of her problems and could take responsibility for them. So could I stop worrying about her allegations about Dawn and the prof? 'What's French like, incidentally?'

'Ego man.'

'So's your violist colleague,' I said, 'James Hallam. He gave a real prima donna performance yesterday evening – really eclipsed young Neil, poor kid. I thought the object of the exercise was to support the student performer.'

'Goes to prove my point, of course. He's not yet hard enough for the rough and tumble of the professional world.'

I flickered an eyebrow in acknowledgement. 'But someone thought highly enough of him to make him leader of the orchestra.'

Fisher looked at his watch. 'Better go. I've got a quartet rehearsal in ten minutes. And, the amount of time we get to rehearse, I don't want to waste a second.' He produced a charming smile, and got up. But I'd rattled him. My fault. I was being nosy, indeed gossipy, and he'd been right to snub me. I'd have done the same in his place, wouldn't I? But I sensed an unease beyond that. And I'd have loved to be a fly on the wall to see who actually led the Boulton Quartet, Fisher or Hallam.

Still, I reflected, as I gathered up my things and headed for the lecture on glassworkers, at least I'd find out eventually – at the Boultons' BMI concert.

Chapter Six

The house felt so empty when I got home that it didn't seem like mine at all, despite the fact I'd lived happily in it for years on my own. I almost felt more at home at Mike's because he'd chosen and arranged and touched everything in it. Sure, I'd chosen and arranged and even loved my things. They weren't all to Mike's taste, any more than some of his were to mine. We'd have to compromise heavily when we moved into our new place. One idea we'd had was to furnish alternate rooms: he the living room, I the dining room, and so on.

Wandering around with a tot of Jameson in my hand, I poked the answerphone without much hope. But there was a short and enormously loving message from Mike, and suddenly my paint seemed brighter. There were also a couple of requests for estimates for catering. The one was for a date on which I was already committed; I arranged to call to discuss the second on my way into UWM the following morning.

It was only then I remembered I didn't want to go into UWM the following morning: I wanted to dodge Rose, and I wasn't welcome in the workroom. Thanks, however, to the conversation with Fisher, I'd completely forgotten all the books and papers I needed to work at home. Bother and bother and bother.

Determined to make it a flying visit, I'd be wildly extravagant – I'd leave the central heating on and return to a nice, warm house.

Warm wasn't really the word for the detached house in Warley I was bidden to. More, stultifying. One of a sixties development on the main Birmingham–Wolverhampton New Road, anywhere else it would have sat amongst its neighbours shuffling with embarrassment. But most of the others had been 'improved' too, extravagantly but not always tastefully. There was a positive riot of glass-fibre Corinthian columns. This particular one had gnomic and other garden additions to what was presumably a ranch house to the point where kitsch became high camp. Even in the glazed porch there were pink Austrian blinds to add to the delights that greeted the visitor – I can never see them without thinking of Alan Bennett's description of them as being like old ladies with their petticoats caught in their knickers.

The front door was opened by a woman of about thirty, tall, with the sort of uncontrolled shock of black hair that makes you think of Pre-Raphaelites. She wore a bright PVC apron over jeans and an open-necked shirt. She pulled her face into an apologetic grimace.

'I can't even find the central heating control,' she said, by way of greeting. 'Hello, Sophie: I'm Sue.'

I shook the proffered hand, which completely enveloped mine.

'Come along in. Sorry about the boxes. But we thought we wouldn't unpack everything till after the party – easier to clean up. Jamie, put that *down*.'

Jamie, a toddler wearing nothing from the waist down, was carrying round a bright red potty, anxious to show off the contents. As an educationalist, I should have been impressed.

'Ah,' Sue observed, rather belatedly grabbing both, Jamie headfirst under her arm, and disappearing into what I presumed was the downstairs loo, from which emerged sounds of protest.

Left to my own devices, I drifted into the kitchen – *kitschen*. Dear God, how long did it take to clean all those curly edges, all those leaded-lights, all those twee things for putting other things on? And they were clean, as a mother-in-lawly fingertip showed. Well, provided I could find a surface to prepare on, the guests wouldn't be at risk from hygiene problems.

My hands were safely back in my pockets by the time the flushing of a loo dominated the squalls. Sue reappeared, again clutching Jamie, but this time to her chest. He still wore no nether garments.

'Potty training,' she said. 'Tea or coffee?'

'Tea would be lovely,' I said, producing my brochure and my notepad and sitting at the kitchen table.

If I expected the cup that cheers, I got liquid compost heap. I wouldn't mind, only people always assume 'herbal' means 'healthy'. All I can say is that a glance at the list of ingredients will show just how 'natural' some stuff is. At least with a decent Darjeeling, you know you're getting leaves and water and maybe a dash of milk.

But I digress.

Predictably, Sue seemed more interested in the vegetarian menu. While she perused it, I found a set of multi-coloured plastic stacking bricks and made a jolly cone for Jamie, who obligingly tipped it over. I repeated the process; so did he. We continued like this in companionable silence until he suddenly toddled off, returning with a different set of stacking bricks, which I turned into a pyramid. This took much more effort to overturn.

'We've just come back to the UK,' Sue said. 'Adrian had a two-year contract in New Zealand. Neurosurgery. We thought we'd rent before we committed ourselves to any particular area of the Midlands. And look what we got! Do take your coat off.'

I needed no second bidding. 'The central heating controls must be somewhere,' I said.

She shrugged, expansively. 'I've tried all the obvious places.'

'We could try the less obvious ones?' I rebuilt both the cone and the pyramid in double-quick time and got up to look around me. 'The utility room?'

53

'Be my guest.'

The instructions for the washing machine languished in an art nouveau frame. There was nothing similar for the boiler. Indeed, no boiler.

'Which is the hottest room in the house?'

'The garage.'

'*Avanti!*'

So there, in a corner into which, for some reason, someone had also huddled a big chest deep-freeze, was the boiler. But there were no instructions. Unless – yes! There they were, beautifully written in a twirly pseudo-italic handwriting that would have had my friend Chris Groom, whose script epitomised elegance and clarity, shaking with hysteria.

'So why didn't I notice them?' Sue asked, hitching Jamie on to the other hip and running a finger along each line.

'Because they look like that Nun's Prayer scroll? Shall I take him?'

Sue was struggling to reach to the control unit. She snorted. 'Not unless your skirt's waterproof. We haven't quite cracked this no nappy thing. Down to about twenty degrees, please.'

While she took a phone call from Adrian, Jamie established me as a favourite master builder. I was happy to oblige for a few minutes, but wished she'd cut short her call so we could conclude the business and I could go on to UWM. It would have been nice to get a positive commitment, but she wanted to talk over the details with the loquacious Adrian in person. Whether she booked or not, I needed her to fill in a short consumer survey for me: where she'd seen my ad., what she thought of my menus, etc. There'd be a follow-up questionnaire after the event – should it happen, of course.

The letters UWM leapt from the A4 sheet I'd handed her to fill in.

'UWM?' I queried, explaining my interest.

'Yes. The staff notice board. I work a couple of mornings a

week in Student Support. Basically I shell out the morning-after pill and homely advice. There's more to me than just an incompetent mother,' she said.

'You don't look incompetent to me.'

'I feel it. All the time. It's so nice going into work and feeling you're on top of something. The worst thing is, Adrian wants more . . .'

I was in a much happier frame of mind when I set out rather later than I'd expected to UWM. There was already talk of car-sharing when it was possible, and we'd agreed to meet up for coffee during her morning break the next time she was in: it would be good to have a refuge from demanding teenagers, hostile colleagues and musical men.

Preferring to avoid as many of each as possible, I slid into the building as if trying to avoid surveillance. No hope of an empty corridor or two: I'd managed to time my arrival to coincide with the end of one set of lectures and the start of another, so the place was heaving. Perhaps everyone would be so purposeful they wouldn't register my presence even if they saw me. And though Rose hove into view, she was deep in conversation with Dawn, the soprano. By this time I was engrossed by two-month-old material on the Local History notice board – and, suddenly, really interested. Why I hadn't noticed it before I'd no idea. The society was organising a trip to see the foundations of Matthew Boulton's Soho Foundry, just down the road in the industrial part of Smethwick. It invited those interested to sign a sheet. While not averse to joining Mickey Mouse and Superman, I was anxious that if Rose saw my name up there, she'd sign up too, with scant regard to her assignments or lectures: she was clearly too weak a student to skimp work. And, to be more honest, I didn't want her there monopolising me or tugging my bag if I moved too slowly or asked questions. I wanted a little self-indulgent half-holiday, where I could have conversations in my head with

55

Mike about somewhere he'd always wanted to visit. So I'd nip back to the Oldbury Campus and the history departmental office to reserve a place in person.

But not, of course, until I'd picked up the stuff I needed from the workroom. A good pile too, since today was Friday and I had a horribly empty weekend stretching before me.

To my amazement, Neil was squatting outside the post-grad workroom, fastening the catch on his fiddle case. He flushed vividly when he saw me, then got to his feet, with a slightly gangly awkwardness I thought he might have outgrown by now.

'I hoped you wouldn't mind,' he began, 'but – you see, it was those staff-student forums you were talking about. I asked the people in there and they said they didn't know what I was on about and that you weren't in and I was to leave a note. So I was just going to write it, but they said would I do it out here.'

Oh dear. So that must be what it was all about – not just Rose's but other students' invasion of their space. They were being remarkably touchy. But then, of course, like me, they had given up a whole year's salary – some had said goodbye to thirty thousand plus – and were paying massive fees to boot. That was why most people on the M.Ed. course were evening-only students, trying to keep a day job going.

'Well, I'm here now,' I said evenly. 'What did you want to ask?'

He shifted as if I'd asked him about how often he changed his socks. 'Well, about what sort of questions get discussed.'

'Depends on their terms of reference, I'd have thought. But all matters of concern on the course. The teaching and learning environment, the content of the seminars and lectures, the lecturers' approach to teaching, that sort of thing.'

'What about – what about individual teachers?'

Alarm bells started to ring so loudly I took a moment to reply. I did not, absolutely not, want to get involved in personal squabbles between students and tutors – especially as I could see both sides of the argument about whether Neil should leave now or finish his course.

'General complaints – if everyone on a course has a problem with a particular lecturer. Confidential complaints – well, I'm sure there's a well-established procedure at a place like this. I always used to tell my students that the first thing they should do was talk to the person they wanted to complain about – see if things could be resolved in a nice low-key way.'

I'll swear I could see the whites of his eyes.

'Failing that, they should talk to their tutor,' I continued.

'But – but . . .' I could see him gathering himself up. 'What if you can't . . . can't.' He came to a halt.

'Then you could either go and talk to the Dean – in which case I'd advise you to take a colleague with you – or make an appointment with a student counsellor. OK?'

It wasn't OK, was it? The poor kid looked utterly miserable.

'Come on, let's go and find where the counsellors hang out. I don't even know how to make an appointment. Do you?' And somehow I got him moving in the direction of Student Support. I was aware, as we set off along the corridor, of the post-grad workroom door opening and shutting.

As it happened, a counsellor was free, so I handed over Neil and headed back. Perhaps, come to think of it, I needed a counsellor myself – to help me overcome these problems with my colleagues. Should I breeze in as if nothing had happened? Or collapse at my desk, sighing heavily and lamenting the demands the kids – not even my own students, for goodness' sake! – were putting on me? Or should I go in guns blazing, asking why the hell they couldn't be courteous to someone obviously in some distress?

None of those seemed appropriate: I didn't want to whinge

and I didn't want to be aggressive. I agonised about it, taking the long way back, and finally deciding the most assertive way was simply to ask Greg what he'd meant by his remarks of the previous day. Then I could respond accordingly. I screwed my courage to the sticking place and walked in. Into an empty room.

Armed for a weekend with all the books I needed, I headed off home, via the Oldbury Campus, where I popped into the history office to ask the secretary to save me a place on the Local History Group trip. There were one or two still available, and she was quite happy to add me to her file, taking £5 from me. She was burrowing in a filing cabinet drawer for a cashbox when the office door behind her opened slightly. The nameplate declared it to be the sanctum of Dr Kenneth Ball. He had a regular column in one of Birmingham's freebie newspapers, managing to bring local history to the masses without making it cheap. It would be good to meet someone who made education slip down so easily. But something wasn't going down easily at the moment: two male voices were raised in a good approximation of anger. I thought I heard the words 'one more complaint' but I couldn't be sure.

My eyes caught the secretary's: she raised hers with resignation.

'The calm, gentle world of academe,' I observed.

'Quite,' she said, counting my cash and stashing it.

The door was slammed shut. Within a few seconds, however, it was open again, with Marcus French striding, if not exactly storming, out. To my surprise he stopped by the outer door, turning back to smile – at both of us it seemed. But he said nothing and went on his way.

The inner door was opening, and Ball emerging. He was a small, neat man, eyes bright with intelligence. So relaxed he might not have heard the altercation within his room, let alone participated in it, he leant against his secretary's desk and looked quizzically at me.

'This is Miss Rivers,' his secretary said. 'It's OK to put her on the Soho Foundry trip list, isn't it?'

'If we've got room, of course it is, Carol.'

'If Mickey Mouse and Superman don't show, I should be all right,' I suggested. 'And I've an idea Gibbon might have a previous engagement, too.'

He raised his eyebrows. 'I suppose it's something that a student knows enough about Gibbon to make a joke about him. Not a lot do, these days. You're not a history student then, Miss – er . . .?'

'Sophie Rivers,' I said, not keen to engage in the Miss/Ms debate. 'No, I'm on the M.Ed. course, but I wanted to go and see a bit of my heritage.'

He grinned. 'Sophie shall go with the Ball. So long as she brings a waterproof, a torch and a pair of strong shoes. Till a week on Monday, then, Sophie.'

I laughed at his little joke, thought of the Thomas Beecham one that French had yet to repeat (*You will, Oscar, you will*!) and bade him good day.

While I was on this site I might as well say hello to an old William Murdock colleague, Luke Schneider, now the UWM bursar. He'd forgiven me for once putting his life in jeopardy and had been enormously kind to me in my first year at UWM. He was on his way to a meeting so we did little more than exchange a smile and wave our diaries at each other, but even that took a few minutes. So I was surprised to find Professor Marcus French in the foyer, apparently engrossed in a notice board, when I emerged.

I wasn't sure about the quality of his smile, still less about what he said. 'You pop up everywhere, Ms Rivers. In the education department, in mine, of course, and now in history. I'm surprised you have time to study.'

'I always make time for important things,' I said, pushing

open the front door, but hesitating on the steps. Rain was lashing down as if someone had turned a hosepipe on the building.

French appeared beside me, opening a golf umbrella. 'Can I offer you a lift, Ms Rivers?'

'My car's within sprinting distance.' But all the same I'd be soaked by the time I reached it.

'In that case,' he said, proffering his arm like a latter-day Mr Darcy, 'allow me.'

I allowed. Safely in the dry haven of my Mazda, I stowed bags and books and gave the inside of the windscreen a polish. And watched the prof drive away in his big Vauxhall, his registration plates fiddled so they appeared to read FRENCH. Hmm. A bit of an ego there. So why had he bothered with me? Surely, surely there could be nothing in Rose's allegations – could there? What if I *had* heard Ball refer to complaints?

Chapter Seven

I so hated weekends without Mike, I spent this one with my head down working, and achieved even more than I'd hoped. I also spent a little time preparing ahead for the buffet. But Monday wasn't much better, of course. If I didn't want to stay in an empty house, there was the alternative of the workroom or the library, both vulnerable to invasion by hostile or needy students. I had to go in for the evening choir rehearsal, of course, so eventually in the early afternoon I tore myself away from Ceefax – Mike had scored fifty-three – and went off to Smethwick. I even took some bread for the ducks on the pool in the park, hoping to while away a few moments discussing the weather with them. Since a squall of rain chose that moment to sweep across the open land, I had to accept their vociferous verdict that they were better equipped to deal with it than I.

To my relief the workroom was empty, so I shook my by now dripping coat and hung it over the radiator. I sorted out the books I'd used over the weekend, and was just going to return them to the library when the door opened and Rose burst in, leaving the door wide open.

'Have you heard the news?'

'Rose! Look, this is a workroom – people aren't supposed to talk in here.' It sounded stuffy even as I said it, but she didn't seem to register I'd spoken.

'Alex Fisher's hurt his hand and won't be able to play in the concert! Do you think they'll let Neil take over?'

I stepped towards her. 'Didn't you hear me, Rose? Whatever the news, however exciting it is, I can't listen to it in here. This is not my private office; it's a communal workroom. And your constant incursions mean my colleagues can't work in it. If you want to talk, we'll step outside, and I'll listen to you there. Come on.'

She gave an enormous flounce, and turned to go, cannoning into Greg as she did so. How he kept his feet or his cool I don't know.

Furious, I apologised for her.

He managed a sort of grin. 'I think I'm beginning to see things differently,' he said.

To encourage the change, I left the door ajar when I followed Rose.

'I meant what I said, Rose. This isn't my private domain. I share it with people who have made huge professional and financial commitments to be here. You mustn't keep interrupting them.'

'I thought you'd be interested.'

'I am. But the news would have kept for the refectory.'

'You're hardly ever there.'

'That's because – like my colleagues in there – I've taken time off work to study. That means a year without pay. And I've got a dissertation to write.'

'But you've got all year. And everyone asks for an extension.'

'I don't intend to. And as I've got other plans for the spring, I have to pack as much work in as I can now. OK. Now, thanks for the news, and I'll see you in the refec some time. Or maybe at the choir rehearsal tonight.' I turned on my heel and pushed back into the workroom – to be greeted, to my relief, to a silent round of applause from Greg.

'Yes,' he nodded, 'I definitely see things differently now. I didn't realise that you were the victim of sexual harassment.'

'Me?' I sat down heavily. 'Sexual harassment?'

'That's what it looks like to me. Oh, five years ago I'd have

62

said the girl had a crush on you. But the official language has changed – even if the passion hasn't.'

'Oh my God. I knew she was – awkward, demanding . . . But—' Never in all my William Murdock years had anyone had a *crush* on me.

'It seems to me you ought to freeze her off fast. Or report her.'

'Report! But—' I shook my head doubtfully. Maybe I'd better have a word with her music faculty tutor, though.

'Tell me she's not making a nuisance of herself. And,' Greg pursued, 'I'd have thought that beautiful young man was somewhat in love with you too.'

This time I shook my head firmly. 'Not him. I think he's got a different sexual orientation. And I fancy he's in a bit of a spot.'

'He's the one you marched off to a counsellor, is he? I have to hand it to you, Sophie – you've been doing your best.'

I sighed. 'Perhaps I should have that on my gravestone: "She always did her best."'

I was just sprucing up in the ladies' nearest the choir rehearsal room when the door opened. Bracing myself for another Rose onslaught, I was relieved to see the slight figure of June Tams, the quartet second violinist, sliding in. It's hard not to have some conversation in such a confined space, so, applying mascara, I said, 'I was sorry to hear about Alex Fisher's injury. How will it affect your concert?'

'Alex? What's that about Alex?'

Her reflection in the mirror was ashen.

I turned to face her. 'I'm so sorry – didn't you know? Look, maybe it's just a rumour.' Seeing she couldn't speak, I continued, 'It was something one of the students was saying.'

'What sort – of injury?'

'His hand. No idea what or how serious. Look, can I get you something?'

She leant on one of the washbasins, breathing deeply. 'I'm not going to sit up,' she said. This didn't refer to posture, but to promotion to first violin, and thus – technically – leader. 'They'll have to bring in someone else.' Turning, she retired to one of the cubicles.

It was time I was in the rehearsal room if I wanted to avoid provoking French. So – spinelessly, perhaps, but after all she was a grown woman, four or five years older than me – I left her to it and took my place on the back row of the sopranos.

Dawn slid quickly in beside me. We exchanged grins, a very pallid one in her case. I wondered if she was short of money, and if an evening's waitressing for me would appeal. It did.

'But I've never done anything like that before. I mean, I'm not an expert . . .'

But she was a very pretty girl when she smiled, and people would forgive her a lot. 'No expertise involved. You just walk round carrying food and smiling at people to encourage them to help themselves.'

'What if they want to talk to me?'

'So long as they don't monopolise you, no problem. And when they've finished feeding their faces and you've helped me tidy away, then you can talk to whoever you want. White blouse, black skirt, hair tied right back . . .'

At this point Marcus French came surging into the room, and though it wasn't exactly the sopranos' turn for a bollocking tonight, we shut up immediately, not wanting to attract any untoward attention. At least I didn't. I might be nearly as old as the maestro – I was sure that was how he would prefer to be addressed – but I'd had enough *Sturm und Drang* for one day. If he became offensive, I would certainly walk out.

Brisk he was, brusque even, but he wasn't vicious. Even a couple of really bad dominoes from the contraltos didn't provoke the outburst I'd have expected. He even gave us sopranos a couple of words of praise.

'What's up with him, then?' I asked Dawn over coffee from the machine.

'What d'you mean, what's up?' She looked at me, startled.

'Well, compared with last week, he's almost tame. Perhaps someone slipped Prozac into his tea. How's he been to you this week?'

Her head jerked back, and she blinked. 'Me? What on earth do you mean?'

'Last week,' I reminded her, 'he behaved to the choir like Attila the Hun initiating a new load of slaves. And you said he'd bullied and upset you.'

'Oh. Yes. I suppose . . . Well, he's been a lot better this week . . . And I got a good grade for an essay,' she added, sounding more as if she'd got a dose of plague.

I didn't tell her I'd already heard. 'You sound almost surprised,' I said.

'Well, I'd worked very hard on it. But an A – well, wouldn't you be pleased?'

'I certainly would. But you don't look very happy.'

'Oh, it's the new batch of reeds. They've got this awful whiny tone, and the prof's saying I should learn to make my own. The trouble is, it takes forever, and . . .'

Out of the tail of my eye I saw Rose heading our way. Excusing myself by saying I needed to recruit other waitresses, I got to my feet and took refuge with Leonore. Having been spared a confrontation with the prof, I didn't want to have one with a second-year student. Although consorting with Leonore might be provocative, it wouldn't be half as provocative as being in conversation with Dawn. The bonus was that she was happy to accept my offer for Saturday night, and knew a friend who'd want to as well.

The second half of the rehearsal saw French a bit fierier, but not outrageously so. So what had been bugging him last week?

Or what had improved his temper this? But now wasn't the time to dwell on it. The last thing I wanted was to produce a false note myself.

Some of the others were off to the local pub, and though they invited me to go along, they clearly wondered where I should park my Zimmer frame. So, almost tempted to tell them my Horlicks and electric blanket were calling me, I bade them good night and set off.

There were several routes home to Harborne: I chose one at random, up Queen's Road and along Hurst Road, till I came to Harborne Road, one of Warley's nicer residential patches overlooking Warley Woods. Even on a blustery, wet night there are always steamed-up cars in lay-bys, and tonight was no exception. I had a sharp spasm of longing for Mike. There might be a message for me when I got back, so I speeded up a bit.

This route saw me turning right at the traffic lights at the Kings Head. I chanced to glance to my left as I waited. There, in the car next to mine, was a profile remarkably like French's. And one remarkably like Dawn's. When the lights changed, I had to creep forward to wait my chance to turn. The Vauxhall accelerating straight away bore familiar numberplates. Oh dear: what if there was some truth in Rose's allegations? And what if French's temper had been improved by the prospect of sex with a student?

The problem was, of course, that if he were having sex with her, there was nothing I could do about it. Unless she told me and asked for help. She'd had a chance to confide tonight, but hadn't taken it. I couldn't very well ask her outright. And – knowing the consequences of a false accusation, however innocently made – I certainly couldn't even breathe my suspicions to anyone else.

There was a lecture on Tuesday morning I didn't have to go to, but thought I might just turn up to anyway. To be honest, I wanted to pick up the news about Fisher's hand injury, and to find out what was happening. After all, if the quartet couldn't replace its leader and had to cancel the gig, they wouldn't be the only ones to suffer. I'd already invested some time and, indeed, some money in the post-concert catering. I didn't want to commit to anything else till I knew the engagement was still on.

As luck would have it, one of the first people I saw as I dripped in from the car park was June Tams.

She flashed me an anxious smile. 'You were right about Alex's hand,' she said. 'Accident with a corkscrew, I hear.'

'Oh dear – a stab wound or tear, not a nice clean cut, then.' I asked, 'Have you changed your mind about sitting up?'

She shook her head so violently her earrings clattered. 'The parts are quite different. And the first violin's very – very exposed. *The Lark*; the Borodin Second. I've no time to learn them.'

The Borodin is one of my all-time favourites, although it's overplayed on Classic FM. Even people not familiar with the music would know the big tune: 'And this is my beloved', from *Kismet*.

'So what on earth will happen?'

'We'll have to find someone who knows it – and hope he fits in with us. Caz is really upset. She and Alex have practised very hard to get their duet right.'

Yes, the lovely movement where the violin and cello celebrate Borodin's wedding anniversary by passing and augmenting the big tune just as if they were singing a love song.

'How do you set about getting a replacement? It's quite short notice.'

'Friends. Friends of friends. But it being a Saturday, which is a big day for concerts, we might not find it easy.'

'So will you cancel?'

'Oh, I do hope not,' she twittered.

Two voices came strongly from behind me. 'Absolutely not!'

Caz and Hallam. The latter added, 'If the worst comes to the very worst, we could always bring in young Neil. He'd do as he was told, at least. Not,' he added, 'that it's any business of yours, Sophie.'

'On the contrary, this month's mortgage depends on it. I'm catering for the reception afterwards.' I was lying about the mortgage. My house had been left to me by a distant relative who wanted to annoy my father. I certainly wouldn't have been able to indulge in a sabbatical otherwise. But it might have been true, and I didn't like people getting stroppy with me.

Caz tossed her golden mane. 'We weren't consulted about the arrangements.'

'French was – via his secretary at least. And it's departmental funds paying for it. So I suppose—'

'What an ego that bastard's got,' Caz said.

'What are we having, anyway?' Hallam asked.

'The usual finger buffet stuff. The nice thing about being so close to Smethwick High Street is that I can get lovely fresh herbs and spices for my samosas and kebabs.'

'God, we always have to be so bloody ethnic!' Caz said.

'I wouldn't have thought canapés and vol-au-vents particularly English fare,' I flashed. 'Anyway, it was French's choice, not mine. Argue with him if you want – there's still time to make a few changes. But please: if you do decide to cancel, let me know.'

'Surely you've got a cancellation clause in your contract,' Caz said.

'I just don't like wasting food,' I said. 'Well, good luck with your hunt.' And off I toddled to my lecture.

I know Vaughan Williams is out of fashion, but his *Songs of Travel* take a lot of beating, particularly when sung by a young man with the clear diction and resonant voice of Dan Langley. I suspected he also had perfect pitch: when I knew him better I might test it. He certainly had one of the nicest singer's bodies I'd come across. Not for him a double chin and a barrel of a tum; if that man didn't weight train, I would, in Black Country parlance, go to the bottom of our stairs. With his voice and his presence, I'd put a fiver on him singing at Covent Garden before he was thirty. No bad for a kid from Dudley.

If I'd been Dawn or Rose I'd have been throwing myself at him. OK, not Rose. But certainly Dawn or one of the other young women. Maybe even Neil.

After a remarkably efficient hour – we'd fallen into step with each other far more quickly than Leonore and I, probably because I was in practice – we had to call it a day because the room was booked. Dawn. I wouldn't have thought her voice was up to recital work. But then, who'd have thought her voice good enough for the prof himself to be accompanying her? Then I noticed her oboe case. I might have been jumping to conclusions. She sketched a smile, dropping her eyes.

A glance at Dan suggested he'd noticed.

'Time for a cuppa?' I asked, resolving to grasp the nettle and ask questions.

The first was, 'What's it like, being a full-time music student?' OK, perhaps I was still wearing gardening gloves.

'OK.'

Well, what had I expected him to say?

'I just wondered if was a happy department.'

He stuck out his lower lip, in the manner of a much younger lad. 'Well, there aren't really enough practice rooms – no one can understand why we couldn't have taken over the whole site and left education where it was. Sorry, Sophie: nothing personal.'

'No problem. What about the teachers? Are they any good? I'm always interested,' I explained, 'being a teacher myself in real life.'

His voice had an angry edge. 'Well, they certainly didn't know what to make of me when I arrived. They might have coped if I'd want to follow in Lenny Henry's footsteps – I was born just down the road from him – but they didn't expect a black baritone.'

Time to soothe the nerve I'd obviously touched. 'Oh, come now! Willard White!'

He grinned. '*Touché*! Well, they're all right now. They treat me and Leonore just fine. The prof's even found some scholarship I can apply for when I've graduated.'

Ah! 'He seems a bit of an enigma, your prof. He was the devil incarnate at last week's choir rehearsal, but quite mellow last night.'

'He's a moody bugger all right.' He dropped his voice and, looking round, hunched closer to me. 'He's got a bit of a reputation . . .'

'What sort of reputation?'

He pulled a face. 'You know . . . with the women on the course. You want to watch yourself, Sophie,' he said, as if only half joking.

I looked him straight in the eye. 'It's no laughing matter, any more than racism is.'

'Some of the girls seem to like it – they make a play for him. And for one or two other lecturers too. It's a tough profession, Sophie. People think they have to take whatever opportunities are offered and make what aren't.'

'But isn't that a bit tough on you blokes? If there are favourites, there must be people out of favour. Unless there's a gay cartel too.'

He snorted. 'If there is, include me out, man! You mean,' he added slowly, 'these girls who are being screwed might be getting better grades and that? And the blokes!'

'I wouldn't know. But you can't really imagine having an affair with a bloke old enough to be your dad – and not a terribly attractive man at that – unless there's some sort of pay-off.'

'What if it's the other way round, though? What if guys like French tell their women that if they don't – er . . .' He stopped,

70

no doubt out of consideration for my advanced years.

'If they don't get fucked, they'll get bad grades,' I concluded obligingly.

He winced. 'That's putting it a bit crudely.'

'It's a very crude thing to do. It's called blackmail.' I let that sink in, then asked, 'Is it just rumours or have any of the women actually said anything? You see,' I pursued, 'you've got the sort of face that people can talk to. I bet you find yourself being treated as a father confessor.'

'Father confessors are supposed to treat the confessional as inviolate,' he said with a solemnity quite at odds with my jokey tone.

'They're also allowed to dish out advice with the Hail Marys,' I countered. 'If one of these women were to confide in you, what advice would you give her?'

'Advice?' repeated this wonderful ringing woman's voice.

I slopped my tea: I'd been so engrossed in our conversation I'd never noticed Leonore approaching. Neither, by the expression on his face, had Dan.

'About becoming a singer,' I lied instinctively, swiftly – all those years of teaching had their uses, after all. Then I regretted it: surely I could trust Leonore.

She sat down, sighing heavily. 'My advice would be to do anything but.'

'But, Leonore,' I protested, 'you've got a wonderful voice – a great career ahead of you.'

'I might have. But even great voices need practice. And we've just lost the next three slots we'd booked, Sophie.'

'"Lost"? How?'

'Marcus bloody French wanted them. Don't ask me why.' She stood up. 'More tea, anyone? I could do with one. Or maybe something stronger.' She glanced at her watch. 'The bar'll be open in ten minutes.'

'You don't want to go down that road, Leonore,' Dan said seriously, clasping her arm, just above the wrist.

'You don't need to,' I said, wondering if I'd regret it. 'I know the acoustics won't be so good; I know the piano needs tuning. But if we can't get practice sessions here, we do have an alternative. My living room.' I didn't add, lest I sound like Lady Catherine de Bourgh, that the house next door was empty.

'Sophie! You angel! But,' she added more soberly, 'I think I should raise this officially. You can't just have lecturers pulling rank over students. The trouble is, I can't really complain to French himself – not if I want to stay on the course.'

Dan and I exchanged glances.

I said neutrally, 'Where I work they have what are called Boards of Study. I explained all about them to Rose.'

This time Dan and Leonore exchanged glances. Hell!

'But if you've got a couple of minutes I could explain them to you,' I continued as smoothly as I could.

Dan looked at his watch. 'Have to take a rain check, I'm afraid. We've got Harmony in two minutes. Coming, Leonore?'

'Shit! I'd forgotten! I'll catch you up. Look, Sophie, can I take you up on that offer? Really? If I can't sort it out here?'

'Sure.' I wrote on a page from my diary. 'Here's my number. Keep it to yourself, though, Leonore.' I was ex-directory, as a private person, that is. But when I'd started my catering business, I'd had to put my phone number on flyers and handbills, of course. Naïvely – goodness knows why I hadn't had another phone line put in – I'd always hoped people wouldn't associate a mere Sophie Rivers with my company, Sabrina Fare. (At the time I'd thought the name allusively and ironically witty, especially given my absence of obvious breasts. It's lingered to become a perpetual embarrassment.)

'Which means don't lose it, either.'

'Especially don't lose it here. I don't want students, repeat any students except you – and Dan, of course, if he has the same problem – to have this. Someone's got – well, a bit of a crush on me, and—'

'Oh, you mean Rose. If it's any consolation, you're in an

honourable tradition: last year she was always making a cake of herself with someone or other. No, I won't let her get her hands on it. Trust me!'

I did. And hoped I wouldn't regret it.

Chapter Eight

It occurred to me that it would have been nice to find out how young Neil felt about his possible elevation to the Boulton Quartet. So as I gathered my things together I looked round the refec. I wouldn't want to interrupt any conversations, still less did I want to attract the renewed attentions of Rose, so I didn't exactly stand on a chair and call his name. From my level, at least, there was no sign of him. Not to worry. Except I always did worry about my student protégés. Hell. Get it into your head, Sophie, that you're no more than a student here, that you have no responsibilities towards these kids.

OK, now I could devote what little morning was left to my own concerns. At least the workroom atmosphere might be sweeter.

It would have been, perhaps, if the phone hadn't rung as soon as I got into the room. Greg picked it up, spoke briefly, and handed it to me, eyebrows expressing all the irritation I thought my rough treatment of Rose had eradicated.

'Sophie – it's Chris Groom here,' came a welcome voice. 'I'm here in Smethwick – at Piddock Road nick. Fancy a bite of lunch?'

'That would be manna from heaven. I'll meet you in your foyer in fifteen minutes.'

Chris and I went back years. We'd been mostly friends, apart from a short foray into being lovers, which was a disaster. But it had always seemed that the more damage we'd inflicted on our friendship, the deeper it had grown. At one time he'd been in charge of the Operation Command Unit of which Piddock Road Police Station was the hub. Now he was in charge of West Midlands Police's MIUs – Murder Investigation Units. The nomenclature changed frequently, but Chris, despite theoretically being in temporary charge only, had been in place several months. Basically he was now a plain-clothes super-intendent with a lot of work. But that would suit Chris down to the ground. He was a highly disciplined man, who relished tough tasks. He was also a kind, decent man – it was too easy to let the role blur the person.

We greeted each other with our usual warm cheek-kiss, and a great deal of pleasure. And from him, a rueful apology.

'I've just this minute been summoned back to Brum for an early afternoon meeting,' he said. 'I'm terribly sorry.'

'When does it start?'

'Two.'

'Why don't we hop into your car and find somewhere to have a bite en route? That way you'll be in spitting distance of Lloyd House, and I can bus back. We can natter while you drive.'

'If you're sure . . .' he said doubtfully. But, I thought, with some relief.

'No problem. On the contrary, it's so good to get away from the angst of UWM that I'd bloody walk back, for the sake of a bit of civilised company.'

'I'm civilised company, am I? Things must be pretty grim there.'

'Not so much grim, more over-emotional . . .'

Chris listened patiently while he was driving but it quickly became apparent as we snatched a pub sandwich that he wanted to talk about something much more serious. No, not a heinous crime, not this time. His own single state.

'You see,' he said, fiddling with the glasses he now wore all the time, 'I've just realised how arid my life has become. I get up, work, go home, work, sleep. It's no life, is it? And I've come to wonder if I need to work so hard, or if I'm using work to fill my life so I don't notice how empty it is.'

I nodded. It was something I'd been worrying about for some time. 'So what are you going to do to change it?'

He shook his head, staring at the plate. Then he managed a fleeting grin. 'Find a partner. Oh,' he said, all in a rush, 'I know I'm getting on, but I'm still fit – I must have something to offer.'

He was also good-looking in a way that looked more scholarly as his hair receded, had a weight-trained body and enjoyed a salary higher than I could imagine, with pension prospects to match. Put that alongside highly intelligent and excellent company. I was surprised he hadn't been snapped up already.

'Offer whom?' I asked gently.

He pleated the paper serviette. 'Someone,' he said, barely moving his lips, 'who'll take your place. I'm sorry – I'm not putting this very well. Sophie. Some part of me will always be in love with you—'

'And me with you, Chris,' I admitted. We had been through so much together that we were as close as brother and sister. But not brother and sister.

'But it's time for me to move on. Just as you have.' He looked me straight in the eye. 'Isn't it?'

I held his gaze. 'Yes. It is.' I'd moved on pretty thoroughly myself. 'In fact I—' I hated not being completely frank with him. But I couldn't break my promise to Mike.

Somehow our hands found and clasped each other's. He turned the emerald with his thumb.

'I need someone to love, Sophie. And someone to love me. Like you and Mike.'

I didn't protest that no two people could ever love like Mike and me. In real terms it probably wasn't even true. 'You're a very special man, Chris. How are you going to find your very special woman?'

He blushed the deepest scarlet I've ever seen. 'How about a marriage bureau?' he mumbled.

I was in the middle of saying all the positive things I wanted when his mobile phone rang. He turned away to answer it.

I couldn't help overhearing his part in the conversation. It alarmed me, but I knew better than to ask outright.

After a few sentences, he switched off, grinning ironically. 'Harvinder. From Smethwick. He heard your voice back there, but was busy and couldn't say hello. That was to repair the omission, and to ask if you knew a UWM student has been reported missing.'

I shook my head. 'Who? Anyone I know?'

'Probably not. A kid in the music department. No reason for you to have anything to do with him, is there?'

'I sing in their choir,' I said. 'And I've got to know one or two.'

'He's a violinist,' Chris continued. 'Neil something.'

My mouth went dry. 'Not Neil Wiltshire?'

'That's right. I suppose you couldn't go and talk to Harvinder?'

'Soon as I can get a bus back.'

'He could come and get you.'

'Regular buses. Hardly any distance to walk.'

Yes, we were suddenly embarrassed with each other. We finished our sandwiches, drained our sparkling waters in silence.

As we left the pub, him turning to the car park, me to the main road and the bus, I took his hand. 'I'm glad you're doing this,' I said, 'But I'm glad you told me first.'

He nodded. 'You and Mike – you're . . .?' He looked at me hard. 'You were going to say something back there, weren't you? Christ, Sophie: you've been and gone and got married, haven't you?'

Staring out of the window at the delights of Cape Hill, I kept hearing Chris's voice. A man as used as he was to winkling out confessions, a man as close to me as he was, would have had little difficulty putting two and two together. Certainly the shock of realisation had thrown his usually concise and elegant phrasing. He was hurt, offended, as much as a friend as an ex-lover. So how would he feel at not having been invited to the wedding? Well, much as all our friends would, I hoped: hurt, yes, but on the whole eventually understanding. He'd probably feel relief too, that he hadn't been called on to witness the marriage. However much he knew he couldn't have me, it would have been quite another thing to have to watch me looking up into Mike's face as we made our vows. He and Mike tried to like and respect each other, but it would be hard to see another man claim as his bride the woman he wanted, just as it would be hard for me when he married – however much I might have schemed and organised new relationships for him in the past. I recognised with a painful pang that it was one thing benevolently to hand over a man I had no romantic use for, quite another to let him show he'd outgrown me by choosing someone for himself.

'You look as if you've lost half a crown and found a rusty button,' Harv greeted me, kissing me on the cheek Chris had kissed earlier. Harv – Detective Sergeant Harvinder Singh Mann – was a slightly built man in his early thirties, not bonily handsome as some Sikhs can be, and sporting neither beard nor turban; a very Anglicised Asian, not surprising since he'd been born and bred not ten miles down the road.

'Well, if someone you know's gone AWOL . . .' I said. Harv was a friend but was also a colleague of Chris's. There was no way I could even hint at the cause of my serious face. 'Neil's an adult,' I continued, as Harvinder led me through to his office.

'I saw him on Friday. It's a bit soon for him to have been reported missing, isn't it?'

'I'd have thought so,' he sighed, pushing a chair in my direction, then perching on his desk. 'But some background – and that's all I want at this stage, Sophie – might help us decide on how to act. Whether to act, actually. Tea?'

Harvinder was even more of a herbal person than Sue, my new acquaintance. I was relieved to be able to decline on the grounds of being awash with mineral water.

'So why the panic?' If I sounded cool it was because my brain was getting back in gear. How many times had parents of my students assumed their beloved kids had been taken by white-slave traders, or succumbed to the wicked lures of London? OK, their anxieties had been real, had got more intense by the minute. But ninety-nine times out of a hundred, the errant offspring had turned up the following morning, having crashed for the night at a friend's and simply forgotten to phone. But there was always the one out of a hundred. I thought of the trauma thc kidnap of one of those ex-students had caused.

He rubbed his chin. 'Personally I think it's too early to worry. The lad's twenty, and should be able to find his way in the world. That's what I told his parents. They come from –' he checked a file – 'Morpeth. They were anxious about him living so far away from them in the first place, but apparently they agreed provided he phoned home on a regular basis.'

'How regular?'

Harv pulled a face. 'Every day.'

'Every day! My God!'

'Not just his parents, but his girlfriend too. Every other day.'

'*Girl*friend!'

'You don't think he was that way inclined?'

'Wouldn't have thought so. But maybe he's AC/DC. Or just

unsure – he's a very young twenty. He could still be having the sort of crush people have on the captain of cricket.'

'Only in this case it's . . .?'

'A violinist – leader of the Boulton Quartet. I'd have a crush on him myself if I were younger – a very handsome man called Alex Fisher. He's thirty-three, thirty-five-ish. Neil's tutor.'

Harvinder slipped off the desk and withdrew to the business side of it, pulling a pad towards him. 'Gay?' he asked.

'Family man. But that doesn't prove anything.'

He pursed his lips. 'Not in a much older man. But there's less pressure not to come out these days.'

'True.' I sat back, looking for another tack. 'He may have panicked. The same Alex Fisher's cut his hand and can't play in an important concert. They may have asked Neil to take his place.'

'So wouldn't that be a wonderful chance for a kid starting his career?'

'Depends. He may have thought he thought he wasn't up to it and done a flit.'

'Couldn't he have said no?'

'The prof – Marcus French – is the sort of guy it's hard to argue with.'

'Any other ideas?'

'He's another reason not to want to play. A possible personality clash with the viola player in the quartet. He's a lecturer called James Hallam. Neil and Hallam played a duet the other evening, and rather than support and encourage Neil, this Hallam more or less humiliated him. I find Hallam a bit of an enigma. He can be very charming, very pro-student, but can, on the evidence of the duet, also be a right sod.'

'Trust you to come up with the precise technical term, Sophie.' He leant back in his chair, twiddling his ballpoint. 'Anything else? A girlfriend – or a *boy*friend in the area?'

'No idea. But something was troubling him at UWM. He was asking questions about staff-student groups, the sort that

81

discuss problems with the way a course is being run. And I know he was actively considering giving up his course to take up a job. In fact,' I straightened, 'that's where I'd start looking. London. He had an offer from one of the orchestras down there to join the second violins even before he'd finished his course. His tutor – Alex Fisher, the one with the hand injury – was dead against it, on the grounds that Neil wasn't ready for the rough and tumble of being a professional.'

'And you can bet your boots his parents and girlfriend wouldn't have wanted him to decamp for the Smoke,' Harvinder observed. 'Which orchestra?'

'No idea. Ask Alex Fletcher. Personal tutors are supposed to be omniscient. And, to be fair, most tutors I've ever come across take their responsibilities very seriously. Even as a mature student I have a personal tutor, though I think her duties would be more academic than pastoral.'

Harvinder sucked his teeth. 'If you had a crush on her, would it make life difficult?'

'For both of us, yes. And I should imagine even more if she was teaching me to do something physical, like playing the fiddle. You know, showing me how to bow, how to stand. Things that could involve touching.' My mind did a nasty somersault in which it offered me the prospect of being tutor to Rose.

He held up a hand to stop me. 'Hang on, Sophie. I'm as British as they come—'

'Black Country,' I grinned. 'Better than mere British.'

'Ah, but at the Black Country comp. I went to they weren't too much into music. Violin – yes, I know what a violin looks like. And a cello. But viola? And fiddle?'

'"Fiddle" is just a colloquial term for any stringed instrument you play with a bow. Even a cello or a double bass could be described as a fiddle. The violin's the smallest in the family, then there's the viola, which is slightly larger and produces a deeper sound. But you still tuck it under your chin to play.

Then there's the cello, which you fit between your knees, and lastly the double bass, which some people prefer to play standing up. And don't ask me why it's double, because I don't know.'

He jotted and nodded. 'Don't you have any wind instruments at UWM – woodwind or brass?'

'I know a woman who plays the oboe, but as for brass, no, I don't know any of the UWM ones.'

'Are they in general as problematic as your – your *fiddle* players?'

'Oboe players are supposed to be positively neurotic, but only about their reeds. Dawn's a bit moody at the moment, but I wouldn't know why. To be honest, I've never known any brass players well enough to comment. We've got some singers at UWM too,' I said. 'I've got to know a couple.'

'And what are they like?'

'The ones I know . . .'

He leant forward to prompt me. 'Yes?'

'Two – both black, as it happens – are lovely. But . . . no, Harv, this isn't relevant to the Neil case. At least, I don't think so.'

The kind, inoffensive Harv, whom I'd never known say more than boo to the proverbial goose, suddenly grew three inches and four years. 'Suppose you stop playing God here, Sophie. I said I wanted background and I want background. I'll be the one who decides what's relevant or not.'

I bit back a patronising retort. He was the gaffer, after all. 'There are allegations of favouritism in the music department,' I said. 'The first I heard was made by a hysterical young woman who, believe it or not, seems to have a crush on me. Most embarrassing.'

He looked at me appraisingly. 'But surely not unusual? You must have been on the receiving end of them before.'

'Not that I know about. Anyway, I've noticed one or two things that might suggest that there is – the prof pulling rank so a student gets more use of the practice rooms than the others, and then giving said student a lift. Oh, and giving her a high grade in an assignment too. But that's all, Harv.'

'You'd be in a better position than us to find out about this, Sophie.'

'Jesus, not copper's nark again!' I was only half joking.

'Paid informant?'

'Surely the police service has more to worry about than the sexual politics of a second-rate university!' This time I wasn't joking at all.

'Let me say it again: I'll make the decisions here.' He said it without animosity, without even raising his usually quiet and gentle voice. But I was in no doubt that he meant it.

'OK. My eyes and ears are at your disposal.' I won't pretend I liked being put in my place like that. Particularly as Harv had always been quite low down the police pecking order, for all he was a sergeant. We'd always laughed and joked together, and indulged in benign conspiracies against Chris. And I hated it when authority figures pulled rank, as he was doing now. The question was, should I let my resentment cloud our relationship? I knew and liked his wife, had chucked their new baby under the chin and generally considered myself a family friend. And here was Harvinder exerting authority!

He must have picked up a tinge of sarcasm, not entirely accidental. His eyes flickered. But then he made an effort I'd been too mean to make. He dug in his jacket pocket. 'Have you seen the latest photos of Inderjit?' he asked.

'Hey! That's the teddy I gave him!' I said, pouncing as a friend should. 'And the teething ring . . .'

'God, don't talk to me about teething!'

We smiled across the desk. Yes, it would be all right, wouldn't it?

Chapter Nine

Chris's astonishing announcement; the little spat with Harvinder – I had so much to think about I almost didn't go back into UWM. But I felt it would be almost dishonourable not to, especially as it was Harvinder who'd made the effort to restore a bridge that my ego had shaken.

Putting my nose round the workroom door, I found the room empty but all the computers humming away, their screens hyperactive with the official UWM screensaver. Even mine? I was across the room dabbing my mouse before I knew it.

Shit and shit! There was a message from Rose, telling me she was sorry to disturb me but she really needed to talk. Why the stupid girl hadn't done what anyone else would have done – written a note and dropped it on my desk – goodness knows. My colleagues would really have loved the whole performance. In my mind's eye I could see her switching on the machine, sitting herself down, tapping away – all the while giving, no doubt, an irritatingly audible commentary. Blast the girl!

Oh dear. What had happened to me? Surely I should be feeling sorry for her. But all I wanted to do was put a duvet over my head and pretend that she wasn't vulnerable, needy and even a tad unhinged. I just wanted her to grow up and let me get on with my life. I was beginning to feel, God forgive me, as if she were stalking me. I'd better get myself to a counsellor – someone like Sue – and talk.

Meanwhile, still fizzing, I typed something on my own account, and printed enough copies for every desk.

Dear Colleague,

I'm sure you've realised by now that I'm being harassed by Rose Dungate and would more than appreciate your help in keeping her out of this room. If we can't manage something unofficial, I shall have to report her to the uni authorities, but I don't want to make a song and dance of it until we've tried informal methods.

I'd be more than grateful for your help, which should ensure a quieter workroom for us all.

I didn't add a dour PS to the effect that one of the other people who'd knocked on my door was likely to be classified a Missing Person and was therefore unlikely, alas, to be bothering me in the foreseeable future. Oh God. Poor Neil – where on earth could he possibly be?

Clearly the music department was where I needed to be. Ostentatiously clutching my piano music folder, I toddled along as if to claim a practice room I'd reserved. There was no booking, of course, but it would give me an excuse to run my finger down the chart to see who was doing what and where.

By an irritating coincidence there was a room free right then. But I dawdled anyway. Yes, there was evidence that several names had been erased from the booking chart, which was usually filled in using the pencil that hung by a string on the board to which the chart was attached. And guess whose name replaced them. Dawn's. By another coincidence, a slot before hers the following morning was free in room nine. If I booked the room and hung about long enough after my session, I could see who was going to accompany her. If it was only another student, I might be able to grab a word before they started. If it was Marcus French himself – though I couldn't believe he'd be so blatant – then what? I could scarcely tackle him about possible abuse of staff power. That would be no more than a diplomatic way of telling him I thought he was bonking a student. I booked the room anyway. I'd have to think on my feet.

In the end, I did the sensible thing: I filled the next hour with exercises. If I thought for a moment about other things, the fingers went all wonky and I had to start again.

I'd have hit the rush hour splat in the middle if I'd set off for home immediately I'd finished. Besides which, the lunchtime water was a long way away and I deserved a reward after all those major and minor arpeggios – harmonic and melodic. One thing I couldn't recall was whether Harvinder had told me to keep quiet about Neil's disappearance. On the whole, it would in any case be better for someone else to announce it. If it was general knowledge people wouldn't be able to keep their mouths shut anyway. Imagine Rose resisting the chance to wax dramatic over it. Oh God – Rose. I hadn't danced immediately to her tune, had I? What if she was miffed, and decided to snub me – something I'd been longing for for days, of course. I'd better go and if not exactly seek her out, be available should she wish to descend on me, as it were.

There was no immediate sign of her in the refec, but Dawn was there, chewing her hair and doing nothing much else. I could drift over, couldn't I? But – wouldn't you just know it? – Greg and Myra, another of my post-grad colleagues, caught my eye and waved me over. I could hardly refuse. But before I sat down with them, I excused myself, and popped over to Dawn.

She looked glum.

'You OK?' I asked.

She nodded.

'You're sure? You look a bit down.'

'Another assignment. And another open rehearsal tomorrow,' she said. 'Mozart. Flute and Harp.'

'Wonderful!'

Dawn shook her head. 'Not with our flautist. Jasmine Carr. Believes in playing with Expression. You know a woodwind section should sound like a unit within an orchestra – well, she thinks we're there to accompany her.'

'And she's got more rubato than a rubber band?' I suggested.

'Quite.'

'So you're expecting French to give her a rough time?'

She shrugged, and returned to her hair. 'Not as rough,' she said at last, 'as she'll give the harpist. Poor sod, trying to follow her.' She snorted. 'Watching her playing's like watching a bloody belly dancer.'

'Trying to pull him?' I asked neutrally, making, in the meantime, a resolution to be nowhere near any belly dancers.

'Well, he's drop-dead gorgeous, but—'

I interrupted her: 'Another student?'

'No. Part-time staff. Not a lot of would-be harpists around, I suppose.'

'No parties for them to go to?'

She didn't pick up on the allusion. 'Trouble is,' she continued, with a malicious grin, 'she hasn't realised he's gay!'

'What if he wasn't? I mean, if she – pulled – him. Seduced him. Couldn't he end up in the shit if the university authorities found out?'

She looked blank.

'You know, staff at places like this aren't supposed to have relationships with their students. It was a hanging offence at my old college.'

'But we're all over eighteen,' she said doubtfully.

'It's to do more with power than with age,' I said. 'Isn't it?'

Her finger found a strand of hair to worry into her mouth. Oh God: I really ought to pursue this.

'I had this student once,' I lied. 'Fancied him like mad, right from day one. But I think it's dodgy, sleeping with someone whose assignments you've got to mark. It's too easy to be

88

influenced by the way the relationship goes.'

'But you—'

I could see she was trying to point out that I was about a hundred.

'He was a mature student,' I said, warming to my mythical past. 'Even so. No way.'

She dropped a tissue, bent to retrieve it, looked at her watch on the way up and clapped her hand, plus tissue, to her mouth. 'Got to go! Late!'

'May see you at that open rehearsal,' I said. 'Oh,' I called her back, 'I see you've booked a rehearsal room tomorrow: what are you working on?'

'The prof thinks I ought to improve my performer's skills. Oboe. He thinks I should prepare for a recital in the summer.'

'Wow! He must think you're good. If ever you need an accompanist, let me know!'

She barely flapped a hand in response. 'See you,' she said.

Greg and Myra, however, renewed their smiles as I joined them, Myra pushing half a KitKat at me. What with her earth mother image, and her regular reading of the *Guardian*, her choice of commercial as opposed to wholefood snack rather surprised me.

Still it was a peace-offering. I'd better eat it, although I knew I shouldn't.

'I didn't realise,' Myra began, pink with the effort, 'that you were trying to avoid those young people.' But her eyes slid over to Dawn.

'Only Rose. I natter to the others because I'm a musician manqué. Eng. Lit. got in the way.' Eng. Lit. and my unwanted pregnancy. Well, I suppose giving up music was a small price to pay for having brought Steph into the world. I wondered how he and Andy were getting on now, still stuck inescapably in each other's company. 'I accompany a couple of them and sing in the choir – we're in a concert at Symphony Hall soon.'

Both looked impressed.

'The other thing is,' I rattled on, though not terribly relevantly, 'is that I'm catering for a reception after the UWM quartet's concert on Saturday. At the BMI.'

'I didn't even know they had a quartet,' Myra admitted.

'Oh yes. The Boulton.'

'Bolton? Why Bolton, not UWM – or even Smethwick?'

'Boulton as in Matthew,' I said. Surely I didn't need to explain. Surely everyone had heard of him and his fellow industrialists. Except Boulton was so much more than that. But two blank looks suggested I'd better say something. 'The Local History Group are organising a trip to see what's left of his foundry. And if you haven't been to Soho House, you're in for a real treat,' I added. 'It's been most beautifully restored. Out in Hockley.'

Myra shook her head. 'Not my sort of thing, industry. I'm more into Art.'

Ever helpful, I said, 'There was a fascinating costume exhibition last time I was there. And a display of embroidery by women from the Asian community.'

'Really? I must make a note.'

We both knew she wouldn't go. But we had a workroom to share, preferably amicably, so we continued to chat. She was anxious about her cats – all five of them. Greg loathed cats, but had a thing about cockatiels. I offered my short but meaningful relationships with a rat and a gerbil. We got on like a house on fire, even if our conversation was scarcely what you'd expect of three experienced career teachers well into post-graduate qualifications.

I hung about long enough for Rose to find me, had she been looking, but there was no sign of her. I didn't know whether to be irritated or relieved. As I was in the lobby heading for the car park, someone else hailed me, however – James Hallam.

'Sophie! Look, I was out of order earlier. Sorry: this first violin problem's really getting to me. Whoever we suggest, the

90

prof vetoes. I think he's going to wish one of his mates on us, the bastard.'

'The trouble is, you haven't much time to argue, have you?'

'Hardly any. God, what a bugger. We don't get time to practise enough as it is, and then this happens.'

'Will you keep the same programme or go for something that makes fewer demands on the leader?'

'Depends who French comes up with. With all due respect to you and your mortgage, I'd rather cancel and be damned. Better that than offer Joe Public a crap performance.'

'Quite. And the concert hall in the BMI won't forgive any lapses in ensemble – the acoustics are terribly dry.'

He didn't ask how I knew. 'We haven't even had a chance to practise there, you know. The BMI said we could have a room the whole day for a peppercorn fee, but French vetoed it.'

I looked at him hard. 'It sounds as if he's doing his best to wreck the evening. Have you looked at your contracts recently?'

He frowned. 'Why?'

'I just wondered if there was a clause that said your contract could be terminated if your playing fell below standard.'

'What? Jesus, that'd be a bit devious – even for French.' He bit his lip. 'I'd better go home and check – though what good it'll do me I don't know. If we're crap, we're crap.'

'If you're nobbled, you're entitled to be crap. It becomes constructive dismissal, I'd say. You are all in a trade union, aren't you? Musicians' Union, or AUT or NATFHE?'

He shook his head. 'Come on, Alex isn't going to slice his hand just to please French.'

I grinned. 'Of course not. I'm letting my imagination run away with me. Right, better be off then. Good night.'

To my surprise he called me back. 'You're serious about this union thing, aren't you?'

I sang, '*They can't get me, I'm part of the union!*'

Small my voice may be, but I'm proud of my diction. So Marcus French would have had the full benefit as he turned a

91

corner and joined us in the lobby. How much had he heard of the rest of the conversation?

He nodded without any particular cordiality, and stopped short. 'Hallam, I wonder if we might have a private word?'

Ah, quite a lot, perhaps.

'I'd best be off, then,' I observed. 'Good night, James. Professor French.'

To my amazement, he smiled at me. 'I never thanked you, Ms Rivers, for going to such enormous trouble with the catering for Saturday. I trust all's running smoothly?'

Sheep and lamb time. 'More smoothly than the music side's going, I gather. I suppose top-quality first violins don't grow on trees.'

'I'd still like to bring young Neil Wiltshire in,' James Hallam said.

So he hadn't heard about Neil's disappearance. Unless, of course, he was bluffing. And why, after their last public appearance together, should he imagine Neil would want ever to play with him again?

'His sight-reading's excellent, and he's very malleable,' Hallam continued. 'He wouldn't bring any preconceptions either.'

'Technically I suppose he's up to it. But my secretary's run to earth an experienced first violin from the Mondi Quartet. Tony Masters. Do you know him?'

'Tony? We've played in a couple of gigs together. But I heard a rumour – hasn't he got some problem with his hearing?'

'Not that I'm aware of. He'll be contacting you first thing tomorrow. Now, I'm happy for you all to cancel all your teaching and tutorial work for the rest of this week to facilitate rehearsal. Don't worry, I've cleared it with the Dean.'

Hallam pulled a face. 'Students on the performing musician courses have got assessments coming up. They won't be happy to lose—'

'They'll just have to lump it, Hallam. I hate to use old-

92

fashioned terms like this, but the honour of the faculty's at stake.'

Before my startled eyes he transmogrified into James Robertson Justice in an old film like *Raising the Wind* and back again.

'Point taken, Prof. Now, when did you want to see me?' Hallam looked at his watch to imply it wouldn't be that evening.

'Let's say eight thirty tomorrow.'

'I have to take my children into school. Nine thirty would be better.'

'Indeed.' The temperature dropped below zero.

Oh, yes. James Hallam had better join a union – any union – pretty damned fast.

All three of us walked out to the car park together. The area supposed to be reserved for staff cars was the far corner from where I'd parked the little Mazda, but French stuck with me, even when Hallam waved and made for his Renault Espace.

'You've got a much better voice than I realised,' French said.

'It's one thing to warble to a friend,' I said truthfully, 'quite another to do it at an audition.'

. Nodding almost absently, he watched me fish for my car-key. 'So you and Hallam are friends, are you?' He rather leant on the word *friends*.

Had I said something wrong? I didn't want to commit Hallam to something he might not feel and which might not do him any good.

'Perhaps I should have said, "When nothing depends on your singing",' I conceded.

'I think you should work on that voice,' he said. 'When is it Hallam's coming to see me? Nine thirty? Why don't you come at ten? I know you're not really part of the department but you're certainly helping two of our best singers. The least we can do is find a voice teacher for you.'

Chapter Ten

Kicking myself for not bringing in a takeaway, I was opening a bottle to help me gear myself up to cooking. Funny how I can cook for a hundred without turning a hair, but how cooking for just me can be an intolerable chore.

As if in response to a prayer, the phone rang.

Chris. 'Have you eaten, yet?'

Us and our synchronicity! 'I was in mid-ponder,' I said.

'Indian or Chinese?'

'Whichever's most convenient.'

'Forty minutes?'

'Beer and wine already chilling.'

Forty minutes to the second, he rang the bell with his usual pattern, so I'd know it was him and not some unwelcome visitor.

'So why didn't you two tell anyone?' he asked as he stepped into the hall, dominating it, as usual.

'Because we couldn't decide on any of the things that would have been important to other people – big or small, pretty dress and morning suit or everyday clothes, even religious or civil. And then with the time for him to go to Pakistan getting steadily closer, we just got a special licence and went and did it.'

'How's Aggie taken it?' He carried the bag – he'd plumped for curry – straight into the kitchen.

'She doesn't know,' I admitted.

'God Almighty! You know she loves you like a grand-daughter.'

Aggie had been my next-door neighbour for years. Now she'd left suburban Harborne and was living near one of her granddaughters in sheltered accommodation in rural Worcestershire.

'No one knows,' I said quietly. 'Except the two witnesses – absolute strangers.'

He fished the foil dishes out, putting them in a roasting-dish I had ready, and stowing them in the oven to keep warm. 'But why – for God's sake. All your friends—'

'Our friends will be invited to the blessing,' I said. 'I know I'm not much of a Baptist, and I don't think Mike's a terribly good Methodist, but we – we do want people we care about to witness that. And come to a monster party afterwards.'

'Even so—'

'Wine or lager?'

'If it's Beck's, yes, please.'

I passed him bottle, then a glass. Chris wasn't a man for supping direct from a bottle.

'But you owed it to people—' he continued.

'Chris,' I said facing him squarely across the table, 'we did it that way because we wanted to. We – we had to.'

He went so pale I was afraid he'd need the smelling salts he always carried. 'You mean you're – pregnant!'

If ever I'd needed proof that Chris and I weren't compatible, it was that conventional assumption. Not so much conventional as old fashioned. But that was Chris.

'No. I mean that Mike and I are thousands of miles apart when we wanted to be together.'

He flipped the tops off the Beck's and passed me mine. 'So you wanted to make sure of him.'

I winced. And realised how angry I was. Let the words be as brutal as I could make them, then. 'For God's sake, if he wanted to fuck other women – if, for that matter I wanted to fuck other men – do you suppose a crappy bit of paper would stop us? Neither of us is wearing a wedding ring, after all. We'll exchange those at the blessing. Chris, we wanted to be man and wife. That's why we did as we did.' I turned from him, swallowing hard. I didn't want him to see how near to tears I was, though he'd know from the way I was shaking that I was deeply upset.

For a few moments, neither of us spoke. When the threat of tears had subsided, I turned back to him. 'With a bit of luck, you'll be able to bring whoever you meet through the agency along to the party. To show her we're over each other.'

It took some time for the atmosphere to ease. We got through the poppadams and dips in silence, and his pakoras and my chicken chaat were pretty tense affairs. It wasn't until our usual bicker over whether one should use a fork or simply use naan bread to scoop up the prawn saag and lamb passanda that we started to talk more freely, and then it was easier to stick to the Neil Wiltshire business.

'So no one at UWM knows he's missing?' Chris leant over to the fridge for two more lagers.

'Someone must do. You can't imagine Harvinder not checking that he'd simply had enough of feeding BT's profits, that he really has bunked off. I'd have thought the someone might be the Professor of Music. But it might well have been the Dean of Faculty, who might in turn have told everyone to keep mum. And what about the students he lives with – in hall or in a house? It's odd, though: at William Murdock rumours would take wing of their own accord. The entire student body would have advance access to the most confidential information.'

'It's a good job you're not there any more,' Chris observed. But he grinned when I looked up at him.

We were back in friendship mode. Just about. So I was taking a risk when I said, 'You will keep it under your hat. Not a whisper. I want all our friends to learn at once. Not even a hint to Aggie.' I knew he visited her as regularly as I did, like an honorary grandson.

'Especially not Aggie,' he agreed.

I got into UWM horribly early the next morning, knowing that the time I was spending sniffing round for Harvinder could have been spent on either my dissertation, or, more probably, preparing items for Saturday's buffet. Who in their right mind would spin out a cup of coffee for ten minutes hoping to attract the attention of someone they'd been systematically avoiding for the best part of a week? I wove interesting scenarios involving Rose and Neil having waltzed off to London together, playing Dittersdorf concertos until they both realigned their sexuality and lived happily ever after. Or, indeed, stay exactly the way they were and *still* live happily ever after.

Meanwhile, my coffee palled and I was being subjected to increasing temptation by the basket of fresh croissants that had just appeared on the servery counter. I pulled myself to my feet, and padded off towards the post-grad workroom. If my route was notably devious, no one but me seemed to be around to observe it. I even popped into the ladies' most frequented by music students, but found neither Rose nor Dawn. I'd scanned the notice board at least five times when at long last I heard someone call my name. But the voice had a Leeds accent.

'Hi, Leonore,' I said, really pleased to see her. 'How goes it?'

She pulled a face. 'Really, really badly. Oh, Sophie, I've done the worst ever thing, and you are going to want my scalp.' She grabbed a fistful of braids, jangly at the ends with pretty beads.

'I do already: it looks really good. Swap for mine anytime.'

'Frankly I do know someone who could make a better job of your colour,' she said. 'And the cut's growing out round the back. My ma wanted me to be a hairdresser,' she added by way of explanation. 'And it doesn't half come in useful – I work at a salon when bloody French lets us have an evening or a Saturday free.'

'Saturdays! Surely he doesn't expect—'

'Well, the Symphony Hall concert's going to mean extra rehearsals, right? And I can't see any other time free.'

She was right, of course.

'Anyway, Sophie, I've done this dreadful thing. And I'm very sorry.' She looked it. 'You know you gave me your phone number? On that bit of paper? Well, I put it in my purse to be absolutely safe—'

'You didn't lose your purse? Oh, Leonore, how awful for you!'

She rolled her eyes. 'Uh-huh. I was digging in it for a receipt and put all the bits of paper on the table, like you do. Right?'

Suddenly I felt a lot less sympathetic. 'I suppose the table'd be in the refec?'

'Right. And who should come along but Rose.'

'And she makes some excuse to talk to you, since she's seen us together, and when she goes you put all the things back in your purse—'

'And when I try to find your number it isn't with the other pieces of paper. But there were lots of other people round, too. Dawn, Dan, Doug, Siobhan and a load of people I don't think you know. I can't be sure . . .'

'When did all this happen?'

'Yesterday. You mean,' she beamed, 'she hasn't phoned you yet? I may just have dropped it after all?'

'I'm sure you did. Anyway,' I said bracingly, 'I'm sure I can deal with the odd phone call.'

For the first time Leonore looked really worried. 'I'm sure you can. But not necessarily from Rose. Her brain's really twisted, man. All this sex stuff.' She patted her temple.

'You mean all this stuff about women bonking French to get good grades is all in her head?'

'I mean her saying you and she are having a passionate affair.'

'What! How dare she!'

'Oh, no one believes her: don't worry about that. After all, she's always done it – fancied someone and chased them round and then found someone else.'

'Any idea why?'

'I'm no psychologist, Sophie. But you should have seen her parents. Freshers' Week they turned up. Sneering that this place wasn't Oxbridge or Guildhall or something. My mum nearly thumped *him*.'

Oh dear, I should have been more supportive, shouldn't I?

'But this phone number,' Leonore continued. 'I'm really sorry.'

The more I made of it, the worse she'd feel. 'Forget it. If it's only temporary, there's no problem. And this business about bonking with French to get good grades – that's all in her head too?'

She dropped her voice. 'If you ask me, that's real enough.'

'Has he propositioned *you*?' If I were looking for evidence, which of course I wasn't, Leonore'd be a cracking witness.

'I don't think he fancies black birds. Besides which, I've had As in all my assessments, and I've got As or Bs in all my assignments – he can't take those away. *No, no, they can't take that away from me,*' she sang. 'And I'd do him for racism if he tried. And win.'

I was sure she would. 'What about other women?'

'There's Dawn, of course—'

'You're sure? You're not just guessing?'

'Found her in the loo yesterday unwrapping a pregnancy test.'

'Could be her boyfriend?'

'Who lives in Worcester and is currently touring with those ice-dancers. I don't think so, Sophie.'

'Shit. Poor kid. Anyone else?'

'Plenty of rumours.'

'You need more than rumours to act. You need names, and not just names. Names of women prepared to stand up and tell the world what's been happening. Not easy, Leonore.'

'I'll keep my ears open. Meanwhile, if I grovel hard enough, can I come round one evening to yours for that practice you promised?'

'We can do better than that if you're free later this morning,' I said. I ought to have been more assertive about the phone number business, perhaps. But the woman had warned me and telling her off would get us nowhere. All the same, there was an irritated niggle in my mind which told me that though her career was paramount, it was best if she pursued it for the time being on UWM premises. 'I managed to book a practice room. And guess who's booked it for the following hour: Dawn.'

'That's great,' Leonore said happily. 'You'll be able to talk to her about her baby.'

Like hell I'd talk to Dawn about her baby! Not because I didn't like her, didn't want to help. No. If Dawn wanted to talk about her baby – always assuming, since pregnancy tests can be negative as well as positive, that there was a baby – then she should talk to her doctor or the Student Support people. Someone like Sue would be able to ask all the right questions and listen for the subtext of the answers. Not Sophie, mother of Steph, given away at birth, and probably the better for it. Not Sophie, who'd breathed to all too many desperate students that there were alternatives to a pregnancy that would disgrace them and their family in their community, and which no one need know about. Not Sophie. No way. Not if Dawn were to get the impartial support she needed. Hell and hell and hell. I was ready to weep for her.

But I must pull myself together. I had to go and see Professor French, didn't I? About a voice teacher. For a moment I toyed with wiring myself up with a tape recorder to obtain evidence. OK, there was a small problem in that I didn't have such a tape recorder. In any case, he was hardly likely to proposition me the first time we met. Which assumed he'd wish to proposition me – after all, I was nearer his age than the girls he was alleged to be involved with. I was a tough, stringy old bird – at least, for a man had a taste for nubile nineteen-year-olds.

'I'm afraid she's been after you again,' Greg announced as I went into the workroom. 'I told her you weren't due in today. She's got it very badly, you know. I hope I did right.'

'How badly?'

'Puffy eyes, dripping nose.'

'Just as likely,' Myra declared, 'to be a common cold.'

'But she seemed upset,' Greg insisted.

'She always seems upset,' Myra pointed out. 'How on earth did you get involved with her?'

'I haven't, not in the sense she'd mean. All I did was talk to her in the ladies' loo one day. That seemed to make us instantly best buddies in her eyes. But not, I hasten to add, in mine.'

Myra coughed meaningfully and looked hard at Greg, who responded by getting up and sneaking out. 'She says you made a lesbian advance,' Myra said. 'Touched her up.'

'Damn it, I'm a married woman!' I expostulated, before I could stop myself. 'Shit! Myra, forget I said that. It's true, but I don't in any circumstances want it known at the moment.'

I'll swear her nose twitched.

'We haven't told our families yet,' I pursued. 'There are good reasons, and I beg you to respect them.'

'Of course I will,' she promised. But I suspected she crossed her fingers behind her back. 'As far as Droopy's concerned,' she said, with a briskness that surprised me, 'I'd talk to the uni authorities – there's a lot to be said for getting your blow in

102

first, you know. Your tutor, Student Support, the Dean – anyone. Because when that weak, wobbly sort of girl sinks her fangs into you, you'll find people believe her because they're sorry for her.'

I toyed with mentioning Rose to Professor French at our ten o'clock meeting. But I decided it was better not to introduce the idea of sex into any conversation with him – even lesbian sex, lest he conceive the idea of converting me to heterosexuality. In any case, I felt more shaken by the news about Dawn than was compatible with calm conversation.

I'd presented myself outside his room a few minutes early, in the hope of a few words with James Hallam. He seemed inclined to trust me, and if it was official that Neil was missing I suspected he'd tell me. But there was no sign of him. French admitted me as soon as I knocked. His desk was the unnaturally tidy sort that always makes me wonder about the state of the owner's alimentary canal – in purely Freudian terms, of course. He stood up when I knocked and entered, gestured me to a chair and referred to a single sheet of paper on the blotter in front of him. Blotter? Where was his computer? Ah – over on a side table.

'I've spoken to Jane Taylor,' he said. 'She's done wonders for women with mature voices like yours. Unfortunately with the forthcoming assessments, she's too busy to take on any new students at the moment. But she's promised me she'll contact you, and arrange an hour or so when the tumult and the shouting have died down.'

'Thanks,' I said. And meant it.

Neither of us, it seemed, wanted to prolong the interview, apart from the usual courtesies. I picked up my bag, and left, closing the heavy oak door behind me. As I set off down the corridor, a terrible wail followed me that I feared would penetrate even the most soundproof of doors.

'Oh God! Not you. Oh, Sophie, I thought better of you. You

bitch! You cunt!' And the full thirteen stone of Rose launched itself at me.

Chapter Eleven

I haven't been friends with police officers over the years without learning one or two dodges when it comes to people trying forcibly to waylay me. I might not weigh in at much more than eight stone, but it was Rose, not me, who ended up in an ungainly heap on the floor.

I suppose it was the shock of the unexpected attack: I felt angry, shaken, upset – and suddenly desperate.

'Get up,' I said, ready to pass her her bag and files when she'd struggled to her feet. 'Right. Now, Rose, you and I are going to have a little chat.'

'I don't want to talk to a whore like you. Letting French—' she yelled.

I kept my voice down. 'Be quiet. We need to talk because you can't go round saying things like that about people.' If only we could talk it through with someone impartial who was also kind and understanding. Yes, someone like Sue, who might be technologically challenged, and whose tea I might disdain, but whose heart I was sure would be in the right place. If not Sue – and perhaps being acquainted with me might make it embarrassing for her – someone else who could invite Rose to reflect somewhere safe on what was driving her.

'Do you understand me?' I pursued. Because if she didn't, she'd have to try to understand a solicitor's letter. 'Go and tidy yourself up,' I added more gently, 'and I'll see if we can talk to a counsellor. There may be one free now.'

'I don't need to see a counsellor.'

'But I do. I'll see you there in five minutes, shall I?'

'I – but I—'

'Off you go, now.' I stood arms folded and watched her trail off. Poor kid. What had driven her to this? Most of my lesbian friends were the most together people you'd wish to meet. Perhaps, despite what Alex Fisher had said, this was the first time she'd truly acknowledged her sexuality. I just wished she'd had a happier time of it.

As I started off in the opposite direction, another young woman came down the corridor towards me: the second clarinet in the student orchestra. We exchanged the cautious smiles of people who three-quarters recognise each other. Knocking the prof's door, she was admitted very swiftly.

Of course she was admitted swiftly. He'd admitted me swiftly. I felt no warmth to the man, but remembered my initial protestations to Dawn: to become a prof, a teaching, administrative and creative role, you had to be pretty efficient. Which might just mean getting people through their appointments with the maximum speed – as he'd completed mine. If only I could talk to Dawn. If only I could trust myself to ask the right questions.

Sue wasn't available, but someone called Kev was. A thin young man – oh, he'd be about twenty-eight – whose jeans and desert boots reminded me of my student days, he sat us down and looked at us curiously through a pair of those fashionable spectacles with very tiny lenses. They did unnerving things to his eyes.

'I just want to make it clear to Rose,' I told him, after giving a brief resume of the situation, 'that while I'm happy to be a friend and colleague, I do not have any other feelings for her.'

We were in what I presumed was a standard counselling room, a narrow, featureless rectangle with the high ceiling and partial ornate cornices that showed it was a mere segment of something much grander. There were four easy chairs, a tasteful print, a wan parlour palm and a coffee table round which the three of us took up position.

'That's not what you said at the start,' Rose said. 'Not when you touched me. Not when you tried to kiss me.'

'When was this, Rose?' For all I was trying to be calm and reasonable, I was far from feeling either. There was something about the counsellor's expression, something about his body language, which alarmed me. Nice, matey Kev.

'In the toilets. We were talking about concertos for two instruments,' she told him. 'Mozart, Bach. And then she said she'd like to play a Dittersdorf concerto with me. But first she'd like to play another sort of duet. And she put her hands up my T-shirt and felt my breasts.'

I shook my head in disbelief. 'We talked music. Full stop. And any physical contact between us took place later when you were upset by an assignment grade.'

'What sort of physical contact?' the counsellor asked Rose, not me.

'She kissed me and—'

'Oh, no, I didn't—'

'Let Rose finish, please, Sophie.'

'She kissed me and ran her fingers down my back . . . into my jeans. Round my bum. And then she pulled away and put her hand down the front of my jeans . . .'

'Inside?'

I wished the young man looked less – interested – in the details.

Rose nodded. 'I tried to push her away. I'm a virgin, you see. But she leant me against the wall and rubbed – rubbed me . . . She brought me,' Rose said, her face rapt. 'There and then. And then she took me along to the canteen to buy me a coffee and to help me with my assignment. But she refused to help any more after that. I wouldn't let her touch me any more, you see, and she said if I wanted help, that was what I had to do. Only this time properly. At her house. I didn't want to. I was afraid of what else she'd want to do. She asked Leonore as well.'

'Leonore?' he prompted.

'She's another student,' I said. 'Keep her out of this.'

Rose turned swimming eyes to me. 'But she's taken you from me. I've seen you together.'

'You've seen me with a lot of people. I don't have a sexual relationship with any of them.'

Kev leant forward. 'No?'

'Even if I did,' I added, goaded, 'it would be none of your or Rose's business.'

Rose flared. 'It is my business! After the things you said, the things you've done—'

'For God's sake!'

Kevin raised a minatory hand. 'Sophie, it's obviously very difficult for Rose to say this sort of thing. Give her some space. In fact, I'm wondering if this three-cornered conversation is the best way of proceeding. I'm inclined to ask you to see me on another occasion, Sophie. Let's make an appointment, shall we?' He reached for his diary.

'There's no point, Kev. Rose has told a whole tissue of half-truths and lies. I can't make her unsay them, and I can't make her unbelieve them. But she mustn't spread them any further.'

'They're not lies!'

Exasperated, I turned to Kev: 'To put your hand down someone's jeans, front or back, would require a certain amount of co-operation, I'd have thought. Buttons and zips,' I said patiently. 'And I'd have thought anyone capable of hefting a bass was more than capable of flooring me, if I'd ever attempted such a thing.'

Perhaps I'd scored a point. Kevin's eyes had followed mine to the belt straining round the waistband of Rose's jeans. I added, 'Whatever fantasies she's woven, Rose must stop disturbing my colleagues in the post-grad workroom.' Damn, I'd pushed too hard.

'This attitude isn't very helpful, Sophie,' Kev began.

'I've got evidence,' Rose announced. 'How about that? Evidence! You gave me your phone number!'

'If you have my number it's because you got hold of it from someone who dropped it,' I said. 'She's already apologised to me for losing it. In any case, I don't think you should be talking about allegations and evidence. You see, if you start talking about evidence, as if I were somehow on trial, I shall start talking about witnesses.'

Rose yelled triumphantly, 'There weren't any witnesses when you – when you—'

'Fended you off,' I said quietly. 'Look, Rose, I really think you need some help coming to terms with your sexuality—'

'That's quite out of order,' Kev snapped. 'All counselling is non-judgemental. Counsellors never give advice.'

'I'm not a counsellor,' I pointed out, trying to keep my voice from rising. 'I'm the one who instigated this discussion. I wanted to talk where Rose would feel safe and where there'd be support for her. I have been the victim of harassment which has interrupted the work of fellow students and I've now had purloined something I gave in confidence to someone else. The funny thing is, after all this, I find I'm now demonised and transformed into the villain of the piece.'

'You were in a position of authority over this young person and have abused her trust,' Kev shouted.

I held out a hand to silence him. 'Hang on. Hang on. How am I in authority over her? I'm a student here. Same as Rose is. And she has, not to put too fine a point on it, made my life a misery this last week. And possibly worse: unless she undertakes never to phone me, I shall have to go to all the fun of changing my number.' Mike had constantly warned me to use a separate line for business: why had I never listened?

'Look, Sophie, calm down. This is a counselling session, not a court of law.'

'How long have you been doing this sort of thing, Kev?' I was on my feet, arms akimbo. 'Because I was a part-time counsellor for years at my old college and I never ran a session like this. And my supervisor – I assume you are supervised? – would have had kittens if I had.'

'Don't you threaten me!'

'For God's sake, I'm not threatening anyone! I'm just saying that I came as – if you wish to pursue the legal imagery – a plaintiff, and suddenly I'm the accused. Non-judgemental: we both agree that's what counselling should be. So why are you judging me?'

He shifted in his seat. 'I'm trying to get at the truth.'

'"What is truth? said jesting Pilate." You're not supposed to be after it anyway, whatever it is. You're supposed to provide support for an unhappy young woman who has to change her behaviour because it's affecting other people. Even if we had had the torrid affair she alleges, I'd have the right to terminate it without being pursued and harassed—'

'So you admit you've—' Rose pounced.

'I admit nothing. Kevin, I've got to go. I've an appointment—'

'With Leonore!' she cried. 'That's who with. And everyone knows she's a dyke.'

I took a deep breath. And another. 'I'm not privy to Leonore's sexual inclinations. If she's gay – I think you'll find that's the preferred term, Rose – or if she's heterosexual, it's all the same to me. All I'm doing is accompanying her on the piano. A word in private, please, Kevin, before I go.' I held the door open, meaningfully.

Poor lad. He was way beyond his depth, wasn't he? He trailed after me.

'What do you propose to do now?' I asked, closing the door after us.

'You've no right—'

'We've got a very unhappy, possibly very sick girl in there, and you waste time talking about rights!'

'But—'

'Go back to square one, Kev. Forget the truth, forget taking sides. Just deal with her professionally. Personally, I think she needs more help than you can give her. Don't be ashamed of referring her to someone more experienced.'

'How dare you!'

'I'm sorry. I was out of order there.' God, how I hate that expression. 'I'm terribly concerned for her welfare, Kev. And – as long as she has my phone number – I'm concerned for mine too. So I'd be obliged if you'd extract a promise from her now.'

'Stop trying to tell me how to do my job.'

I took a very deep breath. 'If you don't do your job properly, Kev, I wouldn't like to have to answer for the consequences. I'd hate to see you in a coroner's court explaining that you were too busy searching for the truth to notice that disturbed and vulnerable young woman might become suicidal.'

His eyes widened: perhaps I'd at last got through to him.

'I suppose I could ask her to give me whatever she's written it down on.'

'I'd be very grateful,' I said, as humbly as I could. She might well have memorised it, of course, or have it written in several places. That's what I'd have done, with anything I considered as precious as she considered my number.

I stood staring at more tasteful prints – Constable as opposed to Monet – trying not to drum my fingers and tap my toe. He returned, awkwardly, with the sort of diary a young girl might have chosen, all pink flowers and cute animals. It was open at yesterday's page. The number was scrawled very hurriedly. The interesting thing was it was scrawled down wrong. One digit wrong, as if she'd copied it down from an awkward angle and couldn't tell a 7, which I always wrote crossed in the continental way, from a sloppy 9. I frowned at it for a few seconds. God

111

knew whom she'd get if she phoned that number. And God forbid she started to make the sort of calls I expected of her to the wrong person. Perhaps I should have shared this with Kev. But I wanted closure and I wanted it fast. I tore out the page.

'Thanks, Kev. Now, please, please, impress on her that she absolutely does not use it.'

'If she does?'

'I shall be forced to take legal action.' I left hanging in the air the possibility that he might be involved too. 'The important thing is her mental welfare, Kev, isn't it? And her physical safety too. Thanks for your help,' I added with as little irony as I could manage.

It was hardly surprising that my session with Leonore took some time to get going. I was desperate for a coffee, but refreshments of any kind were absolutely forbidden in practice rooms. No one would need to know about the bar of chocolate I bought from a machine, eating half straight off, and saving the rest in my bag for an unspecified later. Leonore was patient and indeed compassionate at the start, but became more and more ruffled herself. After all, it's no fun for a quasi-professional to be messed around by an incompetent amateur.

'Let's take five minutes,' she said at last.

I broke the last of the chocolate in two and passed her half, stowing the telltale wrapper deep in my bag.

She peered at my hands. So did I. There were still little red half-moon shapes on the palms where I'd dug my nails in.

'You'd better tell me,' she said, kindly but firmly, looking hard under her brows. 'Shit, it's that bloody phone number, isn't it? Oh God, what's the stupid cow done?'

It was I who'd forced the issue, wasn't it? If I'd kept quiet, there wouldn't have been that crazy interview – interrogation, more like.

'Things got a bit out of hand. She's very upset. I took her to a counsellor.'

'Looks more like you need a counsellor. Sophie, all this is my fault and I'm really sorry.'

I pulled myself upright. 'Did I see something on the notice board about Alexander Technique lessons for you singers?'

She pulled a face. 'What's that got to do with anything?'

'Let's just get our necks free, and lengthen and widen – isn't that what you're supposed to do? – and sort out that bloody Schubert. Right?'

The remaining half-hour sped by with hardly a slip between us. We both realised that we'd achieved so much we shouldn't try and push any further. In any case, Leonore had a seminar to prepare for, and I, of course, wanted to waylay Dawn – should she want to be waylaid. And should I want to waylay her. The morning's trauma had reminded me all too clearly that people can get the wrong end of the stick terribly easily. And that it was from Rose that I'd first heard the rumour, the allegation, against French. To pull down any sort of investigation about his ears might end his career: be he as innocent as I, mud would stick – far worse mud, given that, unlike me, he was an authority figure and more than capable of helping or hindering someone's career. He wouldn't be the first teacher to be brought down utterly by an allegation of sexual misconduct.

Dawn's welfare excepted, I didn't want any part of this. It was one thing to snitch for Harvinder and try to locate a missing boy, quite another to interrogate a no doubt unwilling young woman, who was more than entitled to tell me to mind my own business. I stepped out into the corridor and, closing the door firmly behind me, set off for the temporary haven of the workroom. Even talking to the kids about Neil Wiltshire would have to wait.

Chapter Twelve

I'd got precisely four yards down the corridor before someone called my name. Dawn. I turned and managed a smile. Hers was, if anything, more pallid than mine.

'You all right?' I said. In the Midlands, this wasn't really a genuine enquiry, and it was almost bad manners to respond with a detailed report on your health. It was more polite to respond, 'Fine. Orright?' Even my version elided *you* and *all* in a way I'd never dream of in any other idiom: *Yoorlrigh?*

She went even paler, managing a nod. 'Sophie – I—' She stopped, looking over my shoulder. Someone was coming.

'Lunch in the refec at twelve?' I asked, longing to turn to see who it was.

'Coffee, anyway. See you then,' she mouthed over her shoulder, as she let herself into the practice room.

I did little more back in the workroom than look at the previous day's *Guardian* – all teachers pounce on it to scan the jobs pages, as important as those in the *TES*. I wondered why, given the William Murdock situation, I wasn't bothering. Goodness knew I should have been. Happy though Mike would have been to support me, his own career couldn't last much longer: professional sportsmen and women wear out their joints faster than the rest of us, so injury, if not youthful talent crowding up, tends to push them out of top-rank competition before they reach forty. I know many of the previous generation of great cricketers played many years longer, but they didn't have so many matches to play, certainly at international level.

In any case, what was a woman of my generation doing, even thinking of being kept by her partner? I should be preparing to support him as he retrained for a new career. But the more I flicked through the adverts, the sicker I felt. Something very nasty was happening to me, a road-to-Damascus moment, less dramatic than the original but alarming all the same: a voice in my head was announcing with great clarity that I didn't want to go back to the maelstrom that Further Education had become. I listened to it very carefully. There was no doubt about it. I folded the Education Supplement carefully and replaced it on Myra's desk.

Brooding over my future, I'm afraid I completely forgot about Dawn till ten minutes after I'd promised to meet her. I sprinted to the refec to find her surveying the menu board as if it were a timetable for the day's executions.

'Sorry,' I panted, as I stood alongside her.

'It's OK. I've only just got here. Not very hungry, really. I think I'll just have a coffee.'

I looked at her sideways. Her face looked very pinched. Was she one of those students who tried to save money by eating less? 'Things always look better,' I said, sounding horribly like my mother, 'with some food in your stomach.' I picked up a tray. 'My treat. What will you have?'

She gave a little gasp. 'No, it's all right—'

'I've got something to celebrate,' I insisted. I had. This strange and sudden decision. And maybe my theory was right: she found an appetite for lasagne, chips and salad, rounded off by chocolate sponge. Unfortunately, the refec's chocolate sponge was unbeatable, and I found myself succumbing too – though I limited myself to tuna salad for my main course. We tucked in, in what seemed like a companionable silence.

Try as I might, I couldn't think of a subtle, unobtrusive way to ask if she was pregnant. And by whom. Hoping I could

116

somehow lead into it later, I said innocently, 'I don't seem to have seen young Neil around recently. Has he got the flu or something?'

She looked up startled. 'You're right. And he never misses a single lecture. One of Nature's goody-goodies. I bet he even irons his own shirts.'

'Shirts? But you're all T-shirt people here.'

'Concerts,' she said. 'But he probably irons his T-shirts too. I can't work out why they've made him leader, though – you know, the orchestra. My gerbil's got more leadership qualities than he has. At least you always know he's heading for food.'

'Why do you think he was given the position?'

She touched the side of her nose. 'Not what you know but who you know.'

'And he knew . . .?'

She flushed. 'Just silly gossip, that's all.' She picked up her bag, as if ready to leave.

'So you don't just have to be the best violinist in the orchestra? All those solos, and everything?' I asked as if I didn't know already.

'You actually have to lead. Like in the trenches. The officer who has to take his troops over the top. It's a leader's job to liaise between the conductor and the band. Some conductors have just no idea . . .' She sounded ineffably world-weary. 'And if there's a problem with one of the players, you know, not playing very well, it's up to the leader to sort it out. And personality clashes. That sort of thing.' She returned to the last of the chips with vigour. She looked up with a sudden frank smile. 'My dad used to lead one of the London orchestras. Then he got MS.'

'How awful. I'm so sorry.'

'Well, it's in remission at the moment, and he says he makes far more money selling antique prints than he ever did in the band. He's at home more too – he was always travelling when I was a kid.'

117

'But it hasn't put you off? You wouldn't mind being a nomadic musician?'

She looked down, her face taut again. 'If I'm good enough. There are some of us who've already been approached by orchestral managements . . .'

Though it wasn't very tactful, I saw my chance. 'Wasn't there a rumour that Neil had?'

'Oh, but only rank and file. No, Martin Goldsmith's already had a trial for first clarinet with the CBSO.'

'Wow.'

'He didn't get it, actually, but it only goes to show.'

I was torn. I had to drag the conversation back either to Neil or to her. Time to flip a mental coin. Neil.

'You don't suppose that's where Neil's gone – to do an audition or something?'

'Just before assessments? He'll be bloody strangled if he has. In fact, his not being here anyway means he's likely to be strangled. His tutor's very conscientious. Have you met Alex? He's – he's terribly good-looking.'

I wondered what she'd meant to say.

'He's the leader of the Boulton Quartet, isn't he? The one who's hurt his hand.'

She leant forward confidentially. 'If you ask me, that's why Neil hasn't been around recently. In case they ask him to take over. He'd wee himself at the thought. Well, wouldn't you? I mean, there's nowhere to hide, is there?'

'Hide?' I prompted disingenuously. 'I mean, he leads your band; he takes the fiddle part in the Mozart Sinfonia Concertante – he's a pretty good player.' Except when James Hallam was around, of course.

'Chamber playing needs a different technique,' she said. 'You have to listen more, look more – at each other, not just at the conductor. You need to blend, not stand out as something special. Actually,' she confided, 'I like chamber work much better. But there's not all that much call for oboes, not in the standard chamber repertoire. And I'm not a good enough pianist for a solo career, either.' She added with infinite misery, 'I suppose I shall end up teaching.'

I wanted to shout, *Oh, no, you don't!* Instead I asked, 'What about developing your piano skills? No, not as a soloist!' I added, as she opened her mouth to protest. 'As a singer you understand the needs of the voice. Why not turn your skills to recital work – supporting other singers? A good accompanist is worth his or her weight in gold.'

She pulled a face. 'There aren't all that many woman accompanists, are there?'

'Jennifer Partridge always used to play for her brother.'

'But the really big names are always men. So there we are . . .'

'No, we're not. We're on the verge of changing all that. Damn it, if a sausage fingers like me—'

She giggled, at last laughing with full-blooded hoots. 'Sausage fingers! I've never heard that before. Oh, how wonderful! Sausage fingers!'

I couldn't help joining in a little, though I found the image no more than mildly amusing. It struck me as she continued to chuckle that she was so relieved to have found something in her life to laugh at that she was rather overdoing it.

'Anyway,' I said at last, 'I know two people who are so desperate for an accompanist they've even been using me. And you ask Leonore if I'm not crap. You've got to be better.'

'I don't know . . .'

'Why not try her? Talk to her about it, at least – an hour out of both of your lives isn't going to spoil an assignment or ruin an assessment.' Please, please, talk to Leonore about it. And maybe you'll start talking about other things, too. Like sexual harassment. 'And there's Dan too,' I added helpfully.

'Not Dan Langley! But he's gorgeous.'

'Gorgeous as they come. Coffee?' Having signally failed to

achieve anything, it was time to do some work, not least for Saturday.

'My shout,' she said.

I'd better not patronise her by insisting on buying that too. When she'd settled again, I managed, 'It's none of my business, Dawn, but I thought – well, that you haven't been looking yourself these last couple of days.'

'I'm fine,' she snapped.

I'd have done the same in her place, I suspect. But I continued, 'Great. But you know I'm not really attached to the music department . . . And sometimes it feels easier to natter to people outside a situation – people not involved . . .'

This time she bit her lip. I held my breath. All those years of ministering to young people exerted pressures even greater than my determination not to stir up trouble.

'Dawn!' came this enormous bellow across the room.

Hell.

'Sorry,' she muttered. But she stood up, waving with more vigour than I'd have thought her capable of half an hour ago. 'It's Doug!'

Another three-quarters familiar face came our way. This one belonged to the principal bassoon, an affable-looking young man with the height and physique to bowl for England – and, as I recalled, a voice like a foghorn.

'Doug, this is Sophie! Sophie, my bestest friend Doug.'

'There are some people,' he said with a slow smile and an even slower burr, 'who say bassoonists don't have any friends, like.'

I shook my head, smiling at memories of my own younger self, when my bestest friend was a bassoonist called George. 'Surely that's viola players,' I said, trying not to think about George's murder, which even after all these years I could hardly believe. A wonderful kind man, he was struck down on a building site because someone thought he was someone else.

'What's viola players?' asked a cold voice very close to my head. James Hallam.

At least I thought we were on good enough terms for a silly crack like that not to count. 'Oh, all those jokes on the Internet,' I said.

Neither of the students contradicted me.

In fact, I had a distinct sense that Dawn was diving in to rescue me when she said, quite pertly, 'We were just saying that we haven't seen Neil Wiltshire for a couple of days. Any news of him, Dr Hallam?'

Dr Hallam, eh? Whatever had happened to first names, *de rigueur* in almost every educational establishment I'd known in the last fifteen years – schools excepted, of course?

'Flu or something, I suppose,' he said lightly. 'I hope for God's sake he doesn't come back before he's fit and give it to the rest of us.'

'Goodness, yes,' Dawn agreed, adding a nervous little giggle. 'Imagine that running round the choir, Sophie, before the big concert.'

I produced a capable shudder.

'Haven't seen much of Alex this week either,' Doug observed.

'He's cut his hand, silly,' Dawn reminded him.

'Sure. That means he can't play. But I wouldn't have thought a little cut would have stopped him giving seminars. There's a notice gone up saying he's cancelled them all for the next two weeks,' he added, with what sounded almost like relish.

Hallam compressed his lips. 'I'm sure he's acting on medical advice, Doug. And I'm sure Professor French will be trying to find substitute teachers – instrumental and academic.'

'Will you be taking any?' Doug asked.

Hallam looked as puzzled as I felt. Why should a bassoon player be taking such an interest in the activities – or lack of them – of a string teacher? 'My timetable's overfull as it is,' he said crisply. 'Now, if you'll excuse me . . . Oh, Sophie, might I have a word?'

I felt like an errant student myself, trailing after him. For he made me trail – no side-by-side conversational affability.

'Are you quite sure it's proper,' he asked, as soon as we'd left the refec, 'for you to be mixing so much with these young people?'

'It'd be very strange if I didn't,' I retorted, 'since we're interested in the same things.'

'But –' he had the grace to flush – 'you're a mature woman. And they – they may be getting the wrong idea. A word to the wise, that's all,' he said, turning quickly on his heel and running up the stairs.

There was no way I'd embark on an undignified chase after him. But it wasn't his neck I wanted to wring. How could he have got hold of that? Only one way, as far as I could see. Kev had not been the most secret and most grave counsellor he should have been, had he? And while I'd never in my life made a complaint against a colleague, this might be the day I changed all that. After all, I was no longer a teacher, was I?

I was already on my way to the Dean's office when I came to my senses. Gossip. Everyone would know about Rose's claims. Hallam had simply been giving me a genuine bit of advice, hadn't he?

Chapter Thirteen

'I think he may indeed be missing,' Harvinder said, sitting in my kitchen and watching in fascination as I peeled the skin off drumsticks so I could marinade them. They could sit happily in the fridge absorbing flavours for a couple of days while I turned my attention to other snacks.

'No news from any of those London orchestras he might have been trying for?' I finished the last and wrapped all the remains up tightly, dropping the mess into a carrier bag that Harv reluctantly held open. I turned to scrub my hands at the sink.

'You're being very thorough,' he remarked as I reached for the nailbrush.

'I always am when I've been handling raw meat of any sort. Think of what the average chicken can pass on! I certainly don't want any untoward happenings at my functions. In fact, I keep a separate chopping board and even a separate knife for chicken.' I showed him my lovely Sabatier specimen.

He shuddered. 'I hate knives.'

'But you're a Sikh?'

He laughed. 'Can you imagine the police letting me carry my sacred knife?'

'They let some officers wear turbans.'

He stroked his beardless chin. 'I think I'd have difficulty making a case. Anyway, watch what you do with that, eh?'

'Why do you think I don't have a block for all my knives

123

like a lot of people do? I don't want to advertise to Burglar Bill what he could use as a getaway weapon. If I could be bothered to sort out a lockable kitchen drawer, that's where they'd be. Was it anything in particular,' I added, filling the kettle, 'that put you off knives?'

'My first stiff had been knifed. A hell of a lot of blood for a rookie to deal with.'

'My first stiff too. You never forget the smell of blood, do you?'

He shook his head, shuddering. 'Imagine being a pathologist. Imagine working in Blood Transfusion. Imagine even being a butcher! You know, I wouldn't even fancy doing what you just did.'

'I'd draw the line at drawing poultry, though I know my mother and grandmother used to. Now, let me just put this lot out in the dustbin . . .' I picked up the carrier, tying the handles.

Washing my hands again, I asked, 'Coffee or tea?'

'I suppose you haven't any herbal?'

I kept some just for him, as it happened, a selection in a caddy I proffered. He chose something citrusy, by the smell. I went for the Ian Dale option. When I'd first met Ian, then a detective sergeant, I'd sneered at his surprisingly prissy choice of tea: Earl Grey, served very weak, with the thinnest slice of lemon. Now I knew him and it much better, I'd learnt to make and enjoy it his way.

We withdrew to the living room.

'If your unofficial sniffing round hasn't done any good,' he said, sitting in an armchair, 'I'm going to have to come in officially. His room is as tidy as if he's due an army kit inspection. His landlady—'

'Landlady! Doesn't he house-share like the other kids?'

'Seems his mother knew someone down here and asked her to take him in. He pays rent, but he's on a right cushy number, believe me.'

I shook my head. 'Kids at that age are entitled to rough it a

124

bit, if only in the name of self-discovery. Plus you couldn't take your girlfriend back with a landlady who knew your mother listening for every creak of the bed. Or boyfriend, of course,' I added, in the name of equal opportunities. Or maybe not.

'What about this idea of him having a crush on a teacher?'

'If I start theorising, it may well push you in a direction you shouldn't be going. What I will say is that one woman I spoke to thinks that the idea of leading the quartet has scared him into lying low. Someone else thinks he's got flu, which might well be the official line. What is interesting is that no one seems to have gone round to his digs to find out. Or even called him – kids have mobiles these days like people of my generation had acne.'

'At least,' Harv said, drawing a reflective finger over a couple of deep scars on his cheek, 'acne's a private plague. So no close friends. A loner or plain lonely?'

I shook my head. 'I don't know him well enough. Harv: much as I want to help, I can't. I'm friendly with them but not friends, to turn your phrase. We're different generations. I'm not even in the department. Why don't you talk to the staff there? His tutor, especially?'

'Alex Fisher? Because Alex Fisher's not in town.'

I stared. 'What?'

'His wife says that he kept trying to play despite the cut, so she dispatched him to his brother in Scotland for a few days.'

'Weird. As one of the students pointed out, a gammy hand shouldn't stop you teaching. But one of his colleagues insisted he'd been signed off – for a couple of weeks, I rather think. Must have been a very serious cut. But then only an idiot would try to practise with a bad cut.'

'I'll talk to his GP. Though you know what these medics are like. Confidentiality.'

'Otherwise known as privacy. Come on, Harv, surely he's on the phone wherever he is. As I said, everyone's got a mobile.' I smiled wryly. 'OK, I'm teaching my grandmother to suck eggs, aren't I? You've tried both: the brother's phone's out of action, his mobile's switched off. Sorry.'

'Plus there's no reason to harass a man on sick leave. No, I've got to try other teachers there. But they all say no one knows him like his personal tutor.'

'Which is probably true. I suppose there aren't any young people – notice the gender-free term! – who might have visited him? Under the eagle eye of this landlady?'

'She says not.'

I scratched my head. 'What sort of house is it?'

'A semi, not unlike this. Except it's joined to its mate by the living room, not the hall, not like this. Why?'

'Practice. He'd need to do hours of practice. There are rooms at UWM, but not enough. People reaching his standard would need to put in at least three or four hours a day somewhere.'

'You think one of the neighbours might have been driven mad by all the racket . . .'

'It'd be a top-quality racket. But I'm sure it could drive anyone mad. I met this bloke once who'd had an hotel room next to someone playing the fiddle for hours on end, and was driven to call the management to complain. Seems the guy in the next room was Menuhin. And good though Neil Wiltshire was, he was no Menuhin.' I grinned. 'What I was really wondering was simply where he played. Just curiosity.'

'But if neighbours could hear him, they might have a better idea than the landlady when the playing stopped – in other words, when he actually left the place.'

'Eh? Doesn't she know?'

'Away for a few days looking after a grandchild. The kid's crèche had been vandalised.' He looked at his watch.

'And you should be off duty here and on duty back home,' I said, getting to my feet.

We walked to his car together, standing, in quite a balmy evening breeze, for a final natter about Inderjit's precocity.

When the rain had stopped, it had left a clean smell and a starry sky. We talked about the River Severn's major floods, about Inderjit's first visit to the swimming baths, about all the things friends talk about when they want to wind down. As he prepared to drive off, however, I said, 'Remember you're on your own for a couple of days. I shan't be going into UWM till after the concert. Too much to do for the buffet.'

So it was all the more irritating to get back inside the house to find a new message on my answerphone. No, it was too late for one from Mike. But not, it seemed, from my diligent and conscientious tutor. She would like to see me on a matter of some urgency, she said. She'd expect me at nine the following morning.

Well, I can't pretend to be anything other than irritated. OK, irritated and a touch alarmed. While the professional teacher part of my brain was applauding her for leaving such a discreet message – she wasn't to know I lived alone and would be the only one to pick up the message – the temporary student part was wondering what in hell was going on. Given James Hallam's enigmatic comments, the conclusion had to be that Kev had indeed seen fit to spill confidential beans, presumably with the pro-Rose gloss that had so worried me. However much I told myself I was the innocent victim of a sick woman's fantasies, I found myself turning the whole thing over and over in my mind – to the exclusion, of course, of sleep. Even my usual technique of making myself get up to do something I loathed doing – in this case sorting out my tights and socks drawer – didn't return me to the sort of slumber I craved. After all, UWM internal problems apart, I had a buffet to organise.

So it was in a less than affable mood I presented myself to Carrie at nine sharp the next morning.

She was already at her desk, from which she showed no signs of rising when I entered. I could see no chair the opposite side for me, but I had no intention of standing before her in 'when did you last see your father' mode. To do her justice,

127

when I parked my bag on her desk and looked around, she flushed, and waved a hand at a chair, which I dragged up. Still her own side – hadn't she heard of interviewee-friendly techniques? – she bit her lip and fiddled with a sheet of paper.

I felt for her. Bollocking was never my favourite occupation, especially if the student happened to be older than me.

'What seems to be the problem?' I asked, after the few seconds of embarrassed silence stretched into a minute.

She shifted, not meeting my eye, but keeping it glued to the paper. 'I've had a formal complaint about your behaviour. I've been asked to tell you that you may be suspended from the university.'

'For goodness' sake! What am I alleged to have done?'

Still not meeting my eye, she said, 'You've been fomenting student unrest. This is very foolish of you, Sophie. This isn't the student action sixties and seventies, you know. Telling people to organise and claim their rights. You must be off your head.' She got to her feet. 'Damn it, you're supposed to be a professional teacher! How would you like it if I came to your place and stirred up muck against the staff?'

Everything about her shrieked unease, so I decided to play on it. However much I wanted to scream and plead – and I did, a great deal – I took a deep breath, exhaled slowly, and said, 'Far from fomenting student unrest, I've been trying to defuse the situation. I presume we are talking about the music department?'

'Faculty,' she corrected me.

'Whatever. I sing in the choir; I accompany a couple of their best singers. And everyone sees me as a mother confessor bringing all sorts of complaints against the staff to me. I advise them to talk to the staff concerned or to raise non-personal issues at their Board of Study. What's wrong with that? You can't tell me,' I pursued, 'that you wouldn't have done anything different yourself.'

She turned to face the window, arms clamped across her

128

body. 'We're talking malicious gossip about a particular staff member here.'

'Are we? Who?'

'For God's sake, James Hallam, of course.'

I got up and joined her by the window. She half turned, but no more.

'You do realise I've not the slightest idea of what you're talking about. I quite like James Hallam: I thought he quite liked me. What am I supposed to have said? And why on earth should I want to spread malicious gossip about him, of all people?'

'That's for you to explain.' She returned to her study of the refectory bins: I hadn't realised that her view was so insalubrious.

'There is another member of staff whose name's on a number of lips,' I said slowly, remembering his presence in her room when I'd had my last tutorial; I had to tread extremely carefully if I wasn't to offend her as a friend of his. 'But when I've heard it, I've always rebuked those bandying it around. Careless talk can cost jobs, can't it?'

She continued her surveillance of the bins.

'OK,' I said, trying not to crow at having regained the initiative, 'you've put the complaint to me. I've denied it. What next?' I counted to thirty. 'Come on, Carrie, there must be some official procedure. Even dear, ramshackle old William Murdock has a system in place.'

She returned to her desk the long way round, so she didn't have to face me. 'I'll see what I can do. Talk to people. Tell them you're not happy.'

What on earth had happened to this bright, sparky young woman I'd so much admired and respected?

'I'm incandescent, that's what I am. Carrie, I don't want you to smooth things over. If there's a formal complaint, I want a formal chance to rebut it. And in doing so I shall naturally name the person about whom I have heard complaints, and bring witnesses to support me. To whatever official tribunal or committee or whatever I'm summoned. As for this crap –' I managed a dramatic gesture at the paper still on her desk – 'forget it.' I sat down and leant forward, gentle and non-threatening as if our roles were reversed. 'Look. I can see that this has upset you: you've been put in an intolerable situation. What's going on, Carrie?'

'I don't know what you're talking about. Now, just get out, will you? I'll tell the authorities you've had formal warning of suspension if you persist. I'll say you've apologised and—'

'No, you won't. Because I haven't.'

'In that case, I shall have to suspend you.'

'I don't think you can. Not without due process. Tell you what,' I said, as magnanimously as I could, 'why don't I make myself scarce for a couple of days, and give you a chance to find out what's really going on here? Then you can summon me before the Dean or whatever if you still think you should.' I stood up. 'All right?'

She stared at the sheet of paper as if she'd find the answer materialising before her eyes.

'The alternative,' I said, sitting down again – any flies on the wall must have been holding their sides laughing at this up-down-up pantomime – 'is for you to tell me what you know now. So we can deal with it together.'

'Sophie, I . . .' She looked hunted.

There was a knock at the door. Without waiting to be invited, who should walk in but Marcus French.

'Thank you, Carrie,' I said, winking at her, but with no hint of humour, 'I'll wait to hear the university's next move.' But I couldn't resist it. I turned to French. 'You'll be glad to know,' I told him, 'that preparations are well under way for Saturday night.'

Chapter Fourteen

Peter Andrews had worked wonders with the kitchen area, so that despite my resolve not to use it, I could lay out my serving plates and trays, and stack the empty food boxes without worrying about what they might touch.

'I thought it would be easier,' Peter said, when I thanked him for his efforts, 'if I closed this bar and confined the audience to the theatre bar, which is where I'll be if you need me. Then you've got all evening to do what you need down here. All this food – enough to "coldly furnish forth the marriage tables". Sorry about the split infinitive. I must say,' he added, looking at the plastic boxes and ready-napkined serving plates, 'it looks as if you'll be able to knock everything together in five minutes.'

'Especially with this team,' I grinned as the UWM students presented themselves: Leonore and Dan, plus a friend of Leonore's called Siobhan, a red-head who Leonore insisted was less fiery than she looked, and Dawn. There they were, looking brisk and efficient but all in mufti, at about ten past seven, much to my surprise. They weren't needed till nine thirty, but had other plans in mind, it transpired.

'We thought,' Leonore said, 'we could sneak in the back of the concert hall and hear the quartet. The word is they've brought in some crony of the prof as first violin. And the word is that he and the others . . . don't exactly hit it off.' Her smile was positively gleeful.

'Whether you want to listen is up to you. We're mob-handed, so we could simply leave everything till the interval, whiz down and do our stuff, then whiz back up for the second half.'

'You sound a bit doubtful, Sophie,' Dan observed.

'Well, I know no one can wander in off the street and help themselves. But I'd rather be safe than sorry. Let's hear the first half, have a drink – just the one, mind – in the interval, and then we've just about time to listen to the Barber *Adagio* in the second half. But I'd like us all downstairs at action stations after that. You've got to allow time to change into uniform, remember, even if it means missing the Borodin. I know, it's one of my fave pieces too,' I admitted, as Leonore pulled a face. 'It makes me think about my bloke and how much I miss him.' Still, another month and we'd be together. 'Hang your uniforms up over here. I've got these disposable plastic aprons and gloves for handling food.' I put them on a table alongside the coat hooks just inside the bar. 'OK. So enjoy the concert. Enjoy your interval drink, which is on me. Then sneak out before the Borodin, change, lay out food, uncork the bottles, and be ready with big grins and trays of drinks and nibbles for the second the applause dies away. Military precision time!'

They responded with big grins and salutes that would have won medals. All except Dawn, that is. I really must try to talk to her soon. She no longer looked ill, but clearly there was something wrong.

As I took one last look round before following them upstairs to the Lyttelton Theatre, I was feeling, however, less cheerful than I hoped I sounded. My exit line from UWM on Thursday morning had been satisfactory at the moment of delivery, but in retrospect seemed childish. It wasn't in my interests to provoke anyone, particularly as I was convinced that Carrie was unhappy about what she was doing. What the hell was going on? Who was instigating such a stupid course of action? The other thing that was niggling me was a couple of phone calls cut off as soon as I'd answered. Dialling 1471 had inevitably elicited the information that the caller had withheld their number. I always have a frisson of fear that Burglar Bill was phoning to check if the coast was clear. But I try to calm myself by waxing irate with the grammatical inexactitude. That was better: anger was always better than apprehension, wasn't it?

I was roused from my reverie by Joe and Josephine Music-Loving Public, pushing open the doors, swanning in and looking about them. A swarm of other people, all ages, all sizes, came in hard on their heels.

'I'm sorry: the bar's closed just now,' I said. 'If you want a drink you'll have to go up to the theatre bar—'

'But we've come all the way down here,' objected a middle-aged lady, uncomfortably plump, her feet already overflowing from her shoes.

I held the door open and pointed down the passage. 'No need for the stairs. You'll find a lift just there,' I said. It wouldn't accommodate anything like the whole group, but that wasn't my immediate concern. What I'd just realised was that though I could close the bar doors, I couldn't lock them, not without Peter Andrews, and he was in the bar I'd sent the punters to. Shrugging – the reception staff would keep out any strays off the street, since the building was open only for the concert and in general concertgoers were a law-abiding lot – I did what any self-respecting teacher would have done. I nipped back into the kitchen for one of those easels and nicked a piece of someone's drawing paper, left innocently for the next class.

BAR CLOSED
OPEN AT 9.30 FOR
A PRIVATE FUNCTION

There, that should do it. Seeing the time, I grabbed my bag and legged it up the stairs, to find Peter remonstrating politely but firmly with a smart-looking woman who wished to take her glass of wine into the theatre.

Not my problem. I slipped into a seat at the side, towards the back, so as not to disturb anyone when I slipped out later. I couldn't see my team of waiting staff, but I was sure they'd be with their mates somewhere: there was a little gaggle of young people leaning on the rail behind the back seats, as if it were a prom concert.

I've always loved the hush before a concert starts. It's a very noisy hush before a symphony concert, of course, with the musicians tuning up on stage. A chamber group tends to tune up together in private, unless they have to retune to a piano. The grand was firmly under its cover tonight, however, pushed to the side of the auditorium nearest the passage to the bar. The musicians would come in from the green room the other side.

They should be coming in now, in fact. The anticipatory hush deepened.

What I for one didn't expect, but should have done, of course, in the circumstances, was to see Marcus French step forward. The bright top-lighting made his face more interesting than it was, his cheeks disappearing into daubs of shadow. He coughed briefly, then, having gained our attention, simply announced that the first violin this evening would be Antony Masters, substituting at the very last minute for the indisposed Alex Fisher. The quartet regretted having to make a change to their programme: it would now open with the *Adagio* from Barber's String Quartet, would continue with the Borodin Quartet in D, and end, after the interval, with the Tchaikovsky Quartet also in D. French sat down.

Masters led in the ensemble, striding confidently ahead of June Tams, who, droopy-haired and under-made-up, looked every inch a second fiddle in her greenish long black velvet skirt and faded T-shirt; a very elegant James Hallam, and Caz Byrd, whose petunia-pink long silk dress made me drool

134

with envy. The men were wearing dinner jackets and conventional black ties. They bowed as one and sat down to have a final pither with the music already on their stands – bending forward the corner of a page to give a quicker turn, that sort of thing.

And then they started.

To describe the performance as disappointing would be massively to understate its awfulness. The piece is best known in Barber's own version for a full string orchestra, or even, these days, as a choral piece, *Agnus Dei*. But indeed it did start out for just four string instruments, so presumably Barber thought four was enough to hold the passionate soaring line. Byrd and Hallam did their best, gave it their all, in fact, but neither Tams nor, more especially, the inappositely named Masters was anything other than scrawny in tone. Tams looked wide-eyed with panic, as if aware how exposed she was even on the second desk. And she was utterly unprotected. Half the time Masters gave the impression of never having laid eyes on the piece before. Even if he hadn't – and as I said, it was more usual to hear it in the concert hall in a much richer version – he should have been able to sight-read it better than that. And although Hallam wasn't known for helping struggling violinists, this time he had his eyes on Masters as often as he could spare them from his music. If they ended the work together, it was probably owing to an obvious effort of Hallam's will.

The applause that greeted the last bar was probably as much to signal relief as anything.

If I slipped out now, I could escape the murder of the Borodin.

Too late. Masters announced another change of programme. Tchaikovsky first, then Borodin after the interval. God knows why. The *Andante Cantabile*, played with the strings muted, can sound thin with the best of ensembles. Again, it has a separate orchestral life these days in a better-

135

nourished arrangement. With the modified Boulton Quartet it sounded emaciated to the point of skeletal.

More extremely polite applause.

It was only the good manners and general age of the audience, my young colleagues excepted, that could have prevented a stampede to the bar. I was tempted to gather up my team for an illicit but consoling swig from the bottles I'd brought in for the reception. In fact, I felt a tube fitted up as a drip-feed was the most appropriate antidote to the poisonous noises these so-called professionals had emitted. It was no good reminding myself that at the best of times, in the best of conditions – and the hall's acoustics were even drier and more unforgiving than I'd expected – the quartet couldn't be expected to sound like the Lindsays or the Endellion. As Hallam had pointed out, they had minimal rehearsal time and were primarily teachers and academics, not just performers.

By the time I'd decided I'd better join the scrum for drinks, there was no sign of my team. Nor, when I fought my way in, could I see them in the bar. What I could see was that Peter Andrews was on his own behind the bar, trying to serve drinks and coffee and take money. I battled over to him and dodged under the flap.

'Barman's just phoned in sick,' he said.

'I'll pour, you take the cash,' I said.

' "Never . . . was so much owed by so many to so few".'

Despite that crack, we worked as a team – if a rather slow team – till everyone was served. I relished the evil grin he gave as I poured the last scalding coffee and he pressed the bell for time. Happy to be spared the second half, I collected glasses and cups while he donned vivid yellow gloves and ran hot water.

'That's funny,' he said, after a few minutes, 'I can't hear any music this time.'

I paused. Neither could I.

Which wasn't surprising, as I found out when I nipped round to the back of the auditorium to discover what was happening. There wasn't any music because the musicians hadn't returned to the stage.

It was hard not to imagine a most god-awful row going on in the green room. Eventually French – whose department's reputation was at stake, after all – slipped from his seat and, in a curious crouching lope, crossed the auditorium and slid towards the green room.

The buzz from the audience, no matter how middle-class and polite its members, was increasingly hostile. Any moment now it would be money-back time. And then the reception would start rather earlier than planned, if, that is, Marcus French had the brass neck to go ahead with it. It seemed he did.

He returned to stand between the second violin and the viola stands.

'Ladies and gentlemen.' He didn't need to cough for our attention this time. It was his for the asking. 'I'm afraid that because of the sudden indisposition of one of the ensemble, the rest of the concert can't go ahead. If you have paid for your ticket, perhaps you'd be kind enough to leave your name and address with the reception staff so that we can send you a refund. If you are a guest of UWM, perhaps you would be kind enough to descend to the bar, where the reception will commence in ten minutes.'

Thanks a bunch for the warning, Marcus. So where were my assistants? Thank God for mobile phones. I ran Leonore to earth in a nearby bar. She hadn't been able to face the ritual slaughter of a favourite piece. She and the others were back on duty almost as soon as I was.

It was only when I was halfway through the de-clingfilming process that I noticed Dan was weighing in without apron or gloves.

'Sorry, Sophie – there weren't any left.'

I shook my head in mid-rebuke. I was sure I'd brought

sufficient, but could have been mistaken. Anyway, the four of us could more than manage, so I set him on bottle opening.

To my amazement, the guests seemed remarkably tolerant. They fell on the buffet like locusts, and French unbent enough to compliment me on my work.

'What happened backstage?' I asked, topping up his champagne.

'Hallam – indisposed,' he said.

'Hallam!'

But he'd turned to talk to someone else.

It was only when we'd watered and fed everyone and were gathering trays to top people up that I managed to ask Leonore if she knew what had happened.

'The word is that Hallam simply walked out,' she said, eyes agleam with the scandal. 'Not a word to anyone. Just did a runner.'

'Just like that?'

'Can you blame him?'

'What about the others?' I looked around. Caz, still in her silk dress, was being fawned over by a City Father; June was pale and apparently tearful; and, surprise, surprise, there was no sign of the egregious Masters.

After half an hour or so of eating and drinking, French took up position at the end of one of the U-shapes, tapping a plastic fork on a glass to gain our attention.

'Ladies and gentlemen,' he began.

But that was as far as he got.

Slowly but inexorably the panel framing the niche behind him began to swing forward, like a large door. It gathered pace, and as it did so some of us could see why. James Hallam was pushing it open, that was why.

Or, more accurately, the body of James Hallam was pushing it open. As his torso tipped forward to carry him into a swimmer-like plunge into the room I could see the knife sticking out of his back.

Chapter Fifteen

Human bodies contain a lot of blood. James Hallam's gushed not from the knife wound in his back but from his mouth and nose, cascading and splattering down as he plunged from his hiding place on to the bench seat. There was a sickening thud as he toppled to the floor. No. Series of thuds. Each limb made its own separate thump.

The subsequent silence was shocking. Then noise erupted as if at some bizarre football match after the blackest of goals. Someone had to do something. My hand had already found my mobile, and even as I covered my ear against the first screams a calm Brummie voice told me the police would be round straightaway. But someone had to stop all these witnesses leaving the scene. Someone with authority. I looked in vain for Marcus French. Before I knew it I had dragged across the doors the table on which I'd earlier put the aprons and gloves and had scrambled on it. Years of projecting should have made my voice carry. All I could manage was an inadequate squeak. But even that stopped the front row of would-be escapers, just for a moment.

'Ladies and gentlemen!' Perhaps the time-honoured formula would strike a middle-class chord. 'The police are on their way. They want you to stay where you are. It's vital you stay where you are. Please: is there a doctor here?'

Where was Peter Andrews? He'd bring an air of calm competence to the proceedings. There was another surge, and who could blame people wanting to get away? I could see blood on clothes, hands and faces. I'd have been desperate to find a loo and clean up – even more desperate to bunk for the security of home where walls didn't part to reveal dead men.

'The police want you to stay in here,' I repeated. If they got as far as the front door, the reception staff might be browbeaten into letting people go. Which reminded me: no one at all must leave, not just the people here. The place was sufficient of a labyrinth to allow the killer to be lurking, waiting till he could mingle with other concertgoers and leave unnoticed. Internal phone? I didn't know where it was, let alone the number for reception. But I had the main phone line programmed into my mobile. I used that. There.

By now Marcus French had pushed through to me. I jumped down from the table, then gave him a hand up on to it.

'Ladies and gentlemen,' he began. His face seemed to crumple as he realised that there was nothing to say. He gulped from his glass, then realised he was swigging celebratory champagne. Perhaps he'd thought it was brandy. He held it away from him and stared. At last he found help. 'I think I can hear the police,' he said.

I supported him as he descended, and then found myself taking his entire weight as he crumpled into a dead faint.

I had just enough strength to lower him gently, then to pull the table from the doors, to admit two police officers. They were probably younger than Leonore and Dan. She was an Asian woman not much taller than me, he a white kid with an unforgiving haircut and vicious spots. How they refrained from clutching each other in panic I don't know. They could never have been confronted with a scene like this before. There was a space around Hallam's body big enough to admit no doubt as to what had happened. His blood had soaked upholstery and carpet. The smell fought with stale tobacco and aged cooking smells. Someone had been sick. I realised it was only my efforts to calm everyone else that had kept down my own nausea. When I knelt it wasn't to check French, it was to prevent a fainting fit of my own. It wasn't just a dead body, was it? It was what was left of a human being who made lovely music, who liked some students and whom I'd half liked myself. James Hallam.

I straightened. 'You'd better get the paramedics to look at this man too,' I said.

'They're on their way, miss,' the Asian girl said. 'Who's in charge?'

'He is. Professor Marcus French.'

'Who are you then?'

'I'm just the caterer.'

'Any idea who – he – is?' She nodded at Hallam without actually focusing on him.

'James Hallam. He works – worked – at the University of the West Midlands.'

I wouldn't have known where to start, any more than they did. One of them – the girl – picked her way across to Hallam and touched his neck. We all knew it was a waste of time. Six inches of polished knife handle told us all it was a waste of time. Before they could make fools of themselves – and everyone would have forgiven them – we all heard what we'd been waiting for, and saw through the filthy window the far side of the collapsed wall the most welcome of blue strobing lights.

The first people through the door were in fact the paramedics. It took a couple of seconds for them to establish there was nothing to be done for Hallam, so they could turn their attention to Marcus French. There'd be others to treat too: although the room was quieter than I'd have expected, little hysterical wails and quiet sobs broke out.

I was still nearest the doors when they burst open again. I turned to face a man who flashed his ID and muttered his name. Minett. It looked as if he'd come in a hurry: his suit and shirt were badly in need of ironing. But then so was his face. It didn't have a straight plane anywhere on it. Even his body needed pressing. He'd let his shoulders collapse into what looked to be a permanent hunch. With him was a neat woman in her late twenties. She made a beeline for the uniformed pair.

Because someone had to, I gave Minett the tersest account I could manage. I also told him what I'd told security, to be rewarded with what in another face might have been a smile.

'And you've ID'd the body?'

'James Hallam.'

'Why's he all dressed up?'

'He was playing in the concert here tonight. He was also a music lecturer at the University of the West Midlands.'

'And you're the administrator here?'

'I think he's washing up in another bar,' I said. 'I'm just an outside caterer. Sophie Rivers.'

As if he hadn't registered what I'd said, he asked, 'Is there anywhere else we can put these people?'

'Only the theatre they've just come from. Up all those stairs and a few more.'

'Lift,' he said, as if I were stupid.

'There's only one and it holds four people at most. In any case,' I added, 'if the killer stabbed James somewhere else and had to bring his body down here, wouldn't he have used the lift?'

His eyebrows undulated. 'They'll have to walk, then.'

'Some of them might just walk out if someone doesn't . . . shepherd them,' I observed. 'Or go into the loos, which is where . . .' I tailed off as delicately as I could. Apart from anything else, I'd no idea where Hallam had been killed. 'Which is why I kept everyone in here till you came.'

Perhaps it was the reassurance of having a more solid police presence that freed people up. Perhaps it had been Marcus's example. All around the room people were sipping their drinks; to my amazement, some were reaching surreptitiously for nibbles. But how long they'd be patient who could tell?

'Would you like me to keep them fed and watered till you can talk to them?' I asked. 'In the theatre? So your people can get busy here?'

Many more police officers were making their way in.

'Good idea. Take up as much food as you can manage, you and those kids – they're your waiters, yes? And some drink. But we don't want them pissed.'

'I didn't buy enough booze to get them pissed,' I said.

I was just about to lead the way when he said, 'Hang on a minute. I take it those waiters know the way?'

I called them over. Yes, they'd be happy to carry on upstairs. I think they'd have volunteered for anything so long as it got them away from this room.

'Leonore, show a couple of officers where you're heading, will you? Then come back for some food. Dan, Siobhan – trays and a couple of bottles. Dawn, a few spare plates. But all of you, stay out of this room unless the police say you can come in. They may prefer to pass stuff out to you. I'll be up as soon as I can.'

Minett made a terse announcement that his officers would interview people as soon as they could. In the meantime, if they'd like to take their glasses upstairs, they could wait in more comfort there.

Since French had now returned to the vertical and was trying to regain face by treating anyone within earshot to an acerbic account of the inadequacies of the police, the paramedics turned their attention to other people. The woman who'd led the premature invasion of the bar was now an alarming colour, her cheeks almost purple. Goodness knew what that signified. I was just relieved that expert help was at hand.

'Yes?' I prompted Minett, who'd shut up French and dispatched him with the others.

'Tell me where everything is. Entrances, exits. Stairs. Fire exits. Even lavatories.'

I shook my head. 'I hardly know my way around. The person

you want is Peter Andrews. He's the duty administrator tonight. I told you: I think he's upstairs somewhere.' I'd have expected him to have come bustling down by now. OK, the theatre bar was his responsibility, but I couldn't imagine him not ensuring that everything ran smoothly at the BMI, his responsibility or not.

'What about the boss?'

'He's called Hendry. I've never met him.'

'So you wouldn't know how to get hold of him.'

'Peter Andrews again.'

'Let's go find him. In a bar, you said.'

'It'll be closed now.' I gestured at the wine bottles. 'No point in staying open when there's this for free.'

To my surprise he stuffed half a dozen opened bottles into a box and picked it up. Not to be outdone, I loaded as many chicken joints as I could on to a tray and set off up the stairs. We were both carrying too much and aware of the distance to go to attempt much in the way of conversation.

I had enough breath to call out as we entered the bar, 'Peter? Peter? Are you there?'

Sparkling glasses lay on tea towels on the bar, covered by another tea towel. Yet another lay drying over the taps, while Peter's yellow gloves rested on the tiny draining board. A meticulous man, Peter.

I parked my chicken legs on the bar beside the glasses, Minett choosing a table for his load. No sign of anyone. So much for that good idea.

'Watch a lot of TV, do you?' Minett asked.

'No. Why do you ask?'

'Because you'd have said if you'd ever been in the police but you seemed to keep your head. Not letting witnesses wander off, warning me off the lift – that sort of thing.'

I could have pointed out that lots of people would have done the same. As it was I said, 'I've some good friends in the service.'

'Oh. Now, any other ideas where this bloke Peter might be?' Minett demanded.

'His office, I suppose. Though how you get there from here I'm not at all sure. You need a ball of string to find your way round this place.'

'Or crumbs,' he put in, to my surprise.

'Apparently it's three distinct buildings knocked into one. Hence all these different levels.'

Minett looked around at the dated décor. 'Sort of expect the Bee Gees to come over the PA system, don't you? OK, let's get back to wherever you need to start from to find this bloke's office.' He gestured me to precede him. 'Friends in the service, eh? Now, would I know any of them?'

As if on cue I heard the sound of familiar feet running lightly up the stairs.

'You might know this one,' I said. 'Detective Superintendent Chris Groom.'

Chapter Sixteen

'I was having supper with Harvinder and his wife when the call came through,' Chris said. 'And he told me you'd done the catering. So I thought I'd come along myself. Hello, Trevor, how's things?'

Despite Minett's effort to hold himself straight, he still looked like something from the bottom of the ironing basket. 'Under way, sir.' He coughed meaningfully and looked sideways at me.

Chris did too: I was meant to make myself scarce. I would soon.

'Miss Rivers here's been very useful, sir,' Minett put in, as if in mitigation.

'Why don't I begin spreading this food around while you two get up to speed?' I suggested graciously. 'I suppose I could always ask one of your officers to bring up more if we run out.'

Minett managed a grim smile. 'We won't be removing anything from a scene of crime.' So what about the wine and chicken legs? Chris hadn't been there then. 'I think you'll find there are fewer punters now. All we're doing, sir, is taking names and addresses and letting them go home. If we need to we can take statements when they're feeling better. I should think this evening will put them off concerts for ever.'

'Tell me about it,' I said, picking up my tray and heading towards the little corridor to the auditorium.

'Hang on, just one more thing,' Minett said. 'Peter Andrews' office? And the lavatories?'

'I'll give this to one of my waiters and be straight back,' I said.

But I didn't get that far, because the corridor was occupied by Peter Andrews' body. Someone had hit the back of his head very hard.

I think the reason I stayed upright and didn't drop the tray in panic was the thought of him being pelted by all those chicken legs. I wanted him to have some dignity, even in death. And then I found, as I put the tray carefully down and knelt beside him, that there was still a pulse. What I couldn't find was my voice. Grabbing the wretched tray, I hurtled back into the theatre bar. 'Medics! Fast!' I managed to squeak.

By now the chicken legs had taken on a bizarre life of their own, jittering drunkenly round the tray. I looked at them for some moments before I could make a connection with my hands. So it was they that were shaking. And the rest of me, come to think of it. Hands pressed me firmly down on to a bench seat. I stayed put, silent. The less fuss I made the quicker they could get Peter seen to. The green-clad figures went about their business. Chris and Minett plunged deep into various conversations, mobiles and radios in action.

Someone must have filled one of Peter's nice clean glasses with wine and passed it to me. By the time they prepared to carry him out, I was staring at dregs, anyway. I didn't want to look at Peter in case I completely lost it. But he made a tiny gesture with his hand as if he wanted to say something.

'"Death has a thousand doors to let out life",' he announced weakly. 'But I don't intend to go through any of them yet.' He flapped a hand at me. 'Interesting concert, Sophie. But I'd book a better group next time.'

That was some advice French should certainly take. I took his hand and squeezed it. He managed to hand over his keys to Chris, and then lapsed back into unconsciousness. I had the distinct sense that the paramedics weren't going to waste any more time.

'What was all that stuff about death?' Minett asked.

'A quotation. An Elizabethan playwright, I'd say. But don't ask me which. Not one of the famous ones, anyway.'

'Funny thing to say, when you're being carted off to hospital.'

'A very positive thing to say, in his state,' I countered. 'OK. This food. I suppose I'd better take it round the long way.'

Leonore, Siobhan and Dan were sitting disconsolately in the auditorium when I eventually got there. Everyone else had been allowed home, but they'd stayed to help me, they said. They'd been paid till midnight, after all, Dan added, and it was only just ten.

It felt much later than that to me.

Why had Siobhan kicked Dan? Ah! No Dawn. Well, if she were pregnant, I couldn't blame her for slipping off early, even if it did mean more work for the others.

'I'll go and see when we can go back into the bar,' I said. I saw their faces. 'You won't have to go in again. You'll stay outside and I'll pass stuff out to you. Then all you'd have to do is ferry it to my car, which is in a space just outside. Meanwhile, there's a great big piano here – if it's in tune, why don't you fill the place with decent sound? Make up for the crap we had earlier?' And then I remembered what had happened to one of the musicians, and wished I hadn't been so free with my musical criticism.

Minett was standing outside the basement bar when I went down. I took the circuitous route since I was sure Peter's corridor would be cordoned off. The lift was switched off too – not that with my need to shed calories I'd ever have used it anyway.

'Am I allowed in yet?'

'Sorry. The SOCOs want absolutely everything preserved.'

Even the spare food? 'No problem,' I said. 'Is Chris still around?'

'Somewhere. He'll be bringing one of his teams in, I suppose. Pity, I'd have liked to run with this.'

'Couldn't he draft you in?' I hadn't even registered his rank. Sergeant or detective inspector, presumably, since the teams were headed by DCIs.

'Always a chance, I suppose.' I don't suppose his face ever looked particularly cheerful; it looked positively hangdog now.

'I'll be back in a few minutes, then.'

'Hmm. All this running around. Imagine, only one lift in a place this size. And a piddling little one at that.'

'Room for our killer and poor Hallam's body?' I prompted.

He looked at me sideways. 'If Superintendent Groom chooses to discuss cases with you, that's his business.'

It was. And it would be unfair to press a stranger, even if he'd been happy enough to pick my brains earlier. Especially as Chris was just strolling into earshot.

Not, of course, as I told myself forcefully as I toiled up the stairs again, that this was any of my business. At least, as I heard the sounds of singing in the distance, I hoped it wasn't. There was the remotest of chances, wasn't there, that people I knew were involved?

As I got nearer the auditorium the sounds took shape. Loath to disturb the singers, I slid to where the students had stood for the first half of the concert.

'*Bess, you is my woman now*,' Dan was singing, and Leonore, at a slightly higher range than I'd heard her before, was assuring him that Porgy was her man. The term spellbinding is overused, but it's the one I'd have chosen to describe their performance. Siobhan had been trying to accompany them, but had the sense to realise that no accompaniment was better than a bad one. She was sitting perfectly still.

Only as the moment drew to a magical close, and I was standing with tears pouring down my face, did I realise I wasn't alone. Chris emerged as silently as I had from the corridor. I stuck out my tongue to catch a tear unaccountably dripping from the end of my nose. He passed over one of his beautifully laundered linen squares. I mopped.

We both looked at the stage. For a woman supposed to be a lesbian, Leonore was doing a remarkably good job of a heterosexual embrace. It was only when Siobhan coughed that Dan pulled himself away. But their hands still clung together.

Chris gestured me out into the corridor with a swift jerk of his head. Emotion often made him brusque. Just now, brusque was fine by me.

'No reason for you to hang about,' he said. 'We'll get someone to take a statement tomorrow. Unless you've anything you think we need to know urgently.'

'There was one point when I was alone in the bar and a load of people barged in,' I said. 'Apart from that I was always with other people.'

'Can you remember any of them?'

'One of them was a stout middle-aged woman whom the paramedics had to check over after they – after they dealt with . . .'

'The incident?' Chris suggested drily.

'The incident. I didn't take any notice of them – I was too busy shoving them out so I could nip upstairs to listen to the concert.'

'I don't need to tell you to come back to me the instant you remember anything at all. OK. Off you go.'

I looked towards the singers. 'It seems a shame to disturb them.'

'Any reason for them to hang round?' He could be very curt when it came to responsibility and duty.

'I'm sure someone's collected their names and addresses. They had a dreadful shock this evening, poor kids. Are all the members of the audience OK? I mean, chamber music doesn't seem to attract a youthful audience, and some of those there

151

tonight looked decidedly green. That one the paramedics had to see to—'

'Nearly as green as you, you mean?'

'Peter's head wound, the music – it all brought back George's death,' I said. George, my bassoon-playing friend, had been as close to me as any human being, even Mike or Chris. It had been his murder that had brought Chris and me into each other's lives.

He managed a slight nod of acknowledgement. 'Are you going to call those kids or are they going to stay here all night?'

I called them.

It was a pain having to leave plates and knives and bottle openers behind. But it meant I didn't have to smell that blood again.

By now Hendry, the chief administrator, was in the foyer, terribly worried about Peter Andrews, anxious about his insurance, wondering who'd finally clean up all the mess. In other words, a perfectly normal decent man. He was probably just the far side of fifty, dapper in jumper and slacks. His hair flopped about a bit, not unlike Minett's; very alert, bright eyes shone from his face. Chris didn't seem pleased to find me listening in on the conversation, innocent though it was.

'Well?'

I flapped an ironic hand and left in silence.

If emotion made Chris curt, it made me bossy – not, I suppose, that I needed too much encouragement. Perhaps when I ceased to be a teacher, the bossiness would evaporate. It was much in evidence that night, however, as I insisted that the kids take taxis home, pressing extra fivers on them to emphasise my point. I also gave them my home number with instructions to phone me at any time if they needed me. They were to pass it on to Dawn too. She'd already left, Siobhan whispered, as soon as the police had said they'd finished with her. They'd promised to cover.

'So I gathered. Don't worry, I don't think she's very well.'

Dan said, 'I bet Marcus French is sweating cobblers at the moment.'

'You mean he'll get it in the neck for booking Masters or whatever his name was?'

'Oh, that too, I suppose. No, I was thinking of the Old Bill. "Ve haf vays of making you talk."'

'Oh, shut up, Dan,' Siobhan suggested. 'I know they used to have flaming rows, but that doesn't mean he killed him.'

'Rows?' I repeated, ultra-casually.

'Oh, real humdingers,' Leonore said, tightening her clasp on Dan's fingers.

I thought of what I'd said about constructive dismissal. 'Any idea what they rowed about?'

'Just didn't like each other, I suppose. That's what the Old Bill will want to talk to them about, isn't it?'

'Mind you,' Siobhan added, 'they'll want to talk to us too. You know, standing at the back of the hall. I mean, no one would have noticed if we'd gone and killed him and then come back.'

'They'd have noticed the blood, stupid,' Leonore said. 'You'd be covered in it, wouldn't you? Your hands and front, anyway.'

At this point their taxi arrived. It spared me having to admit that the killer might not be too bloody – not if he'd worn my missing plastic gloves and apron.

Should I go back in with the theory? No, the police weren't stupid. They'd almost certainly find them bundled up somewhere. Come to think of it, where had we women left ours? In one of the bins in there? I went back.

I felt rather like a twelve-year-old waiting outside the Head's study as I hung about in the foyer while a uniformed officer went off in reluctant search of Minett – not Chris, who was, after all, an administrator, and a temporary one at that. But it was Chris who appeared, grim-faced at finding me so importunate. But he brightened when I told him about the apron. It tied up, he said, with other evidence, which he did not disclose.

'But you do realise,' he said with more emphasis than was perhaps necessary, 'that it's all the more vital that you remember who came into the bar before the concert? Tell me, did you lock up when you'd got rid of them?'

I shook my head. 'I just left a notice outside.'

'So anyone could have got in.'

'Anyone.'

'Provided they knew there was something in there they wanted. Sophie, for God's sake start thinking about those people. Or rather,' and his face softened, 'don't think. Let the memory creep up on you. Right?'

'Right.'

There was still a great deal of activity, and I knew better than to hang round getting in the way. We bade each other a cordial good night, and I returned to my car. Halfway to Harborne, however, I knew I couldn't face going home. At the end of the High Street I turned towards Bournville, and Mike's house. Although I had to make up the bed, although I knew I was being fanciful, I felt closer to him there, and found his duvet a good deal more comforting than I'd have found my own.

Chapter Seventeen

If I couldn't cherish Mike, I could cherish his plants. I picked off a few dead leaves and watered them before I set off home for what should have been a mega washing-up session, had not West Midlands Police detained even dirty glasses. All I had to do now was some big plastic boxes, which I'd emptied and returned to the car before the drama began. At least I'd be spared the usual binning process: the police had also laid claim to all the rubbish, just in case. Lucky them – all those half-chomped chicken bones.

Before I did more than empty the car, however, I checked the answerphone. It was brimful of messages: Harvinder twice; Chris twice; Mike a new one to add to all the others I couldn't bear to wipe; Sue, from Student Support, saying she'd been asked to do extra hours to counsel students and staff present last night, and I was welcome to call her; Marcus French – where'd he got my number from? – and Leonore. All left return numbers.

Starting in order of seniority, I called Chris, to be diverted several times before I gave up, simply calling his mobile and leaving a brief message. Harvinder, on the other hand, answered first ring.

'Copper's nark here,' I said drily.

'Hi. Thanks for phoning back, Sophie. Now, have you time to pop round for a few minutes?'

I ought to make a token objection. 'At nine on a Sunday morning?'

'Whenever you're up and dressed,' he conceded sarcastically, 'so perhaps we should say eleven thirty? That would allow you to apply a modicum of make-up as well?'

He was already laughing, so I responded in kind.

'Provided I don't bother curling my eyelashes. OK, Harv, I've got a list of phone calls to make as long as your arm, but I should be with you by ten.'

He coughed, delicately. 'Would one of those calls be to Chris Groom?'

'It would be, only I've left a message to call me back.' I waited for a response. What was Harv up to? 'Do I gather that you'd rather I'd spoken to you first? I could leave my mobile off it would help.'

Another silence. 'I don't want to be deceitful . . .'

'It's switched off and I'll let my answerphone screen incoming calls,' I said. 'Provided you promise to tell me why when I see you. Chris's friendship's very important to me, Harv.'

'I know.' And he cut the call. Weird.

I expected that Leonore would simply want advice on how to deal with the police, in which case I'd have told her to tell the plain and simple truth. As it was, she wanted to tell me how wonderful Dan was in bed, and ask about the morning-after pill.

Marcus French – who would have got my number, of course, from UWM – was conveniently engaged. I didn't avail myself of the ring-back option.

As for Mike, I knew better than to try to phone on a match day. But I allowed myself a quick gawp at satellite coverage of the first test match. Yes, there he was, a distant figure sitting in the pavilion padded up ready to bat. I blew him a kiss and set off for Smethwick.

'There's got to be some connection between the two crimes, surely,' Harvinder said, passing me a mug of Blackcurrant Bracer.

I jiggled the little bag until I'd got a brew of a satisfactory colour, dumping it in the nearest bin. 'Why do you think that?' I asked neutrally.

He sniffed his herbal brew – it smelt like the stuff I give my houseplants as a treat – with every appearance of appreciation. 'Well, it would be a great coincidence if two such things happened unconnected in one not very big university faculty.'

'True. But Chris would say you're jumping the gun, Harv. You mentioned two crimes. But we have only one, surely, which one of Chris's teams or units or whatever they're called will be investigating. That's the indubitably dead James Hallam. But all Neil Wiltshire's done is go missing.'

He leant forward confidentially. 'I want to get on to one of those teams, Sophie. It would mean a big step up in my career.'

'Promotion? I thought you had to have a spell back in uniform before you could go back into CID at a higher rank?'

'Even as a sergeant—'

'Even longer hours, even less of your family?'

He pulled a face. 'But it's getting noticed by those who matter, isn't it?'

'You've got to get noticed in the right way. And you know how Chris hates assumptions. Look, Harv, you've no evidence at all that anything nasty's happened to Neil. Have you? Or do you have some you haven't told me about?' I looked at him as if he were a bright but lazy student.

'That's where you come in,' he said dropping his voice furtively. But then he remembered he'd been authoritative with me before. He straightened. 'You know about music and musicians, Sophie. I'd like – what I'd really like is for you to come with me and check out Neil's room.'

'Me! What for?'

'You know I wouldn't know a bass from a bassoon.'

I grinned. 'The musical version is B flat from a bull's foot. Hell, Harv, you're taking a chance, aren't you? Chris doesn't like unofficial sniffing round.'

'He gets you to do it!'

'That's because it's he who's breaking the rules. He doesn't like me to sniff around without his say-so, believe me. But if you're prepared to take the risk,' I concluded, 'I'd love to.' It was the lure of other people's lives, wasn't it, the glimpses into strangers' rooms from the top of the bus?

'Let's go,' he said. 'But leave that mobile switched off, will you?'

He was on his feet reaching for our jackets before either of us could finish our tea. I didn't argue.

At least I found how someone could practise the violin for hours on end without attracting complaints. Neil had practised in a garden shed. It was a very superior shed, dry enough to keep garden tools without the slightest hint of rust, and curtained and carpeted, if in a rather juvenile mode.

'Used to be my youngest's Wendy house,' Mrs Cole, the landlady, explained. She hadn't turned a hair when we'd turned up on her doorstep. But then, there was no need for her to. Her house was as immaculate as if she'd just spring-cleaned it, and she herself was neat in a jumper and skirt. She'd be about sixty-five, at a guess. 'All the dollies' tea parties we had in there . . . Of course, my Ron grabbed it for his tools as soon as she outgrew it, God rest him. But it seemed the very place for young Neil. And now there's no sign of him. What do you think's happened to him, miss?'

'That's what we're trying to find out, Mrs Cole,' I said awkwardly. If I was an oracle, I was an oracle on false pretences. Harvinder had introduced me in an uncharacteristic mumble, the clear implication being that I was a colleague. I'd chosen to satisfy my nosiness first, before allowing Mrs Cole to lead us to the much more conventional bedroom. It was as tidy and clean as the rest of the house. Tidy! Clean! Was it really a young man living here? I thought of the ash-covered tip that constituted Steph's bedsitting-room in his adoptive parents' posh house. I thought of the amiable clutter that constituted our bedroom, though that, of course, was clean. They: our bedrooms in both houses.

Neil occupied the back room, overlooking the garden and the shed.

'A place for everything and everything in its place,' Mrs Cole observed, patting the built-in wardrobes and dressing table.

To my embarrassment – but then I remembered I was supposed to be a police officer, snooping legitimately – she opened drawers and showed me beautifully ironed T-shirts, paired socks and folded sweatshirts. Another drawer held files, all marked on the top with their contents. Music was in box files on the bookshelves. His violin case stood proudly to attention in the corner furthest from the radiator.

It was an unwritten law amongst musicians that no one ever touched anyone else's instrument without permission, let alone played it. So I felt I was taking a liberty in picking it up, laying it on the bed and flicking open the catches.

'I hope you're not going to mess with that,' Mrs Cole said sharply. 'It's his pride and joy. I ran a duster over it once – only a nice bit of wax polish – and he got really cross.'

'Has he just got the one, Mrs Cole?' I asked, lifting the fiddle free of its packing and unwrapping the silk scarf it was swathed in. I didn't know enough to say how old it was, certainly wouldn't presume to run a bow across it, but the worn patches on the lovely honey-coloured varnish suggested it was old and possibly valuable.

'Oh, yes. Makes enough noise on that when he puts his mind to it, he does. But he's a lovely lad. I wouldn't want to give the wrong impression. If ever he got cross, which I've only known once or twice all the time I've known him, two years or more now, he was still polite, if you see what I mean.'

'I'm sure he was,' I smiled. Then I realised I wasn't supposed to have met him. 'All his friends and teachers say what a nice lad he – is.' I was in danger of revealing things with my tenses, if I wasn't careful. I'd nearly used the past. I ran a finger over the fiddle's belly, picking up a light dust of resin. Then it was time to swaddle the fiddle in its wrapping. As I laid it gently back in its case, I wondered who'd be the next to play it.

All Neil's clothes were in place, all his books. No wonder Harv was sure something was wrong. But for me, the final nail in the coffin of hope was that fiddle: no one would have left an instrument like that behind if he didn't intend to come back – an instrument clearly loved and cherished.

Harv was inclined to hang around, but I wanted to be out of that room and its sad relics.

'OK, Sergeant,' I prompted him. 'Thanks, Mrs Cole.'

'You wouldn't like a nice cup of tea? I always have one with Neil at this time of day, when he's here, of course. It's a habit I got into with my Ron, bless him.'

Harvinder hesitated.

Maybe there was something else she could tell us? But I didn't like my role in this. And I had something urgent to tell Harv. So when he caught my eye, I shook my head minutely.

'I'd hate to take any more of your time, Mrs Cole,' he said gently. 'Particularly as you were so helpful when you spoke to my colleagues the other day. We'd best be on our way.'

By the front door, she said, 'You will ask if there's anything else, won't you, miss?' And then her face sagged. 'Or tell me – if . . . if . . .'

No, being a police officer was one job I wouldn't want.

'Well?' Harv prompted me, fastening his seat belt and pulling out.

'Call Chris and get into one of his bloody teams. That's what you want, isn't it?'

'What's up? Come on, Sophie, it isn't like you to lose your rag.'

It wasn't. So what had made me now? A sense of being

160

used, being invited along as some spurious expert, to confirm what Harvinder, a very bright copper, knew anyway? But then I reminded myself that I'd used him to get into someone's rooms. A voyeur, that was what I was. No, it wasn't Harv I was angry with, it was myself. I turned away, not keen for him to see I was ready to weep – perhaps with grief, in fact, not anger. I'd liked poor innocent, naïve, vulnerable Neil. He'd brought out my protective side.

'There's not the remotest chance he could have been kidnapped, is there?' I managed.

'No note.'

'There's been time?'

'He's been gone at least eight days now – plenty of time for anyone to get in touch if they wanted to.'

'Still nothing definite about a last sighting?'

'No. As you could see, no sign of a struggle in his room. In any case, his parents are comfortable but not loaded.'

'No chance, then. Shit. Harv, you knew, didn't you? A room left as tidy as that? His fiddle left – that's the clincher, isn't it? It knocks the London orchestra theory bang on the head for one thing, and – no, wherever he went, he'd want to take that. I think he popped out – you know, to the pub or something – and never came back.'

'My theory exactly. You see, Sophie, if you bought it, I think Chris Groom will.'

Back at Piddock Road Police Station, he took my elbow as he guided me through the corridors back to his room. Not his exclusively, actually. He shared it with DI Peter Kirby. But Peter's desk was notably clear. He was on a course, Harvinder said when I asked. It had been the wrong question, hadn't it? There must be some needle between the two men I didn't know about – Peter certainly specialised in upsetting people. Or needle between Harv and someone else – he'd not been quite himself since the start of what was now clearly a case. For once, I wouldn't ask personal and embarrassing questions. We had more important things on our plate. In fact, I even had a couple of chocolate biscuits on a plate, plus a cup of proper tea.

'Blood sugar levels,' he said tersely. 'And when you're feeling better, Sophie, I want to go through everything – *everything*, mind – that's been going on at UWM.'

There was an abrupt knock at the door. Harv had got as far as 'Co—' when in walked Chris Groom. He might not have been wearing uniform but he looked every inch a senior officer. In Harv's place I might have had a quiet quail, and I would almost certainly have waved goodbye to promotion to one of Chris's teams.

'So that's where you are, Sophie,' Chris said. 'And why, may I ask, did you leave your mobile switched off?'

'Because Harv and I didn't want any interruptions, Gaffer.' It always disconcerted him when I addressed him as if I were a junior officer. 'You remember that missing person? Neil Wiltshire? Well, he was from the same faculty as James Hallam.'

Chris pulled up a chair and sat astride it. 'A murder and a missing person in the same faculty. That doesn't sound too much like a coincidence, does it?'

162

Chapter Eighteen

'If Neil Wiltshire had killed James Hallam and then disappeared,' I said, 'it might have made some sort of sense.' Now he was here, Chris might as well make a morning of it and hear the whole lot. 'Hallam treated Neil very badly in front of the whole music faculty—'

'And in front of you? An education student?' Chris interjected drily, peering over his glasses. He fished out a fountain pen. Harvinder passed him a writing block. 'Thanks.'

'Yes, as it happens. It was an open rehearsal. Anyone can go. In fact, you have to if you're a music student.' I felt a silly *frisson* of something like guilt: I'd skipped the rehearsal for the Flute and Harp Concerto, hadn't I? Promptly I told myself off. I wasn't attached to the department. *But I might have seen something useful! Not your job, Sophie*, I concluded sternly. 'Neil and Hallam were playing the Mozart Sinfonia—'

'The one for violin and viola? Hmm. Both good musicians, then.' Chris looked impressed. Harv wisely stayed silent. 'So what went wrong?'

'Basically Hallam ignored Neil for the whole of the performance, both when he was correcting orchestral faults and, more to the point, when they were playing—'

'Hang on. How can you play a piece like that, virtually a duet, and ignore the other half of the duo?'

'Good question. Pity Hallam's no longer here to ask. But Hallam wasn't the only one Neil had a problem with. He disagreed radically with his personal tutor—'

'That'd be Alex Fisher,' Harvinder put in.

'That's right. There was talk of Neil leaving UWM before he'd finished his course to take up a job with a London orchestra. Fisher opposed it: he said – and he had a point – that Neil was too young, that he wouldn't last five minutes in the cut and thrust of London.'

'And Neil didn't like this opinion?' Chris asked, writing.

'No. Not according to Fisher.'

'We've not been able to talk to Fisher yet, Gaffer,' Harv said. 'He reported sick last week with a cut hand. Seems he had this constant urge to practise, so his wife packed him off to Scotland. His mobile doesn't seem to work up there. Until last night's incident, I didn't think I could justify bringing him back for questioning. Now I'm not so sure.'

'I'm sure the MIT's budget will rise to it,' Chris said crisply. 'Would you want to go and get him yourself or talk to him up there or what?'

Harv gave an unexpected grin. 'I could try something cheaper: tell his wife to go and get him.'

'We'll think about that one. Anything else I should know about?'

'For a start,' I said, 'I think I might be suspended—'

'Come on! Surely you'd know. And you'd know *why*.'

Harv and I exchanged a quick grin at the appropriation of his words. But I was quickly serious again. 'I say might because there's been no written notice, no proper hearing, no proper anything, in fact. Apparently someone alleged that I was stirring up the students.'

'Not you, Sophie – you never stir up anything!' His smile countered the sarcasm. 'Who were the complaints from?' he added more seriously.

'My God!' How on earth could I have forgotten? I looked at them both in turn. 'The complaint was put to me by my tutor, Carrie Downs. But she alleged – and God knows where she'd got hold of this from – she alleged that I'd been both fomenting student unrest and spreading malicious gossip about Hallam.'

'You should have told me this earlier, Sophie,' Harvinder said severely. He didn't add, though it was implicit, that had I done so he'd have kept me miles away from Neil's digs.

'I – I know this is hard to believe but the allegation was so silly it hardly registered with me. Hallam did say something odd to me at one point, warning me against getting involved with the young people, but I assumed it was in connection with something quite different.'

'Which was . . .?' Chris asked, his voice as expressionless as his face.

I told him about Rose's harassment and about the scene with Kev. Again, virtually no reaction, though I'd have expected hilarious guffaws when I told them about the lesbian aspect.

'Let's get back to Hallam for a minute,' Chris said. 'You came back to BMI on Saturday to say one of your aprons and a pair of gloves had gone missing. At what point did you register they'd gone?'

'Only when Dan, one of my waiters, started to handle food without them. Just after the interval.'

'Where did you spend the interval?'

He was taking this very seriously, wasn't he? My God, it was as if I'd become a suspect!

'In the theatre bar. The barman hadn't turned up so I helped Peter Andrews till the end of the interval, when I went back to the auditorium. As soon as Marcus French announced the rest of the concert was cancelled, I called my waiters – I had four – on my mobile—'

'Why?'

'They couldn't listen to the quartet, it was so awful. So they'd repaired to a pub somewhere.'

'All of them? Together?'

'I don't know for sure. All I know it that they reappeared together.' No point in telling Chris to ask them: someone already had, of course, and I was merely confirming what they'd presumably said.

'So you phoned them from the auditorium?'

'That's right. I hadn't seen them in the theatre bar and they were nowhere to be seen upstairs. When French told the audience the second half was cancelled, he also said that I'd be serving refreshments in ten minutes. So it was all-hands-on-deck time.'

'He didn't give you any prior warning?'

I shook my head. 'I phoned and then legged it downstairs to start taking clingfilm off plates of food.'

'Which is when you realised you were an apron and a pair of gloves light.'

'Yes. When Dan started to unpeel film. Usually I take plenty of spares: don't know why I didn't this time.'

'Are you sure you didn't?'

'I don't know. I'd count out at least five aprons, ten gloves. I usually add spares. But I truly couldn't swear either way. I mean, they're thin plastic: they stick together.' I looked at their implacable faces. Not hostile, just withdrawing any feelings of friendship that might prejudice their judgement.

I clapped my hands to my head. There was something else I'd forgotten, wasn't there? 'Peter Andrews,' I said. 'How is he?'

'Hoping he'll confirm your alibi?' Harv asked unpleasantly.

I held back a gasp. Occasional spats notwithstanding, we were friends. I'd have to try to talk to him, to find out what was the matter. And if he was like this, I'd have to choose my moment with some care.

Chris shot him an unreadable look. 'He must have a remarkably thick skull. That blow could have killed him, the medics say. He's been in and out of consciousness all night, but the prognosis is good. He said that he'd been quoting Massingham, by the way.'

'Good.' I couldn't stop myself blurting, 'Chris, I was a suspect then, wasn't I?'

He managed a brief smile. 'Technically you still are. But while everyone except Renault claims that size isn't everything, I think it might be a factor in this case. But I'd rather not talk about that now.'

Size? Well, apart from anything else, it would be hard for me to have lugged someone Hallam's size very far. What I couldn't work out, come to think of it, was how anyone had lugged him that far without spilling blood everywhere. As soon as the body had fallen forward, there'd been that huge gush. Could he actually have been killed in the bar? Behind the BMI equivalent of an arras? Peter Andrews would have a plethora of apposite quotations.

'Confidential evidence?' I hazarded, wondering now how he could possibly have been persuaded to walk down there anyway. Or even, since not everyone shared my prejudices, descended in the lift.

He nodded, managing a ghost of a smile. 'Confidential evidence.'

Harvinder coughed decorously. All this was as highly irregular as my trip with him. 'Would it be preferable in the circumstances for this discussion to end?'

'I think we can pump Sophie for some more information first,' Chris said, smiling easily for the first time this morning. 'Let's talk about the student unrest you're supposed to have been fomenting.'

'That's easy, because I've done the opposite of foment. I've tried to solve problems without getting in any way involved myself. I'm too old, Chris. The students want to treat me as staff; the staff don't know how to treat me. Anyway, various students came to me with complaints about various teachers, but I told them that the Uni must have procedures and they should follow them. That's all. I gave the same response to that pain in the arse Rose, to Dan, the waiter whom you heard singing, and – yes – to Neil Wiltshire.'

'Neil! Whom did Neil want to complain about?'

'No idea. An informed guess would be Alex Fisher, of course, his tutor.'

'Of course. Other staff?'

'Amongst others, Professor French. He's both the professor and conductor of the student orchestra, an irascible man with a bob on himself, Harv. I should imagine you made his acquaintance last night, Chris.'

'"A small man drest in a little brief authority",' Chris observed. 'If Peter Andrews can come up with quotations after a blow like that, I should be able to,' he added, as my eyebrows shot up. 'Even if I've misquoted it!' He yawned. 'Any chance of a coffee, Harv? No, not your herbal tea, thanks very much. It's the one decent thing about Lloyd House: they don't have that cat's piss there! Sophie, you look as if you could use some decent caffeine.'

Harv may well have suspected it was a ploy to get me on my own. Neither of us mentioned the earlier tea and biscuits. But Chris merely got up and stretched, yawning hugely again, and pulling up Peter's padded chair to replace the hard one he'd occupied so far, sitting back in it the conventional way.

The coffee was no better than average canteen, but it was warm and wet and therefore welcome. While we sipped Chris and I talked lightly about West Bromwich Albion, a team which had caused us much heartache in the past but which was now making good progress up the First Division. Only when we were well into their chances of promotion did we remember that Harv didn't like soccer. The gossip ended swiftly.

'Let's get back to French, shall we?' Chris suggested. 'You said you'd fielded some complaints against him.'

'They were more rumours than complaints – rumours that he'd award good marks in return for sexual favours.'

'Evidence?'

I sat back in my chair to think it all through. It didn't come clearly, and I was glad I'd had the coffee to prime the cells. 'To be honest, I've personally had very little contact with him. The only time he summoned me to his room was to offer me singing lessons—'

'*Singing* lessons? But you're an English teacher!'

'That doesn't stop her singing pretty well. Even so, Sophie, that takes some explaining.'

'I thought so at first. But he said he was grateful to me for accompanying Leonore and Dan. And the lessons weren't with him, but with a woman voice teacher, who's too busy at the moment anyway. Oh, and he escorted me to my car once, in the pouring rain on the Oldbury Campus. To be honest, on that occasion I did have the distinct impression he'd been waiting for me.'

'How did he know you were there?'

'I'd been in the local history office to book a place on a trip tomorrow.'

'A trip?' Chris's eyebrows capered.

'Yes. To Smethwick!'

'But you're *in* Smethwick,' Harv objected.

'Yes, but this is a special bit of Smethwick. Almost not Smethwick, actually. Almost Handsworth. The Avery Berkel works.'

'Ah! The site of the Soho foundry,' Chris said.

'Why special?' Harv asked.

'Because Matthew Boulton – the man who owned it – was so important. I mean, we're talking world heritage here, not just a tatty bit of the Black Country. I thought it would be nice to go and have a look round. Any road up,' I continued, entitled, I thought, to use a Black Country expression which I knew irritated Chris, 'while I was booking my place, who should erupt from the office of the guy running the trip but Marcus French.'

' "Erupt"?'

'It sounded as if he'd been having a row with Kenneth Ball, the guy who writes that local history column for the freebie paper.'

169

'OK. Anything else about French?'

'All the students are entitled to book sound-proofed practice rooms for an hour at a time. He's cancelled several bookings and inserted another student, a woman called Dawn Harper, on the grounds that he thinks she should work towards a recital this summer. Now, Dawn is the one whom the wretched Rose alleges has let French into her knickers to get better marks. And the one I believe I saw in French's car after choir rehearsal one night,' I added.

'Why would he risk being seen with her? Surely they'd do their illicit bonking on university premises?' Chris asked. 'In a practice room? So no one would overhear anything?'

'Or maybe that's too risky, or maybe he prefers a bit of comfort,' Harv suggested. 'You're sure it was them?'

'It was certainly his car. But I couldn't swear it was Dawn, not in a court of law.'

There was a pause.

Chris's stomach filled it with an immense rumble. He looked at his watch. 'I've got a lunch meeting with some of the DCIs to see which of their teams is going to take this on. I'm sorry. We'll have to leave this here. But I'd like you to talk about this lot, Sophie, with whoever takes over. OK?'

I ignored a stricken look on Harv's face. 'Fine. I could do with a break, to be honest. Only my break involves washing up after last night.'

'You haven't done it yet? Not like you to leave a job like that hanging over you.'

'No,' I agreed.

All three of us rose to our feet, Harv obviously intending to escort us out of the building. I thought I'd do better without him.

'No,' I said. 'Listen to that rain. You stay put. Chris has got to get wet anyway. He can get my car released.'

'But—'

What was the matter with the man? His interpersonal skills

were usually better than that.

'Thanks, Harvinder. I'll be in touch,' Chris said. 'Ms Rivers?' Just like French he proffered a courtly arm.

I took it until we were out of sight. 'You know he's pissing himself with anxiety lest you don't get him in to whatever team ends up with this lot.'

'I know. He ought to be there too. But with Peter on this course, we can't reduce CID over here any further.'

'He's done so much it would be criminal not to let him.'

'I'll have to think about it. It doesn't just depend on me, you know. The acting operational commander here might have something to say.'

'Go on, be selfish, just this once. He's a good cop, you know that.'

'But quite erratic and edgy recently. Any idea why?'

I sighed. 'I'll try to find out. Meanwhile, couldn't you—'

'Don't press me any more, Sophie. Apart from anything else I'm late and we're both getting soaking wet. Take care of yourself.'

'And you. Hey,' I called him back, as he was half in, half out of his car, 'did you do anything about – about the agency.'

He blushed deeply. 'I was supposed to be meeting my first date tonight.'

'"Supposed"?'

'This case . . .' he shrugged.

'Look, Chris Groom, this case is just a matter of death. But tonight's a matter of life. Your life.'

Chapter Nineteen

I hate washing plastic boxes. You can only get about three on the draining board before you have to dry them. And then you start all over again. I ought to be able to regard it as therapy or penance or something positive. I can only ever see it as a miserable chore the only good thing about which is that it rounds off a job. This time I hadn't even been paid in nice crisp notes after the event. I'd got to make out formal invoices to submit to the faculty secretary, who would pass them to the university accounts department, who would . . .

Hell, I hate washing plastic boxes.

I was on the last one when the phone rang. My impulse was to let the box go hang, and dive for my last chance of hearing a human voice today. But what was an answerphone for, if not to ensure I did the last of the washing up uninterrupted? All the same, I listened with half an ear, only to hear the caller ring off when the machine clicked in. Bother. And if I knew the workings of fate, when I pressed 1471 I'd find whoever it was had withheld the number or that BT did not have the number. I was right. Not sure whether to be anxious that someone might be trying to scare me by this means or be irritated by someone playing silly buggers, I plumped for not being scared.

I tutted, therefore, with irritation. As I did, something dawned on me. To be honest, I was so embarrassed by my stupidity I flushed as if someone were there to see me. Why had it not registered till now that I'd given no thought at all to the other quartet members? The women must have had an even more dreadful shock than I had, having worked with Hallam as part of a tight unit. I could imagine that poor June would want to merge with the wallpaper, but I was surprised that Caz hadn't had something to say. In fact, purely as a bit of sisterly kindness, I could always phone June, couldn't I? To find out how she was. Tams wasn't a very common surname, and not everyone was as paranoid about strangers discovering their number as I. I reached for the phone book, and found a Tams, J, in Bearwood.

'You seemed so calm, so – so competent,' June said, pouring tea in her kitchen. 'Keeping your head when everyone else – well, could you blame them?'

June lived in a terraced house just where the not-yet-so-fashionable Bearwood was about to merge with the snazzier Harborne. I wondered where she could practise, without disturbing neighbours close enough to provide through the party wall a heavy metal thump as background to our conversation. No shed for her, I'd have thought, at least not a cosy one like Neil's.

I accepted a stale packet biscuit, but shook my head at her compliment. 'On the contrary, I almost passed out,' I said. 'In any case, I never knew him as well as you must have done. How long . . .?' I dropped my voice, suspecting that June might think it more appropriate to speak of the dead in hushed tones. For all she couldn't have been more than six or seven years older than me, she seemed more like someone of Mrs Cole's generation.

'About a year. I joined the university as a Boulton Scholar, you see, on the strength of my thesis on the Abbess Hildegarde. Boulton Scholars are required to be not just teachers but practising musicians.'

'That's a pretty rare combination,' I remarked as if hearing the information for the first time, but declining another biscuit, all the more firmly when I saw the sell-by date on the end of the packet.

She blushed with pleasure. 'And I've got teaching experience too. I've done a bit of everything, Sophie. I started off fresh from the Royal Academy with the Hallé. But I didn't really enjoy the touring and the irregular hours. My poor cats never knew when to expect me. So I became a peripatetic teacher.'

'State schools?' Not a very good move, given all the redundancies when the Thatcher team decided music wasn't necessary for children's development.

She nodded. 'But the work got less and less . . . Fortunately a premium bond came up, just when I'd forgotten I'd got any. So I cut my losses and went back to study. Which is what Professor French tells me you've done.'

So when had they been talking about me?

'Nothing as scholarly as that, though,' I said, ashamed at having dismissed her as a nonentity. 'So you must be the most recent of the quartet.'

'That's right . . .'

So what was the problem there?

'It must have felt very strange, joining a group who were already established. How does one set about fitting in?'

'Well, so much depends on the leader, of course. And I must say, just within these four walls . . .'

I nodded. 'Of course.'

'Well, Alex Fisher is – he's inclined to be a little arrogant. And James: he didn't like being told what to do. Not at all. Nor Caz. Absolute fireworks, sometimes.'

'It must have been very uncomfortable for you.'

'Uncomfortable! Many's the time I thought of resigning, but I wouldn't give them the satisfaction.'

I looked around the kitchen, extended into the scullery to make one good-sized room. The flooring had worn thin, the china was cheap but not especially cheerful and the ceiling had a big brown patch over the stove. I'd not seen much of the rest of the house, but my route from the front door, opening straight on to the living room, and then via the back room, had led me over threadbare carpets and past fifties' furniture not yet chic. If June had reasons not to resign, not giving the other members the satisfaction of getting rid of her might not be the main one. On the other hand, why had she let the place get so tatty? I knew roughly what the university pay scales were, since they were more or less in step with further education ones. Perhaps the premium bond win hadn't been quite enough: perhaps she'd had to go into debt.

'Didn't rehearsing within earshot of the prof restrict their bickering?' I asked.

'You'd have thought so, but no: on and on they'd go, all about a bit of bowing or how many repeats you should play in Haydn. Not worth arguing about, if you ask me.'

But wasn't that precisely the sort of thing chamber players ought to argue about? Music, and how to play it? I remembered Hallam's contempt for Neil during the Mozart. Neil was a fine musician, potentially probably better than Hallam himself. So how had June fared at his hands?

'So you just kept your head down and got on with your job,' I suggested.

She beamed with relief. 'Exactly. Anything for a quiet life, I always say. Oh, Ludwig, you naughty boy.' A large cat poured himself through a cat flap apparently three sizes too small and made straight for the litter tray, which he used, noisomely. He made a token gesture at covering his deposit, and then exited whence he had come.

I could think of nothing germane to say.

'Goodness knows what'll happen now,' she said. 'You see, we're really all supposed to be on the same contracts. I mean, we're supposed to be appointed at the same time and leave at the same time. What's happened, of course, is that some people – like James Hallam – had his contract extended and extended, goodness knows why—'

I smiled deceitfully. 'You must have some idea.'

'Seriously I don't. No, really. I mean, Professor French likes a bit of respect.'

'From everyone? I overheard him and Kenneth Ball yelling at each other the other day—' I began.

'Oh, he's let that newspaper business go to his head, I expect. And he's not a professor, which Professor French is, of course.'

So was the theory I'd put before Hallam, constructive dismissal, not as wild as it might have seemed? I could scarcely suggest that, however. What I might float was another part of my theory – that French had imposed a poor player on the ensemble in the hope the resulting fiasco would rebound not on him but on the quartet.

'Quite,' I said. 'But of course, Alex Fisher wasn't there for the concert, was he?'

'No. We had that awful Masters. Such a pompous, conceited little man. Caz says he kept trying to look down the front of her dress. She reckons he wore a wig too.'

How had I failed to notice something like that?

'The funny thing is,' June continued, dropping her voice and leaning forward as if trying to pass a message under an enemy agent's nose, 'Alex is supposed to be in Scotland, but I'm sure I saw him the other day when I was shopping in Harborne. They've got a Marks and Spencer there now,' she said, as proudly as if she and Bearwood could bask in the reflected glory. 'A Food Hall, at least. Still, I must have been mistaken, I suppose. But it was someone just like him,' she added, plonking her mug on the table with a little dab of defiance.

'They say we've all got doubles,' I said. All the same . . . 'You didn't think much of Masters, I gather?'

'Well, could anyone? But he's a friend of the professor! And he has a good reputation. He's played with some professional quartets – full-time ones, I mean. But he'd no idea. Really, no idea. And dashing off like that without coming to the reception.'

'Would you have stayed,' I asked drily, 'if you'd given a performance like that?' I hoped I implied that she was miles better than he.

She seemed to take it that way. 'Perhaps not. But he positively charged out of the building. He'd been to look for James – well, Caz and I couldn't look in the gents, could we? And then Professor French went looking as well. But there was no sign of James's things, none at all, so we thought he'd had a tantrum because Antony was so bad and gone home without telling anyone. And all the time . . .' Her voice, which had been rising alarmingly in pitch, now cracked. She couldn't keep back tears.

Silently I passed her some tissues from my bag.

She mopped, and sniffed hard. 'Those poor students seeing it: awful for them. Mind you, most of them had gone to the pub, hadn't they? So they wouldn't have been at the reception.'

'I don't think they'd been invited. Wasn't it supposed to be a profile-raising event for the media and councillors and so on? The great and the good generally?'

'That's just what I told Rose when I saw her, actually.'

'Rose!' Forget this quiet, low-key interrogation: I wanted hard information and I wanted it now. 'What the hell was she doing?'

'Looking for you, of course. She does get these crushes on people. Last year it was on Alex. And on James.'

'Why me?' I wailed. 'Not exactly part of a pattern!'

June looked at me thoughtfully. 'If you ask me, she'd have a crush on anyone who showed her the tiniest gleam of encouragement. She's not very bright, you know. She needed an enormous amount of help just to get through to this year, and she responds to the helper by falling in love with them – staff, and, oh yes, students. Poor child: she hasn't got much going for her, has she?'

Ashamed, I agreed.

'On the other hand, as I kept telling her, making a nuisance of yourself with people only annoys them. She listens to me, you see, as if I were some sort of schoolmistress.'

Poor frumpy, nervous June. But she had enough imagination to see beyond Rose's unprepossessing behaviour and to try to channel it.

'Anyway, I told her on no account was she to gatecrash, which is what I think she meant to do. I think she went off to the pub in the end.'

'I don't know how you did it, but thank you. It would have been dreadful if she'd made a fuss when I was supposed to be working.'

'That's what I told her. "You'll only get another public snub," I said, "and no one will like that." Not that I'd think you'd be as unkind as James. Oh dear, speaking ill of the dead . . . And Alex: he reduced her to tears on several occasions.'

'How serious are these crushes?' I asked. 'I mean, do they last long? Will she soon be over me?'

She bit her lip. 'They don't last long, but – I think I should warn you she can get quite vindictive. Alex didn't dare leave his car in the car park. And I believe she phoned his wife and said all sorts of things.'

'Why didn't the university sack her?'

'Retention,' she said drily.

'You mean bums on seats? My God! I'd heard of that sort of thing happening in further education but never in higher!'

'We need funds too,' she said.

So how had quiet little June managed to prevail? 'Rose's got all the sensitivity of a Sherman tank,' I reflected. 'How did you manage to stop her when no one else has managed it?'

She gave a little smile, which suddenly broadened, transforming her face. 'I reminded her she had an assignment coming up. And that I was marking it.'

'Oh, June!' We beamed at her wickedness. We even had another biscuit to celebrate. But I found myself becoming anxious for her: it sounded as if that was one thing Rose could complain about legitimately.

I was just leaving, Ludwig having made another deposit in the tray, when I asked, very casually, 'How's Caz taken all this?'

'Well may you ask! She went off last night with some nasty little Brummie councillor, don't ask me why.'

If it had been the one I'd noticed her with, I didn't need to.

'And this morning I only got her answerphone when I phoned to find how she was. It must have been about eleven, too.'

'Well, if you get hold of her, tell her how sorry I am,' I said, reflecting that with the best will in the world I didn't see how I could casually phone Caz to offer woman-to-woman support. Not with our niggly history.

'Of course. Now, Sophie, remember what I said about Rose. The best we can hope, to be honest, is that she finds someone else to fall for as quickly as possible.'

We kissed each other's cheeks and I set off, wondering if I should decamp to Bournville for a while. There was no reason not to, except the big plastic boxes waiting to be stowed properly. Them, and a fundamental objection to being drummed out of my own home.

Chapter Twenty

My answerphone might be bubbling with messages, but it couldn't compete with the test match highlights on Sky. Mike had taken a good catch to dismiss a major Pakistan batsman, so I saw him four or five times in slow motion from a variety of viewpoints. The England innings started disappointingly with the fall of a couple of wickets, so I even saw him batting, though going very much against his natural inclinations with a dour and dogged few overs. He was not out at the end of play, so I should be able to watch the rest of his innings if I was prepared to skive the following day. I was very tempted. After all, why should I want to go into UWM in the morning? The afternoon trip was another matter. For one thing, because Marcus French had left a further message on my machine. Would I be kind enough to come to his room at nine thirty? I wasn't sure how kind I felt.

As I made a reflective cup of tea, I cogitated about my threatened suspension. The whole thing stank, of course. Could Carrie Down's attempts to suspend me have originated from someone else? She'd never pretended the complaints had come from the Education Faculty. The more I thought about it, the more I realised that in my terms she'd been decidedly remiss as a tutor. I'd have wanted to hear the student's side at very least, and I might even have attempted some sort of negotiation before coming up with any nonsense about suspension. So why had she behaved so badly? Who had made her? Well, the obvious candidate was someone who obviously had power over her: the man who marched into her room as if it were his own and read her paper without a by your leave. French. Perhaps I would have to go into UWM, but to see her first, then French. It might well be, of course, that French didn't want to talk about my alleged behaviour in Smethwick but about my very real behaviour at the BMI. Perhaps he might even want to thank me for holding the fort when he couldn't manage a squeak. Damn it, I'd even saved him from injury when he passed out. But was French the man to acknowledge debt to anyone else? I rather thought his ego would have difficulties with the concept.

It would have been nice to have someone to chew the whole thing over with. Any other day the first person I'd have turned to, assuming, of course, I couldn't talk to Mike, would be Chris. But Chris was on his First Date – if he had any sense, that is. No Aggie these days: although we spoke regularly on the phone, our conversation was pretty one-sided, since she was now too deaf to take in more than about forty per cent of what I said. In any case, university politics wasn't exactly her main area of expertise. I'd lost touch with most of my William Murdock colleagues. Many had moved to jobs in other parts of the country rather than stay in doubtful security in Birmingham; some simply resented my ability to take not just one but two sabbaticals, even though this second one was funded by UWM itself. I was still a member of NATFHE, the lecturers' union, but it seemed more an NUS matter, since I was currently a student. Even if I'd had an emergency contact number, I wasn't sure I wanted advice from a kid Steph's age. Harvinder? I'd an idea he'd be pretty unhappy if I disturbed what should be a family evening in. So I was left with the professional but still I hoped friendly offer of support from Sue.

Sunday night? Well, I could simply suggest a car share the following morning.

To my enormous relief, she accepted with alacrity, no questions asked. I'd pick her up at eight fifteen the following morning.

'Provided you don't mind my picking your brains while I drive,' I added, conscience a-twang.

'Not if you don't mind talking catering ditto.'

'Except –' I smacked my head: how could I have forgotten something so important in five minutes flat? – 'I shan't be able to run you back. Not till late. Sue, I'm so sorry! It's not going to work, is it?'

There was a little pause. Sue cleared her throat. 'You sound as if you need a listening ear. It so happens that I'm on my own this evening. Adrian's got an emergency on. Now, as you know, UWM have offered immediate counselling to anyone involved in last night's events. So if by any remote chance you wanted to talk about that, I could claim overtime for every minute you were round here. Provided you were prepared to initial a little sheet saying you'd needed help and for how long we'd talked. Of course,' she added, with no detectable irony in her voice, 'we'd have to sign off before we talked catering. We couldn't expect UWM to pay for that.'

'You know, Sue, there's some interference on the line. It couldn't be your halo causing the problem, could it?'

Jamie was at the grizzly stage of tiredness when I arrived, and swatted my constructions to the four winds before they were anything like their full height. Sue gathered him up, causing a full-throated squall, of which she took amazingly little notice, and headed upstairs. I enjoyed five minutes with the *Observer*, and wished I'd thought to eat before I set out.

It was a good job I declined Sue's offer of an evening drink: she poured herself the stiffest gin I'd seen for some time, and knocked back a second without slurring a hair. She accepted as quite reasonable my explanation that I was driving.

'Which lot of business first?' she asked, kicking off her

shoes and putting her feet on the sofa. 'I tell you, Sophie, I go into work for a rest these days.'

'Catering?' I suggested, not even pretending to be disinterested. 'If you want to go ahead, that is?'

She narrowed her eyes. 'I don't suppose your prices include cleaning up afterwards?'

'Only the mess my team and I make. But I dare say you could very easily come to some private arrangement with the students. One of them might even want work on a regular basis. Not just cleaning but baby-sitting,' I added.

She flapped her arms and grunted. 'That's the nearest I'll get to flying pigs,' she said. 'Maybe when he's potty trained . . . OK, fifty guests, with your vegetarian menu. But I would like just a few meat dishes, but not offensively meat, if you see what I mean.'

I didn't quite, but would work on it. 'All the meat I use is organic, if that helps.'

That agreed, we settled a date and she produced a file from a heap of detritus behind her sofa.

'OK. UWM business. You have to sign here now – time counselling session starts – and then initial at the bottom when we've finished.' She even dimmed the light and put a box of tissues within my reach. Suddenly she ceased being a gin-swilling exhausted mother: she was an alert professional. Had I needed counselling, I'd have been happy to confide. I took a deep breath and began.

'Firstly, I think I should make it plain that I'm not really here to be counselled, whatever that form says. I'm here to talk as one adult to another.'

'But – oh, well, OK.'

'As you know,' I continued, ignoring the interruption, 'I'm something of an oddity at UWM. I completed almost all my assignments last year, but not my dissertation, which in fact is practically ready for submission. So I have a lot of time on my hands.'

184

'You live on your own?'

'No, but my partner's away at the moment. I tend to spend time in the music faculty – I'm in their choir, and play the piano for a couple of singers. Because I'm older, some of the students see me as an auntie figure, and they've come to me for advice on a number of different issues. They also gossip. The gossip has one thing in common. Sex. There's a persistent rumour, Sue, that staff in the music faculty are demanding sex in return for good grades. Now, I know I can't ask you who's come to you for advice – though I have pointed a number of students in the direction of Student Support. But I wonder if I can ask if you've picked up similar information.'

She looked troubled. 'I'm not sure that you can. We're talking confidentiality here, Sophie.'

'Of course. Which is why I phrased my question as I did.'

'But confidentiality ought to extend to people against whom the complaints are made. After all, they may be quite innocent.' She spoke so carefully I almost smelt a rat.

'Agreed. After all, I'm the victim of such a complaint myself, as I suspect you know. Come on, Sue: I know about co-counselling. And I know about referring up to supervisors. Kevin will have had to talk to someone, but I suspect he may be in deeper than he'll have admitted. In fact, if I'd seen Rose in the state she was the other day, I'd have been thinking about immediate referral to an outside agency.'

'We can't talk about other people, Sophie.'

'I'll try not to. But it may not be possible. First, someone needs to know about all this alleged sexual blackmail; secondly, I'm concerned about Rose, both for her sake and for mine. The thing is, Sue, she was at that concert last night and she's known to have had a crush on the man who was murdered. A crush that was rejected. So the police ought to know about it. And – since I've rejected her – I'm personally involved too. And some part of me would like the police to know if I'm at risk. Though, to be fair, she made no approach whatsoever to me last night.'

Sue clutched her forehead. Perhaps the gin had cut in at last.

'I'm out of my depth,' she said at last.

She looked it. And perhaps I was being unfair. She was new to the staff, and worked only part time. And it was Sunday night.

'Can we leave those problems on the table, then?' I asked. 'You see, I've got another, more immediate one. As you may also know, I'm being threatened with suspension for—'

'I think you'll find it's more than a threat,' she interrupted me. 'That's why I suggested you came round tonight. Because I think you may find the security staff turn you away if you come in tomorrow.'

'You're joking!'

She wasn't.

'But Marcus French has asked me to see him tomorrow morning – which was why I wanted your advice. You see, I suspect it might have been on his say-so that I was suspended. I wondered if I'd compromise myself if I went to see him. Or if,' I added slowly, 'he might be about to offer me a way out of my unpleasant situation.' Now that was an interesting idea. If only I could get miked up: maybe it wasn't too late to contact an old friend of mine who was extremely big in surveillance and protection systems. He always assured me that any self-employed person ought to be available for business twenty-four hours a day.

'It'd be your word against his if he did.'

I pounced. 'So you have had complaints against him!'

She flushed. 'I didn't say that.'

'I know you didn't. Not in so many words. But there was a clear implication, Sue, wasn't there? Entirely off the record?'

'I suppose you might have interpreted it that way. But I'd deny saying even that.'

'Oh, it's my post-traumatic stress making me jump to weird conclusions. I suppose you need to make some record of this conversation for the authorities if you're being paid weekend rates?'

She looked genuinely shocked. 'I wouldn't have volunteered for the scheme if I hadn't thought it was entirely confidential. I'd make notes afterwards for my own use if you were a – a real client.'

'In that case, in all seriousness, I'd like you to write down that I was terribly worried about Rose. And I'm pretty worried about Neil Wiltshire too,' I added. 'This disappearance of his. Something must really have upset him. I suppose he wasn't one of your clients too? You see, if he was, the police will want to know.'

'In that case,' she said, stiff with embarrassment, 'the police will have to ask me, won't they?'

Gavin was amused by my phone call, but clearly didn't want me calling round at his seriously stylish flat over in Moseley. Given his enthusiasm for the golf course in general and holes in one in particular, I wasn't surprised. But I was touched when he told me he'd drop off a very easy-to-use device early the following morning. He was en route for the M5, he said, so it wasn't far out of his way. I didn't argue, though from where he lived I certainly wouldn't have used a route with all those lovely rush-hour bottlenecks.

He arrived just before eight, sank one of my coffees, showed me how to wear and activate the little machine and was off. He gave me one of his usual bear hugs and Holly-wood kisses, but it took no more than a token protest to make him desist: he must be really in love at last, at least for this week.

So I was on my own, in every sense. Well, at least I had the Soho Foundry visit to look forward to. I checked my torch and stowed walking boots in the back of the Mazda. I also sub-stituted a fleece and waterproof for my usual rain jacket. On impulse, I ran back for my camera: there was always a chance there might just be something worth recording on film.

Chapter Twenty-one

Despite Sue's warning, I found it very disconcerting to be intercepted by security staff who'd hitherto maintained such a low profile as to be virtually invisible about the place. They'd been briefed too: I was escorted straight to French's domain. The door was flung open immediately. That friend of Dawn's, Doug the foghorn, was in mid-harangue, it seemed. But he shut up at once, and went off quiet as a lamb.

French retreated to his chair, the far side of the desk. He nodded me to an upright one opposite him. To give the little microphone a better chance, I partly unzipped my waterproof and fleece. The room was hot enough to justify such an action. Only as French's eyes gleamed did I realise he might place another interpretation on it.

'This is very unfortunate, Ms Rivers,' he said. 'A charge like this against a highly regarded student such as yourself.' If the row with Doug had upset him, he showed no sign of it.

I nodded, watchful.

'Particularly in view of the recent circumstances.'

'Dr Hallam's murder, you mean?'

'Exactly so.' He bit his lip: he might have been as genuinely upset as he'd appeared on Saturday.

I waited. It seemed best not to offer him any sort of lead or prompt, lest someone later interpret it as entrapment. Or could only the police be guilty of entrapment? Suddenly my visit seemed nothing less than foolhardy. Why hadn't I called Chris or Harvinder this morning to tell them what I was doing?

'I need not say how impressed everyone was by your – your sang-froid on Saturday. Particularly as with a charge like this against you, you must have been seen as a prime suspect.'

'It depends who made the charge, Professor French.' I tried to keep any menace out of my voice. 'And what exactly the charge is. If that's the correct term anyway: it's one I tend to associate with the police. Dr Downs said I'd been fomenting student unrest, then seemed to imply that I'd been spreading malicious gossip about Hallam. Now, these aren't quite the same thing. Which is it?'

He never had an impressive front; now he looked positively shifty. 'The two aren't mutually contradictory. You encouraged students to complain about Dr Hallam's sexual advances.'

Now was not the time to mention the name on people's lips had not been Hallam's. 'To complain to whom?'

'Does it matter?' he asked pettishly.

'I'd have thought so,' I said reasonably. 'After all, if an official complaint is made to a senior member of staff it would be investigated, and if the allegations had substance, action could be taken. If they didn't, action could be taken against people spreading the rumours, couldn't it? Then – and only then – you could certainly suspend whoever they were. But I don't see how you can suspend me. Firstly, all I did was counsel my fellow students to say nothing against *any* member of staff –' I allowed myself to stress the word very lightly – 'that they weren't prepared to substantiate in a formal inquiry. Secondly, I'm not a student in your faculty, so I don't see that you can have any jurisdiction over me. Had the education professor taken it into his head to suspend me, there might have been some logic. Always assuming there was some foundation.'

'After all I did for you!' he said. 'I gave you a highly lucrative contract; I offered you voice lessons. And now you query my right—'

'I don't query your right to do either of those,' I said. 'One was a straightforward catering job. My tender was no doubt more competitive than other people's. The other was unexpected, but a gracious gesture, I thought, to acknowledge the help I was giving to two of your students. But neither has anything to do with a suspension for a quite spurious reason.'

'Oh, I've no more time to waste on you! Any sort of remorse – an apology! But you're too bone-headed! You have to play the little barrack-room lawyer.' He stood up and strode round to the door, but though he held the doorknob, he made no attempt to open it.

Still seated, I swung round to face him. 'So if I were to apologise, I might be reinstated and all this expunged from my record?'

'It depends on the sincerity of your apology.'

Ah! The little microphone probably picked up my quickening pulse rate.

'I'd have to think about it.' I bit my lip in apparent anxiety. 'Apologising for something I've not done . . . The thing is, this has caused me problems already. The police—'

'The police! How would they know anything about it?'

'They asked about any connections I might have with Hallam, of course. I'm sure they asked you too,' I added ambiguously.

'I didn't say anything about it. Come on, Sophie, I'm sure this can all be smoothed over.'

I hoped the mike caught the slight caress in his voice as he let go of the door and leant closer to me.

'Let me think about it, Professor. I – I've never been in this position before.'

'How long would you want to think?'

I'd started on the little-woman act so I might as well continue. 'It's so difficult . . . At least a day.'

He returned to his desk and flipped open a diary. 'Shall we say five this evening? No, I shall be preparing for the choir rehearsal. Shall we discuss it after that? I take it you'll be attending?'

'If you can tell security to let me in,' I said. I gathered up my bag and got to my feet. 'Now, if I agree, will you need some witness to my apology, or will a written one do?'

'Let's discuss that when you've made up your mind,' he said smoothly.

'Very well.' I paused by the door. 'Actually, there's something I'd like to ask you, if I may. The violinist that replaced Fisher: why did you recommend him?'

'What business is that of yours?'

'Just mild interest. I'd have thought a man running a department as good as this would have chosen a better musician.'

He smirked a little at the compliment, but then pulled down the storm clouds again.

'It's absolutely none of your business. Good day, Ms Rivers. Until this evening.'

It was only as I shut the door behind me that I realised how tense I'd got. I waggled my head and shrugged my shoulders a couple of times. As I did so, Carrie Downs rounded a corner.

I couldn't manage a welcoming smile, nor did she attempt one.

I was out of the building in thirty seconds flat, heading for Piddock Road and the protection of Harvinder Singh Mann. No, I was quite sure no one was following me, that no one had any reason even to suspect what I'd been up to. But I was unaccountably nervous, and kept checking the rear-view mirror for a car labelled FRENCH or one driven by a fluffy blonde. No, nothing. But I was anxious, horribly anxious. As it happened, Harv wasn't there. I hoped, crossing all available digits, that he was being signed up for the MIT or MIU or whatever that would be investigating Hallam's murder. So I handed the envelope to the duty receptionist, a man whose age, haircut and beer-belly suggested ex-forces, with the earnest plea that he should put it into no one's hands but DS Mann's, or, if he should drop by, Detective Superintendent Groom's.

'It may just be,' I added, trying for casual, but probably not achieving it, 'that someone could turn up claiming that it's theirs. But I don't think you should believe them.'

'Don't worry, miss,' he said, with a wink as expansive as his waistline.

I stepped briskly back into the street, looking around me. No: no sign of French parked anywhere near – but then, he wouldn't have brought a car with such an identifiable number-plate. I'd no idea what Carrie Downs drove, but there was no car occupied by a woman, anyway. No, nor man, neither. Peter Andrews would have capped the Grave Digger allusions, wouldn't he? And pointed out I'd got the man-woman equivo-cation in the wrong order.

What was it he'd seen that would make someone sock him like that? Or, more accurately, who?

I dawdled along the High Street in the comforting presence of the morning shoppers, coveting some wonderful saris and salwar kameez, not to mention the bright Indian gold that shops along here specialised in. Not that my skin tone and hair colour would have done any of them justice, but the colours and textures were so gorgeous it was a pleasure simply to see them. I could have treated myself to some bags of spices, but with Mike away it would have been a wasteful indulgence: I preferred to buy a little and often, using the coriander or cumin before it lost its intense new smell and taste.

I'd carefully not reminded French of the Soho Foundry trip, lest he use it as a lever to encourage me to decide to 'apologise' on the spot. So I simply presented myself in the Avery Berkel factory complex at the pre-arranged time. There were about twenty of us there, mostly young but a couple of mature students like me, all sensibly shod and warmly dressed and carrying serious torches. Although we stamped our feet and blew our fingers, it wasn't in fact cold, just windy. Some of the self-set buddleias still had residual flowers, and nothing was as dead as it should be at this time of year. At last a Volvo estate pulled up along my Mazda, disgorging Kenneth Ball and a tall, square-built bearded man in his late forties whom he introduced as George Demidowicz, the industrial archaeologist who knew more about this site than anyone else. Whether it was with a view to hiding his light under a bushel or simply to keep warm, Demidowicz immediately donned a hard hat, dishing out one to each of us from the tailgate of Ball's car.

When they'd all been adjusted – yes, there were the clever-clogs who wanted to wear them at a rakish angle or even back to front – he led the way briskly past what looked like state-of-the-art industrial premises, opposite which was a row of cottages in which, according to an unobtrusive plaque outside, William Murdock had once lived. Touched, I took a photograph. I felt almost valedictory, as if it was the great man's presence I was leaving, not just a college named after him.

I galloped to catch up with the rest of the group in a big open space, roughly triangular. To one side was James Watts and Company's brick-built mint, now abandoned, but, according to Demidowicz, the scene of some exciting archaeology. To our right, as we stood with our backs to the modern part of the site, was what was left of the Foundry. It was an unprepossessing mixture of old brick and modern corrugated iron and steel-framed windows. As the first slash of rain pattered on my hard hat, I wondered why the hell I was there. Particularly when Ball admitted the arrangement for handing over the key had gone pear-shaped, and prepared to traipse back. Demidowicz, however, was made of sterner stuff, and found, behind a buddleia unaccountably sporting thorns – ah! a bramble had insinuated itself along the branches! – a door he could squeeze through. We followed.

If you looked at what was closest to you, you saw a sad office, with long-redundant health-and-safety notices still pinned to the walls. There were even a couple of dirty mugs and a pair of boots. If you turned round, you saw an expanse of what Demidowicz told us was sand: we were almost on the site of the first huge furnaces, from which molten metal would have been poured into casts, the casting pit now, alas, floored over. I was so overwhelmed by the sheer size of the place that I wandered slightly away from the rest of the group simply to gawp, so I missed what he was saying about the industrial processes. And I'm afraid that was the position for much of the visit: had there been a test paper at the end of the visit, I'd have failed lamentably. It was as if a fourteenth- or fifteen-century religious architect had guided the pen of his 1795 industrial counterpart, so great was the height and sweep of the place. The roof wouldn't have been out of place in a cathedral. Despite the scale, there was remarkably little visible support: traceries of metal rested on slender pillars. Was it disappointing to learn that the roof was a nineteenth-century alteration? A Belfast roof, according to Ball. Well, cathedrals had been changed for the better as time went on – why not a factory? Whoever had constructed the roof, it was amazingly light and airy, at least a third made up of glass panels. One part even had what looked remarkably like a clerestory. The erecting shop – what a homely term for another vast space – had high brick walls. Window embrasures, no longer holding glass had they ever done so, rose in three storeys, getting smaller with each level, like those on elegant Georgian houses. George said he hoped when funds came through it would make the exhibition hall at the heart of the heritage site. I saw it as a banqueting room, glittering with glass and silver wear.

But now we were being herded into the vaults under the pattern stores. If you needed a thread or crumbs to ensure your safe return in the BMI, what would you need here? Even twenty torches gave no more than adequate light, and there were regular clunks as people not much taller than I collided with beams or lintels. We were too busy worrying about where our feet were going – the ground was slippery with broken glass or even damp – to think about our heads. On one wall our torches picked out a giant mycelium, blindly, purposefully, carrying dry rot throughout the building. I suppressed a shudder.

'What's it like without torches?' someone asked.

'We'll see if you like. Is everyone happy with that? You're sure?' Ball asked. No one demurred.

'*Quite* sure?' Demidowicz pressed. 'OK. But only for a minute.'

We switched our torches off.

The darkness was absolute. It was in its way as awesome as the lovely light buildings from which we'd come.

And one of our number started to have hysterics. 'It's crawling everywhere. Everywhere!' he began to cry.

All around, torches sprang back into life.

I'd no idea who the man was. Demidowicz and Ball did their best to calm him down; a woman suggested slapping him back to sense. But there was nothing for it: someone had to take him back to daylight. I didn't even think about volunteering. I wasn't responsible, I didn't know the way, and I wanted my fiver's worth. In whichever order!

Ball eventually offered to shepherd him back to daylight, and a convenient pub right opposite the works entrance for a brandy. Two or three other people suddenly announced they'd rather go back too. So it was a somewhat reduced party that Demidowicz led through another couple of sections of the foundry's entrails.

He was making purposefully for a doorway on the far right when I smelt something sweet. God, any moment I'd have hysterics like that bloke earlier. You couldn't get the smell of blood in a place like this, and there was no way I would acknowledge a belief in ghosts, especially to myself, though there must have been industrial accidents aplenty in a place this old. I talked myself out of the idea; thought of the health-and-safety legislation that made even visitors wear hard hats. I followed the others, marvelling at the way Boulton had recycled ash as a filler to level a badly sloping site, looking at the old but empty storage rooms for patterns – great wooden shapes, Demidowicz told us. Then we turned back.

This time I had to turn my torch in the direction of that smell. Waiting till the last of my colleagues had stooped their way out of the door, I turned my torch on a passageway. There. Nothing to worry about. Just a cascade of the most enormous chains I'd seen outside the Black Country Museum. I switched on my camera, preparing to take what I hoped would be a dramatically lit still life. Bits of industrial litter, even half an old cardboard box lay on top: perhaps I should leave them as they were – a photo vérité – or should I move them? One photo with, one without. I pushed at the cardboard: what did it hide? Not, now I looked closely, the source of the smell of blood, and the other smells of death. A pale hand protruded, with the long, strong fingers and short nails of a fiddle player.

Chapter Twenty-two

'Neil!' I really lost it. I couldn't stop screaming his name, as though he might yet hear and come back. But no one could have a hand as cold as that, be buried under so many links of iron, and come back.

Even as I started to claw the chains off, I knew I shouldn't. I should be preserving the scene. Sobbing with impotent anger, I squatted where I was, wringing my hands.

Eventually I was aware of a hand shaking my shoulder, firmly but not unkindly. 'If you're afraid of the dark,' Demidowicz said, 'why on earth didn't you go with others? Staying on your own like this, you're putting other people at risk too.' His voice became increasingly stern. When he hooked his hand under my elbow, I had little choice but to stand.

At last, I had enough control to play my torch on what I'd seen.

'Bloody students and their practical jokes,' he said. 'Come on, let's get you some fresh air.'

'Not a joke,' I managed. 'Real. And I know who it is under there.'

'Come on: pull yourself together.' He was still patient.

I had to do it. I bent and touched that hand again. Pulled gently. Half an inch of wrist appeared. A chain slithered.

'What's that smell?' he asked, his voice now catching my anxiety.

'Blood,' I said flatly. I swallowed. 'I'm as sure as I can be without seeing the poor kid that it's a student who went missing from UWM a week or so ago.'

'Let's get out of here. As soon as we're back in daylight I'll call the police.'

Gripping his arm, I said, 'No one must come in till they do.'

He managed a dry laugh. 'Do you think anyone would find their way in without Ken Ball or me?'

'Someone did.'

The story we hatched as we picked our way back to the others was that I'd had an attack of asthma and would have to sit quietly till I'd got my breath back. George – we'd rapidly got on to first name terms – would escort the others back to the pub and Ken Ball, and come back for me. Meanwhile, I'd call the police and give them details. He'd return to show them—

God, I'd throw up if I weren't careful. There was nowhere to throw, that was the trouble, and I'd hate to give someone the job of clearing up my vomit after me. Deep breaths, that was the answer, of the familiar Smethwick air, the smell of which was still much the same as it had been when I was a child. I'm sure some environmental health expert would be able to tell anyone interested what chemicals gave it its individuality.

OK, the others were now out of earshot. Time for my phone call. Since I didn't know which DCI was in charge of the team investigating Hallam's murder, I did the obvious thing. No, nothing as sensible as dialling 999. I called Chris Groom on his direct line.

To see not just Chris but a whole police team arrive was wonderfully reassuring. They'd acquired hard hats from some-where – perhaps George had recovered the students' and had redistributed them. Off they went, regulation torches agleam, uniformed and plain-clothes officers alike. Then a young carrot-headed woman with a medical bag arrived; she needed my hat and torch. To do her justice, when she emerged, she cast a highly professional eye over me, checking my pulse and tersely suggesting it might have been more sensible to keep me somewhere warm. I'd have been more than happy with the pub, but it seemed that the management of Avery Berkel, through whose foresight and generosity the whole site had been kept for posterity, were prepared to go an extra mile and offer me and the police team coffee from the machine in their foyer. Not just any coffee. Good coffee. If the cups were plastic, they sat in little holders with user-friendly handles. Comfortable chairs to sink into. And heating, when I thought I'd never be warm again. The reception staff didn't turn a hair at the muddy boots, just regretting that their senior colleagues were detained in a meeting and couldn't come to greet us.

'I told you Black Country people were the salt of the earth,' I remarked to Chris, who came eventually to join me, getting himself a hot chocolate before he did so.

'I've never disputed it. I've simply reminded you that Black Country people are also renowned for cock-fighting, dog-fighting, racism, sexism and incest,' he said. 'Ah, you're looking more yourself now. But someone has to give us a preliminary ID before we bring in next of kin to do it properly. Are you up to it? The quicker it's done, the sooner we can end his family's ordeal. I promise you, you won't have to see the wound.'

'Which is in his back?' If only I could keep the analytical bits of my brain engaged, perhaps I could deal with the ID.

'The fatal one. There are others. He fought very hard, Sophie.'

'Hallam – Hallam—' I gestured to my nose and mouth. 'Blood all over Hallam's mouth and chin. Has Neil . . .? Because, if he has, I don't think I could.' I swallowed hard. Mustn't be sick, not here.

He looked at me hard. 'Come on, Sophie, that's not like you.'

'I knew him. He's the same age as Steph.'

'In that case,' he said crisply, 'you owe it to him to help us find his killer as soon as possible. But the police surgeon says all the blood remained in the chest cavity. He's not hideous, or I wouldn't ask you. You know that.' He might have been a caring uncle supporting a nervous niece.

Zipping myself firmly back into my thick layers, I allowed him to take the cup and pull me to my feet. To my horror he passed me hard hat and torch.

'I haven't got to go back in there?'

'We're still waiting for the path,' he said. 'What's that for?' He stared at the camera I was holding out.

'There are some photos in there I definitely want developed properly,' I said. 'But there's one I never want to see again. I took a photo of that pile of chains before – before . . .'

His eyebrows hair-high, he passed it to a grim-faced man with a quickly opened polythene bag.

How my feet took me back on to the site, and then underground, I didn't know. Chris knew better than to be kind to me any more – he'd know it would reduce me to tears – but he was remarkably distant, disengaged, as if he'd forgotten I wasn't one of his team, that I was entitled to have sensibilities without the sensible police precaution of counselling against post-traumatic stress. Counselling? Well, you could count Kevin out and I wasn't too sure where Sue stood either.

I didn't even notice the wonders that had so entranced me earlier. We penetrated in the cellarage all too quickly.

Whether for my benefit or for theirs, or simply because there wasn't a lot of point shining torches round unnecessarily, the officers hanging round had only a couple of torches switched on, neither pointing towards the chains. No doubt they'd be sorting out a generator and rigging up lights.

Someone had found bits of tarpaulin from somewhere to cover everything I might not want to see. Chris gripped my upper arm – a couple of weeks ago he'd have gripped my hand

– as I bent, turning my torch on Neil's face at the very last
minute.

The grip tightened as I staggered.

'Well?'

'It's not Neil,' I whispered.

'What?'

'No, it's not Neil. It's Alex Fisher.'

'Come on, Sophie,' Harvinder said, making me jump. I'd no
idea he'd been in the team. 'Alex Fisher's got a doctor's note. I
was supposed to be going up to Scotland to question him.'

'Question away,' I said. 'But I doubt if you'll get many
answers.'

I neither knew nor cared where they set up their incident room,
which seemed to be the chief topic of conversation as we
headed back to the cars waiting to take us back to Piddock
Road, and its CID room.

'You are absolutely sure it's Fisher?' Harvinder asked me, at
irregular but irritating intervals.

At last I cracked. 'For God's sake, you must have seen
photos of Neil – did they look anything like that poor sod back
there? Well, then. Sorry if it messes up your theory, but perhaps
it wasn't a very good theory anyway.'

Chris said coldly, 'Don't I recall your telling me that it
would have made more sense if Neil had bolted after killing
Hallam? Well, looks as if that might be a theory with legs.'

'I don't believe he would,' my lips said stiffly.

'Whether or not, we have to find him. Soon. The search
isn't for a missing person any more. It's for a murder suspect.'

To do him justice, Chris unbent a little when a couple of hours
later he drove me back to the Avery Berkel works to collect my
car.

'You've had a nasty shock,' he observed, unnecessarily,
perhaps, but with enough sympathy in his voice to suggest that

he still had at least a modicum of humanity pumping round his official veins. 'Are you sure you ought to be driving?' Perhaps a smidgen would be nearer the mark.

'Don't know how the car will find its way home without me.'

'One of the lads would have brought it round later. So what are you planning to do now? Jet off to join your husband?'

'I thought you understood the H word was off limits,' I said. 'You wouldn't want to use it when anyone might hear, would you? The same applies to W and M words too, if you don't mind.'

Husbands, wives, marriages – they seemed to belong to an impossibly suburban world in which people didn't get knifed to death. But then, Fisher was a husband, with a wife. Who was now a widow. So how would she feel knowing that he wasn't alive and kicking his heels in some Scottish glen?

'I suppose the pathologist didn't come up with a possible time of death?' I asked, my train of thought having gone on its own tracks – after all, had June not said she'd seen Fisher in Harborne, with its Marks and Sparks Food Hall?

'I've no idea. I'm just the administrator, remember.'

'You could have fooled me. I thought the only thing administrators dirtied their hands with was their budget. Bombing round derelict world heritage sites isn't a usual thing for a desk-bound cop to do.'

'Ah, but I'd always wanted to see it,' he said. 'I shall be leaving everything to the team dealing with the case now.'

'Case or cases?'

'I shall make a possibly unwarranted assumption that they're related. If that meets with your approval?'

I ignored the sarcasm. 'Depends on what the path. says about the knife wounds, I'd have thought,' I said, to irritate him. 'Not to mention the time of death. Of course, the temperature must be very stable in a place like that. It'd be almost as good as stuffing your stiff into a fridge.'

'"Your stiff." Only an hour or so ago you were in tears over Neil.'

'When he *was* Neil. I'm sorry it's Alex Fisher. I'm sorry it's anyone. But I can't deal with it all if I think of the deceased –' I shot him a sideways look – 'as someone I had lunch with and chaperoned against importunate students. Isn't gallows humour how you people deal with it?'

'Possibly. But that hardens us – possibly diminishes us as human beings.'

'Perhaps in the present circumstances that's just what I need.'

It wasn't. What I wanted was the comfort of Mike's body, round me, on me, under me, in me. I wanted warm living, loving limbs, breathing chest and belly. But I could hardly say that to Chris, and in any case, there was no hope of it. Dimly I registered I didn't know the test result. Half a planet away, life and death involved runs and wickets, not cold dead musicians.

I swallowed a sob.

He must have noticed. 'Shall I run you down to Aggie's?'

'No spare room. And her heart's not that good.'

'Surely there must be someone.'

'Hardly any of the old crowd in Brum now.' The William Murdock diaspora had left me bereft. I hadn't noticed the exodus of my friends when I was happy. I'd seen Shahida and Tanvir decamp to wonderful jobs in the States. I'd waved goodbye to— No, as Peter Andrews would no doubt have pointed out, *That way madness lies*.

'What about Ian?'

'Testing the climate in Spain.'

'Do you want me to stay? Spare bedroom, of course.'

I managed an affectionate laugh. 'Without Aggie being there to tut over your car through the gap in her curtains, it wouldn't be any fun. In any case, how would your date like it if she found you were sleeping at an old flame's?'

'She was a nice woman,' he reflected. 'A decent woman.'

'Are you seeing her again?'

'Who knows? With this case—'

'Which you are administrating, not investigating, Chris Groom! Go on, phone her when you get home.'

'You know,' he said slowly, 'I might just do that. When I've set up the incident room, of course.'

Chapter Twenty-three

During the appalling drama of finding Fisher's body, I'd completely forgotten the lesser drama of French, of course. In fact, had I not had an irate phone call from Harvinder on my mobile, just as I was getting into my car in Avery's car park, I'd simply have gone straight home to a cosy cocoa and an early night.

'I'm supposed to be clearing my desk here before I move into the MIU,' he said, 'and what do I find but some enigmatic package with my name on it in your handwriting.'

'MIU? That's marvellous,' I said, hoping I'd injected a reasonable amount of enthusiasm into my voice. Chris still did have a human side, then.

'All the same, what's this package?'

'Have you had any tea yet?' It was, after all, the time when some people ate – about six thirty.

'I haven't had time.'

'In that case, play it back to yourself and then I could explain over a quick sandwich, couldn't I?'

I switched off the phone before he could reply.

Remembering my manners, I turned to smile and salute the security guard to thank him for opening the barrier. But the gesture was wasted: he'd ducked right to the back of his little hut, and I found myself waving at the back of his head.

God knew, I needed some support at the moment, and

if the best I could get was a rushed conversation over a canteen sarnie, that was better than nothing. Besides, I added, apologising to the Mazda for crashing its normally imperturbable gears, it wasn't as far to Piddock Road as it was to Harborne. And Chris might have been right about my driving. My concentration was positively premenstrual in its paucity.

In the police station reception area, Harvinder greeted me with an unexpectedly warm smile and a kind hug. I wouldn't refer to his earlier edgy behaviour unless he did. After all, he wasn't a man for blood, and the smell had been inescapable back in the foundry. Perhaps he owed his silly argumentativeness back in the cellars to the fact he'd been trying not to throw up – just as my cantankerousness was a defence against tears and terror.

'This conversation you taped – it's you and the prof, right?'

'Right. The one who's suspended me.'

'And he wants a private conversation with you late tonight to discuss your apology, right?'

We fell into step, heading for the canteen and – yes, hot soup, an altogether more attractive option than the salad I'd normally have opted for. A couple of people I knew vaguely flapped their hands in my direction; a couple more came over to rib Harv on his move. But such was the turnover in personnel these days I'd no idea who most of the officers were – any more than they would know me.

'Are you going to go?' Harv pressed me.

'That's what I want advice about. What's your reading of the form French would want my apology to take?'

'Doesn't take much to work that out, Sophie. He wants you lying back and thinking of England, to put it politely.'

'My feeling exactly. Which I'm not keen on. But somehow even to turn up suggests I'm acquiescing.'

'If you turn up alone, sure. But not if you come along with someone else.'

'Like who?' All my loneliness washed over me again, flooding my eyes.

He reached and squeezed my hand. 'Poor Sophie; it's been a pretty crap day, hasn't it? Now, I was wondering how I'd do as a friend.'

'You! That'd be wonderful.' And it meant we were friends again.

'Well, more like knight in shining armour. You know this little gadget transmits, as well as just recording. It must have cost you an arm and a leg, by the way.'

'More like an arm and a leg-over. Gavin's got this unrequited passion for me, he says, and rents me things like this remarkably cheaply. Mind you, I paid a lot to have my house fitted with burglar deterrents, so perhaps he considers this part of the after-sales service.'

'The word on the street is that he's really smitten after all these years. So perhaps your second theory's the right one.'

'Wow. Do we know anything about her . . .?'

Harvinder's ostensible reason for wanting to talk to French was, of course, to tell him about this afternoon's discovery. He'd lurk out of sight – perhaps in a practice room – and listen to our conversation. If things got hairy, he'd charge in. He assured me that the police had ways of dealing with locked doors, should that contingency arise. In any case, surely the loud announcement that he was outside should depress any surges of academic testosterone.

I felt too dim to take in all of his carefully explained plans, but returned his reassuring smile the best I could as I started up the corridor housing French's office. I wasn't expecting a pleasant discussion – after all, however good my excuse, I'd just missed a choir rehearsal, something bound to irritate even the most mild-mannered professional. And that was another strange thing. After his incandescent temper at early rehearsals, he'd been decidedly less vile. Not polite and loveable, but not vitriolic. Perhaps someone had indeed complained and made him tone down his behaviour.

'You!' He flung at me, as I put my head round his door after the usual swift summons.

'Yes, me. I—'

'You *dare* to show your face? Have you any idea what the time is? You miss a vital rehearsal and swan in, looking as if you've just got out of bed!'

What I wanted to tell him was that I'd just been finding the body of one of his valued colleagues, but Harv and I had agreed I wouldn't mention the murder unless French did.

'I wasn't sure whether I'd be welcome till I'd apologised,' I murmured.

He looked at me appraisingly. 'So you're prepared to apologise, are you? Well, well.' Rather to my surprise, he returned to his side of the desk, making, as he sat, one of those irritatingly complacent steeples with his hands. His executive chair, all leather and chrome, tipped back slightly.

'I wondered what form you'd want an apology to take,' I said, sitting down. It might have been on the edge of the seat, but it wasn't nervousness: no, I was ready to run. 'And an assurance that you'd be able to remove any trace of this from my academic record.'

'Dear, dear, still demanding your rights. What a naughty girl.' By now, one of his hands had disappeared beneath the desk; the other was fingering his chin.

'The two must go together,' I said firmly.

'Well, let me see. How shall we get into the files? I'm not *au fait* with computers, Sophie, but I'm sure you are. Can you work that clever little animal in the corner?'

I looked where he was pointing. Inasmuch as any computer can look elegant, this did – one of those with a flat monitor.

I shook my head. 'You'd need passwords to get into personnel files.' I produced a winsome smile. 'How did you get this complaint put on my file, Professor? Because whoever put it on would have to take it off again.'

By now he was coming round the desk, holding out an inviting hand. I had a fair idea where the hand had been, though his flies were zipped.

'Let's see what we can do together, shall we?'

I stayed put. 'You must have completed some form or other,' I insisted.

'I knew you were a clever girl.' He fished in his in-tray, flourishing a piece of paper over his head. 'And what have we here? Come on, my dear, you apologise properly and you can tear it up yourself. You'll enjoy that, won't you?' He returned to his chair; his hand returned below the level of the desk. 'Now, just come round here, Sophie. So we can do this properly.'

I hesitated, but only long enough for him to produce another smile. Yes, as soon as I was his side of the desk, I could see what he wanted. What I couldn't see was any sign of a condom.

'So I get forgiven if I suck you off?' I tried to sound neutral.

'I'm sure we can find some other ways to persuade you. You do like sex, don't you, Sophie? As soon as I saw you, I knew you did. A bit of a goer, aren't you, Sophie? You like a bit of cock. And isn't that a fine upstanding bit of cock? Of course, if you were silly enough to try biting it, you'd find I'd get really angry. You'd find just how angry I can get.' He'd dropped his voice to a low monotone as he started to jerk himself off. 'There, you just kneel down there and say you're sorry.'

Tempted to rap back that I'd like to make him pee through a catheter for the rest of his life, I simply shook my head. 'That's blackmail, Professor. I'm prepared to apologise in writing or in front of witnesses but not to do that.'

'We could do something else if you prefer. You've got a lovely arse, Sophie. Made for fucking. Why don't you get those filthy trousers off and bend over for me?'

'Let me make this plain, Professor: I will not have sexual intercourse with you in any form.'

'Won't you, indeed? We'll see about that.'

My scream was genuine. He got up more quickly than I could have imagined, knocking me backwards. I could trust to the belt and the tightness of my jeans to protect me, not to mention some well-targeted kicks, till Harvinder came to the rescue, but French wasn't aiming for my crutch. He was kneeling on my arms, ready to thrust into my mouth. When I clamped my jaw, he hit me hard.

However I responded, however I fought and wriggled and kicked, I couldn't shift him. But just at the moment when he grabbed my nose, hard enough to break it, I heard the wonderful sound of the door opening.

Having had one sort of flash, I didn't expect another – this one from a camera. Evidence collected, Harv went into battle. He was hardly taller, no heavier than French – but he tore him off me and threw him across the room.

'This is what they used to call extracurricular activities, is it?' he asked, as French subsided, breathless, against a wall. 'Oh, for God's sake, sir, tidy yourself up.'

I liked the 'sir'.

'What are you doing here?' French managed.

Reasonable question. I'd have liked to phrase it differently: *What kept you so long*?

'I came to discuss a sudden death with you. But it seems we have something else to discuss instead.'

To my amazement French ignored what should have been extraordinary information. 'Come on, officer.' He addressed himself to his flies, and then struggled to his feet. 'Miss Rivers is an adult. We were merely indulging in a little adult behaviour.'

'Indeed?' The more I watched him, the more Harvinder grew in stature. 'In that case, you and Ms Rivers might prefer to talk about it separately. At Piddock Road Police Station. They have a rape suite there.'

At first, as French clutched his throat and chest, as he started to gasp, I thought he was having us on. But Harv was quicker on the ball than I was. He was summoning an ambulance even as I started to jeer, before French's knees buckled and he slumped to the floor.

'Heart attack,' Harv was saying. In a second he was on his knees, loosening French's shirt and thumping his chest. 'Sophie, help me resuscitate—'

Which is how, minutes after fighting the bastard off, minutes after clamping my jaws against him, I came to have my mouth pressed firmly against French's.

The police surgeon who insisted on examining me found it richly amusing too. Carrot-head turned out to have a name: Lynn. She told me off in the kindest terms for not cosseting myself after the shock earlier in the day, but finally admitted there wasn't a lot wrong with me that a hot chocolate and twelve hours under the duvet wouldn't put right.

'Except,' she continued, sitting on the sofa opposite the huge squishy armchair they'd offered me, 'you may well get flashbacks. Now, if you do, avail yourself of the services of Victim Support. There's some wonderful folk working for them. And if you want to talk about your more recent adventure, you know that Pam or Eileen will always be there for you.'

The women who'd stayed with me in the rape suite nodded as one. Pam was a thirty-something willowy African-Caribbean; Eileen a shorter, almost dumpy white woman, in her early forties, at a guess. Neither was in uniform.

'But it wasn't rape,' I insisted. 'At least not within the meaning of the act.'

Pam looked me straight in the eye. 'Rape isn't confined to penile penetration of the vagina, Sophie. Not as far as the victim's concerned.'

I nodded soberly.

'Now, where are you going to stay tonight?'

213

I knew what they were getting at. They didn't want me to be on my own. I wasn't exactly lying when I said, 'Over at my bloke's.' No need to tell them he was half a world away.

'We'll take you there.'

'My car?'

'One of us will drive it.'

'Yes, please,' I said simply. It would be such a relief simply to be taken and put and organised and not have to worry about anything except filling a hot-water bottle.

'Have you got anything to help you sleep?'

'I've got some homeopathic pills.' Plus, if I needed my usual insomnia therapy, Mike's sock drawer, which he'd left in chaos. Fatigue and warmth and hot chocolate and some remarkably filling fruit cake were making me drowsy. Little spurts of brain activity kept pulling me awake, however. 'Any news of Marcus French, by the way?'

'You don't want to worry about him.'

I sat up straighter. 'But I do. I don't want him to die and poor Harv take the rap for scaring him to death.'

'I don't think the DPP would give it five minutes' thought – not since you recorded everything!'

'Even so . . . But he'd have to be investigated by the Police Complaints Authority anyway, wouldn't he? Not very nice.' It would have been so easy to lapse back. 'The other thing,' I said quickly, in response to quite a sharp jab from my brain, 'is that French knew about the Soho Foundry trip. So maybe he knew about the Foundry. So maybe it was he who . . . No, that won't fadge. He was surprised as anyone when Hallam's body fell through the wall . . .'

Clearly neither woman had the faintest idea what I was talking about. I had a pretty hazy idea myself. 'Would you mind simply writing it down and passing it on to Harv?' I managed to ask. I hauled myself to my feet. Another little flash – a really irritating one. 'Would you mind, since I'm not going home, if I paged my answerphone? Just in case?' In case of what? I didn't know. Maybe I didn't even want to know, since I wanted to do it in the company of these kind women. No, when I'd skipped through Mike's messages, there was one I didn't want. A silly woman pretending to be ghoulish, laughing as if she were pretending to be Mr Rochester's mad wife. I told the machine to replay it and handed the receiver to Pam.

She looked completely blank, but I knew that laugh. It was Dawn's. Perhaps she wasn't pretending after all.

Chapter Twenty-four

'We've got to talk to her tonight, haven't we?' I said, all my years of being a personal tutor to endless vulnerable students stiffening my lip and straightening my spine.

Eileen held her hand out for the handset: 'May I?'

The machine responded to my muffed instructions by returning to the start of the recording – an especially lascivious message from Mike. I skipped it, and the next, until Dawn came on again.

While Eileen listened, Pam looked sideways at me. 'I thought you said you wanted to sleep with your bloke.'

'Said I wanted to sleep at my bloke's. His house, as opposed to mine. Quieter there, and no one would know where I was. But it sounds as if I'm not going anywhere yet, doesn't it?'

Pam and Eileen looked at each other and sat down. I sat. Or rather, my legs folded and my bum found something soft.

Eileen leant forward. 'You look too washed out to do anything except sleep for twelve hours.'

'"My word, you do look queer",' I said. Neither was old enough to recognise the line. It might even have been a bit low-brow for Peter Andrews. I grinned. 'Another slice of that cake and you won't recognise me.'

'What do you actually want to do, apart from eat cake?' Eileen asked.

'Get hold of Dawn Harper's number and phone her – find

out why she left that "message".' I inserted quotation marks with my fingers.

'Dawn Harper. Who is . . .?'

'A music student. Voice, oboe, piano. Rumoured to be . . .' I sought for a suitable expression other than the crude one which had sprung to my lips. 'They say she's sleeping with Marcus French in order to get good grades. I'd insert the words, "having to". Seen in a car with him. Seen with a pregnancy test. Boyfriend not in the picture at the moment – on tour with some show.'

'So why should she laugh like that?'

'She probably spoke to French tonight. Or vice versa. I shall be all right, honestly, when I've raised the blood-sugar levels again.'

'Do you know her number?'

'No, but I know a man who does. He won't enjoy being phoned at home at this time of night, but that's tough. He'll have access to all the UWM student records, including phone numbers. God, aren't I a fool?' My old William Murdock mate Luke Skywalker – OK, now Luke Schneider, Bursar at UWM – would have wiped my record clean as soon as blink. Well, maybe. With a bit of persuasion. But not the sort of persuasion that French had demanded. I suppressed a shudder. It was a good job my experience of oral sex with Mike had been so good that French's activities hadn't put me off for life.

'Sorry?'

'Nothing. Shall I phone him or will you?'

Luke can look so compassionate when he puts his mind to it that it's all you can do not to throw yourself into his arms and weep. Even the kindness of his voice over the phone was enough to make tears come to my eyes.

'Of course I can access UWM records from home, Sophie. No, don't apologise. I understand the situation entirely.' The part of it I'd chosen to tell him, at least. 'Poor girl. Poor little girl.' He was inordinately proud of his own daughter, and tended to imagine any crisis affecting her, not an anonymous student. 'Just give me a few minutes . . . Oh, this laptop – you have to get the screen at exactly the right angle, and when I think how much it cost UWM . . . Ah, there we are.'

My pen was poised. But he said nothing. No doubt he was tapping in passwords, scrolling down screens.

'Are you ready? Phone number? Or address?'

'Both,' I said firmly. I dreaded having to go round to her home, but if she didn't answer the phone, I'd have to, wouldn't I? However professional and compassionate Eileen and Pam were – and as far as their treatment of me was concerned, I couldn't fault them – Dawn had phoned me, not them. In the present scale of disasters, hysteria came pretty low, but there'd be dozens of police officers and – well, given the state of the health service – several medical staff dealing with higher priorities.

Just when my mind was wandering off on its own, Luke's voice started to dictate, very slowly and clearly, Dawn's details. She was sharing a house in Londonderry Lane, within easy walking distance of the uni, though far enough from Piddock Road to justify a car, at least at this time of night. Just for good measure, I got him to give me her parents' number and address.

We dialled the local one first.

It was a young man who answered the phone. From the sound of him he was stoned or drunk, so it took several minutes to elicit the information that he supposed Dawn was in but that she hadn't had no pasta, like, with the others. If I'd asked him to go and get her, he'd probably have forgotten the reason for his journey by the time he reached the top of the stairs.

There was no doubt that Pam and Eileen were intrigued and aware that their behaviour was irregular: all they were supposed to be doing was taking me safely home. The detour was unauthorised. But I said enough on the way to persuade them that Dawn was just as likely to have been a victim of sexual violence as I nearly had been – without my self-defence skills (which hadn't worked anyway) and without Harvinder's 'chance' appearance on the scene.

When we arrived at the house, a solid, Victorian semi, the door was opened by a bleary-looking young man with waxed hair and a plectrum clamped between his teeth. The smell of pot was overwhelming. In fact, the atmosphere was so thick we didn't need joints of our own. So how would the policewomen react? Reach for their cuffs or smile blissfully as they inhaled?

Dawn occupied the rear bedroom, according to plectrum teeth, who resumed his avocation as a bass guitarist as soon as we started up the stairs, playing the same chords over and over again. Presumably that was what bass guitarists did. Loudly, and at eleven o'clock at night. Poor neighbours. Poor housemates.

A jolly ceramic plaque screwed lopsidedly to the door announced that it was Dawn's Room. I tapped, and, hearing no response either way, looked from Pam to Eileen and back to the door. I opened it gently. Dawn sat in the middle of the room, huddled before an unlit gas fire. Although her clothes looked no more than damp, a dark patch on the carpet suggested they'd once been wet. Her hair had been left to dry of its own devices. There was an odd smell about the room. Not as if she'd wet herself, though that wasn't impossible, but still distinctly unsavoury.

Leaving the women on the threshold, I took quick steps towards her, and knelt beside her. 'Dawn?' I put my arm round her to shake her gently. 'It's Sophie. Can you tell me what's the matter?'

She might have been made from the mud of which she smelt.

'Come on, you'll catch your death, as my mum would have said. Let's get these wet things off you. Is there anywhere you can have a nice warm bath?'

One of the officers coughed, reprovingly. No, possible rape

220

victims couldn't have baths, could they?

I tried something less controversial. 'Up you get. Come on now.' Everything I said had this boo, boom, boo, boom accompaniment.

There was no response. Perhaps the experts should have a go. God knows I wasn't at my patient best, and something had caught my eye. On her bed lay an envelope torn open to reveal what looked like twenty-pound notes. It sat beside a teddy bear with a lopsided grin.

A movement behind me made me turn quickly. Pam had disappeared. The noise stopped abruptly. Ah. Then, even better, Pam reappeared with a mug of coffee in her hand. I'm not sure that anyone would positively have wanted to drink from it, but at least it gave Dawn something to wrap her hands round. Pam, kneeling the other side, coaxed her into an occasional sip. Eileen foraged in the detritus on the floor and came up with some dry clothes. I reached for a thin towel drooping from a chair by the window. Somehow, infinitely patient, the women coaxed her out of her clothes, into ones I warmed, old-fashioned, in front of the gas fire, which responded greedily to my coins. They stowed the clothes in a fresh bin liner they sent me to the kitchen to retrieve. It must have been about the only fresh thing there.

I was quite out of my depth. A week ago I could have dug deep, come up with resources to support her. Now I could scarcely manage to keep awake. There was no way I could question her, counsel her, whatever. What I knew I ought to do was offer to stay with her, or offer her a bed at my place. But I couldn't. Not tonight. I tried to justify myself: she needed proper support, not a knackered amateur's. But it might take hours for an emergency social worker to turn up, and my body wouldn't hang on for much longer. In any case, what could a social worker do? Locate a doctor? Find a friend to be with her? The finger was pointing at me again. I sank on to the bed, shifting irritably whatever I'd sat on. It took me a second to register that it was that envelope. A quick check told me there was upwards of four hundred pounds in it, a lot of money for a student.

Pam and Eileen withdrew to the landing for a muttered discussion. The ideas I overheard sounded remarkably like the ones I'd been having, so I wouldn't have minded joining in, but my legs refused to stand up. Not yet midnight. But it felt as if it had been a long day.

The bass guitar thudded into life again. A flurry of footsteps on the stairs, a couple of sharp words, and it stopped.

'Threatened him with Environmental Health,' Pam said tersely. 'Noise pollution,' she explained when I blinked.

Dawn hadn't uttered a word during the whole procedure. Dry at least, she collapsed on to a once-beige beanbag. She picked up her mug, and managed two or three more sips. Pam found a brush, which she applied to that mess of hair.

'I think you need to talk to someone, maybe see a doctor,' she said gently, at last. 'What do you say to that?'

Dawn nodded.

'There's a nice warm room at the police station,' Pam continued, 'where the police surgeon will check you over. Would that be all right?'

Another nod.

'And we could phone your parents—'

'No. No.'

'Maybe tomorrow when you feel better?'

She managed another nod.

The women helped her to her feet. 'OK, let's go.'

It took several moments for me to register that she meant me, too. We both let ourselves be taken, passive as the teddy bear, which Eileen gathered up too. Pam took the sack and the envelope full of notes.

To my irritation, I fell asleep in the car. A few hundred yards and I couldn't keep awake that long! A bit of rapid reshuffling at Piddock Road found me in my own car, but in the passenger seat, Pam at the wheel. We were tailed by another car, driven by goodness knows whom.

'Just take me home,' I said. 'It's closer and intruder-proof. I'll be all right there.'

'I'll come in with you, just to make sure, and then I'll stand on your doorstep till I hear you lock me out,' she said.

I didn't argue.

I wonder how they know when they've reached the North Pole. Or the South Pole, come to think of it. All that snow whirling round and they're looking for – what? A cairn, these days? Actually, as my morning brain cleared, I realised I felt more like the Pole than like an explorer. I was at the middle of a snowstorm and all around me people were looking for clues. No, that wouldn't do either, because they weren't looking for me, but for a double killer. And for who or whatever had reduced Dawn to the catatonic state she was in last night.

It was that thought that got me out of bed and into the shower. I don't have as much water pressure as Mike, so my shower's an altogether less vigorous affair. I'd have welcomed his little hot needles. Never mind, I had at least rejoined the human race, and that before eight thirty. I chalked it up as an achievement, though possibly the only one likely today. I hoped Dawn had had a similar deep sleep, wherever she might be.

I was just tossing up between toast and muesli when the phone rang. I picked up the handset, having plumped for toast. It was a woman, a WPC from Piddock Road who had, she said, taken over from Eileen and Pam. Dawn had had a bit of a nap, but wanted to talk to me as soon as she could. Before she'd even phone her mother. Would I fancy a bite of breakfast over at the station?

I didn't think I could drive anywhere till I'd eaten and, in any case, I'd back my organic wholemeal bread against their large white any day, so I merely agreed to come over in half an hour

223

or so, traffic permitting. That way I'd catch the post too – and yes, a wonderful funny, long letter from Mike. I read it and put it in the box file with the others I'd saved. One day I'd show him how good a cricket and travel writer he was, and shove him towards a new career. Even if I'd given up teaching and couldn't support him.

Dawn appeared to have spent the night on the rape suite sofa, but had more colour than last night. The new WPC – Sybil – brought us a tray of tea and coffee, and withdrew to a discreet corner.

'You mustn't let him,' Dawn said with no preamble. 'You mustn't.'

No need to ask who 'he' was and what his intentions were. 'I won't,' I said.

'But he told me what he was going to do to you. Said you'd be more fun than me. Said – he said I'd have to get a lot better if I was going to get decent grades. He told me the sort of thing he wanted me to do. He wanted – you know – up my – in my—'

I sensed rather than saw movement from Sybil. She was right – there was no point in Dawn working herself up again.

'Don't worry, Dawn. He won't be able to do any of those things to anyone else. In fact, he won't be doing that to anyone for a bit.' I explained – though not in detail – how Harvinder had interrupted French with his trousers down.

'He was trying – going to put . . . it . . . in your . . .' She shuddered, then reflected bitterly, 'Mind you, at least you don't get in the club that way.'

'He's got you pregnant?' I feigned shock and horror, as if I hadn't known about the pregnancy test. 'Didn't he use a condom?' Surely a man in his situation wouldn't have risked pregnancy or – more likely, perhaps – being infected himself. Not that I'd seen any sign of one. Perhaps he trusted my oral hygiene.

'Oh, yes. But one tore ... He's given me money for an abortion – I don't know if it'll be enough . . .' She sat back helplessly.

'Do you want an abortion?'

'Would *you* want his baby?' A spurt of anger; it seemed healthier than her previous inertia.

'In that case, I should have thought the National Health should oblige – in a situation like yours. But you must get proper counselling, straight away.'

'But what'll I do with the money? If the abortion's free? Would I have to give it back?'

I stared. 'Keep it, for God's sake.'

'But—'

'Have you any idea how much a professor earns?' When she shook her head, I told her.

'But he said that was all he could afford for the time being.'

I looked at her very hard. 'You didn't blackmail him or anything, Dawn?'

She stared at me as if I'd suggested she take up lap dancing.

'No, I'm sure you didn't. Look, love, as soon as the police have finished talking to you, you get down to your GP or the university health centre or whatever. I could drive you if you like,' I added, crossing mental fingers, 'or I'm sure one of Sybil's colleagues would.'

She nodded. So did Sybil, when I glanced at her for confirmation.

'Just tell me one thing,' I said, getting up. 'How did you get so wet last night?'

She flushed so deeply I almost apologised for causing her so much pain. But I had to know. Her soaking had clearly been what had pushed her from just managing to her present state.

'Doug,' she whispered at last.

'Doug? That's the bassoon player?'

She nodded. 'I had to tell someone, you see, and he's my bestest friend, so I told him. I went to the park and fed the

225

ducks with him and told him there. And he didn't say anything. So I asked if we were still friends, and he picked me up and threw me into the pond.'

So much for Doug the gentle giant. I'd like to talk to Doug. And, come to think of it, while I was about it, I'd like to ask him why he'd been so interested in the activities of Alex Fisher – or rather, the lack of them. It would have been odd for any student to cross-question a lecturer about another lecturer's teaching commitments. It had been even weirder for a wind player to be so interested in a string player's timetable. It seemed as if he'd been making a distinct point. Had he some complaint against Fisher? Or was he finding a way to needle Hallam? Whatever it was, now they were both dead, the little conversation had suddenly become much more interesting. As had the conversation I'd interrupted in French's room.

'S'pose I deserved it really. He and my boyfriend are mates. He wanted to know if I'd told him yet – Ross, I mean. And I said I hadn't, and that's when he threw me in. And he just walked off. You know, I just wanted to lie there. In the water. Just go to sleep.'

I took her hand and held it. 'Thank goodness you didn't. You can get over this, Dawn. And you will. There'll be plenty of people ready and willing to help you. Let them.'

She picked up her teddy bear. Poor kid. But if I cried for my own past, that wouldn't help her, would it?

'Those women last night . . . they were policewomen?'

'Plain-clothes officers. Like Sybil. They showed you their IDs, love, and said who they were,' I added for the record.

'I wasn't taking much in, was I? But they were so kind. Even when I said I was pregnant they were kind. Even when I said he hadn't exactly raped, but . . . I didn't think you were supposed to have sex if you were pregnant?'

'You're not supposed to have sex *ever* if you don't want to. Did you want to have it with French?'

'Of course I didn't!'

226

I glanced at Sybil. I didn't want to muddy any evidence she might have to give in court. My knowledge of the law being very hazy, I'd no idea whether what French had done constituted rape, but he'd certainly blackmailed her. And how many others?

Suddenly Dawn's lips quivered and she started to weep into the bear. 'I want my mum,' she sobbed.

Back in the car, I buried my head in my hands. If only I hadn't been so prejudiced against Rose, if only I'd talked properly to Dawn earlier instead of constituting myself a mini detective, how much suffering I could have spared Dawn, other women – and, indeed, myself.

Chapter Twenty-five

What I'd do now, where I'd go, I'd no idea. Funny, I'd almost have welcomed having to take Dawn back to her room, as her mother no doubt would, and giving it the spring-clean of its life. OK, it wasn't spring, but a lull in the wind and a no doubt temporary break in the rain had left the weather mild and invigorating.

UWM held no appeal at all today. It would no doubt be swarming with police personnel entitled to do the sort of sniffing round I'd been doing as an amateur. What about a day of doing nice normal things at home? I could clean the car, maybe do some light autumn pruning; the gales must have shaken my poor shrubs and bushes to the tips of their roots. Then I could clean the kitchen floor, with which I had a love-hate relationship: it showed every splash and stain but came up beautifully when mopped. There. A nice, low-profile, thera-peutic day in view. I started the car, changed from some etiolated Radio Three countertenor strangulating Dowland to 'Sempre libera' on Classic FM and headed for Harborne.

I was so intent on pursuing my domestic plans that I half resolved to ignore the red light of my answerphone. But of course there'd probably be a message from Mike. There was: a gorgeous soppy one, topping up my energy reserves as if I'd never felt low and lifeless. But there was another. From DCI Minett. Would I favour him with a call, at a convenient moment?

Just now, I couldn't see a convenient moment. There were a muddy car out there, a border full of battered roses, and a lavatera tossed like a South Seas clipper every time the wind blew.

I supposed I could always put the Mazda through a car wash. And it wouldn't hurt to leave the garden till it had dried out a bit more.

In the end, I compromised. I dealt a few savage chops to the lavatera, disposing of the leaves in the compost bin (the branches chopped small in the dustbin) cleaned the long-handled secateurs, locked them and the gardening gauntlets in the shed, made myself a cup of tea and then, after I'd put a load into the washing machine, which I should have done before I started everything else, I found a convenient moment. I didn't realise how badly I'd been neglecting domestic trivia recently. Later I could have an evening ironing in front of the TV. Yes, and a glass of wine to help. No bodies, dead or alive, to worry about.

The phone rang.

'Ms Rivers? DCI Minett, here.'

'Hello,' I greeted him brightly. 'I was just going to phone you. I've just picked up your message.'

'It's taken you long enough,' he said, 'seeing that you left Smethwick a good two hours ago.'

So we didn't get off to the best of starts. I was so angry with myself for feeling guilty – damn it, answerphones were designed to enable people to return calls when they wanted, and who was he, in any case, to behave as if he had some authority over me? – that I nearly snarled. Apologise I would not.

'How can I help you?' I cooed, saccharine replacing the acid I wanted to use.

There was a pause, perhaps while he reassembled the things he'd wanted to say before I'd wrong-footed him. At last he said, 'It would be helpful if we could go over the recent events with you.'

'Of course. Any in particular?'

'There's no need to be facetious, Ms Rivers. I'll be round in half an hour, if that's OK. You won't be going anywhere, I presume?'

'Not now I know I have a visitor. Unless I can nip out for some milk. Mine's gone off. The corner shop's less than five minutes away.' To be honest, I didn't know why I wanted to wind him up. Or did I? Wasn't it to disengage myself from the whole thing? Weren't my efforts in house and garden simply displacement activities? Didn't I simply want to throw everything in the air and go and join Mike? Not that I'd have been especially welcome out in Pakistan at the moment – a possible distraction when the last thing the team needed was distracting. And I had to remind myself of other wives, most of them younger than I, many with tiny children, who were dealing with their loved ones' absence with a calm and equanimity that belied their years. There was always the grim chance that the police might not let me go, either. I added, before Minett could speak, 'I'll be back well before you can get here. And I'll have the kettle boiled waiting for you.' Or did that sound like grovelling appeasement?

'I'll be with you at twelve thirty,' he said, unappeased even if it did.

I was pottering round the kitchen when the doorbell rang, thirty minutes almost to the second after Minett had put the phone down. None the less I checked the spyhole before I opened the door: I was in that jumpy sort of mood. He'd brought with him an African-Caribbean officer who looked startlingly like Viv Richards, the great West Indian batsman, in his handsome heyday. Sergeant Ellis. Like a Spanish hidalgo's, his features were as straight and sleek as Minett's were crumpled and battered.

I showed them both into the living room, offered tea or coffee, both of which were declined, and sat down opposite them. I'd spent so many hours of my life talking to the police recently, I really wasn't sure why Minett should be here at all.

'Is it true you've not yet made a statement?' he began.

I must have looked as gormless as I felt. 'I seemed to spend yesterday afternoon and evening doing nothing else,' I said. 'Fisher's body, the attempted rape . . .' I enumerated on my hand.

'But not, with due respect, Ms Rivers, the murder on Saturday. Goodness knows how it came to be overlooked.'

'I spoke at great length, albeit informally, to Chris Groom on Sunday. And to DS Mann. In any case, I should imagine you and your colleagues had quite a lot of statements to take, and they probably wouldn't be materially different from mine, any of them.'

'Possibly not. But Superintendent Groom said . . .' He coughed, consulting his notes with apparent disbelief and disdain, a gesture I didn't credit for one moment, 'there was something you had to creep up on.'

So there was! The group that invaded the bar. The woman with the high colour, several other women, indeterminate. There must have been some men. I closed my eyes. Were there any men?

I shook my head with embarrassment. 'You don't need to tell me how important this is. Someone in that group almost certainly registered that there was protective clothing within reach. He or she must have gone back to pick it up, and put it on to – to kill . . .' I allowed my mind to shoot off at a tangent. 'But why should James Hallam have stood still while his murderer got dressed up?'

Minett managed a bleak smile, crumpling his features even further. 'The post mortem came up with some interesting facts, Ms Rivers.'

'Don't tell me: you can't say what they are. But let me think.' If I wanted to get the body undetected to the bar, let alone up behind the false wall, I'd have to be very strong or very cunning. I'd try to get the body down while it was still alive and walking. To do that, I'd have to persuade it that it was in its interests to walk. 'I suppose there isn't a small knife wound to the throat?' I asked. 'Hallam's throat?'

Hole, as Gavin would no doubt say, in one. 'Why would you ask that?'

'Because –' I got up and walked behind Minett – 'that's how you'd have got Hallam to go down into the bar. By holding a knife to his throat.' I demonstrated with my index finger, to Minett's alarm and the ill-suppressed amusement of Ellis. 'Right?' I returned to my seat. 'I bet you've got other evidence to back it too.'

'I told you before: if you want confidential information, ask your friend the Super, not me,' Minett said.

I returned to my chair. 'Four or five women. One of them very tall, but she was in the middle of the group. And two or three men. One not very tall. Could have been Marcus French.' I sat down with my eyes shut.

When I opened them, both men were staring at me.

'The group that came into the bar,' I said. 'Sorry, that's how it comes to me. When I'm thinking about something else. There were no *young* men. Except I think, now I come to think about it, that there might have been a security guard. But he couldn't have been there more than a second because if he had I'd have buttonholed him and got him to lock the bar. Neil Wiltshire, the music student who's disappeared, certainly wasn't there. One person who doesn't seem to have been is a woman called Rose Dungate, though I know she was in the building somewhere. June Tams—'

'She plays in that quartet, doesn't she?' Ellis checked.

'Right. June told her not to come down, at least after the concert ... I'm sorry. This is of far more concern to me than to you.' I explained about her crushes: Fisher and Hallam last year; me this. 'But I couldn't swear that she was anywhere other than the auditorium, where she was supposed to be.'

'What's she like, this Rose woman?'

'Tall as your sergeant. Strongly built. Plays the double bass.'
The officers exchanged glances.

'Was she the tall woman in the group that came down?'
I pressed my fingers to my temples. 'Surely I'd have recognised her!'

'I'm surprised you can't be more definite, I must say,' Minett observed sourly.

'I was concentrating on preparations for the buffet. Really hard. Catering for a do that size you get something like first-night nerves – you have to exclude everything else or panic. I only really registered one woman, the one whom the paramedics had to treat on Saturday. Presumably they'd have kept a record of her name and address. Routine, I'd have thought.'

'It is. But it seems when the call went out for emergency action upstairs to assist Peter Andrews, whoever was responsible for keeping the notes put them down. And they'd gone when they phoned my officers to pick them up.'

'Of course,' Sergeant Ellis put in, his voice remarkably light and high for a man of his build, 'there may be nothing sinister in that. The patient herself could have seen them there and picked them up.'

'You've asked her?'
Minett pulled a face. 'She never went back up to the Lyttelton Theatre, did she? She just bunked straight off home.'

'Come on, the place was alive with policemen. How did she get away with that? Oh,' I said, to spare him corporate embarrassment, as it were, 'she'd just toddle off and when she was challenged she'd say the police had already spoken to her.'

'Which we had, of course. But not to recover the details.

And the paramedics, for God's sake, have forgotten them! There might not be anything sinister in this, of course. She might just have wanted to go home and not realised the significance of what she was doing.'

I pulled a face. 'A guest. She'd be on the guest list, maybe. But you must have been able to talk to other punters – got some idea of who went downstairs before the concert.'

'The trouble is, no one's very definite.'

'No reason why the high blood pressure patient should be either,' added Ellis. 'It's just that it would be nice to tie up the loose end. You mentioned a guest list, Ms Rivers. Any idea if there was one, and where we'd find it?'

'Easy. The music department secretary. I can't remember her name off hand, but I've got to soon – I still haven't invoiced the Department for Saturday yet.' I clicked my fingers in irritation. God, another sign of getting old! Forgetting names! 'Jean. Jean Ford. She doubles as French's secretary. I wonder how much she knows about his extramural activities. How is he, by the way?'

'Still in hospital.'

'For quite some time, one trusts? Until he's really well? Until he's well enough to stand trial?'

'You know they try to get folk out of hospital as fast as they can these days. Throughput or something. But he's one scared man, that prof – that's what they said at this morning's briefing.'

'Scared of whom? One of the students?'

Minett fidgeted. 'I do wish you wouldn't ask us these questions, miss. You know we can't tell you the answers.' Then he grinned. 'To be honest, he won't tell us. Not even the sex of the person concerned. Which isn't a lot of help if you're trying to protect him.'

'What a stupid bugger,' I agreed. 'So we're all hunting for a student – male or female, but reading between the lines someone with height and muscle. And a grudge against French.'

'So – assuming that's the case – how wide would you say the field was?'

I shrugged. 'I'd like you to zap out and arrest Rose! But I don't think she's ever favoured him with her adulation. Except she got murderously angry when she saw me coming out of his room.'

Ellis leant forward, linking his fingers loosely between his knees. 'What about big men, Sophie?'

'I can't think of any.' Nor could I. My mind emptied completely.

'Dan Langley. How would you see him?'

'Why?'

'We ask the questions, remember, Sophie,' Minett reminded me, without rancour.

I pulled a face. 'I see him as a lovely young man with some problems caused by other people's racist attitudes.'

'You mean he's got a chip on his shoulder?' Minett asked.

Ellis didn't so much as blink.

'I meant exactly what I said. I find him charming.'

Minett didn't quite sniff his disagreement but might just as well have done. My God, had Dan somehow put himself in the frame? Or had Minett trodden on sensitive corns? Perhaps a word with his boss . . .

Goodness, I had been letting things slip, hadn't I? 'Who's the DCI in charge of your team, by the way? Anyone I know?' But I knew the answer would be negative. Any of my old mates would have been in personal touch, wouldn't they?

'DCI Betts. Not long down from Manchester,' Minett said. He managed a crooked grin – well, it would have been hard for him to manage any other sort. 'Which is how I managed to wangle my way into his team: needed someone with local knowledge. Same as your Harvinder Singh Mann. Who *isn't* going to be suspended pending a complaint from our friend French.'

'My God, if they suspended him I'd be out there banging on

the Home Secretary's door. His intervention saved me from a very unpleasant experience. I'm very grateful to him, very grateful indeed.'

I might have said it before, but not to these two. They seemed to have registered quite early on that I might be on the side of the angels. This would be some sort of confirmation. And it had the enormous bonus of being true.

'Well, that's what friends are for, isn't it?' Ellis smiled. 'To be there for one another.'

No wool pulled over his eyes then.

'What's this Betts like?' I asked, as an off-hand non-sequitur.

The folds deepened round Minett's eyes, which I took as a sign of interested amusement. 'You're not going to try to tell him how to run his inquiry, are you? The word in Lloyd House is that's what you did when Chris Groom was a DCI.'

'Can you imagine *anyone* telling Chris Groom how to run an inquiry? Well then.'

'I can imagine you trying. And I can imagine him listening. Why do you want to know about Betts?'

'I'm at a loose end this afternoon. I was going to take Peter Andrews some flowers, if he's up to visitors, that is. Betts permitting, too.'

'He's not been able to remember anything of the assault on him,' Minett said obliquely. 'Of course, a different visitor might just – help jog his memory. The medics'll only let you stay five minutes, though.'

'Five minutes is more than adequate to hand over a bunch of flowers. After all,' I added innocently, 'I may have no longer than that. It depends how long it takes you to write down my statement.'

I found somewhere to park at the Queen Elizabeth Hospital and battled my way against the latest squalls of rain. If only I'd spent longer on the garden this morning. If it continued to rain like this, both lawns, Mike's and mine, would become quagmires, and I'd be able to do nothing till the spring – by which time I'd be in Sri Lanka. And by which time, now I came to think of it, we might be together in one house, with a quite different garden to worry about. Rather than pruning things that would be staying, I ought to be potting up the shrubs and plants I wanted to take with me. As far as the house went, I'd better get on with some book-sorting. It was easier to get rid of no-longer-precious books in small doses to Oxfam and Harborne High Street now boasted not simply the famous Marks and Sparks Food Hall but also a specialist Oxfam bookshop. The trouble was that as I took a bagful in, I tended to come across other books I couldn't possibly do without, leaving with at least as many as I'd got rid of. I wondered, as I tried to protect from the worst of the gusts the flowers I'd brought with me, how soon Peter would be up to reading. I had some vague but probably erroneous suspicion that reading was bad for you if you'd been concussed.

I found him in a side ward, eyes closed, apparently listening to a portable CD player or possibly asleep. The WPC at his bedside was halfway through the *Guardian* crossword, her dark hair slipping from its knot where she'd scratched her head with her pencil. When I coughed gently both looked up.

'"Sohrab and Rustum", I think,' Peter murmured. 'But my memory's so foggy at the moment . . . Matthew Arnold,' he added. 'These headaches, Sophie.'

Under the swathes of bandage, he didn't look good. I leant across the bed to kiss his cheek.

'They're still monitoring me for blood clots,' he said. 'With my blessing. I'd hate to end up paralysed or whatever. But they say every hour without one is more than an hour further into the clear, so I let them watch while I wait.'

'I'll go and see if I can find something for those flowers,' the WPC said, pink-tinged about the cheeks, passing me her chair.

'That would be more than kind, Tessa,' Peter said. He smiled at her, managing what looked like a conspiratorial wink. 'I thought I heard Dr Hale's voice a minute ago.' He waited till she'd gone. 'I hope he knows as much about female hearts as he does about male brains. Talk about head over heels . . .' He seemed to make an effort, which was the last thing he was in all probability supposed to do. But then he subsided and allowed his eyes to droop again. 'I sent my wife home,' he said. 'Poor Helen, she's worn out. And now Rod's gone down with glandular fever – his first term at Stirling. The fees . . . Not to mention the train fare. And a whole term wasted. Maybe more.' His eyes opened again. 'Your dissertation . . .?'

'In abeyance for a couple of days. All this has been a bit of a shock, Peter.'

His CD player started to slip. I made a successful grab for it.

To my surprise he sniffed. 'Nice perfume, Sophie. It might be true what they say about losing your sight. That your other senses go into overdrive to compensate.'

'But your eyes—' My God, had his assailant blinded him?

'Just more comfortable to keep them shut, that's all. Nothing to worry about, they say.'

'Thank heaven for that!'

He continued, 'I've never gone in for differentiating between perfumes till now. But young Tessa wore something that made me feel instantly ill. In contrast with Helen, who wears, she tells me, some aromatherapy stuff with lavender. And Rod's girlfriend – now hers is more like yours.'

'It sounds as if you've been well off for visitors.' I felt embarrassed. We hardly knew each other but he seemed to be getting remarkably free with confidences.

'So what's your perfume called? I could get some for Tessa

239

when we part company. Much nicer than today's, though she assures me it costs an arm and a leg, even in airport shops.'

'Mine's made by Lancôme. Ô,' I said, trying to make my lips form the right French vowel, but unsure about the precise influence of the circumflex accent.

'Eau? Water?'

'Just the letter Ô. With a circumflex.'

'Let me smell it again.'

I put a wrist near his nose. Ô was Mike's favourite, a light perfume, best for summer, perhaps. But I tended to wear it all the time now.

Peter reached for my hand and gripped it. 'I think you should call Tessa,' he said. 'I've just remembered something the police should know. And,' he added, 'maybe you should call the doctor too. The pains in my head . . .'

A false alarm, insisted the doctor, stepping back into the corridor where I was waiting with Tessa. He was so blue-eyed and tanned and Australian that he might have stepped straight off a soap-opera set. What surprised me was that he was not only in a prosaic Birmingham hospital, but that he seemed to consider himself available to patients. My limited experience of such situations was that if you were particularly lucky you might after several minutes' agonised hunt run down a trainee nurse already doing two other jobs. Maybe he was available to this particular patient because of the pretty girl guarding him.

'That's what you get with concussion,' he said. 'And if someone's never been prone to headaches, well, it comes as a surprise. But maybe you'd better let him have a bit of a kip.'

'Can I just say goodbye?'

'Why not?' He turned to the WPC, looking as wrapped up in her as she was in him.

So I tiptoed back in, taking Peter's hand gently.

'Sorry about the panic,' he murmured.

'No problem. What did my perfume make you remember?' I knew he'd have to tell Tessa, but there was no reason why I shouldn't know too.

'Did I want to tell her something?'

'Hmm. Just before I called that doctor. Something my perfume reminded you of.'

But he was already drowsing into sleep.

Chapter Twenty-six

'Perfume or aftershave?' I wondered aloud to Tessa, while inside the ward a nurse – yes, a real nurse, dragon tattoos undulating down his forearms – checked Peter's vital signs again. 'Whichever it was, it smelt like my perfume.'

'It isn't very strong,' she observed, somewhat disparagingly, I thought. Well, if she liked the big musky breed, she wouldn't like this light floral fragrance, would she?

'Hmm. It wouldn't be a very manly aftershave, would it?'

She scratched her scalp, a little more hair detaching itself from the bun. 'Why is it so significant anyway?'

And yet she could tackle *Guardian* crosswords . . .

'Because Peter associates it with his bang on the head. So there's a chance the assailant was wearing it,' I said patiently – or patronisingly, from the look on her face. Bother. I hadn't meant to irritate her.

The nurse emerged. 'He's fine. But I think you should let him have a bit of peace and quiet.'

'I've just said goodbye,' I said. 'See you, Tessa.'

It was only as I headed down the stairs that I realised that I'd seen nothing of the flowers since she headed off with them looking for a vase. Love!

Almost without my turning the wheel, the little Mazda headed off towards the city centre. What I could do was nip into the big Boots or Rackhams and go round trying perfumes and aftershaves like my Ô. I tried my usual parking places, but eventually had to settle for a slot down Newhall Street. My route to the centre took me not very far from Margaret Street and the BMI. Just as my car had brought me into town, so my feet organised the diversion. I don't know what I hoped for – another poke round the BMI would obviously be out of the question, since the police would almost certainly still be *in situ*, and if they weren't, then anything of interest would have gone anyway.

Not that I even knew what was interesting.

The Victorian buildings seemed almost as vicious at funnelling wind as high-rise ones are known to be. Putting my head down and slinging my bag over my head and shoulder like a schoolgirl's satchel so I had hands free to hold my skirt down and my collar together, I charged into the mini canyon of Margaret Street. And, quite by chance, into Harvinder, as he left the BMI, stepping on to the pavement without really looking. We steadied each other, laughter replacing any snarls as we recognised each other. But then his eyes narrowed in official-looking suspicion.

'I'm on the skive,' I announced, before he could embarrass us both by starting to cross-question me. 'A bit of Christmas shopping, before everyone else starts.'

'Don't you believe it,' he said, drawing me quickly into the shelter of the BMI doorway. 'Cards, lights everywhere. As for trees, I saw my first late September. At least Hindus don't start celebrating Diwali so far ahead.'

'There must be less money in it,' I suggested, 'for the bloated capitalists who've made Christmas so bloody commercial. At least,' I conceded, 'our city fathers seem to have one thing right: the Diwali lights metamorphose nicely into our Christmas ones.'

'I wonder,' he responded, 'if we could persuade Jews to celebrate Hanukkah and Muslims Eid with lights – then we could be totally economical.'

'And indeed ecumenical,' I concluded. 'Peter Andrews said something half-interesting when I took him some flowers,' I added, with a conversational scrape of gears. 'Do you suppose DCI Betts would be interested? Something's reminded him of the assault. The WPC guarding him didn't seem overly impressed, mind you, so perhaps—'

Looking positively shifty, he stepped back into the street. 'Have you got time for a coffee somewhere?'

I pointed to the Museum and Art Gallery. 'There's the Edwardian Tea Room in there.'

If anything the wind was worse as we turned towards Chamberlain Square, and we were swirled up the Art Gallery steps. The effort of closing the heavy doors behind us was more than repaid by the stillness within the entrance hall, our footsteps loud against the stone stairway – but then they were completely drowned by a tidal wave of primary-school children sweeping towards us. Withstanding the buffets, we dived through the souvenir shop into the calm of the industrial gallery and thence into the tea room. There'd been yet another reorganisation of the servery and tills, but at last we lodged ourselves in a quiet corner and I could look interrogatively at Harvinder.

'Not like you to want to keep information to yourself,' I observed, stirring a calorie-laden but comforting hot chocolate.

'Who said I did?'

'Look, Harv, we've been friends for ages now. I know when something's wrong. These last couple of weeks you haven't been yourself. Do you want to tell me what's up?'

'Nothing's up.'

I favoured him with the direct, eyebrows raised stare I'd used with great success with my students when I wanted to query what they were saying and encourage them to tell the truth. It went with a half-conspiratorial little grin, the head slightly to one side.

He dropped his eyes and jiggled his tea bag. 'I don't know what you're on about.'

'How's Inderjit?' I tried.

'Fine. Well, he's got a bit of colic. Or it's maybe his teeth coming.'

'Not much sleep?'

'What's sleep?'

Ah! 'It's what "knits up the ravel'd sleeve of care".' I raised a chocolaty cup to Peter Andrews.

'I wouldn't know. I'm sorry, Sophie. I really am so bloody tired. But don't let on to anyone, repeat, *anyone*, will you?'

I shook my head.

'So what's this about the assault?' he continued.

'So little it's hardly worth mentioning, perhaps. Except you told me to give you information and let you make the decisions. I wear a brand of perfume that reminds Peter of a smell around the time of the assault.'

'So find the perfume, find the assailant.'

'Except in the first instant it'd point the finger at me.'

'Find a *matching* perfume, find the assailant.'

'Possibly. To be honest—'

'About time!'

'I was just off to Rackhams hunting for a match – preferably a male match.'

'Spray your wrist and sniff?'

'Hmm.'

'Wouldn't work. Scents smell different on different skins.'

'Back to square one! I'll just go and get some Christmas presents, then.'

'Maybe not square one. When we get to the search-warrant stage we'll check for perfume. Or aftershave.'

'Was that an afterthought?'

'No.'

'So you're not looking for a woman?'

'She'd have to be a very strong woman, wouldn't she? Oh, we're just going round in circles, Sophie, though I'd not say that within earshot of anyone in the service. It'd be a capital offence.'

'Nothing to pin it on Marcus French?'

'No, more's the pity. It'd be good to see him sent down for a nice long time, wouldn't it?'

'It'd certainly improve the quality of prison music! Nothing to point the finger at anyone?'

He poured himself a second cup of tea, the pot dribbling in his saucer. I waited while he added milk and stirred. 'I really dare not say anything. Except that we're looking for someone strong.'

I bit the bullet. 'In the interests of my own safety, I'm going to ask you something. And you may have to ask your DCI Betts for an answer, so I'll put it very formally. Rose Dungate—'

'The one with the crush on you,' he observed. 'And she plays the double bass – is that it? – and is what you might call a strapping wench.'

'Spot on. You'll have heard from other witnesses that she also had a crush on Hallam at one time. And one on Fisher. Both of whom are dead.'

'So you want to know if you're likely to end up dead?'

'Quite.'

'I'll talk formally to Betts. It seems to me,' he continued, sounding more like Chris Groom with every syllable, 'that you've got a legitimate question here, which the police should answer.'

'Thanks, Detective Sergeant Mann.' We grinned at each other. As I got up to go, I thought of something else. 'For sleeping, there are always earplugs, so you and your wife could take it in turns to deal with Inderjit. And I've got some wonderful homeopathic sleeping tablets.'

'Would they really help?'

I sat down again. 'Better than lying awake all hours when the baby's fast asleep.'

He nodded.

'I always choose three o'clock for the best of my worry sessions,' I said. 'I can get really worked up over trivial things. Or, of course,' I added more soberly, 'serious ones.'

He leant across and squeezed my hand. 'You're a nice woman, Sophie. Maybe getting some more sleep would help.'

'If it doesn't, you know where I am. Now, is Inderjit celebrating Christmas, because Auntie Christmas wants to know...'

The shops were already so brash with decorations I wanted to turn tail and run. A glance at my watch told me that that was what my parking meter would soon demand anyway. A House of Fraser teddy bear – reduced if you spent sufficient in the store – reminded me of Dawn's bear, and Dawn, of course. She'd been through so much and had still more to endure. On impulse, I bought some perfume for her, and a bargain bear, which looked reproachful when the assistant told me how cheap he was. Even if her mother had already taken her back to wherever home was – somewhere you could sell antique prints from, presumably – Pam and Eileen would know where to find her and would forward the gifts. But it would be nice to hand them over myself, and to reassure her that her friends would still love and care for her whatever had happened in French's room. A quick call established she was still in Smethwick, still, as it happened, in her digs. Her mother had decided to wait till the rush hour was over before tackling the drive home.

Traffic was already snarling up as I set off for Smethwick, but I got there without incident, and parked right outside Dawn's house.

Dawn, clean and well scrubbed, with shining hair tied neatly back, opened the door herself. Tears were obviously not far away, though, so I reached up and hugged her.

If Dawn looked better, her room had undergone a miracle transformation, a variety of conflicting smells and a heap of dusters testifying to Mrs Harper's activities. She stripped off rubber gloves and turned to me smiling, a woman not much older than me with well-cut Titian hair and the sort of face that looked good even without make-up. With, her eyes and cheekbones would have been lovely.

'I want it nice for her to come back to,' she said. 'The doctor says she'll soon be able to. She'll have the – the op. as soon as possible. In the meantime, she'll come home with me – her dad'll want to spoil her a bit. And as soon as she's well, she can get on with her course. When she's good and ready.'

I had an idea that termination procedures were so efficient these days that some women actually had the operation at lunchtime and were able to complete their day's work. But Mrs Harper was right about the spoiling part, at least.

'At least she won't have to face French about the uni when she does return,' I pointed out. 'With a bit of luck,' I added, smiling at Dawn, 'you won't have to see him again till he's between two big security guards in the dock. Your chance to put him behind bars.'

She bit her lip. 'Won't it be scary? Court?'

I thought it would be terrifying, particularly if French's counsel were allowed free rein, but said bracingly, 'With Pam and Eileen behind you, not to mention your family and friends, you can do *any*thing, Dawn. And I'll be there giving evidence too, remember. And some of your mates.'

Not surprisingly – Dawn was no fool, after all – she didn't look impressed.

I sat on the bed, stripped down to mattress cover and bare pillows and duvet. Black sacks bulged behind the door. But Mrs Harper couldn't have had a clear run. In one corner was a card table with a little piece of machinery on it – a miniature version of the sort of thing an ironmonger copies your keys on, a pile of thin bamboo slivers and a Stanley knife.

'I didn't know you made your own reeds,' I said. In fact, I rather thought she didn't. My late bassoonist friend had always made his own, rather despising those who couldn't.

'I've just started,' she said, picking up a couple and comparing them. 'After French said I should work for a recital, Doug said I should make sure my reeds were consistent.'

'So you actually went and bought one of these machines?' I asked, trying to sound ingenuous, but probably failing. After all, I knew that George had paid a great deal for his, and that was years ago, when he wasn't a penniless student but an orchestral principal.

She shook her head. 'Oh, no. I borrowed it. All I had to buy were the uncut reeds and the knife.'

My brain was spurting off in so many directions I didn't know how to control it. I took a deep breath. Dawn was the most important person right now: I must address myself to her problems, and to do that I must unfortunately draw her attention to them.

'I suppose you haven't remembered anything else about the BMI concert, have you? Like who else was there?'

Her eyes filled with tears. 'I thought you were my friend!'

'Of course I am! What's—'

'The police!' She swallowed. 'They've been on and on at us all about alibis and things.'

Mrs Harper moved protectively towards her. Any moment she'd cease to be a polite and grateful acquaintance and become a fierce mother telling me to get out.

'It's just that it's important you tell them about buying a craft knife, Dawn. They're out there grasping at every clue. No matter how innocent that purchase was, you must tell them before they find out.'

'But they said Hallam had a kitchen knife sticking out of his back! And no, I was at the far side of the bar and I didn't see it!'

I passed her some tissues from my bag. 'I'm so glad you didn't. You've been through more than enough recently.' From the tail of my eye I could see Mrs Harper's hackles subsiding.

They might go up again any minute now, however. 'But you know that someone else has died.'

Her eyes widened.

'They probably didn't want to tell you when you were so upset. But they've found another body.' I'd better be careful. I didn't want to muddy police waters. But surely it would be all over the papers by now? 'Knife wounds,' I added. 'And I've no idea what sort of knife.'

She went so pale both her mother and I started forward. 'Not Neil? Oh, don't say it was Neil!'

Neil the victim or Neil the perpetrator? 'It wasn't Neil's body,' I said carefully, getting to my feet. Casually strolling over to the table, I touched the machine. 'Someone must care for you a great deal to lend you this.'

'Oh, that's just Doug. Doug Leigh. You know, my bestest friend.'

'Lovely lad,' I said to Mrs Harper, over my shoulder. *Apart from his habit of dunking his friends in ponds.*

'She'll need her friends when – when she's through all this.'

'There are some smashing kids at UWM,' I said, telling her what she no doubt wanted to hear. I turned back to Dawn. 'Did you manage to fix up some sessions with Leonore?'

She shrugged pettishly. 'I tried yesterday. But she and Dan were all over each other. If you want one you get both.'

'How were they? I ought to have phoned but . . .' But I'd been busy, hadn't I?

'They said the police had given Dan a bad time – racist pigs!'

I didn't point out that the same racist pigs had treated her as tenderly as if she'd been their daughter. But clearly Dan and Minett hadn't exactly become bosom buddies. I hoped for the sake of the service – and for the rest of us! – that Minett had been stroppy not because of racism but because they were looking for a big killer. And Dan, incontrovertibly, was big, and, just as much to the point, had been at the BMI. Moreover, and now I too must have gone pale, as a Black Country lad he might even know about Soho Foundry and its cellars. As we'd seen, a few locked doors were no bar to access.

But I didn't want Dan to be a murderer. I didn't want him harried by interrogators till he said something stupid. I liked him. I wanted him to sing at Symphony Hall, at Glyndebourne, at the Sydney Opera House, at the Met. I wanted him to take that lovely Dudley voice all over the world. So I'd better get round to proving him innocent. Even if that meant proving someone else was a cold-blooded killer.

I suppose that was what I'd wanted to do all along.

Chapter Twenty-seven

If only I had a police ear to bend. And an officer willing to share information with me, of course. While I could see a number of my young acquaintances in the frame, the official investigation might well have eliminated them entirely, and be ready with quite another suspect. It wasn't fair to pump Harvinder further, I couldn't see Minett or Ellis ready to spill any unprofessional beans; and I'd never even met Betts.

It would have to be Chris Groom, wouldn't it? I'd have to swallow pride and principle, and see how far I could presume on our long friendship without risking his new relationship or my new marriage. If I could offer him something he'd not come across, it would be a nice gesture – in this case, some hard facts which I could access as easily as his team, but which they might not have thought about. I turned the car for UWM's Oldbury campus, stopping only long enough to phone Luke Schneider to warn him I was on my way.

'Student records?' he greeted me in the foyer, as I shook my umbrella. 'I don't like it, Sophie, though I know you're as honest as the day is long and as silent as the grave.'

I wrinkled my nose at his clichés, as he'd known, probably hoped, I would. 'It's not as if I want contemporary information – not yet, at least,' I conceded. 'And if anything might stop these appalling killings, isn't it our duty to look at them?'

He hitched his shoulders in a huge, self-parodying shrug. 'So what do you want?'

'For a start, their UCAS forms – I want to look at the personal statement supporting their application. That's all.' UCAS was the central clearing system for all kids wanting to go on to university. The applicant completed part of a composite form, the school completed the rest, and the whole lot was sent off with a large cheque. UCAS photocopied the forms and distributed them to the university admissions tutors on the students' wish lists.

Luke looked at his watch. 'I don't have a problem with that. But others might. Why don't we have a bite to eat while everyone goes home? The canteen over here isn't as good as the Smethwick one, but they do a decent salad . . .'

No lunch told me I couldn't resist.

So what with food and family gossip, it was another forty minutes before he unlocked the storeroom and then the filing cabinets where the application forms were kept. They were photocopied and reduced by UCAS before they were sent out, so the piles weren't as immense as you'd expect. UWM's admission tutors would have made their decisions on the basis of the teachers' confidential references and on the students' personal statements. These days more and more universities were simply making standard (and often very high) grade offers, relying less on personal information. But the students still went through the hoop of writing about themselves and their interests and ambitions. As Luke thumbed through, I could see lengthy handwritten screeds alongside terse computer-generated affairs with bold headings and bullet points. Dan, Neil, Rose and Doug – they were the ones I wanted: Dan because I wanted so much for him to be innocent – though I could see he had the opportunity, if no clear motive; Neil because I wanted any hint as to what might have happened to him; Rose because of her past involvement with the two men. And Doug because one lunchtime – it seemed weeks ago – he'd asked a very pertinent question about the absent Fisher's teaching commitments, because as a reed-maker he'd need to use a sharp knife accurately and – last but not least – he'd baptised poor Dawn. But his anger about her pregnancy would surely have been directed against French. I'd interrupted which was at least a loud discussion, after all. Did he have some sort of logic? That if French saw his colleagues dropping like flies, he'd get more and more terrified? Perhaps the ruin of the Boultons' concert was a threat in itself – or simply a desire to humiliate French, as head of faculty. There – another reason to phone Chris later, to make sure French had protection, louse though he was. After all, I didn't want an untimely second heart attack to prevent him hearing the nastiness of his university sex life being exposed to the world. What I couldn't work out was why the women – I presumed it was more than poor Dawn – had succumbed. What had happened to self-esteem? Still, with no grants, tuition fees to pay, and an uncertain profession ahead of you, there must be temptations to short-cut your way to good grades and perhaps good contacts that I'd simply never imagined.

'Why do you suppose there's anything at all relevant here?' Luke asked, as if, files in hand, he'd had another spasm of anxiety about revealing anything.

'Because kids put down all sorts of things in their personal statement designed to impress. There's quite an art in getting them to put the right things. I had no end of a job trying to dissuade one lass from writing about her passion for Gérard Dépardieu, and then there was another who thought that reading "books, not too hard", might curry favour. There was another I censored, because it used the F word in connection with someone of the same sex.'

'You'd have let it through if had been heterosexual sex?' Luke found a table for the file, opening it and riffling through it for the ones I wanted. 'What little hobbies can possibly incriminate them?'

I shook my head. 'Goodness knows. Nothing, with a bit of luck. I'd much rather the killer were some crazed guy off the street than someone I know. I'd even rather it were a member of staff. At least they'll have lived part of their lives. These kids have everything to live for.'

'So why are we doing this?'

I tried not to sigh. He was right to protect confidential information. 'Like I said, in case someone might want to kill again. And in case – just in case – an item on one of these forms will give us an outside chance of working out who that person is.'

'Here you are – goodness, why separate the men from the women? Dan Langley.'

Dan had gone for a rather prolix affair, talking about his love of music ever since members of the CBSO had visited his school ten years ago. He listed membership of various choirs, some TV appearances. And then he mentioned swimming, tennis and weight-training – nothing his physique wouldn't have suggested. It was tempting to look at the confidential report his school had produced, but I turned it over resolutely. Later, perhaps, if nothing else came up in anyone else's statement, I'd look at those. Doug Leigh next. His was typed, but not well: he was an all-round sportsman, it seemed – again, not a surprise if you looked at him, but not all that many musicians risked their hands on the rugby field. He'd done a bit of everything, it seemed: a couple of choirs, the county youth orchestra. Nothing there. I was aware of a *frisson* that might have been either disappointment or relief.

Neil Wiltshire had been to a choir school and then a specialist music school – hadn't he told me that? – and had handwritten his in beautiful italic script. Oh dear – as a tutor I wouldn't have been especially happy about this one. Interests: reading and writing poetry (unpublished), guppy breeding. Did I believe that one? It looked like application form padding to me.

Nothing stood out on Rose's statement, either. No martial arts, no sculpture, no – hell, we had one thing in common. She liked cooking. Did that make her handy with a knife? It hadn't turned me into a blade-wielding ripper: no reason for it to have done so to her.

'Nothing?' Luke prompted me. 'You want to see the teachers' references?'

A glance at my watch told me that I was making Luke work hours of unpaid overtime.

He caught my eye, and produced another shrug. 'Oh, in for a penny, in for a pound.'

In reverse order, Rose's teachers estimated only moderate grades at A level, but insisted that she was worth auditioning. She'd not mentioned her Girl Guides activities on her part of the form, silly girl, but here they were – she'd completed the Ten Tors walk, for one thing. She must have learnt survival techniques at one point then. But surviving the elements was hardly the same as bumping people off. Apparently she was moody – I'd endorse that, but wasn't sure a supportive tutor would have mentioned it – had some difficulty establishing appropriate relationships – you bet she had! – and had lost a lot of weight. Jesus, what did some of these teachers think they were doing?

Neil had had the voice of an angel, had sung solos on major recordings with the cathedral choir until his voice had broken and had had at one time a vocation for the Church. (He was applying for *music*, for goodness' sake!) He was well organised and, with support, would overcome his natural reticence to become a violinist in a top-rank orchestra. Nothing about any extramusical skills at all.

Doug, who came from a Herefordshire farming family, had shown quiet determination to overcome family opposition – they'd made him study physics, chemistry and biology in the lower sixth in the hope he'd become a doctor – to a musical career. He had genuine leadership qualities, as was shown by his role in the lower sixth expedition to France for speleological research.

'What's speleology?' I asked Luke. 'Caves?'

'You're the English teacher.'

I jotted it down anyway. It was the nearest I'd got to eighteenth-century cellars until I found the next sentence which included the words historical society. Then there was the biology A level – not that all biology students would learn sufficient anatomy to become killers. There was the farm background, though . . . Was I on to something? Apart from the fact that some teachers weren't as conscientious about supervising personal statements as I'd always been.

Dan was – I groaned at the cliché – a gentle giant, now he'd learnt to control his passionate personality. Oh dear. I didn't want 'passionate' to turn out to be a euphemism for 'violent'. A good prefect, a leading light in the Christian Union who'd once been chosen to meet Nelson Mandela, he was a strong defender of the rights of younger and weaker pupils.

Strong enough to bump people off if he didn't like them?

I thrust the sheets at Luke. 'I'm only asking this so that we can both go home: any chance of photocopies?'

'Absolutely not. The material's totally confidential. Oh, is that my phone ringing?'

I was sure it wasn't, but he scuttled off, leaving the door open so I could see the photocopier sitting temptingly just outside. What a kind man.

I'd finished, stowed the copies in my bag and filed the originals in their file by the time he returned. We exchanged farewells without any reference to my evening's work.

Chris stopped off at ten, clutching fish and chips for five thousand, though he insisted he'd bought only two normal portions. I fell on mine: the salad I'd had earlier had barely registered in the void of my tum.

'These fell off the back of a shredder,' I said when we'd disposed of the paper and had settled in the living room with glasses of Chilean Sauvignon Blanc. 'Trouble is, I don't know if it was worth picking them up.'

He held the photocopies at arm's length, reading even as he fished for his reading glasses. 'Why did you get these? Apart from your incurable nosiness, that is.'

'Because, unless your team's got evidence to the contrary I'm obviously not going to be party to—'

'You haven't suborned Ralph Betts yet?'

'Not even met him. Minett and Ellis seem decent enough guys, though I haven't attempted to suborn them either. Or anything else them.'

'You must be feeling ill.'

'Maybe old. Certainly – yes, certainly tired. What with one thing and another, life's been quite eventful these last few days.'

'It might yet get more eventful. Harvinder tells me – not Betts – that you're feeling vulnerable because you spurned Rose's advances and because Hallam and Fisher, having done the same, ended up dead. Do you really see Rose Dungate as a killer, Sophie?'

That wasn't the sort of question Chris usually asked.

I replied carefully, 'As I told you, she was in a very emotional state last time I saw her. Who can tell what people with deep and unrequited feelings might do?'

'Yes or no?'

I stared, eyebrows raised. Not Chris's sort of question at all. 'Yes,' I said at last.

'It's just as well, then, that we've got a call out for her.'

'What?' I felt very cold.

'She's disappeared, Sophie. Off the face of the earth. Come to think of it, exactly the same way as Neil Wiltshire disappeared.'

'Anything about their disappearance in common?'

'You mean like leaving her fiddle behind in an unnaturally tidy room? Well, she didn't take her bass with her, and her room was a tip. No note from either of them to suggest suicide. What do you think's happened to them?'

'As for Neil . . .' I stared at my glass. No point in mincing things. 'I wouldn't be at all surprised if some rambler found his body at the bottom of a cliff one day. Any musician going anywhere for any length of time would have wanted his fiddle or whatever with him. To keep it safe. To play it, for goodness' sake.'

'My feeling exactly. But suicide?'

'My instinct tells me he couldn't deal with his sexuality, poor kid.'

Chris nodded. 'Now, what about Rose?'

'If she topped herself it would be where I would discover the body – now, that is, she can't leave it for Hallam or Fisher to find. A vengeful woman even in death, I'd say. Or, to be more precise, that's what June Tams tells me. She's the second violin of the Boulton Quartet. Somehow or other, she managed to stop Rose bothering me – well, gate-crashing the reception, to be precise. Funny, because June's about the least forceful person on God's earth.'

'So you're more afraid of falling over a body than of being one?'

'I didn't say that at all, Chris. Nor will I, until you've established once and for all that someone else is the killer. Incidentally, much as I loathe him, I hope French is being protected very thoroughly.'

'Not only protected, Sophie, but also moved to a secret location. Betts managed that even without your assistance!'

'*Touché!* OK, so he should. A professional cop . . .'

He picked up the photocopies again.

'Are there no staff suspects?' I asked. 'What about Mrs Fisher, insisting her husband was alive and kicking in Scotland when all the time he was dead and buried in Smethwick?'

Chris gave one of his rare smiles. 'Between ourselves, he *was* alive and kicking. We have witnesses. See, the police do check out these things.'

'So June Tams could have been right, then. She could have seen him in Harborne.'

'When?'

'You'd have to ask her. I don't think she told me exactly. There wasn't a lot of love lost between her and Fisher – or between members of the quartet as a whole, from what I can gather.'

'According to Betts' team, it was a pretty unhappy department. Well, if the boss is neglecting his departmental duties and spends his time shagging everything in a skirt—'

'What about trousers? I suppose French wouldn't be AC/DC, would he? I was thinking about Neil . . .'

Even before I'd finished, Chris was making a note.

'I suppose Betts' team didn't pick up anything about the sexual proclivities of the rest of the staff? Like whether Hallam and Fisher demanded the same favours as their boss?'

He made another note. 'What would you think?'

'If they did and if he found out, no wonder he and Hallam used to have shouting matches! The more promiscuous men around, the more chances of one of them being found out – and an investigation unearthing his activities.' Somehow I didn't see Ken Ball indulging in sex with students. Could their now possibly have been because some of Ball's students had complained about French? 'Maybe you should talk to colleagues outside the faculty too,' I said.

Chris made another note. 'Anyone in particular?'

'Dr Ball,' I explained.

'But would the students – er – succumb in such numbers?'

'Even back in my university days, there were strong rumours that if you wanted a First, there was a certain member of staff you had to be nice to. And these poor kids have far more invested financially in their courses than you and I did, Chris.'

'So the fear of failure – my God, the fear of actually being failed by the bastards demanding sex – would be even greater! Poor kids.' He looked at me with a mixture of shrewdness and shyness. 'Did anyone come on to you – French apart, that is?'

'Well, although I wouldn't in the least describe them as having made passes at me, they were both friendlier than I'd have expected. But they were both attractive, probably sexually active men. Attractive to both sexes, possibly.'

'No complaints, then?'

'No complaints. Except,' I added darkly, 'against my tutor, who seemed entirely under French's thumb – but perhaps that's another matter. French and his department. Have you found any other women prepared to complain about French – or anyone else?'

'More your line than mine, I'd have thought! Seriously, we've got trained women officers talking to all the women, but yours is a familiar face.'

I shook my head. 'I feel very ashamed, Chris. Apart from Dawn, I know nothing of these kids' lives. They made me a sort of friend, but I don't know anything about their families or friends.'

'Generation gap,' he said briefly. 'You know about Harvinder's family, you're virtually part of Ian's – you know he'd hoped to give you away.'

'Thanks for reminding me,' I said sarcastically. 'Chris, we may have let down our friends, but getting married is really a matter for the two people involved. Some clergymen are still sniffy about divorce – and you know this is Mike's second time round.'

'People have big register office affairs.'

'We didn't want that.' Time to get a grip on the conversation again. 'So, does Rose have a family and do they have any ideas?'

'None about her sexual aspirations, from what I gather. Of course, we wouldn't send PC Plod to barge in asking if they knew their daughter was a confused dyke.'

'Want a bet?'

'Things *are* better these days, Sophie.'

'I know they are.' My smile was conciliatory. 'Pam and Eileen down in Smethwick deserve medals the way they dealt with Dawn. And with me, come to that.' Chris would remember compliments to his team, and would almost certainly pass them on, both to the individuals concerned and to people with influence over their careers. 'Now, on my checklist I'm left only with Doug. And since you haven't told me the intimate details of half the music faculty, which makes me assume there aren't any obvious suspects there, perhaps we should talk about him.'

'It'll be a pretty one-sided conversation since I hardly knew he existed, but talk ahead. Provided I can have another half glass of that Sauvignon Blanc . . .'

'To sum up,' Chris said fifteen minutes later, covering his glass when I offered a top-up, 'he's got some knowledge of anatomy, is interested in history and caves and really flipped when Dawn told him she was pregnant. He's very big, didn't like some of his lecturers. But the salient question – which I don't think you've touched on – was whether Doug was at the BMI on Saturday. Did you see him?'

'Surely he'd be on Betts' list of witnesses. Minett seemed very thorough, very conscientious.'

'So he would. And if he somehow managed to scarper, then he'd show up on the cross-referencing of witness statements. This isn't like you: you usually have a quite disconcertingly good memory.'

'Even if I have to creep up on it!' I smiled.

'You didn't do very well this time!'

'You've checked already!'

'I was hoping you'd do better, I must admit. I don't suppose you can recall seeing this Doug there?'

I topped up my glass. I drank, savouring the fruit and the aftertaste, and sat back, closing my eyes. 'I'm sure he wasn't in that mob that wanted pre-concert drinks. The only youngish man I saw then was a security guard. There was a big bunch of students knocking round at the back of the Lyttelton Theatre. I sat at the side, so I couldn't have seen them without turning round. Most of them didn't return after the interval, and who could blame them?'

'So he could have been there without your knowing – literally.'

'Oh yes. But wouldn't he have needed to come down to the bar before the concert to get the apron and gloves – assuming he knew they were there?'

'Only if he hadn't already provided himself with some beforehand.'

'But how come I'd only got four pairs?'

'You could, as you said, simply have counted them out incorrectly.'

I subsided, pulling a face.

'The big question – and to my astonishment no one seems to have thought of this – is how the killer knew that the wall with those embrasures was false. And that you could conceal a body there. Gloves, apron – if the killer relied on those, it would make the murder an opportunistic affair. But no one could have relied on finding such a convenient – if ultimately unsuccessful – hiding place for the corpse. Whoever killed James Hallam knew more about the BMI than most people.'

'And,' I added, 'whoever killed Alex Fisher knew more about the Soho Foundry than most.'

'It certainly narrows the field a little. As I shall point out to Betts tomorrow. Oh, Sophie, I wish I could get out from behind my bloody desk and do some real work for a change!'

Chapter Twenty-eight

Chris didn't exactly check under all the beds and inside the wardrobes before he left, but, in an unconscious parody of Pam, the WPC, he certainly waited on the doorstep till he heard the click of the Chubb lock and the slam of the bolt. Then he waved a cheery goodbye through the spyhole and set off.

So we were almost back at square one. Two missing students, two dead lecturers. And when I thought of 'we' I should really have thought of 'they' – the police. With all the technology, all the other resources at their disposal, they were still no further forward than they had been on Saturday. What was the adage – if they hadn't made an arrest within twenty-four hours, it might be twenty-four months before they made one? Not very cheering. And very frustrating, being a copper's nark and feeding in information but – oh yes, quite rightly – getting very little back. Defence Counsel would love it if the police had to disclose they'd been chewing things over with me with a nice cup of tea, herbal or otherwise.

My breakfast toast found me equally gloomy. If I'd been a possible prey in the past, I'd always had some idea of who might be the predator. I couldn't believe it was Dan. Rose was a possibility, but I saw her more as an impulse killer, if killer she were. Essentially I was as ignorant now as before – except, if Doug were the murderer (big 'if'), then at least he wouldn't be after me. Would he?

I could see he might be after French. That would make sense. But unless Hallam and Fisher had had a greater part in Dawn's life than I knew, I couldn't see why they'd been killed. Unless young Neil had blown a fuse. But then, surely he'd have done it swiftly, unpremeditatedly – and so guiltily he'd have owned up? Back to Doug, then: the man who'd chucked his best friend in a pond.

Clearly I needed to talk to Dawn again. In my role of nice kind older friend, I might just phone her, to see how she was now she was back home – wherever home was.

Her mother answered the phone, and had no hesitation in summoning Dawn, who seemed pleased that one of her colleagues was still concerned about her.

'It's out of sight, out of mind,' she said, as if she were Luke. 'It's as if I'd never existed.'

'Did you tell people where you'd be going?' I asked gently – after all, she'd probably not been into UWM to tell people she was leaving Smethwick.

'I suppose not. But someone at the house would have told them, always assuming they'd bothered to phone.'

'Not if they got that pot-head who plays the bass guitar,' I said. 'He was completely out of it on Monday. That's one reason why I came round.'

'I suppose . . .' She swallowed a sob. Then the phone clattered and I heard her running off.

However irrational she was being, I wanted to help. She'd been treated unforgivably badly, was pregnant, was little more than a girl. The least I could do was phone a few of her mates and alert them to her illness; I didn't have to be specific as to its nature.

Mrs Harper's voice replaced Dawn's. 'I suppose you couldn't pop round for a cup of tea, could you, Sophie? She'd kill me if she knew I'd asked, but she's really down – just as those nice policewomen said she might be. Ten minutes ago she was even wondering if she ought to keep the baby. And her dad and I don't think that's a good idea, do you?'

'I'll have to see what else I'm supposed to be doing,' I said cautiously. I wouldn't be able to resist the opportunity to ask pertinent questions about her friends, Doug in particular. But getting into arguments about unborn babies was not something I meant to do.

Undaunted, Mrs Harper gave me the address. They lived just to the south of Redditch, which, though for students relying on public transport might not be easy, wasn't inconvenient by car.

I decided to hop into UWM first – to spread the word that cards and even a collection for flowers would be welcome. And – oh, yes – to keep my eyes open in a way Chris would publicly condemn but secretly approve.

One opportunity I certainly wouldn't resist if it came my way – would positively engineer, come to think of it – was asking Carrie Downs what the hell she'd been up to. I could have been melodramatic and observe that she'd broken the tutor-tutee compact. In fact, if the words I'd have chosen would have been less emotionally charged, that was what she'd done. Tutees are supposed to be able to trust their tutors, not just for their academic judgement but as human beings.

Though her car was in its usual parking space, she wasn't in her room when I tapped – I tried the door, just in case. Locked. Another stronger, braver soul might have applied a forceful shoulder, but however brave you might be, five foot one doesn't allow that sort of action, not even with the added avoirdupois of recent months. So I toddled off in search of her, running her to ground eventually in one of the private study carrels in the music library. She looked at me with cold resignation, shrugged and, gathering up her books, came out to join me.

'Refectory or your office?' I asked.

Scowling, but clearly recognising defeat when it kicked her in the teeth, she led the way to her office.

'Let's not mess about,' I said, closing the door behind me. 'You know why I'm here. I want to know why you let Marcus French manipulate you like that.' When she compressed her lips and turned away, I added, 'It's all right to talk now, surely? Now he's safely in hospital?'

'Thanks to that bloody policman! I'm sure he'll be lodging a complaint. Brutality.'

I kept my temper. 'Were you there, Carrie, when the police officer came in?'

'Of course I wasn't.'

'Well, I was. And I've never been happier to see a policeman. As for the complaint, I rather think that any brutality came from French, not from the police.'

'I don't get you.'

What planet was this woman on? Thinking a little brutality – if only linguistic brutality – wouldn't come amiss, I said, 'He was demanding oral sex with me. You know what that means: he wanted me to suck his cock. And I'm particular about which cocks I suck. I like to know where they've been. And I rather think French's has been in rather more places than I like in a sexual partner.'

'Shut up and get out!' She didn't sound very convincing, however, especially as she was addressing the kitchen bins at the time.

'Look at me. Watch my lips.'

She continued to face the window.

'Marcus French tried to blackmail me into having sex, and you, wittingly or not, were a party to it. What does that make you, Carrie?'

'Get out!'

'It makes you his dupe or his accomplice. Which, Carrie?'

'I shall phone Security!'

'Do that. I shall, of course, make a call to the police.

And another, come to think of it, to the Dean. It's about time someone lodged an official complaint about the way this place is run. I just hoped your name wouldn't be on the paper.'

'Now who's blackmailing people?'

Uninvited, I sat down. I wanted to fold my arms across my chest but thought that too combative. So I laid my hands, to all intents and purposes relaxed, in my lap. 'Isn't it about time you talked to someone on your side?'

Perhaps it was the gentler approach, perhaps it was the realisation that she wouldn't easily get rid of me, but at last she turned and hovered her side of the desk.

'Carrie, it's no business of mine what you and French get up to in your private lives. Though I must say I wouldn't want my lover strolling into my room and sitting down to read my paper when I was conducting a tutorial.'

She flinched: perhaps she hoped I'd forgotten that episode.

I waited for a moment before resuming, 'To my mind, that wasn't so much intimacy as a display of power. Is that how you see it? What hold does he have over you, Carrie?'

She bit her lip, turning away again. I wanted her to sit down and face not just me, but her situation, whatever it was.

'You must know he's reputed to be fucking his way throughout the undergraduate body – at least the bodies of those women needing better grades. You must know his attitude to the Boulton Quartet is ambiguous in the extreme.' I hesitated – was this the time to pursue that line? I'd risk it. 'He makes them practise where he can hear them, and then he lands them with a so-called professional who can't even get his fiddle in tune. Why?'

She shrugged. 'That lot are a liability. It's time to start again from scratch.'

So I'd been right to tell Hallam to get union protection. 'So he goes for a public humiliation, after which he can push them or wait for them to jump. Or kill a couple of them . . .'

'That's nothing to do with him!' she said, facing me at last. She leant heavily on the desk before groping behind her for her chair. Pulling it forward, she collapsed on to it.

'No?'

'Of course it isn't! It can't be!'

To my ears she sounded more desperate than convinced. This time I did fold my arms. 'No?'

'I mean, how could he? He was with guests all the time at the concert.'

'Are you sure?' I hadn't noticed her there, had I? 'Were you there?'

'It was an official function.'

Which sounded like a negative. I shot her a glance of sympathy. How dreadful to be the unofficial woman. And then my eyes narrowed – could she simply have been evading the question? I was sure she hadn't been at the reception afterwards, but that didn't mean she hadn't been in the auditorium. What if she and French had acted in concert? I winced at my mental pun. Would they have been strong enough to overpower Hallam? And it would have made donning apron and gloves and getting him into the space behind the false wall very much easier. Why hadn't I thought of that? At least I had one consolation: the forensic evidence the police had access to was much more reliable than my mere theorising.

'And how could he possibly have known about the foundry place?' Carrie continued.

'There's a witness to a meeting he had with Ken Ball – the man who led the unfortunate expedition,' I said. 'Apparently they had some sort of row. Was that because he'd already planted a body there and wanted to stop the visit?' I'd no idea how far that tied in with police information about Fisher's movements, but – I nodded mentally to Luke – I've never been reluctant to draw a bow at a venture.

'It was about a student. Someone doing combined Honours,

history and music. She'd made some stupid allegation to Ball and Marcus went over to try to sort it out.'

'An allegation about sex? Carrie, hasn't it ever occurred to you that there might be an element of truth behind all these allegations?'

She shifted as if the chair had suddenly grown spikes. 'Students are always saying things like that. They don't work hard enough and they see other people getting good grades so they make up—'

'Do you think I made up what I told you earlier?'

'Maybe you misinterpreted . . . or you . . . Some women lead men on and then pretend to be surprised when men take them up on their offer. Look at all this date rape business.'

Where had this woman been? What century did she live in? What sort of woman was she, into whose vocabulary, let alone her consciousness, sisterhood had never penetrated?

'Marcus faked a charge against me, pretending that he'd reported me to the university authorities. He hadn't, by the way. The relevant form was still on his desk when I went to see him. He said he'd tear it up when I apologised – the oral sex bit – or when he'd punished me – which probably involved anal penetration. I didn't wait to find out. He got you involved. Apart from anything else, how could an education lecturer possibly act on the say-so of someone from quite a different department?'

'Faculty,' she said automatically.

'Come on, Carrie. Open your eyes and look at Marcus French. There's no smoke without fire, you know.'

Her chin shot up and her eyes narrowed. 'No? Tell me, Ms Sophie Rivers, about your affair with Rose Dungate! You're not on very safe ground when it comes to allegations like this.'

'That fabrication is irrelevant.'

'So why should I give credence to those against Marcus? Tell me that.'

I said, very slowly, as if speaking to an idiot, 'If I hadn't had Rose all over me like a rash, I'd have drawn to the attention of the authorities the rumours about French straight away. But I knew how awful it was to be on the receiving end of a trumped-up allegation. I didn't want to believe anything bad about a fellow teacher.'

'So you're not having an affair with Rose? And you're not sick of her and have got rid of her? Well, I'm sure the police will be glad to know.' She put her hand on the telephone.

Thank goodness I'd already told Chris and Harv about the Rose problem. Thank goodness I'd had Sue minute my anxieties about Rose's mental health, with my signature alongside.

As if sensing my tension, Carrie produced a smile. It was not a kind, understanding one. 'Of course, what I have to tell them may not be news. I know they've been speaking to Kevin.'

Who clearly hadn't considered himself bound to treat what had been discussed as confidential. Well, I wouldn't expect him to conceal material from the police, but it sounded as if he'd chewed me over with Carrie. Not nice. I just hoped he'd been as free with my suggestion that Rose was sick and in need of professional support as he probably had been with his accusations against me.

As for Carrie's kind hints, I thought back to my hectic weekend. There was something to be said for having spent every waking hour in the company of others, particularly when those others happened to be police officers who might be relied on for alibis.

'What a pleasant pair you are, you and French,' I observed. 'I came here to see what I could do to support you at a difficult time, Carrie. French tries to rape me; you add insult to injury by trying to blackmail me. At least, I suppose that's what you were doing. OK. I'll be off, now.' I got to my feet, the only position from which I could stare down at her. What I saw

272

wasn't attractive. She'd gone a pasty white and had started to
tear at a scab on her hand.

'Come on, Carrie,' I said, embarrassed for her, despising
her, pitying her. 'Wouldn't it help to tell the truth? To bring
everything out into the open at last?'

Chapter Twenty-nine

Whether or not I'd find any of Dawn's colleagues there, I needed the refectory and its good strong coffee. Carrie had come up with nothing more, of course, except a pithy suggestion that I should go away. By then I'd had enough anyway. Carrie might have been a good teacher, but as a human being she was a mess. I thought of Toscanini's dismissal of Richard Strauss: 'To Strauss the musician I take my hat off, to Strauss the man I put it back on again.' Which took me to the next item in my collection of other people's insults. Sir Thomas Beecham had demanded to know the name of a musician in his orchestra who was making a mess of a solo: 'Mr Ball? How very singular.' Had French ever applied that to our Ken Ball? What had really gone on in Ball's office? Probably not a lot different from what Carrie had said, and I had suspected.

More to the point – yes, I could feel an excuse coming on – how had he coped with the débâcle of his Soho Foundry trip? Of course, he hadn't seen the body, so perhaps it hadn't been so bad for him. George Demidowicz – it must have been as unpleasant for him as for me; but no doubt the police would be offering him support, and in any case, I didn't know his phone number.

Ball, now: I knew where he hung out. Practically on my route home. He might know if French had ever had access to the foundry – or if anyone else had, for that matter.

'Sophie? All right?'

I looked up, blinking. 'Hello, Dan! How are you?'

He sat down beside me, stirring sugar – how on earth could anyone consume so much and stay so thin? – into milky tea. 'Not so bad, considering, as my old mum says. I mean, it's great with Leonore, but the police, man – they haven't half been fucking us about something shocking. Bastards. I keep telling them, man, I'm a fucking singer; I never had anything to do with those bloody fiddle players. But they don't give a shit!'

I looked at him, raising an eyebrow. It wasn't like Dan to indulge in such language. 'Is that what you'd say to your old mum? Who can't be all that much older than me, by the way!'

'Sorry, Sophie. But they really got to me.'

'So I see. Why do you think they gave you a hard time? If, as you say, you've not come into the closest contact with Hallam or Fisher—'

' 'Cause I'm black. Oh, they say it's 'cause I'm big and I work out and I was fucking there on Saturday and I wasn't wearing my pinnie like a good boy – thanks a bunch for that, Sophie!'

'All part of the service,' I said. 'Leonore all right?' I added more quietly.

Dismounting from his high horse, he produced a sheepish grin. 'She's great. Thanks, Sophie, for . . . Don't want to bugger up her career by getting her pregnant, whatever the stereotype says. How's Dawn, by the way? Leonore says she's in the club.'

'Keep it to yourself. It's not good news, nor how she got that way. In fact, she's gone home for a few days. She could do with a few cards, a few phone calls.' I wrinkled my nose. 'I suppose even new men don't organise flowers?'

'I could ask Leonore, if you think it's that bad.'

'I do. Here, pop that in her envelope for starters.' I passed ten pounds in pound coins. Students didn't have money to spend on essentials, let alone on gestures to their ailing friends, but I didn't want a telltale tenner giving away my part in it.

Dan raised an eyebrow, but grinned, as if he understood. 'Sure, man. But you could hand it over yourself. Here she comes.' And he got to his feet with a smile of purest delight.

Leonore was in the centre of a whole bunch of students, apparently wrestling with the intricacies of harmony, each singing the odd notes while the others came in higher or lower. As soon as she saw Dan, she beamed back, but she made no effort to come over. In fact, she gave extra attention to a woman I didn't know. Oh dear, this relationship wasn't going to be the plain sailing an old romantic like me favoured. Behind Leonore's group straggled more music students, amongst them Doug. Would he come to my table, or would I have to go to his?

Eventually Leonore detached herself from the others and came our way, accepting if scarcely returning Dan's enthusiastic embrace. However, she did take his hand when she sat down, and listened to his version of my request.

She stuck her hand out for the money he said he'd collected so far; she probably didn't see his enormous wink – yes, he had understood, bless him. 'If I'm going to get this sorted today, I'd better get on with it,' she announced, getting up and neatly avoiding the hand heading possessively for her bottom. She plunged back into the group she'd entered with, drawing everyone's eyes as she stood on the table, using a coin-filled coffee cup as a tambourine – the Carmen of Smethwick. Dan was on his feet with the others, clapping his hands and catcalling. I thought it was time to shift my seat so I could keep an eye on Doug. So I was completely at a loss when a woman's voice screamed from the main doors, 'Sophie! Sophie Rivers!'

I turned – I suppose everyone did, as the singing became raggedly silent – to find Rose slinging down her bag and racing towards me. Right arm upraised, she looked like an avenging Valkyrie.

'Sophie! Where have you been? Why didn't you call?'

Was that a knife in her hand?

'Why didn't you phone me back?'

Keeping the table between us, I said, in as normal a voice as I could manage, 'I didn't know you wanted me to.'

'Liar!' She picked up a chair and crashed it on the table. 'I left all those messages. I told you to phone back. I wanted you to!'

Now wasn't the moment to remind her I'd threatened her with the law if she so much as tried to contact me. At least the chair-smashing had alerted everyone else. I could see people either side of us, and a couple of men were inching closer to Rose, one Dan, the other Doug.

Tears streamed down her face. Her hair hadn't seen a brush for days, nor had her face seen water. Her clothes were filthy. She smelt.

'Why didn't you phone? I kept ringing! I kept on and on ringing. All I got was this man's voice! Why didn't he tell you?'

'I don't know, Rose. I don't know.'

Someone else was running out through the main doors – perhaps to call Security. And someone else was yelling into a mobile phone for an ambulance and police. Mistake. She took a couple of steps back, ready to bolt.

She had to stay put. I had to make her.

'Why did you want to speak to me, Rose?'

'You helped Leonore. You did. Didn't she?' she turned to the others to demand. 'And Dawn.' She crossed her fingers. 'You were like this with Dawn. You fucked Leonore and Dawn and you wouldn't fuck me.'

'I haven't fucked anyone—'

'Of course she hasn't,' came a strong woman's voice. 'She's a married woman. Doesn't go in for that sort of thing.'

Rose collapsed, mouth agape.

'Come here, lovey. Let's have that phone of yours before

278

you drop it. There.' And Myra enveloped Rose in a huge maternal embrace.

'She didn't phone,' Rose sobbed into her shoulder. 'She never phoned.'

What might a bit of logic do? I took the phone from Myra, and looked at the number in the display. Yes, it was the same of mine, except for one digit. 'That's why I didn't phone back, Rose,' I said gently. 'You dialled the wrong number.'

Knowing that a large bunch of flowers would soon be on its way, I took Dawn the Rackhams perfume and teddy bear. Her mother let me into a beautifully converted barn. Clearly there was money in antique prints; clearly lack of funds hadn't been the reason for Dawn not wanting to spend money on food. Perhaps she'd been saving in the belief that she'd have to pay for the abortion herself.

Taking my coat, Mrs Harper showed me into the family sitting room. The room was recently decorated, tastefully lit and as immaculately tidy as a hotel lounge except for Dawn languid on the sofa. No wonder Mrs Harper had given Dawn's digs such a good going over. She brought us tea, Dawn squirming with embarrassment, and left us two girls on our own. I was ready to squirm too, suspecting that what I was supposed to do was talk Dawn into an abortion.

What I did do was tell her about Doug's part in my rescue this morning. I censored much of what had happened, just assuring her that all the students were fine and that Rose was being cared for. She was too bright to know that Rose would be kept anywhere voluntarily, but we didn't use ugly words like sectioned.

'Do you really think Rose might have done it? Them, I mean. The murders?'

'All I know is that she's a very sick woman. She's been sleeping rough somewhere, and needs a lot of TLC. And God knows what her phone bill will be. She kept on phoning the same wrong number.'

'Why didn't whoever she was phoning report her?'

'I don't know – I suppose you can get calls intercepted? Anyway, whether he or she did or not, she's now being looked after.' But not, presumably, being questioned by the police, unless some psychiatrist could be found to say that she was only partly mad, and could understand and respond to questions. At least she was in secure accommodation, whatever her situation. And I felt much better. I might never really have suspected Rose of two murders, but I'd never quite ruled her out either.

Since I'd missed lunch, I indulged myself on an extra slice of Mrs Harper's excellent cake – imagine, finding time to cook like this when your daughter was in the middle of such a crisis! Or perhaps that was what mothers did: they showed they were there by making huge fluffy sponges.

'So is everyone missing me?' Dawn asked plaintively. 'Truly?'

'I asked them not to phone this afternoon when I was down. But I'm sure they'll be in touch soon.'

'Have you told them about – about . . .? I'm seeing a consultant tomorrow, by the way. Do you think they hate me? Do you think they'll despise me if – if . . .'

'I have a feeling that you weren't the only one French blackmailed, Dawn,' I said. 'What do you think?'

She pulled on her lower lip. 'Apart from you? Well, I think Andrea – she's a clarinet student – and . . .' She listed five other women. Then she got up and checked the door was shut. 'Sophie, I want you to promise, promise, promise not to tell anyone else. Especially Mum. She'd really freak. I mean, she's being great. Really kind. But I know she really disapproves. You know, her own daughter having sex with a man.'

'She loves you, Dawn – she'd rather you'd had wonderful sex with a young man you loved.'

280

She blushed. 'That's just it. I did. He was really special. Really wonderful.'

I had a terrible idea I knew what was coming. ' "Was"?' I prompted.

Her eyes flooded. 'I thought I was special too. But then I found out he was sleeping with other people. Sophie, he was even sleeping with *men*!' She swallowed. 'I was so worried I went off and had the test. You know: Aids. But it was OK.'

'Thank God for that!' I leant across and squeezed her hand. 'It must have been terrible for you.'

'It was. I never – not after that . . . But I didn't want him to be dead, Sophie! But imagine it, knowing you'd shared a man with Rose—'

'Rose!'

'He said she'd threatened to blackmail him if he didn't! But I don't know, she's such a loser, but he – he turned out to be a shit . . .'

I passed her a tissue.

'Oh, and he had sex with Neil. I felt so sick! I swore I wouldn't sleep with anyone except a real boyfriend. And I stuck to it. I've been loyal to Ross, even though we don't see each other very much. I'm not even on the pill. Then there was French, and then I had to. Or he'd have ruined my career before it even started.'

'Could he really have done that?'

'My assessments . . . and he had to write my references! And he knew everyone in the music business . . . One word from him, and I'd never even have got an audition.'

'So who was the other man? Hallam?'

'Oh, no. He's *old*. Was old.'

'Fisher.'

'He was so lovely and – oh, Sophie, imagine him being dead.'

I let her weep for a few minutes, realising with a shock that they were the first tears I'd seen for any of the dead musicians.

'Did Hallam ever try—'

'Oh, Sophie, he was terrible. Bought me flowers and came on really heavy.' She managed a bitter laugh. 'Do you know, I even threatened to report him to the Professor? And do you know what he did? He laughed! I didn't realise why till a couple of months ago, of course. Bastards! That's what men are, bastards. All of them!'

'Some of them,' I amended, gently taking her cup and saucer from her. But she made a grab for the plate – there was still some cake on it. Poor Dawn, initiated into womanhood the hard way but still a child.

'Ross isn't, I suppose,' she conceded, through the cake. 'No, he's lovely. And Doug's sweet. Really kind.'

'Except for Monday?'

'Except for Monday.' She picked up the teddy bear and straightened its bow tie.

'How did you feel about telling a man? You know, girls' talk?'

She looked at me as if I had completely lost it. 'He's my *friend*. I tell him everything.'

'Even about –' I tried to swallow my disbelief – 'even about having sex with other men?'

'Oh, he was brought up on a farm. He knows all about that stuff, doesn't he, Bear?' She made the bear nod.

'Doesn't he ever get – well, jealous?'

'Why should he? We're friends.'

'How does he get on with Ross?'

'Wonderful! They're mates. Except they've had a bit of a falling out about something. But it'll all blow over.'

'He must be a very special young man,' I suggested, feeling an absolute louse and wishing I didn't have to do it, but knowing that someone had to. 'I told you he and Dan were first on the scene when Rose blew her fuse today.'

'He never liked Rose. She had a bit of a crush on me, you see. I – I don't think she's quite made up her mind yet.' She

282

held her hand face down, rocking it from side to side. 'That's the only thing I've ever heard him lose his cool over. Gay people. Either sex. Unnatural, he said.'

My God!

'Playing the bassoon's a bit of a far cry from farming,' I observed, while my thoughts raced. The most unpleasant one was the realisation that Doug had almost certainly overheard Rose's accusations about Dawn and me. He wouldn't like to think that I'd had sex with his goddess, not if Dawn was accurate about his views.

'Oh, he could have done lots of things. He was the captain of rugby at his school and went in for orienteering and was in that thing for training officers, only he didn't want to go into the army. Oh, and he actually got a write-up in the papers for some cave rescue he did in France.'

'Any idea why he didn't like the STC or OTS or whatever it's called these days?'

She nuzzled the bear's ear. 'Funny, that was one thing he'd never talk about. Anyway, he managed to persuade his parents he didn't want to take over the farm, nor become a doctor, 'cause that was the next idea they had – a doctor or a vet – and he came up to UWM. We met at the freshers' disco. But we've only ever been friends.'

'We all need friends,' I said easily. 'I don't know what I'd do without mine.'

'He'd do anything for me, just as I'd do anything for him,' she continued.

'Has he ever asked you to do anything for him? Recently?'

For a second she looked me full in the eyes, much as I imagine a rabbit must look at that last car. Then she blushed scarlet and fiddled with the wretched bear again. 'No.'

'Are you sure?'

'It's him that does things for me,' she said.

On automatic pilot I wittered away about the times my friends had been there for me. But all the time I was doing sums in my head, and I didn't like the total they all came to.

What I didn't like most of all was the fear that on top of all she'd had to put up with, Dawn might be about to lose her bestest friend.

Chapter Thirty

I'd dealt with being scared before, and I could deal with it now. The essence was to make sure that anyone who could alleviate any danger to me, real or perceived, should know, and that until I reached a place of safety, I took no risks whatsoever.

So my first move on leaving the Harpers' house was to pull into a lay-by and reach for my mobile phone. It would have to be Chris: he'd have authority over everyone else, and, more to the point, would credit my theory, even if, please God, it was ultimately proved wrong. All his numbers were programmed in: I tried the Police Headquarters one first. No luck. His mobile? It would take a message. I left one, anyway, and then tried his home. Another message there.

All right, it'd have to be Harvinder. I had only his mobile number – and had to leave yet another message. This was getting irritating. And alarming. I fossicked through my organiser for Minett's card. Yet another message.

They all said roughly the same thing. That I had reason to believe that Doug Leigh might be involved in the musicians' murders and that he might equally regard me as his next target. I would make my way back home and await their instructions. I'd added to Minett that my house was less vulnerable than most, thanks to the security systems I'd had installed.

I reminded myself of this every time I checked my rear-view mirror. No, I wasn't being tailed. I didn't expect to be. There might be a reception committee outside my house, of course.

If there were, I could always drive straight to a police station and ask for help.

It wasn't like me to be as rattled as this. I'd had bad moments before, panicked before, to be honest. But I'd always felt, deep down, that I could cope, that I'd survive. This time I wasn't so sure. Perhaps, I admitted, as I overtook a lorry, that in the past I'd known that my death wouldn't matter overmuch. It still wouldn't, in the great scheme of things, but now I loved people who'd very much rather I was alive. Steph had grudgingly become a friend, even if I'd never be his mother, as far as he was concerned; Mike would be as devastated by my death as I would be by his. He'd be angry too. He didn't like my habit of interfering with matters best left to the law, even though he shared my nosiness and love of finding solutions. Well, he did the *Guardian* crossword puzzle for daily pleasure.

So it wasn't just self-preservation that put me on my toes, it was reluctance to hurt others. Trust me to prefer altruism to self-interest, I told myself, as I pulled on to the M5. And now, since rain was swirling in great swathes, just like the rain in movies you never quite believe, I'd better think about another sort of self-preservation – alert, defensive driving. It wasn't as if I were in any hurry to get home . . .

Putting the car away in the garage didn't seem an alternative to leaving it on the road and scuttling for the shelter of the house, not with the torrential rain and the darkness already falling. No, the security light showed no one lurking in the shadows – not that any trees or bushes provided cover for intruders, not any more. And the door was reassuringly locked. I locked it behind me.

The answerphone announced several messages. The best was Mike at his soggily sentimental best. The rest were from the police officers I'd roused. I was to call Harv and Minett as soon as I had anything positive to report. I was to call Chris full stop.

I did. This time he was engaged.

Despite my attempts to reassure myself that all was well, I still felt uneasy. When the phone rang, I jumped so much I slopped my tea.

One voice I didn't expect was Mrs Harper's. 'I just wanted to thank you for coming this afternoon. You've done her so much good.'

I demurred.

'And getting her friends to rally round like that – that nice boy Doug came round with the most gorgeous bunch of flowers.'

'Is he still there?'

'No. I did suggest he stayed for supper but he said he had to work this evening. A responsible job, he said. It's nice he's doing so well and can still think about my little girl.'

'Well, he would, wouldn't he, if he's in love with her?'

'Him! In love! But I thought—'

'I'm sure he is. Dropping someone in a pond doesn't sound like the action of a disinterested friend to me.'

She took time to digest the idea. 'But Dawn says she tells him everything – that's not very kind of her, is it?'

'I'm sure she doesn't have an inkling. She can only talk about Ross!'

'And you, Sophie! She was telling him – well, we both were – how kind you'd been. I warn you,' she laughed, 'he didn't think much of that teddy you gave her. He said she ought to have a real animal. But with her being away from home during term time, and the strongest chance she'll be moving away when her career takes off . . . And with her father not being in the most secure of health . . . No, I told him I thought the teddy was the best thing she could have.'

In other times, other circumstances, I think Mrs Harper, not Dawn, would have been my choice of friend. As it was, I feared she might have been saying the worst possible things at the worst possible time. After a few more sentences, I was glad to hang up.

Chris was still engaged.

I made myself behave normally: I switched on Radio Four for the *Six o'Clock News* while I prepared the ultimate in comfort food, cheese on toast. Since this – in my book – involved rubbing bread with raw garlic and drizzling it with Worcester sauce, it wasn't the sort of thing you could eat if you were expecting close company – vampires apart, of course.

Not fancying the programme after the news, I switched on the TV for the BBC local news. Nothing to alarm or excite. Yet I felt so uneasy, garlic-breath notwithstanding, that I went round twitching all the curtains I'd so carefully drawn. No. No cars, no motorcycles I didn't recognise as my neighbours'.

I gave Chris another try. This time the phone rang and rang with no reply. Ditto his mobile.

I'd no sooner returned the handset to the cradle than it rang. I pounced, ready to make some silly quip. Before I could do so, however, a calm but purposeful male voice interrupted me. 'Miss Rivers? Miss Sophie Rivers? This is the police here. We understand you were involved in the discovery of a body at the Soho Foundry the other day. We're continuing our investigations, of course, and wonder if you'd come down to the foundry to help us.'

'I'd be delighted, officer,' I responded, my heart thudding so fast, so loudly I thought he must have heard it. 'When?'

'I'd be grateful if you made your way over there now.'

'I'm in the middle of something, officer, but I'll come as soon as I can. Nine-ish, shall we say? Whom shall I ask for?'

A moment's silence.

'Oh, just make your way to the main gate. I'll meet you there.'

'Are you sure you want to go through with this?' Chris asked, as I wrestled my fleece and cagoule over the body armour I'd been all too delighted to borrow. My only fear was that it didn't cover enough of me: if my head was dragged back, my throat would still be vulnerable.

'It's the best way to trap him, isn't it?'

'That's not the most positive answer I've ever heard.'

It wasn't the most positive I'd ever given. To be honest, I felt like Hamlet, preparing for his contest with Laertes. I was determined that no one would know how ill all was here about my heart. And being a woman, I could be troubled by the gain-giving. Peter Andrews could have quoted line by accurate line. Biting my lip, I said out loud, ' "If it be now, 'tis not to come. If it be not to come, it will be now." '

Chris looked sternly at me. ' "The readiness is all"? I promise you, Sophie, that if you're the tiniest bit uncertain, you don't have to do this.'

'Get me to Smethwick, and I'll see,' I said.

Chris himself drove my car. We'd swap over before we were in sight of the foundry.

'What made you suspicious?' he asked, as much as for something to say, I suspect, as to find out.

In the same spirit, I replied, 'Well, whoever it was didn't give a name. Nor his station. And your colleagues are in the habit of getting details like that right.'

'So I should hope.'

We lapsed into silence.

'Funny thing is,' I continued at last, a penny dropping after twenty-odd years, 'you know how I love Georgette Heyer's books?'

'Those historical romances?' Chris had the hint of a sneer in his voice.

'Yes. Brilliantly plotted, lovely style, excellent research – usually. But I've just remembered that in one of them she has her characters go to the Soho Foundry – in Soho in *London*. The only mistake I've ever caught her out in.'

'Unlike chummie who made several.'

'Oh, it was Doug's accent too, I think. He'd made his voice higher, and was speaking more quickly than usual. But there was a distinct burr. God, this rain!'

We drove in silence for a while.

'How do you think he lured Fisher here?' I asked.

'Well. A neat little nick to the throat suggests he had the same treatment as Hallam. But there was also bruising to his wrists, as if he'd been handcuffed. Maybe it wasn't so much luring as compelling.' Then he added, 'You know what you have to do. Keep him talking in the open air as long as you can. Keep your distance from him. Your mike's working?'

So he wasn't as confident as he pretended to be.

I tapped it. He flinched.

'OK. Your mike's working.'

My Mike would be asleep by now, preparing for another match, with luck, another big innings. He seemed terribly far away; had he been in Birmingham, would I have taken the risk I was taking now? Was I gambling on having recovered from whatever injury I might be laying myself open to by the time he came home? If so I wasn't being fair to either of us.

'What about the security man on Avery's gate?' I asked.

'Just tell him you're meeting someone. He may not even know there's an operation on. We've got access via the adjoining factory so that Doug sees nothing untoward.'

'Fine.' It wasn't. I'd have liked a friendly guard as well as the police.

'Now, I don't want you to drive straight into the car park or the space between the two old buildings. I want you to stay near your car, as if unsure of where to go. Keep in the open as much as you can. Remember, your body armour will protect you.'

'Against knives as well as bullets?'

'Especially against knives. You've got these mesh gloves on under your mittens, too – you'd be able to grab the knife, in an emergency. But believe me, Sophie, if we have to shoot, we shoot to kill. Don't look round for us once you've located him. Just pretend you believe what he's doing is routine.'

'OK. Is this a good place to stop?' The borders of Smethwick had never looked less enticing.

'Yes.' He pulled into the kerb. He got out but waited for me to shift across to the driver's seat before closing the door as quietly as he could.

I wound down the window. 'What if I can't hack it?'

He reached in for my hand, heavy in its mitt, and squeezed it. 'You've never let us down yet, Sophie.'

Chapter Thirty-one

As instructed, I pulled into the works entrance, waiting, although the barrier was up, as if for further instructions from whoever had summoned me there. When nothing happened, I parked tidly and prepared to get out. But I made sure I donned my hard hat, tucking an extra layer of padding between the rim and my collar. My fleece and cagoule covered most of the body armour – I must have looked like a Michelin Man. I swathed my neck in a navy silk scarf. The torch was a heavy police one, long and heavy enough to sock someone with. They'd done their best, bless them. I slammed the car door, but didn't lock it, tucking the key into a pocket – no bag for anyone to grab or to impede me should I need to run.

Then I set off slowly along the road, as if it were the most normal thing in the world to have a tryst with a solitary unnamed policeman in the middle of a world heritage site. There was plenty of light from the surrounding industrial areas – no wonder you could see cities from space, if this was how they were lit up. The residual cobbles glistened in the sea of mud and smashed tarmac. My footsteps should have rung through tense silence: they pattered against the prevailing, if distant, sounds of heavy industry. I knew the new Avery Berkel works were bristling with armed officers, that more were concealed in the old buildings, though not apparently near the foundry doors, which this time stood invitingly open. There was another contingent behind the tottering corrugated-iron fence separating Avery's from the factory next door. I was protected. If I hadn't been swamped by waves of superstition, I should have quoted the Scottish Play, the bits about courage and sticking-places, but Peter Andrews wasn't there to appreciate them.

I came to a halt at a point I judged to be equidistant between the buildings and listened. Nothing.

Still obeying instructions, I called out, 'Hello? Sophie Rivers here.'

I was to wait for a count of sixty elephants, not looking behind, call again and finally walk slowly back to the car. That was where they thought he'd be waiting, if he hadn't penetrated the buildings. He'd get behind the driver's seat and as I sat put a knife to my throat. I wasn't at all sure about that theory: mine was a two-door car, and I couldn't see anyone getting out of the back seat while still posing a threat to anyone exiting more easily. But perhaps that would be my salvation – in addition to all those armed officers.

As I turned, however, a figure emerged from the shadows. Tall; bulky; grizzled beard: it looked in the half-light as if George Demidowicz were coming to greet me. And he was, one arm behind his back in an arm lock that was tight enough to make him wince every time he stumbled. Another hostage: we hadn't bargained for this. From where I stood, I couldn't see a knife, if the figure holding him had one. This man too had a hard hat, but wore under it a balaclava. I couldn't kid myself it was for warmth. The hard hat had a miner's light fixed to the front.

'Get into the foundry,' balaclava man said. 'Tell her, George.'

George grunted a mixture of assent and excruciating pain.

I stood my ground. 'When you let George go. He's got nothing to do with this.' As if I had!

'Do as you're told, you fucking dyke.' However Doug tried to disguise his voice, that burr came through.

George suppressed a groan.

'I'm not a fucking dyke, but if you have an argument with me – which I very much dispute – you should sort it out with me, not George. How did you get hold of him anyway?' I asked, remembering rather belatedly that I was supposed to be engaging him in time-wasting dialogue, not provoking him further.

'Ball told me his number,' Doug admitted.

'Why should he do that?'

'Something about another trip—' George began. 'Aargh!'

'I told you to get moving.' Doug snarling was like one of Dawn's teddy bears trying to be fierce. But however gentle his voice, I could see the pain on George's face. Was it just the arm-lock, or was there a knife involved too? George wasn't protected by body armour, of course.

'Look, as I said, your argument's with me. I'll be your hostage or whatever. Let George go.'

'Get moving.' Another teddy bear snarl.

A glance at George's face persuaded me. I moved, but as slowly as I dared.

No light, of course, inside, except from my torch and Doug's helmet. On my own I'd have had risked blinding him with the full beam, and cutting and running – if cutting wasn't the wrong term in connection with Doug. But not with an innocent man at possible knifepoint. I'd have to do something else. In the cold and echoing darkness, I tried to think.

'The cellars,' Doug grunted. 'Go on.'

'Where? I don't know—'

George gasped.

Doug said, 'Don't be silly. You've been there before.'

'Silly': such an innocent, naïve word for an overgrown youth who'd already killed two men.

'I'm not being silly. It wasn't dark then,' I wailed.

'Go to the bloody cellars. Tell her which way, George.'

I tried to control my voice again. 'Just let him go, Doug.

He's not involved in any of this. Why—'

'He found the body, right? So—'

I stopped dead. 'But everyone knows where the body was found. You're not being very logical.'

'Just shut up! Get moving.'

By now his voice was beginning to show strain. I might play on it. 'What do you intend to do with me when you get me down there? Because you wouldn't want to do it to George, would you?'

I was rewarded by a sob, Doug's, surely. Then there was a grunt. I spun round. George had fallen heavily, but not hard enough to hurt himself. In fact, with amazing agility for a big man, he somersaulted to his right, heading goodness knows where. But now Doug was on me, throwing himself on top of me as if to protect me from something. Winded, I tried to struggle but all a man of his size had to do was lie on me. He smashed my hand hard against the floor: the torch rolled away. As I dragged a breath in, I smelt a light, sweetish aftershave.

I might have been a rag doll for all the resistance I could put up. He simply hauled me to my feet using my scarf, his arms so long that however hard and far I kicked, whatever I did, it was all useless. When he'd had enough, he changed his grip to my hair, turning me round so he could frogmarch me, my arm now locked, to wherever he wanted us to go. He clamped a huge hand across my mouth for good measure. His miner's lamp shone towards the cellars.

He meant it. He was going to take me to the pitch-black cellars. The chains. The mycelium. The cold steel of his knife. NO!

I fell apart. Completely. Worse than last time. I screamed and wept and struggled. I don't know when he let go of me, if he did, though I suppose he must have done. All I knew was that I couldn't walk another step. I gibbered. I howled. At some point I wet myself. I vomited. And then big yellow blobs swam over everything and I sank God knew where.

Chapter Thirty-two

As Chris walked delicately into the ward, he managed a smile, but his face was so anxious that he might not have bothered. 'I brought you the clothes you asked for,' he said unnecessarily, dropping a Safeway carrier on the bedside cupboard. 'They say you're free to go anytime you're ready. I'll run you home if you like.' He withdrew, drawing the curtains round my bed. I heard his feet retreating a discreet distance.

Hospital. I must have been worse than I realised. Or had Chris just been his ultracareful self? Stiffer than I could imagine, with no reason I could recall, I hitched myself out of bed, letting myself down gently enough for there to be time to inspect my knees. Not a pretty sight, unless you liked red and purple. Nor were my hands. The fingers of the right hand were blue: they were truly sausage fingers now. Thank goodness I'd left the big emerald in its safe at home. I inspected the bag. Poor Chris, having to pick his way through my undies drawers – pants, bra, socks. T-shirt. Jogging top and trousers. Trainers.

I'd have to do without the bra, though. The wrist and fingers refused to bend, and, when it came to it, under the top no one would tell the difference. And someone would have to tie the trainer laces for me.

Chris's bald spot, as he knelt at my feet, was horribly distinct.

Someone at the nurses' station gave me a follow-up appointment card and a professional smile, but then had to chase after me with a polythene bag holding the clothes they'd stripped off me. I'd have been happy to sling the lot on the pile of clinical waste bags lurking in a corner, but Chris took charge of it in a way that brooked no argument. I could bin it later, anyway. Because one thing was certain, I'd never wear any of those things again.

He took my elbow to steady me, but released it when I cried out with pain. More bruises I hadn't noticed before.

'He must have kicked me.'

'He did. But not as much as he wanted. When you got hysterical – we all thought at first it was simply a magnificent piece of acting, by the way – he tried to slap you to stop you.'

I ran an apprehensive finger over my face, and tried – very gingerly – a repeat exploration of a couple of teeth. I could feel a bank loan for crowns coming up. 'Rather hard,' I complained. 'Not exactly your medicinal slap. He was supposed to be a gentle giant,' I added.

'He's gentle enough now,' Chris said. 'The only problem is how soon he'll be fit to plead. If ever. We've got all the evidence we need on your audiotape and film—'

'Film!' I stopped to give an automatic door time to do its stuff.

'Infra-red cameras. And the testimony of all the members of the armed response unit.'

'I thought you said they'd shoot to kill?'

'Not if someone isn't trying to kill them. Even then they shoot to disable.'

'Hmph! So . . . Doug . . . Where did they hit . . .?'

'Nowhere! We knew George Demidowicz was hanging round somewhere, so we didn't want him collecting an odd bullet, and we could see that Doug was too intent on kicking the shit out of you to notice a little extra company so we jumped him. Good old-fashioned teamwork. Not a round fired. And we realised you weren't acting, and the medics – yes, we had a couple of ambulances tucked round the back too – insisted they should give you the once-over.' He zapped his car. 'Look,

I'm going to have to just drop you off – I've got a team meeting in half an hour.'

'It must be an important one if it means your splitting an infinitive like that. Is it about the UWM case? Ah! Thought so! In that case, I'd like to come too.'

He sighed, but since he'd fed me the information himself the sigh lacked conviction.

'And while we're on the road,' I added, easing myself into the passenger seat and discovering my hand couldn't manage the seat-belt fastening, 'you can tell me about George: he is all right, is he?'

'Fine. Very shaken, but fine. He's probably still kicking himself for being deceived, but apart from a very painful shoulder – fortunately one of the medics put it back in after Doug dislocated it—'

'He *dislocated* George's shoulder? Jesus!'

'It was the way he got out of the arm-lock. Anyway, he was trying to pick up the torch to sock Doug when we emerged. He was in so much pain he wouldn't have been terribly effective, but he would have done his best to stop Doug inflicting much more damage on you. Anyway, we patched him up and took him home. He'll be making a statement later this morning.'

If Betts and his team were disconcerted to have an unauthorised visitor wished on them by the superintendent in charge they were in general too polite to show it. Maybe Harv's spontaneous hug helped.

Anyway, they settled me down and found me water and hot chocolate to sustain me, and got on with their debriefing. It was one thing to trespass on the hospitality of old friends, another to interfere in the workings of a load of strangers, so I resolved to keep quiet. Unless, of course, I couldn't.

The mood was upbeat, as you'd expect after a couple of nasty deaths had been sorted, but something, perhaps just my presence, was tempering any hilarity. As Betts, a man with the most pugnacious jaw I'd ever seen and an accent you could grate nutmegs on, stood up to address his team, I looked round. Yes, one or two faces looking distinctly serious. That good-looking sergeant – Ellis? – might have been preparing for a funeral, in fact, something I didn't feel I could blame myself for.

Betts was already in mid-flow. The post mortem on the first body, that of James Hallam, had shown, he reminded them, a puncture mark to the throat. Nothing serious, though it could have been if it had penetrated any deeper. There was bruising to the left wrist, the marks suggesting that someone had gripped it very firmly. Some slight tissue damage to the left shoulder might indicate a recent strain. To illustrate, he jerked his arm up his back as if someone were doing to him what Doug had done to George.

'At this point,' he continued, 'the finger of suspicion was pointing at Daniel Langley, a tall, strong young man who had access to plastic aprons.'

'Plastic aprons?' I interjected.

Betts smiled but not warmly. 'We believe that the killer must have covered himself in something before killing Hallam. One of your aprons goes missing, Ms Rivers, as does a pair of plastic gloves. We believe the killer put them on. But we don't know how he got hold of them even now.'

'Ask another music student called Dawn Harper,' I said, 'But do it very gently because she was raped by Professor French and is now pregnant.'

'Dawn – she was the lass whom Doug Leigh threw into the water,' Minett reminded the team smoothly. 'Supposedly friends.'

Betts made an obvious effort to get back to his narrative. 'Thanks, Ms Rivers. That's the access problem resolved.'

I nodded, and resolved to make no more interruptions.

'I was talking about Daniel Langley. Yes. We couldn't find any motive. Or, since he'd been on duty as a waiter or in a pub with his friends, any opportunity. The next likely candidate was Neil Wiltshire, who had gone missing.' He dropped his eyes, frowning.

My stomach lurched. Had they found him? And was there the remotest chance they'd found him alive?

'Then we found a second body, this time in the Soho Foundry. Now, not a lot of people know about the Foundry, let alone know their way about it. The temporary lighting makes it a bit easier to get about these days, of course, but it's still not easy.'

Minett nodded. 'It's a bit like that place on Crete with the Minotaur.'

I wondered if Peter Andrews would have known a suitable classical quotation.

'But it seems that someone did know about it, and did find his way about. We checked the records of all the members of staff, and the extra violinist that the professor brought in to complete the quartet. There was nothing to suggest that any of them had the requisite expertise, let alone motive or opportunity. Then Ms Rivers had this strange invitation to join a non-existent officer at the Foundry, and she shared her knowledge with us. As you know, we took the incident very seriously, and it was a total success.'

Minett smiled at me, I at him.

'We believe that Leigh conceived a pathological hatred of anyone he imagined having had sexual relations with his friend Dawn Harper. Hallam; Fisher; French. So when one of the students at the university alleged that Ms Rivers had had a lesbian relationship with Ms Harper, Ms Rivers joined his list. Leigh was handy with knives: he used them to make –' he checked his notes as if not entirely sure of his material – 'reeds for his bassoon. He was a keen caver. He knew about anatomy from his life on the farm. He had had – and this is only hearsay; we've yet to substantiate it – a very bad homosexual experience at school when he was in the army cadets or whatever. But how he lured Alex Fisher to the Foundry I for one have no idea. Except that Fisher had a puncture mark to the throat, of course, and damage to the wrists. The forensic team are still taking Leigh's car apart. If there are any fibres associated with Fisher or with anyone else, they'll find them.'

'By anyone else do you mean young Neil?' I asked, despite myself.

Betts ignored me. 'We do know that Fisher already had a hand injury – genuine, according to his GP and his wife. We know he set off for Scotland.'

'June Tams might be able to confirm that she saw him alive and well in Harborne when he was supposed to be away,' I murmured. When that had no immediate effect, I added, 'Do we know exactly how he came to injure his hand? An accident with a corkscrew or fending off an attack by Doug Leigh?'

Betts just about refrained from raising his eyes heavenwards. But Chris, who had been notably self-effacing, now leant forward as if interested in the reply. 'Or indeed by anyone else – such as Neil Wiltshire?'

Betts flushed. 'Mrs Fisher insisted it was the Saturday evening sauvignon blanc, as it happens. And the post mortem found nothing to argue with that. What interested us, sir, was a letter stashed in Fisher's papers indicating that he'd had the Aids test. Negative, as it happens. And we gather that young Wiltshire was a bit that way inclined. That in fact he made a bit of a nuisance of himself with one or two members of staff. According to Professor French, who we know may not be the most reliable of witnesses, Ms Rivers, both Hallam and Fisher had discussed the problem with him. He'd recommended comprehensive and public snubs, provided they were consistent with professionalism, that is.'

I thought back to that rehearsal. Was that treatment consistent with professionalism? 'But—'

'We have two separate, indeed conflicting views of Wiltshire: one that he was a perfect son, tenant, boyfriend. The other –

well, I'm afraid it was altogether less attractive. The young man seems to have had major problems with being gay. As a result, he is known to have visited at least one hetero massage parlour. For more than a massage, if you take my meaning. But he also picked up rent boys. We caught him on CCTV in the centre of Birmingham the Friday before he disappeared. I understand that Ms Rivers was afraid we'd find he'd committed suicide, he was in such an emotional state. We rather think . . . the trouble is, until we can question Leigh properly, we can't be certain. Leigh's got a bit of a penchant for hiding bodies, hasn't he? So while I share Ms Rivers' fear that we shall find him dead, I'd go one further. I'd say he's been murdered. By Doug Leigh.'

'But Leigh's rationalisation – correct me if I'm wrong,' Chris said, '– was supposed to be that he had to rid the world of people who might have had a sexual relationship with Dawn Harper. Surely Neil wouldn't fit into that category! And wouldn't he have started with French?'

'He also broke out of that pattern when he invited George Demidowicz along last night,' I pointed out. 'He's just a nice decent family man: no one could have an axe to grind with him, surely.'

'Not unless,' Chris said, 'he was afraid that Demidowicz might find another corpse in the course of . . . No, surely we checked every square inch of the Soho Foundry site, didn't we?'

For 'we' read 'you', I thought, sympathising with Betts. 'There are an awful lot of square inches,' I said, as if in extenuation.

'I gather Demidowicz is somewhere in the building making a statement,' Minett said. 'Go and see if he's got any ideas, will you, Ellis? So,' he continued, 'we've got this little clutch of killings with no apparent rationale, no – no pattern.'

'Fisher and Dawn had a relationship,' I put in. 'I bet Dawn told Doug about it. He got away with killing Fisher. Hallam had been on to Dawn – he did a spectacular job of polishing him off. If I'd been French I'd have been worried.'

'Except he didn't know Fisher was dead.'

'And he shouldn't have found out that Hallam was dead. Two sex-mad colleagues disappear, and you wonder if you're next in line, I should imagine.'

Chris shook his head. 'But why kill young Neil? Assuming he did. And why crack Peter Andrews on the skull? Which he certainly did. Andrews ID'd the aftershave we found in his digs. Lucky bugger, Andrews – I'm sure that blow was meant to kill him.'

'I suppose,' I said, pointing out the obvious, 'that Peter must have seen him doing something suspicious.'

There was a little silence.

'To get back to Neil,' Minett said tentatively, 'I suppose it couldn't be anything to do with that Aids test Fisher took. Perhaps he associates Aids with gays. Has the wonky logic that when Neil fucked with Fisher he was putting Dawn at risk.'

'But he must have known for ages that Neil was AC/DC. Why now?'

'Back to that learning to kill syndrome,' Chris suggested.

It was the best we could manage. At least, until Doug was able to talk.

Minett coughed. 'Now, I suppose Ms Rivers would like to hear about UWM, and the sexual harassment there.'

'What I'd most like to hear,' I said, knowing what I was saying was irrelevant but incapable of keeping my mouth shut, 'is why a bright woman like Carrie Downs let French treat her and everyone else the way he did. She must have known he was a prize shit, but she let him roll over her and—'

'How can anyone know anything like that?' Betts retorted angrily. 'Psychologists apart, that is?'

'But is there anything in their past they have in common?'

'Nothing, as far as we can see. But they've certainly got a lot in their present, with hotel receipts to prove it. Separate homes still: it'd cramp his style with the students he knocks off if she were anywhere around.'

'But she couldn't be that naïve, could she? When I suggested his sexual behaviour might be . . . unprofessional, she took violent exception. Have your colleagues been able to work out how many women were involved?'

'We're into double figures, so far. Disgusting: those poor girls up for grabs like that.'

I thought back to my teaching days. The shocking truth was that French's trade union, if he were in one, would be forced to defend him, however sickening the vast majority of teachers would find what he'd done. With luck, professors didn't join unions: with luck he'd lose not just his liberty but his job – and his pension.

'I wonder if I might ask you something else,' I continued, with suitable diffidence.

Minett nodded and Betts frowned simultaneously. I chose to notice the former.

'Just a loose end,' I said. 'But I hate loose ends. That lady with the high colour, Inspector – did you ever run her to earth?'

He nodded. 'Turned out she was just a punter with blood pressure who thought she could take herself off. All those man-hours wasted . . .'

Ellis erupted back into the room. 'Mr Demidowicz suggests the pattern stores, sir. They're the furthest part of the site; part that Mr D. didn't take the party to the other day. I've already got people looking, but I think we should join them. I take it you'd like to sit this one out, Ms Rivers?'

'You take it right,' I said with fervour.

It seemed that George had more guts than I. Despite his injuries, he went off to Smethwick, while I stayed to make a formal statement, though my concentration was very poor. I kept seeing what I'd seen before – a strong violinist's hand protruding from ancient rubbish.

I'd just meandered to a close, apologising for the umpteenth time to the patient young PC unlucky enough to have had to prise obvious details from me, when there was a tap at the door. Chris and George. Their faces told me what I needed to know.

'One wound only, apart from a puncture to the neck,' Chris said, pouring strong coffee in his office. 'Very quick, Sophie. They found Hallam's day clothes and fiddle nearby, incidentally.'

I nodded. Then my brain clicked in, as always ready to take over when I had unpalatable emotion to deal with. 'But how did Doug get access to the site? There's a security guard to stop stray visitors.'

'That's something that worried me. But to do him justice, Betts and his team were on to that. You know your constant railing against students not having grants and having to work? Well, guess what part-time job Doug Leigh found. On the face of it, he must have been ideal material for job in security: big, gentle, and phlegmatic.'

'And no doubt he was working at various historical sites,' George put in drily.

'Quite. We could have had corpses concealed at Aston Hall or Soho House – he had that passion for history, remember.'

George shook his head. 'If only it could have been channelled properly.'

'Quite.'

'So that was how he knew about the false wall at the BMI. Chris, I've been so slow.'

'Between ourselves, I gather that some of my colleagues haven't been all that quick either. Sophie, you usually communicate better than this.' He looked at me sharply.

'Only when I'm invited to. I didn't want to – to interfere. Not when I knew hardly anyone.' And Harvinder, a trusted ally, had been decidedly edgy. Perhaps now he was catching up on some sleep, things would be better for him. Otherwise I'm sure he'd welcome a natter over a quiet drink.

Which was precisely what George suggested now. I accepted; Chris demurred. He needed to be with the team. I raised an ironic eyebrow. He nodded. No, I'd never been part of it, had I?

'You'll have to exorcise the ghosts,' George said, sinking the last of his red wine, 'sooner or later. It's a nice afternoon. Why don't we go over there now? Just for ten minutes. You've got to pick up your car anyway, haven't you? And you've got your outdoor clothes and hard hat in that bag. Come on. Won't take long on the bus.'

We were walking slowly to the bus stop when someone called our names. Harvinder. How was I feeling? Any better?

'Let's just say I'm looking forward to Sri Lanka,' I said, wondering if a grin would expose my broken teeth to un-welcome cold air. I risked it. It did. 'And you, Harv – how are you?'

It was hardly the question he could answer in depth with George present. 'Better,' he said tersely. 'Inderjit's sleeping a bit more, thank God.'

'Teething,' I explained.

'Nasty time,' George put in. 'I remember when my daughter . . .'

I couldn't work out whether Harv's offer of a lift was a put-up job or not. Maybe it was all too pat to be a coincidence. But a lift seemed altogether nicer than the jostles of public transport, and, while I'd retained my car-key, it dawned on me that I hadn't locked the car. What if someone had helped himself to it? Hot-wired it and driven it off? But I needn't have worried. The Avery Berkel security staff – minus Doug – might have guarded it specially. When I thrust the bag in the boot, retrieving only what I needed, they raised a cheer. I offered left-handed handshakes to everyone in reach. So my heart was much lighter as we set off to the entrance, still wide open, but garnished with police tape. A word from Harvinder admitted us.

It would have been nice to have a hand to hold as I set off into the cellars. But Harv and George might have been embarrassed, and, in any case, I couldn't have risked a reassuring squeeze. I told myself that this was no worse than Mike going out to face, as he'd once had to, a West Indies fast bowler who'd broken two of his fingers the last time they'd met. After all, nothing of mine was broken, and the fan of mycelium might be no good for the health of the building but it couldn't rot me. I stared at the chains. The chalk and other marks left by the police made the site look more like a stage set than a real-life murder location. They were still busy by the pattern store; a quick look and that was it.

At last we turned round and returned to the great nave of the erecting shop. I lifted my head to the light, and offered my thanks to whoever was up there.

Oxford Shadows

Veronica Stallwood

When the flying bombs terrorised London in 1944, anxious mothers sent their children away to the peace of the countryside to escape the danger. Oxford and its surrounding villages appeared to be havens of safety, but dangers other than bombs menaced some unlucky children – and for ten-year-old Chris Barnes, the result was death.

Over fifty years later, novelist Kate Ivory, searching for wartime love stories as material for her latest historical romance, uncovers Chris's tragic tale. Amongst the piles of old papers in the attic of the house she shares with her partner, George, she finds the child's diary and drawings, and, in an old newspaper, a haunting photograph of a face she cannot forget. But one thing remains unclear – why he died so young.

Never able to resist a mystery, Kate determines to find the truth, but the knowledge comes at a price – the boy's death appears to implicate George's family – and Kate is faced with an impossible choice . . .

'Novelist Kate Ivory snoops with intelligence, wit and some nice insights' *The Times*

'Stallwood is in the top rank of crime writers' *Daily Telegraph*

'One of the cleverest of the year's crop [with] a flesh-and-brains heroine' *Observer*

0 7472 6844 4

headline

Now you can buy any of these other bestselling Headline books from your bookshop or *direct from the publisher.*

FREE P&P AND UK DELIVERY
(Overseas and Ireland £3.50 per book)

Seven Up	Janet Evanovich	£5.99
A Place of Safety	Caroline Graham	£6.99
Risking it All	Ann Granger	£5.99
Cold Flat Junction	Martha Grimes	£6.99
Tip Off	John Francome	£6.99
The Cat Who Smelled a Rat	Lilian Jackson Braun	£6.99
Autograph in the Rain	Quintin Jardine	£5.99
Arabesk	Barbara Nadel	£5.99
Oxford Double	Veronica Stallwood	£5.99
Bubbles Unbound	Sarah Strohmeyer	£5.99
Fleeced	Georgina Wroe	£6.99

TO ORDER SIMPLY CALL THIS NUMBER

01235 400 414

or e-mail <u>orders@bookpoint.co.uk</u>

Prices and availability subject to change without notice.